The Turn
in the Path

John Lea

Published by

OAKLEA BOOKS
THE OAKS, SHELLOW LANE
NORTH RODE, CONGLETON
CHESHIRE
CW12 2NX
TEL. 01260 223255

©John Lea and Oaklea Books 2007
ISBN 0-9553724-1-0   ISBN 978-0-9553724-1-4

Typesetting by Christine Pemberton

Foreword

My earlier books, *Down the Cobblestones* and *My Countryside* captured both the struggle and fun of farm and village life in the early part of the 20th century. Although I included gamekeeper and poacher tales there was not much about the country gentry. And yet the bulk of rural England was still owned and controlled by the Lords of the Manor. They usually owned the whole parish; every farm, every village cottage and they had probably built the church.

Needless to say, nothing happened without their blessing, or more likely the approval of their agent, factor or steward. Whatever the title, others trembled in his presence.

As the century turned that old order was already dying, but perhaps German snipers in the First World War did more to change the English countryside than anyone. The heirs to the country estates were automatic officer materia, and, though they had always gone to war, never in such great numbers. On the killing fields of France German snipers were trained to pick them off; one great Cheshire family lost 13 heirs in those few years. Families that had held lands since Norman times reached the end of their line.

I was determined to capture those changing times, perhaps because I was weaned on the older generation's tales of them. My parents were tenant farmers and although their landlord's estate was not large, it was still impressive. As a boy I roamed the woods and fields and listened to the old estate workmen. It was natural to build this fictional story around the working of such a country estate and, as in real life, it sizzles with sex and ruthless ambition, which in turn create intrigue and violence.

Dedicated to Celia

*Her support and skill with a camera
(cover photographs)
has been inspirational throughout my writing*

Acknowledgements

The inspiration for this story came during a visit to see the snowdrops at Rode Hall in Cheshire. I an indebted to the owner, Sir Richard Baker Wilbraham for taking the time to describe how such a country house was staffed and run during the 1920s. That visit triggered memories of my own youth growing up on a tenanted farm on a similar estate just outside Knutsford. There, the stories told by an older generation, who lived and worked on those old country estates, both fascinated me as a child and later were to colour my imagination.

Even so the estate, village and people in this book are entirely fictional and any resemblance to anyone living or dead is completely coincidental.

A special thanks to Harry Owen for his proof reading and copy editing.

By the same author

Silk or Gritstone
There is a Thomas Hardy feel running throughout this enthralling 1920s tale of business greed, lust and romance. Set on the edge of the Pennines it captures those austere times as it moves between beautiful countryside and industrial silk town.

Down the Cobblestones
A witty and informative look at farm and village life in the early half of the 20th century. A true story complemented by photographs and cartoons.

My Countryside
A sequel to the above, but this time in the middle of the 20th century. Many of the same characters are in these amusing tales from the Author's childhood and later life. Illustrates with photographs and cartoons.

Time to Change
An unusual and humourous mix of short country stories, some true, some fictional.

The Peover Eye
A beautifully produced cloth backed limited edition, this book is a collector's item. Illustrated in colour by the artist G. Ashley Hunter the book follows the Author and Artist as they fish for trout and observe the wildlife along this lovely Cheshire river.

Chapter One

It was done. Rachel had no regrets as she watched Alexander being driven away. After eight years of marriage she had at last stood her ground. A small cloud of dust rose off the gravel as the chauffeur drove sedately down the long winding drive through the Park. Watching it settle Rachel wondered whether all this was the result of marrying an older man. Perhaps, she reflected, as an eighteen-year-old bride had she been just too young to see what kind of man her tall, handsome Army captain really was.

The car was nearing the end of the drive. Soon it would be through the wrought iron gates and travelling past the church where just eight years ago her dreams seemed to have been fulfilled. Unable to tear her mind away from the happiness of that day, she stood forlornly on the gravel comparing it to the last half hour when Alexander came into her bedroom demanding, "Why aren't you packing? Don't you realise that we haven't got much time?"

"I've already explained, I'm not going with you, I must go to visit Hannah."

"Don't be ridiculous, your place is with me."

Rachel remembered turning away to look out of the bedroom window, trying hard not to say the words that would probably take their marriage beyond repair. In this beautiful countryside there was always something to take her attention; this time it was a dairy cow browsing among the parkland trees. As it shuffled slowly forward, with outstretched neck and rasping tongue reaching up high for overhanging oak leaves, the length of its tongue both amused and seemed to calm her.

Feeling that her anger was under control, she turned back to face Alexander but he was checking through his case. It gave her a few moments to look at him and with a shock she realised that she no longer liked what she saw. Oh, he was still the same man, the one on whose arm she had walked proudly; even more proud that he had overcome the pain and discarded his wheelchair, though he had been glad of her supporting arm as they walked side by side down the aisle. But now his fastidiously parted brown hair, straight backed military bearing and what she once thought was the reserved maturity of the

Lord of the Manor all seemed so artificial and pompous.

Meeting his cold blue eyes with a forced smile Rachel said, "Can't you see that now Hannah is so poorly I have to go to her? After all, she is my closest friend and it seems that she hasn't got long. I must put her before London."

Avoiding her attempt to keep eye contact Alexander marched across the bedroom into his dressing room. He returned with some handkerchiefs and, closing his travelling case, said in his precise way, "This may be my chance of promotion. Now that I am behind a desk I'm dependent on the recommendations of those damn civilians. I must join them at that dinner in London on Saturday night." Then turning to point at her he added, "The right impression counts and as my wife I want you with me."

Rachel had to smile. It was just as though he was instructing a junior officer on some exercise or other but then, she thought, that's just what I am, that's what I've been throughout our marriage. Perhaps I should salute and say 'Yes, Captain'.

Although her husband was in constant pain from his old war injuries, she had previously admired the way he kept the evidence off his handsome face. Now she realised that by hiding his emotions from others he also hid them from her. Gradually he had shut her out until they no longer shared any intimacy.

This confrontation, although screaming with tension, had been conducted in conversational tones and was not about her decision to visit Hannah in that T.B. Sanatorium. This was about eight years of marriage that had slowly become a shell without affection. Oh, she knew that he had loved her; perhaps he still did but it was never revealed in any show of sentiment. Even in an argument there was no real passion or an end when they could make up. The next day there was always just an icy pretence that nothing had happened.

Though this time Alexander made it clear that there would be no morning disagreement, icy or otherwise, by saying, "I promised Bestwick that he could have the weekend off. He was to drop us at Crewe station then go on to visit his mother in Whitchurch."

Fond of the tall taciturn chauffeur, Rachel had no intention of upsetting him. Anyway she had heard that Hannah's fiancé, Nathan, was coming to his intended in-laws for a few days so, presuming that he would have a car, she replied in equally icy tones, "I'll find some other way to visit Hannah."

After a last glance round his dressing room to check if he had missed anything Alexander picked up his case and, walking towards the top of the stairs, said, "I won't be back next weekend."

Rachel followed asking, "But what about the estate and the farm? Doesn't that letter from the bank mean that we have to talk? Surely we must make some decisions?"

He was partway down the stairs before he replied, "You talk to the bank. You've always known more about this estate than I have, so you make the decisions! I mean it …. You get on with it!"

Before Rachel could reply he was striding across the gravel towards where the chauffeur was holding the car's passenger door open. Closing the door, Bestwick walked round the car to climb into his driver's seat. Then, without even a glance her way, Alexander was gone.

Now turning back to the house Rachel caught a glimpse of the parlour maid surreptitiously peeping from behind a door and the tension broke. She laughed; at Alexander's pompous departure, at her maid's interest in her affairs and particularly because she knew that her small staff would be well aware of the state of her marriage.

Rachel walked into the garden to be alone. She wondered whether the lack of intimacy with Alexander was beginning to distort her mind because it flew back to her early teenage years after her father had become Steward to the estate. Then, living so close to the Hall, she had mixed with both the young maids from the Hall and the dairymaids working on the farm. Although they were always a bit cautious as to what they said in front of her, those girls had known and discussed most of the titillating happenings in the Hall. That Alexander's parents, the Colonel and Lady Louisa, had separate bedrooms was common knowledge. How often he went into hers was more spicy news, perhaps because it was not very often. The bedroom maid could even tell them if he had stayed with her all night. The teenage girls would then spend ages giggling over their own imaginations.

The subject of sex had never been talked about in her home and hardly mentioned in school lessons, but it had been demonstrated to Rachel when she stayed with Hannah for a few days one Christmas holiday. During the winter months Hannah's father, William Brown, kept his dairy cows tied up each in its own stall in the warm shippen, only releasing them for about a half hour each morning. In that time the men tidied up the cows' stalls while the cows took the chance to drink from the farm pond behind the stack-yard. The two twelve-year-old girls had been innocently playing in the hay barn when they saw that the bull was also in with the cows, so they stayed hidden among the hay trusses to watch. As the cows slaked their thirst in the pond the bull moved among them, smelling at each in turn. One cow turned round, head down to play fight with him; it was obvious that she was on heat because within seconds he just mounted her. No long endearing courtship, just one thrust and that was it. When another cow came teasing and rambling with the bull he just butted her off until he had recovered his ardour. The girls wondered if that was all there was to it? Would it be like that with a boy?

Looking back Rachel found it hard to believe just how little they had known. Neither of them had ever seen a book on sex and with Rachel's mother's health failing it didn't seem right to ask her and Hannah's mother never explained anything to her either. In both their homes sex was a forbidden subject. If William Brown had caught them watching his bull she would have been packed off home in disgrace and s Hannah sent upstairs to bed.

There could have been a more revealing lesson for the two girls the following Easter when again Rachel spent a day with Hannah.

Most years the Browns reared a foal from one of their heavy working horses. Rachel had long been aware that when the foals were born each spring grooms led stallions from farm to farm to mate the mares and get them in foal again. She had known because in a mixed sex class of mainly farm children what the girls were not allowed to watch the boys took delight in describing in lurid detail. This time when Hannah said, "The stallion is coming this morning", Rachel said, "Let's watch. If we hide up the orchard we should see from there."

"If dad catches us we'll be in trouble. You'll be sent home and I'll be sent up to bed."

"It's worth the risk," Rachel said and asked, "Why is he called a groom?"

"Dad told me that stallions' owners usually hire a groom for a few months each spring just to walk their stallions round the district because their own farm waggoner is too busy with the spring work on the farm."

They were hidden behind the orchard hedge when the stallion came prancing into the yard. Mr Brown had to rush forward and take hold of a lead halter at one side while the groom held onto a second halter at the other side. Hannah whispered that he was so excited because he would have smelled that the mare was in season long before he got to the farm. When the Browns' waggoner led their mare from the stable that great stallion, with neck arched and lips rolled back, pranced sideways across the cindered stack-yard. The mare's answering call caused the stallion's loud whinnies to become a screech. His excitement was so great that the men had difficulty holding onto him, especially when he began to rear and lash out with his front legs. It was then that the two girls realised the sheer wild primitive passion of that massive animal.

The two girls were so engrossed they jumped round guiltily when, from just behind them, Mrs Brown said, "If Mr Brown catches you there will be an awful row."

For the two girls it had been awesome to see the primitive force and power of the great stallion. Even as they all walked back to the farmhouse Rachel couldn't help but glance over her shoulder. Although she could only see the stallion's head and shoulders above the hedge she was astonished at his primeval passion. With his majestic head thrown back and lips curled to bare powerful teeth his screeches reverberated through the farmyard.

Rachel would never forget how shaken they both were. Sometime later when they were alone in Hannah's bedroom she asked, "Do you think that a man could have that much fire and passion?"

Hannah said, "I don't know but I don't intend to find out until I'm married."

As Rachel got a little older those young people at the Hall (not just girls because there were trainee gardeners and boys from the farm) also helped to educate her. In fact the cowman's teenage son tried to further her education on one or two occasions. Although she had resisted his advances she knew that he had found some of the dairymaids more receptive to his charms.

***

Sitting now on her favourite seat overlooking the lake, Rachel reflected how all that had been before she began to help Alexander's mother by pushing him out in the garden in his wheelchair. Soon her schoolgirl crush had grown into love and from that love had come the responsibility for this estate and its people. Now she determined that Alexander's lack of affection wouldn't stop her caring for what happened here on this estate.

It was a relief to know that the estate was quite small. If one compared estates by the number of acres owned, Hesston estate with less than 3,000 acres would come well down in the league of Cheshire's landed gentry. It was modest compared to the historic holdings of many of the great Cheshire families; the Cholmondeley family held nearer to 20,000 acres and the Tollemarches about 25,000 acres. Even the smaller estates were usually between 5,000 and 10,000 acres.

Rachel was relieved that the size of their country house was in keeping, needing only a small permanent staff to run it. In the Colonel's days before the Great War there had been a butler, housekeeper, five maids and a cook. Also there had been two or three cleaning ladies working under the housekeeper. Outside, three men with different impressive titles worked in the stables and there were at least five gardeners and a footman. The latter seemed to hang around the front door looking very colourful but she, as a young girl, had never understood his function. On top of that Lady Louisa had her personal chambermaid and Alexander's father, the Colonel, had brought his batman back from the Boer War to act as his valet.

Wars may have brought glory to the Wentworth-Jones family but they had also left dreadful scars. The Colonel returned from the Boar War an absent-minded broken man. Sadly, he died while Alexander was still recovering from his wounds received in the Great War, which meant that when they married Rachel became mistress of Hesston Hall.

Chapter Two

The fact that she had been brought up to do housework and did not expect to be waited on every minute of the day meant that Rachel could manage the affairs of the house with the help of a cook, three maids and a village boy. He came in each day to carry in the logs and coal, before helping the gardener. Bestwick also occasionally helped in the garden, when he had time to spare from both chauffeuring and keeping the temperamental Hall generator going.

Water hens called to each other across the lake and colourful chrysanthemums and dahlias swayed beside her in the gentle breeze but, hardly aware of them, Rachel sat in reflection. Perhaps it was because of Cook that she managed the house so easily. Certainly she was the reason that Rachel had never replaced either the butler or the housekeeper when illness had forced that loyal couple to retire.

Cook was just Cook to everyone, in the village as well as here on the estate. Before working at the Hall she had been the wife of one of their less successful farm tenants. Married later in life, they had been one of the happiest couples Rachel had ever met. They had met when her husband had been the respected head shepherd on a large estate in Derbyshire where she was the cook. After their marriage they took the tenancy of a farm here but he still spoke of his wife as 'Cook'.

Travelling around the tenants with her father had given Rachel a chance to see into most homes on the estate. Cook, a large energetically happy woman, had kept her house the most spotless and cheerful of any around. Her relationship with Rachel was strengthened at village functions. If there was food to be prepared or served Cook naturally took charge and, as Rachel often helped, they got to know each other. "Come on young Rachel, get the jam and cream in these sponge cakes" was the usual sort of exhortation from Cook when Rachel was in her mid-teens but that had to change when, to the surprise of the whole village, Rachel became engaged to the squire's son. Then Cook, with years of professional practice behind her, just added a respectful 'ma'am'.

Unfortunately the ex-shepherd had failed to develop the business skills needed to run the farm efficiently. However it had been his skill in training sheepdogs that was his undoing.

In the early stages of training an eight-month-old pup Cook's husband had taken it out to round up his eight dairy cows. Alas, unbeknown to him the neighbour's bull had broken through the boundary fence and the pup couldn't handle the charging animal. Cook, who had seen it all from the farmyard, ran to let the old dog loose, then on to the stable for their carthorse. While the more experienced dog harassed the enraged bull, Cook riding bareback steered the horse between the bull and her badly injured husband. Then with the dog's help she managed to drive the bull, along with the cows, into the farmyard. Sliding off the horse's bare back to fasten the gate, she ran back to where her man lay struggling to breathe and obviously in great pain. He held her hand for a couple of minutes before dying in her arms.

The doctor later confirmed that the bull must have knelt on his chest to crush his ribs so extensively.

Rachel's old cook had already expressed a wish to retire so the impoverished farmer's widow took no persuading to accept the post.

It was the beginning of a very happy working relationship. At first Cook had lived in a one room flat at the back of the Hall. When the housekeeper fell ill Cook shared her workload with Rachel. Later, when it became obvious that the housekeeper had not long to live, she and her husband (the butler) retired and moved away to live with their daughter. Cook moved into their larger flat and just carried on with that extended role.

The other maids were all farm girls, who had been brought up to do whatever task their parents set them. Although each now had an official title no one bothered too much; if the parlour maid was busy elsewhere Cook would don a white apron and serve afternoon tea in the lounge. If need be, on other occasions she would dash upstairs to help the bedroom maid rearrange furniture. It meant that the whole house was run in a relaxed family atmosphere, at times much to Alexander's disgust.

Rachel had long realised that her friendly staff knew, not just what she did, but often what she was thinking. And she knew that she had been sitting here thinking for too long. It was the news about Hannah that had sent her mind spiralling back to their earlier years. Hannah's parents must the heartbroken.

The fact that the Browns, who had seemed like second parents to her in those schooldays, were now her tenants had not strained their friendship. She decided to go to see them.

***

Striding across the fields from Claybank Farm, his fiancée Hannah's home, Nathan's mood slowly relaxed. By the time that he'd vaulted the gate onto the back drive, which would take him through the woods to both the Home Farm and Hesston Hall, he had come to terms with the fact that he was going to lose his fiancée.

At twenty-eight and just under six foot tall Nathan's lithe movements obscured the power of his compact, sinewy physique. Perhaps swinging a seven-pound felling axe from his early teens had added a graceful co-ordination to his strength.

It was natural to take an interest in the trees and woodland abutting the drive because, as a woodman, trees were Nathan's livelihood. He was surprised how much these trees had matured and changed since his schooldays before the war, when he had spent many happy hours here with Hannah's brother and also with Hamish, the estate keeper.

Not that this was really a back drive. It was in fact the way from the Hall to the town of Knutsford where the Squire and his family shopped and did much of their business. Built two Centuries before to allow the Landowners of the day to ride in comfort through their new plantations, this drive gave a contrast to the front one, which wound through the grazed parkland into Hesston village.

Nathan's father had lived on his grandfather's farm on the next estate but the village school in Hesston had been the nearest to them. From becoming friends at that school, Nathan and Hannah's eldest brother Bill continued their friendship after Nathan's family had moved to Shropshire.

Nathan, having taken time off from his work at the timber company to stay a couple of days with the Browns, had intended to borrow their car to visit Hannah. It was the Browns who told him that they had heard that Rachel was going to visit Hannah the next day. Although he had only met Rachel briefly on one or two occasions he felt that he knew her through Hannah and asked if he could join her.

Nearer the Hall the drive passed between overgrown rhododendron bushes before crossing the dam. Behind the dam a long, landscaped lake ran along one side of the Hall gardens. Leaving the bushes Nathan rounded the bend towards the more formal gardens and saw Rachel striding along the lakeside towards him.

***

After Alexander had so dramatically left, Rachel had gone through various emotions, from despair to a burst of almost uncontrollable laughter at the memory of the pompous way Alexander had marched across the gravel before being driven away. Having worshipped and idolised him from the age of eleven, she wondered why it had all gone so wrong. She recalled the time her Father had become the estate steward and her family had moved to the stable cottage behind the walled gardens. Rachel pictured again in her mind her first sight of Alexander in his uniform: Oh! Her 11-year-old heart had nearly stopped.

Now, as she strode along in the warm early September sun Rachel realised that eight years of marriage to a man who couldn't or wouldn't share his inner feelings had drained that love away. What she had left was a steely determination to do something about the estate. Yes, she loved this old house, these farms and these people; they had become her life. Yes, it was time to take an interest in the estate and sort out the finances.

As steward, her father oversaw the upkeep of the rented farms, supervised the woodland and managed the three hundred acre home farm. At the age of fifteen Rachel had left school to look after her father when her mother's tragic death had ended her plan to go to university. Needing more of a challenge than just the housework, she became her father's assistant, keeping his books and often accompanying him around the estate.

Yes, Alexander was right - she did know a lot about the estate - but from the day of her marriage her father had refused to discuss the estate business with her. If Rachel asked him anything he would just say, "I must only report to the Captain."

Through the first year or two of their married life Alexander had taken an interest in the estate, discussing everything with her, but after taking that desk job in London his interest had gradually fallen away. Rachel, having been taught to observe by her father, couldn't help seeing the decline in their farm in recent years.

It wasn't just the estate that was being neglected by Alexander's absence. Their social life also suffered, not that Rachel had ever been accepted into the county people's circle; perhaps the Hesston estate was not grand enough. Or perhaps it was she herself who wasn't grand enough. At one hunt ball soon after her marriage Rachel had overheard one elderly county dame say, "Of course she is only the steward's daughter."

On other occasions when she had been introduced to some of the 'great' they had acknowledged her and then deliberately cut her out of their conversation. Even so, through the early years of their marriage, she and her husband had developed a circle of friends. In recent years, though, Alexander had been away so much that joint invitations and even entertaining at the hall often had to be cancelled because he was detained in London. Slowly most of that circle of friends had fallen away. There were still the occasional hunt ball and regimental-type occasion when Alexander made the effort to attend. Other than those, some ladies-only invitations and a few shooting or tennis weekends, she spent most days on her own.

Deep in thought, Rachel was not aware of anyone near until she heard the crunch of Nathan's boots when he strode past the overgrown rhododendron bushes. Although they had only met occasionally in Hannah's presence, Hannah's enthusiastic narrations about Nathan made it seem that Rachel knew him quite well.

While shaking hands and exchanging the usual pleasantries Rachel was conscious that, although slightly taller, he did not tower over her like Alexander; it was the power of his personality that impressed. Rachel was just wondering how to say, "I'm sorry to hear that your fiancé is dying," when Nathan said, "I need to go to see Hannah and I heard that you might be going. I usually come in the boss's car but he couldn't spare it for the week. I can borrow William Brown's old car but it would take about three hours to do thirty odd miles in that; can I come with you?"

Rachel liked the direct way that Nathan addressed her, no subservient humble phrases or fawning smile and, despite the graveness of the situation, there seemed to be a twinkle in his grey eyes that emphasized the sun creases on his lean face. Rachel recovered her wandering thoughts to be equally direct. "The chauffeur's taken Alexander to Crewe and is going on to visit his mother. I was walking across to see if I could have a lift with either you or Mr Brown."

Comparing in his mind the Browns' battered old car against the Wentworth-Jones car increased the twinkle in Nathan's eyes. "Ay, this isn't your beautiful Talbot Darracq with its shiny brass headlamps and radiator, all kept lovingly polished by Bestwick. It's not even a four-seater. It's an old 1921 Carden with a two-stroke two cylinder engine at the back and no hood."

To Rachel's, "So what, will it go?" Nathan's face broke into a smile as he quoted William Brown's favourite saying, "Well ...maybe!"

They discussed the route and the starting time, and then Nathan asked, "Will you make two picnics?"

When Rachel looked puzzled he added with another smile. "We can enjoy one when we break down on the way there and the other when we break down on the way back."

Chapter Three

Although it was nicely situated and landscaped, Hesston Hall was neither large nor impressive. Built mainly from Cheshire red brick, the only outstanding feature was perhaps the stone-built porch which, supported by two pillars, broke the uniformity in a stately way.

Nathan pulled up in front of that imposing entrance and left the engine running. As he jumped out of the car, the Cook came towards him with a bulging picnic hamper and while he was stowing it behind the seats a maid brought out a heavy raincoat and weather-proofed hat. Rachel followed wearing a light overcoat cut to reveal the curves of her slim body; it received an appreciative glance from Nathan, as did her broad-brimmed sun hat.

When all was loaded and both were seated, Rachel found that the two seats were intimately close together.

They were motoring through Hesston village when the Church clock struck ten. It was such a pleasant early September morning now and the sun was quickly burning away the mist that still lingered from the cool of the night.

Nursing her sunhat to let the breeze ruffle the natural wave in her fair hair, Rachel was aware that neither of them had yet mentioned Hannah even though she was the purpose for their journey. Perhaps both knew that it would be a heartbreaking visit. To break the silence Rachel said, "I never understood why your family moved away from the village?"

Nathan took his time explaining how Grandfather Dobson's landlord had banned his tenants from shooting rabbits. "As you know, it's a tradition on most estates to allow the tenants to protect their crops and rabbits aren't just a pest, they're a saleable crop, and Grandad's was only a small farm so he was glad of the extra cash they brought in. Anyway, the landlord didn't see it like that. He had wanted the sport of rabbit shooting kept just for him and his invited friends. They were just a bunch of gentry who couldn't shoot so the rabbits multiplied and in the end Dad decided to do something about them."

Engrossed in the story, Rachel began to feel heat from the mid-morning sun. Nathan concentrated on his driving while she carefully donned her sun hat before asking, "How do you mean?"

Nathan continued. "He bought some long nets to use on the occasional dark winter's night. With the help of two friends they caught over three hundred rabbits that winter. The elderly keeper, knowing that the rabbits needed to be controlled, had turned a blind eye; alas, he retired that spring. The following winter the new keeper, who was officious and interfering with all the tenants, soon worked out where the rabbits were going. He must have told the landlord and he in turn came knocking on Grandad's farmhouse door demanding to know if it was true. There was an almighty row."

"Surely he didn't turn your father off the farm?"

"No, because the tenancy was in Grandad's name, but Dad was told that he could never have a tenancy of that farm or any other on that estate. Falling off a stack some years before had left Grandad partially crippled, but seeing that he was allowed to stay on the farm for his lifetime Dad stayed on to run the farm for him. When Mum and Dad got married the large farmhouse was divided into two for both families. I was born in it and lived there until Grandad died."

"You must have left school the same year that we came to Hesston," Rachel said. "I never understood though why you moved so far away."

"The landlord put the word around that Dad wouldn't make a good tenant, which meant that even though he was considered for several farms that reference ruled him out. In the end he managed to buy a small farm in Shropshire."

"How did you get into forestry?"

"The farm wasn't big enough to provide work for both me and my older brother, although I did help to get it tidy in the first year. Dad sold some trees to raise a bit of cash and when the timber merchant came I was laying an overgrown hedge."

As Nathan changed gear to help the little car up a slight incline Rachel asked, "What then?"

"He saw me swinging an axe and told me that he could find work for a lad like me and I've been with him ever since."

"Doing what exactly?"

"I usually go with the Boss when he's looking at potential timber. I'm in charge of falling, hauling, either back to our yard or on to other merchants. I've a team of five horses, a steam engine and six regular men. As well as those men we use contractors to fall some of the timber. We also do some woodland management and tree planting."

Rachel relaxed, enjoying the scenery. Most of the roadside weeds and flowers looked drab with the onset of autumn. Occasionally late flowering trefoil provided a contrasting block of bright yellow. The blackberry season was nearly over but even so in some places the bushes were showing both red and black with the late ripening fruit.

Due to the previous spell of wet weather the corn harvest was far from over. Although bare stubble fields told of the progress of harvest, on others corn stood in kivers (Nathan insisted on calling them stooks) and there were even a few fields of growing wheat waiting for the farmer's binder.

In the warm midmorning sun, farmers were walking through their cornfields feeling the sheaves to check how dry they were. Later in the journey, when the warmth of the sun had dried off the moisture from the night's mist, horses and carts sedately headed towards the cornfields and farm workers began their long day of pitching and loading sheaf after sheaf.

A downward slope gave the little car the impetus to touch 20mph, nearly plucking Rachel's hat from her head. Clutching it, she laughed and pointed to the speedometer, "You broke the speed limit then."

Seeing the crinkles increase around Nathan's eyes reminded Rachel of Alexander's parting cold, expressionless face. Nathan just smiled as the road levelled out and the speed fell back to about 13mph.

When they were passing a block of mature trees she noticed Nathan slowed even more to cast a professional eye over them, explaining, "We are always on the lookout for good timber and there is some in there."

"You talk as though you are a partner. Are you?"

"There's no chance of that. There are two young sons in the business, one works with me and the other one on the merchant side. Me and Hannah ..... well ..... we'd planned to start our own business."

He finished the sentence very quietly but it gave Rachel an opening. "I'd believed that Hannah was going to get better. What's gone wrong?"

"I don't know. As you know I've only been allowed to visit her once a month but we write often. I thought she would be home and cured after twelve months but she suddenly went worse and .... well, I doubt she won't come home again."

Rachel said, "It's been hard not to be allowed to visit. Now we can I suppose it means ...." They both went quiet.

Rachel noticed that the type of farms had changed the further they travelled across the Cheshire plain. She presumed that they were now passing through an area of heavy clay soil because the cornfields had given way to grassland and the dairy herds were larger. There was an occasional herd of about a hundred cows, which caused them both to comment, knowing that these would be cheese-making farms.

Then Nathan asked, "How would you like to run one those large farm houses? Cheese making needs teams of young people to milk the cows and run the dairy. If you put that many youngsters together you get a few problems to sort out."

"You forget that we make cheese on our Home farm, although I don't take an active part in it now. Though my father still manages the farm. With only forty cows most of our dairy work is done by the families of our older workers."

"Is the farm doing well?"

"It doesn't seem to be at the moment, no!"

There followed a long, relaxed discussion about the merits of cheese making, cereal prices and the strengths of mixed farming. When Rachel expressed her surprise at how knowledgeable Nathan was about agriculture, he said, "It was going to be my life and anyway my family's still farming!"

He looked at Rachel staring across the fields and Nathan, with a wave of his hand, said, "You don't seem to miss much, do you?"

"My father trained me to observe. He says that a steward should not only watch his own tenants but also know how others are farming. When we rode together in the trap he made me comment on what I observed. I had to assess how good a farmer was by just looking over his fields while riding by."

Nathan chuckled his reply: "My old Grandad did much the same with me. He'd a struggle to get in and out of the trap so when he went out on business I often went with him. Either to hold his horse or open gates for him. I never saw him read a book. I'm not sure that he could read much but as we trotted along he used to say, 'Country's like a book to them as can read it. Along the road each corner's a new page.'"

"Did you spend a lot of time with him?"

"He liked to mix with people. Market day, visiting other farmers, whatever business he had on if Dad wasn't going and I wasn't at school. Ah, and sometimes I went along when I should have been at school."

"Hannah must have shared the same interest."

"Her Methodist upbringing seemed to prevent her from criticising other people, which seemed a nonsense to me. She was shocked when I said that one of her neighbours was about farmed out. The next day, when she asked her father if it was true, he'd said, 'Well .... maybe, but some farmers can make going broke last a lifetime'. We had a good laugh, and after that she took more notice."

The little car chugged along until they got back into more cornfields. There was constant movement across the fields. Horses were pulling empty carts out to the fields and others toiled home loaded. Men with pikels (Nathan called them pitchforks) were pitching the now dry sheaves onto carts. When they drove past a farmyard more men were unloading and building stacks in the stackyard.

Rachel was enjoying watching the activity and teasing Nathan about his local names for different tools until they caught up with a heavily loaded cart trundling along in front of them. Not being able to pass Nathan had to slow down to the pace of the horse but soon a little steam began to show around the radiator.

"This car's soon in trouble if it's held at a low speed. There's a wide gateway over there - I think it's picnic time."

When Rachel protested that it was too early, Nathan said, "The car's had enough. This isn't your Talbot with its shiny brass radiator; this old Carden would be in the scrap yard if it wasn't mostly made of wood - even the radiator's made from wood."

Steering the car off the road he added, "And it won't start again until it's cooled off."

"How long will that take? Will it be cool in a half hour?"

"Well .... maybe - but more likely an hour."

Sitting on the hedge cop just inside the field gate they relaxed over the picnic. Down one side of the field a waggoner was cultivating the cleared stubble with two horses. It soon became obvious that one of the two horses was just a colt that was being broken in. Rachel had often watched the Browns breaking in a colt the same way. They would get it used to wearing harness and perhaps pulling an old log around towards the end of the summer, timing it so that it would be ready for its first real work on the autumn stubbles. After harvest the stubbles were roughly cultivated to encourage

27

weeds to germinate. It wasn't exacting work for a young horse because the odd mistake didn't matter. Later in the winter any weeds that had germinated would be buried when the field was ploughed ready for next year's crop.

Watching this waggoner it was obvious that he was having a lot of trouble controlling the gangly three and a half year old colt, particularly when the team were turning round on the headland. With time to spare Nathan had walked across the field to look over some trees while Rachel picked a few late season blackberries.

Pausing from the blackberries to watch the waggoner work, Rachel saw a hare spring from its seat just in front of the two horses. Leaping in fright, the colt would have run away had it not been tied to the other. As it was its hind legs became mixed in the chains causing it to kick and lunge about. Nathan ran across to help the waggoner who had run forward to hold the bridles of both horses. Between them they disentangled chains from legs and tried to calm the team down. Nathan then walked alongside the young horse until it settled down again.

About an hour later they were turning into the Sanatorium car park. The last half hour of the journey had passed in silence, each of them deep in thought as to what lay ahead.

They were soon by Hannah's bedside, being greeted by her welcoming smile. Rachel though was not prepared for the shock. Hannah's round, healthy face had always sparkled with her personality. Now her blue eyes looked too large in the shrunken face and her once beautiful smile was like a crease in a sheet of parchment.

They made small talk of home and families until Hannah began to cough. It racked her whole body so much that the nurse rushed in to usher them out to a waiting room.

They sat stunned and silent for nearly a half hour, before the nurse indicated that they could go back in. Nathan rushed to Hannah's side in heartbroken devotion. Rachel, not able to bear watching them cling together, quietly slipped out of the room.

It was the remembered dreams that she and Hannah had shared together that disturbed her. Their hopes to each meet the right man; their youthful growing awareness of sex and Hannah's determination to wait until she was married.

Rachel's mind flashed back to that powerful stallion long ago with sickening realisation that although she had not had to wait long she had never experienced any wild animal ardour in her own man. What she'd had in her teens was a loving companionship for a man that had promised so much. In reality he had failed to bridge the gap between companionship and the intimate fulfilment needed in a successful marriage. Watching Nathan's tender response to Hannah back there in the ward, Rachel knew instinctively that theirs would have been a really happy marriage. Now Hannah would never have the chance to experience what she'd waited so long for. Yet, Rachel thought, after eight years of marriage I'm still longing for some emotional reaction from my insensitive husband. It was more than that, though; Rachel had no illusions about her real need, because in recent months she couldn't resist looking in prams. When any of the tenants had a baby it had been her privilege to take them a small gift but recently she had become a compulsive baby gurgler.

Rachel walked on through the gardens until she found a shaded seat and just sat in a daze. With no brothers or sisters to share her life, her closest friend had been Hannah. In the first few years after their marriage Alexander had tried to keep them apart by taking her off to London or to weekend house parties. To some extent he had succeeded because his friends moved in a different circle to Hannah's. Rachel mused that although she managed to bridge the two societies, she was more relaxed sitting in the Browns' large farmhouse kitchen than the palatial country houses where, in the early years of their marriage, they had spent too many aimless weekends. Nathan found her in the garden and together they went back into the ward only to find that Hannah was asleep. Rachel watched Nathan gently touch her pale face and she did the same knowing that it was her goodbye.

On the return journey they had been travelling for over a half hour before either spoke. Pointing to where three horses were pulling a binder in the warm late afternoon sunshine Nathan said, "That wheat must have been sown in late spring to be so late ripening."

Watching the growing wheat fall over the knife bar before vanishing inside the machine to re-emerge in neatly tied sheaves finally broke Rachel's trance. "Why Hannah? She was so healthy, how could it happen to her?"

Nathan negotiated the little car on to the grass verge to let a horse and cart loaded with sheaves pass by before replying. "When I asked our village doctor that, he said he thought it was something to do with the fact that Hannah never drank milk. I've always drunk it, her brothers always drank it, I'm sure you did too."

When Rachel confirmed that with a nod, Nathan continued, "I had to help milk each morning before school. I used to tip the bucket from the first cow up to my lips and drink. Anyway that doctor seems to think fresh milk gives us some sort of immunity against TB, perhaps because TB is within the herd."

"Are you returning to Shropshire tomorrow?"

"No, the men are thinning out some young trees so my boss told me that his lad could supervise that job. I have the week off."

They were both quiet for a while as the journey continued, until they were back among the larger dairy farms.

Rounding a bend they came up to a herd of cows wandering down the road with just a big dog behind them. Nathan dropped down to the cows' speed but when the dog decided to sniff around the car the cows almost stopped. The car, not happy with this creeping speed, gave a little cough and stopped. Nathan kicked hard on the foot starter pedal to crank the engine over but, alas, it just flooded it. They both said, "Picnic time."

Although the car free-wheeled onto the grass verge it was too muddy from the daily passage of cows for them to sit out on the grass. Nathan reached for the picnic basket and placed it across their knees inside the car.

When they had finished eating, Nathan, deciding that the car still needed longer to cool, stepped out to stretch his legs. Rachel followed by climbing over the seats to jump down onto the clean road on his side.

As they wandered side-by-side down the lane past the dairy farm they were amused to see the farm staff milking the cows out in the open. Cows stood around in the farmyard while ten or twelve workers just placed their three-legged stool by each cow in turn and milked away.

One fidgeting cow suddenly lashed out with her hind leg, tipping an unfortunate dairymaid backwards off her stool. They smiled at the roar of laughter that rose from the other workers while the embarrassed girl used an old sack to wipe the mud from her dress. Seeing the number of cows and the limited building it was obvious to them that there was not room to house the whole herd inside through the winter months. Nathan said, "They must live out throughout the year. That's how all cows were kept until near the end of the last century."

"But it is so wasteful of land. It needs four or five acres to keep each cow that way!"

"Yes, but you have to value the land against the alternative cost of building winter housing," Nathan said.

Rachel pulled a face to dismiss that point of view and they walked on in friendly debate.

Further down the road they picked and ate more blackberries and then found a clean hedge bank to sit on. Rachel marvelled at how relaxed she felt in Nathan's company. They chatted, pointed things of interest out to each other or sat companionably together.

Chapter Four

Sunday morning seemed unreal to Rachel. After a restless night during which Hannah's pale, drawn features had appeared as a vision each time she closed her eyes, the morning found her tired and listless.

Protesting at missing his walk the day before, Digger, their curly-coated black retriever, began to leap around her. Rachel responded by walking down the drive towards her father's cottage in the estate yard. Although her father often had Sunday lunch with her and Alexander, they never discussed estate business until after the meal. The men would then retire to the study with a big cigar and a brandy each.

It hadn't been like that in the early years of their marriage. Then Rachel had taken part in those discussions as the three of them, after a full Sunday lunch, sat relaxing round the dining table. After Alexander had been involved in London for a couple of years his lack of knowledge of the estate's affairs began to show. Not wishing to lose face in front of Rachel from then on he had suggested that he and Thomas retire to the study with their brandy.

"How about Sunday lunch father?"

"There's the Bolton family, you know the ones who have just moved into the village? Well they've invited me to join them for lunch." Thomas added, "But I'll walk with you to church for morning service."

In the hierarchy of country life Thomas Courtney was second only to the squire. Tall, with handsome features and genial disposition, Thomas was also held in respect by villagers and workers alike. Until her marriage Rachel had been very close to him, working for him through the day both in the house and in the estate office. When they had first come to the Hesston Estate Thomas had created his office in an outbuilding at the back of their house. After losing her mother and leaving school to help her father it had been easy for Rachel to work in the office or to slip back into the kitchen to put lunch on. That closeness had faded through the years of her marriage.

With morning church over Rachel was relieved that her father was not coming for lunch this Sunday. She just wanted to be on her own and she really was alone because, unless guests were being entertained at the Hall, the house servants had Saturday afternoon and Sunday off.

Rachel, after making a snack, then tried to relax in front of the drawing room fire but before long a feeling of restlessness prompted her to take Digger for his long walk.

Rachel walked through the farmyard intending to follow the cow lane, which ran between the fields to the centre of the Home Farm. Responding to the sound of laughter and shouting coming from behind the farm buildings, she walked round to lean on the stack-yard gate. A group of young people, some her workers and others from the village, were playing 'scroggen', sometimes called 'peggy'. She'd enjoyed playing it as a teenager in this very stack-yard. It was one time when she could join in without the others feeling that they had to be careful in front of the steward's daughter. Not that they had ever made an issue of it directly with her but there had been many occasions when conversations had stopped when she had approached. On other occasions little signals of caution had passed between her companions.

It was a simple game needing only a short four or five inch wooden peg and a length of shaft, which was usually about a three foot length cut off an old broken pikel shaft. As Rachel watched, one of the lads placed the peg on the edge of a deep cartwheel track so that it was balanced, then hit down on the protruding end to make it fly up and then gave the flying peg a second hefty whack. Rachel could see a mark on the ground every five yards and it was obvious the two teams were taking alternate strikes. The skill was in that he had to shout out, as he hit, how far it would fly. This time his shout must have been correct because the rest of his team shouted, "Scroggen".

Leaving the shouts of "scroggen" behind, Rachel walked on down the cow lane. It was across this block of land that their dour Scotch gamekeeper Hamish released about fifteen hundred young pheasants each year.

The Home Farm grew a mixture of arable crops in rotation with the hay meadows; which meant that fields of corn were intermingled with fields of swede turnips and potatoes. Although the two menfolk in Rachel's life had in recent years tried to keep her from taking an interest in the farm she couldn't help but be aware that all was not as it should be. Some cleared stubble fields lay bare but on others kivers stood in silent rows, waiting for the three weeks needed to dry the straw and harden the grain between cutting and leading them home. Two or three fields still awaited the binder. As she passed one of them a flock of woodpigeons, feeding on an area of wheat flattened by the heavy rain, flew up with a startling clap of wings.

Among the kivers on the next fields a covey of grey partridge ran ahead of Digger before taking to the wing to skim over the nearest hedge and drop beyond it in the growing turnips. Half grown pheasant poults also scattered before them. Because they were so easily frightened by her boisterous dog Rachel put him on his lead so as not to earn the wrath of Hamish. It was not that Alexander did a lot of shooting but he did like to invite a few friends to share the odd day's sport. The first weekend in October was traditionally kept for Alexander's partridge shoot. Then guests filled the Hall for the weekend. The later-maturing pheasants were not shot until November.

Rachel knew that she must give some thought to the Estate's finances but memories of Hannah kept crowding her mind. Hannah's vibrant, joyous personality and her love for Nathan all now seemed to have no purpose. Having seen the deep tenderness in Nathan's love, Rachel asked aloud, "Why is it all being wasted? Why so young?"

Deep in thought, she was surprised when Hamish stepped out from behind a tree. He looked at Digger's lead with approval and nodded his usual greeting: "Missey." Somehow he managed to roll a Scotch 'r' into the word in a way that always sounded like music to her.

"Hamish! How are you?"

She took his throaty, not unpleasant growl for a positive answer and said, "I thought it was your habit to rest on a Sunday afternoon?"

"I thowt I'd told yer' a keeper should'na have habits or routines. If he does then others'll soon learn 'em. I try to be where I'm not expected."

They walked on in companionable silence. Rachel suddenly laughed as she recalled one of the first walks they had had together. It was when her father had asked Hamish to walk home with her from Hannah's. When they set out across the fields in the spring twilight Hamish asked, "Well Missey, what have yer' bin doing today?"

She blurted out, "The travelling stallion came."

Then, conscious that she'd agreed with Hannah not to tell

anyone, she tried to look nonchalant. Hamish had given her a searching look before asking, "Arrr well, and did yer' watch?"
To her shy head shake he'd replied, "Arrr well, yer've got t'learn sometime."

Later on in that walk, they were passing along the edge of the wood when Hamish signalled her to stop. Slowly raising his index finger Hamish pointed further ahead. Rachel looked and looked but couldn't see anything other than some playful rabbits. At least she had known what rabbits were about in spring. Frolicking together, one rabbit, chasing after another, got closer to a bog of young nettles. Seeing a slight movement Rachel realised that a fox crouched by the nettles. Just as her eyes focused on the fox one rabbit ran too close. There was a flash of movement as the fox leapt out then that amorous rabbit hung squealing in its jaws.

Occasionally after that Hamish allowed her to go on his rounds with him. From her father Rachel learned to read the farming business of the countryside but Hamish showed her how, within that farming environment, lesser beings went about their own business. It was a life and death business too. With Hamish she'd watched mad march hares frolicking and boxing before mating. Weeks later she'd watched in horror as a young hare, perhaps born from that mating, was attacked and killed by two carrion crows. Hamish had stopped her from running across to save it by saying, "Arrr Missey, we mun keep th'vermin down but we mun leave what's left to get with th'lives."

That was all in the past. Now Hamish stopped and raised a bushy eyebrow at her smiles. Taking it for a question Rachel explained. "You would only let me go with you if I didn't talk. I used to chatter away non-stop with every one else but with you I was silent".
"Its ne'r silent." Waving his hand at the fields and woods around him Hamish added, "Yer can hear what's going on but only if ye'r quiet."
A whirl of wings stopped them when a covey of partridge exploded from the stubble at their feet. As the covey skimmed over the nearest hedge Hamish, pointing at them, said, "That's why I'm here."
"What do you mean"?
"There's some Gypsies on th'heath."

The heath was a triangle of gorse-covered land where the lane from the village joined the chapel lane. Each spring old Jake Smith and his extended Gypsy family met there for a family reunion.

Colourful friendly men traded horses between themselves and with local farmers whilst their women walked the lanes selling their wares, which ranged from simple clothes pegs to delicate crocheting. Rachel often spent a happy hour chatting to them over their campfire.

"Old Jake's family wouldn't touch our partridge, would they?"

"No, but there's a couple of families on there now who would. Th'beggars use a short net in th'dark. They came same time last year and took five or six coveys."

"But that's at night, so why are you here now?"

"Partridge like your stubble fields and seem to roost on 'em." He added with a smile, "There's more weed seed on 'em like knotgrass, scarlet pimpernel and fat hen. Or maybe it's because your harvest's late, Browns are already working their stubbles. So I've bin slattering a few thorns about your'n."

When Rachel still looked perplex he explained. "They listen to where each covey of partridge is calling out as they settle down at dusk. Then they drag a short net over em in th'dark."

"What do you mean by a short net?"

"It's about ten yards square with two or three weights on one side and a forty yard rope on th'other side. That means with one of 'em on each end o'rope they can walk well clear o'partridge. Then when th'nets over 'em and th'covey flies up they drop on th'net to hold 'em in. So if thorns are tangled in th'net... well them Gypos'll get in a mess."

Rachel could imagine the two men having to extract the vicious spikes from their hands and knees before disentangling them from their net. And they would have to do it all in the dark.

They briefly discussed the prospects for the partridge shoot before Rachel turned to walk on across the fields. "Bye, Hamish."

Hamish's "Bye, Missey" brought another smile from her because others may fawn and bow but to Hamish she had been just 'Missey' when she was a schoolgirl. Now, even though she was married to the Landlord, she was still just 'Missey' and she would never wish him to call her other.

Another hour of brisk walking took Rachel back towards the Hall, tired in mind and body. Realising that she had in fact been mourning Hannah as though she was already dead she wondered if she was. Or perhaps it was nature's way of preparing her to overcome the grief that was inevitably going to follow.

***

In the 1890s the Wentworth-Jones family had given land to the Methodists for them to build a Chapel. But being good church people Alexander's parents made sure that it was built well out of the village. Lying about half way along the lanes between Clay Bank Farm and Hesston village, it was a comfortable mile stroll for the Brown family each Sunday.

William and Lisa Brown had decided to forgo the services this Sunday and instead would go to visit their daughter. Alas, the little Carden refused to start. Their younger son Matt, although used to its whims, failed to coax the car into life. Nathan helped him to strip the fuel system down without success. After watching them for a frustrating couple of hours the Browns reluctantly admitted defeat and retired to the house.

The two young men went through the car's fuel system again. Just as they finished re-assembling it Mrs Brown called them in to Sunday lunch. Matt, who had started towards the house with Nathan, suddenly turned back to give a hard kick on the starter pedal and the car sprang into life. They both laughed, not knowing what they had done to make it work. By then, though, it was too late for Matt's parents to start on the long journey to the sanatorium.

After lunch William Brown, short, stocky and energetic, led his family along the quiet lanes to the afternoon service at their Chapel. Nathan loved these strong, independent people; he had always felt that he was part of them. Walking along with them Nathan was aware, with some sadness, that now he would never become a member of that family.

After chapel the family returned home to enjoy a light afternoon tea before tackling the milking.

***

Monday morning found Nathan back under a cow again. Now that he had been milking for three days he found that his milking grip was returning. He marvelled that even though he used an axe most days, it had taken so long to get back to milking at full speed.

Milking over, they all headed towards the farmhouse kitchen. The sights and smells of this special room reminded Nathan of his family home. Although most of the food was stored just off the main room in a low, cool pantry, in the kitchen a large ham hung on one side of the black-leaded cooking range. On the other side William balanced on a chair to re-hang the roll of bacon from which his wife had just sliced breakfast. Above the mantelpiece several assorted brass pans hung from a beam. That they were burnt black by the fire on one side and highly polished on the other testified to Lisa's house pride.

It was not only the domain of the apron-clad Lisa; this room was the centre of Claybank Farm. In this room business visitors were entertained and deals were struck. With papers and invoices spread over this table William Brown would struggle in the fading evening light to keep abreast of his financial affairs while Lisa would try to position her rocking chair to gather the maximum light from either the window or the oil lamp as she sewed or knitted through the evening. The front room was only used on a Sunday or for special visitors.

Now Nathan noticed the dog stretched out in front of the black-leaded fireplace had relegated the cat onto the tiles beneath the oven door. Highly polished brass handles glinted on a battered oak dresser taking pride of place along one side. In the opposite corner the grandfather clock ticked away life's minutes.

Two plates of freshly baked bread stood waiting on the large scrubbed table. When the men pulled up their chairs a sizzling-hot plate of bacon and eggs was placed before each by Lisa's maid. These, to keep the smell of paraffin out of the kitchen, had been cooked on a small stove in the back kitchen.

Before breakfast William had supervised the morning milking, made sure that the horses were attended to, looked up at the sky and tapped his weatherglass. Now, after mopping up the fat from his plate with a large piece of crusty bread, he was ready to outline the plans for the day.

The oldest son, Bill, was to take two calves to Crewe cattle market with the pony and float. Matt would stay at home to organise the farm workers, who would lead the last field of wheat sheaves in to the stack yard. William and Lisa would take the car to visit Hannah.

Just as they got up from the breakfast table, a boy who helped out at the village post office cycled into the yard with a telegram.

The Browns had thought that they were prepared for the worst but the news still came as a numbing shock. Nathan read the stark message and, wanting to be alone, walked out of the house and across the fields. It was only when he got to the back drive to Hesston Hall that he thought about Rachel. Realising that someone must tell her, he turned to walk in that direction.

***

The need to take Digger for his morning walk each day gave Rachel the chance to enjoy a feeling of freedom in the fresh air.

Leaving the pool to stride out on the gravel drive between the two woods Rachel stopped to watch the local hunt's fields-man rebuilding a jump.

Neither she nor Alexander now hunted but they still allowed the hunt to meet at the Hall. As a teenager she had always ridden with the hounds. By riding astride, Rachel had earned a reputation for her daring and skill on the chase. After their marriage Alexander made it clear that he didn't think it lady like. Not that he actually told her not to, he just hinted that real ladies rode side-saddle. Rachel did try. However elegant it may have looked to others, she never felt confident jumping the big hedges and ditches with just one foot in a stirrup. It still gave her a thrill though to see the hounds strung out on full cry with excited horses stretching out behind.

Looking up now she saw Nathan in the distance and walked to meet him. When they drew closer his face told her the news and without words they just held each other in silent grief.

Stepping back to wipe her tears, Rachel said, "I feel guilty, because I went to visit Hannah and Mr and Mrs Brown couldn't; they must be heartbroken that they didn't have a chance to say goodbye. I must go and comfort them."

"Well I'll let you go alone. I'll just take a walk through your woodland, if you don't mind."

Rachel said, "Of course not," and started on her away deep in thought.

As a schoolgirl she had always been made so welcome in their home. Now, although their landlord, they still treated her with the same open relaxed friendship. Many of the villagers addressed her in a servile, fawning manner that irritated and hurt. Even some that she had played with as a child adopted that demeaning attitude but not the Browns. Nor would they now accept her apologies for going to visit Hannah instead of them, they were just so grateful that Hannah had seen her before the end.

***

On the day of the funeral, with only the village joiner owning a hearse, Rachel insisted that the Browns let Bestwick chauffeur them in the Talbot Darracq. Coming next in the cortège, Rachel rode in silent comradeship with Nathan in the little Carden. Hannah's older brother Bill, his wife Katie and their children William and Madge came after them in the pony and trap driven by Matt. Various relatives and friends followed behind.

Many country families still relied on their horse for transport, which meant that outside the Chapel ponies, standing restlessly in the shafts of their traps, were mixed in with a collection of quaint cars parked along the lane by the chapel. Rachel was amused to see more than one pony tied up to the back of a parked car. She hoped that the wrong one didn't drive off first. Inside, the little chapel was packed with mourners, and others who could not get in lined the path to the graveside.

Without Alexander to share her grief Rachel felt very alone standing by the open grave. The Browns sensed her feelings and stepped one to each side to hold both her hands. She looked across at Nathan's white face but he stared only at the lowered coffin.

Relatives and friends had worked hard to prepare food, which was laid out in the Sunday school ready for the mourners after the service. Those who had travelled some distance made the most of the rare opportunity to greet each other; one moment expressing their condolences to the Browns and the next their delight at meeting an old friend or relative. It would be late in the day by the time some had completed their slow journey home.

Nathan's parents made a particular point of thanking Rachel for supporting him, brushing aside her protests that it was nothing.

**

Whenever Nathan came back to Cheshire, the farming community always made him welcome. Today, though, he found them fumbling for the right words and wanted to get away to be on his own but he wasn't sure what the leaving arrangements were. He could see Bestwick standing by Rachel's car. Was he waiting to drive the Browns home again or just making sure no farmer tied his pony to it? Nathan stood out in the lane uncertain as to what was expected of him when Rachel joined him, saying, "Have you run out of small talk too?"

"I ran out of words some time ago, I just stayed on out of duty to the family. Now I've run out of duty."

"I know, I feel the same. Drive me back to the farm!"

The sun had broken through, warming the autumn afternoon. When the car picked up speed Rachel took her black wide-brimmed hat off, letting the gentle breeze ruffle the natural wave in her short fair hair. Nearing Clay Bank they found the Browns' workers bringing the herd in for milking. The road seemed full of cows just as it had a few days earlier on the journey back from the sanatorium. Rachel couldn't help smiling, "I haven't packed a picnic this time."

"I couldn't eat anything else but I'd love to sit on that hedge cop and not have to smile at or speak to anyone else today."

Rachel squeezed his arm in sympathy then, as the last of the cows turned into the farmyard; Nathan drove past them and parked by the back door. Rachel went inside to make the fire up and put the kettle on ready for when the family got back. Nathan went to find solitude in the garden.

On the Cheshire Plain forty foot is a bank, and Clay Bank Farm house stood about that high above Hesston Brook, which curved round the homestead. The garden sloped gently away from the house for some thirty yards. There a low hedge divided it from the narrow meadow, which in turn sloped down to the brook. The curve in the brook created a lovely view from the garden and that was where Rachel found Nathan.

As she sat down on the other end of the battered old garden seat their eyes met in understanding. In the peaceful afternoon sunshine two young water hens, obviously a late hatching because they were still not fully-grown, ranged out from the tree-lined brook side to pick worms and grubs from the field. From the buildings cows emerged as each was milked and in turn released. The cows meandered singly across the meadow, some to graze and others to satisfy their thirst from the brook.

The peace was at last broken when a hovering kestrel sent the young water hens scurrying back to the brook. Rachel asked, "Would it take a fully grown water hen?"

"I doubt it, but it would take a younger one. I suppose they've yet to learn that they are growing up and are playing safe."

Some time later they heard Bestwick drive into the farmyard so Rachel went inside to make a pot of tea. When each of the adults was settled with a cup and the two children, William and Madge, with a glass of home made lemonade Rachel took her leave.

Chapter Five

Lisa Brown's younger brother, Jack Birtwistle, had offered to give Nathan a lift back home. He and his wife Alice had come back to Clay Bank to help serve out cups of tea to the many relatives and friends who still seemed reluctant to take their leave. Jack, becoming impatient to get back to his Shropshire farm, went to look for Nathan in the garden. Since moving to Shropshire the Birtwistles had been good friends to Nathan, always making him welcome when he called. In fact some of Alice's delicious homemade scones often supplemented his bachelor fare in his little cottage.

When Jack asked, "Are you ready to go Nathan?" He stood up, looked around and answered, "Yes there's nothing more for me here." Nathan had been working on his cottage for a while before Hannah became ill. Using the best-seasoned oak from the timber yard he had used his woodworking skills refitting the down stairs rooms but had yet to start on the bedrooms. Now, when he stepped in through the back door he felt the autumn cold of an empty house and realised with sadness that, although this cottage had been their dream home, without Hannah it was no more than a cold and empty shell.

Watching the flames climb up the chimney triggered a mixture of nostalgia and regret for the wasted years. If only he'd got to know Hannah sooner. Well, that was silly because he had known her from his schooldays. The only trouble then had been that, as Bill's young sister, she'd been a bit of a nuisance. After he moved with his family to Shropshire, travelling difficulties had made his visits to see Bill few and far between. It was at Bill's wedding, when he'd been best man and Hannah the chief bridesmaid, that he'd realised how Bill's young sister had grown up into a very attractive young woman.

Nathan remembered chatting to her through the reception and finding her an interesting companion. The trouble had been that she already had a boyfriend and he was involved with a Shropshire girl. Nathan remembered how after that day he became so restless that he'd ended his relationship with the other girl. Still unsure as to how to approach Hannah he'd let a few months go by before an unexpected letter dropped on his doormat. As he opened it his heart almost stopped when he saw it was from Hannah! The pretext of the letter was to tell him that Katie and Bill were expecting a baby but it was much more than that because Hannah had filled three pages of village gossip and added her views on many things. He smiled as he remembered how his reply had been much shorter, but from then on they wrote regularly.

Visiting Bill and Katie for the christening was the opportunity to see more of each other and develop a relationship beyond just exchanging letters, though Nathan always regretted that their courting had mostly been conducted through the post. The occasional visit in his boss's car had helped to build on their love but those brief occasions had been too far apart.

Perhaps that was as well, Nathan mused to the dancing flames, because they were both warm, responsive people and having to wait until they were married had taken some willpower, particularly because he was not without experience. There had been two or three girls in his life, and he remembered one in particular.

Was he only twenty-one (he struggled to remember, it seemed so long ago) he had gone to fall timber on her father's estate. He remembered stabling his team of five horses in the estate's stables while he'd arranged lodgings for himself and his three men with different estate workers.

Throwing another log on the fire sent a burst of sparks up the chimney, reminding Nathan of the sparks that flew when Natasha came into his life. Tall, blonde and riding astride on a man's saddle, Natasha began to take her morning ride in the direction of his felling operation. The first task in the wood on a cold winter's morning was always to light a fire and put the kettle on. By the time it came to the boil they were ready to gather round it for a break. He remembered with some amusement how that rather sophisticated society girl seemed to think it exciting to tie her horse to a tree and sit by a camp fire drinking out of a tin mug with four tough, rough woodmen.

After those visits had been going on for about two weeks Nathan's men moved across the fields to the next wood, while he stayed behind marking the fallen trees. When Natasha found him there alone she turned on her seductive charm. Before long they were half sitting, half leaning against the pile of large oak tree trunks and if he remembered rightly he ended up with a skinned knee.

From his lodgings with the estate's resident woodman it was just a short evening walk to make a bedtime check on his horses. Natasha began to take an interest in the welfare of her own horse at the same time and though the nights were dark and cold the stable had been warm and dry. Nathan really believed that he'd found true love.

That affair lasted until Christmas. When he got back there after the Christmas break she was gone. He was told that she had gone to stay with her father's cousins but no one knew where. Or if they did they weren't telling him. It was made obvious that Daddy hadn't approved.

About a month later Nathan received a letter from her; there was no address. Headed *'The Cotswolds'* it read, *'Daddy tricked me into going away on the pretext that it was just for Christmas. After Christmas when he wouldn't come to fetch me I was furious but it was perhaps for the best. The hunting is superb here, the ground is so firm and the gallops are long. The foxes are not dodging from one wood to the next like they do in Cheshire. Oh, and we do have some marvellous parties with interesting people coming up from London.*

It was fun. Wish you well.

Love, Natasha'

He'd thought he was heartbroken but when he read that a long gallop across firm ground was better than anything he had to offer his heartbreak soon ended. There had been two or three other affairs before Hannah came into his life.

He and Hannah had been engaged twelve months, found the cottage of their dreams, fixed the wedding day for late spring and then Hannah caught the flu. Months went by, the wedding day got closer but Hannah still seemed tired and listless. The flu had left her with a cough that didn't seem to get better.

Nathan's agony was great when he remembered how, just a month before their wedding day, her doctor had diagnosed TB.

For those first few months of her stay in the sanatorium he'd found it hard to work on the house. It had been Hannah's optimism and encouragement that motivated him to start again. She particularly asked in her letters for him to describe what he'd altered and how it looked.

Now it was all a waste. The fire seemed unable to dispel the feeling of icy cold loneliness in the little cottage.

***

There was some surprise the following day when Nathan arrived back at the timber yard; they were not expecting him back until the following week. Nathan didn't tell them that he just couldn't sit in a cottage full of memories. His boss, who was just walking to his car, expressed his sympathy and explained that he was late for an appointment but Anthony would bring Nathan up to date with events.

From his schooldays Tony, the eldest son of the boss, had been Nathan's companion. Whatever the weather, each school holiday Tony had been out with Nathan's timber-felling team. Always respectful and obedient as a boy, not that there was room for any other attitude when falling tall timber, Tony had developed into a strong, likeable character. In fact it had been Tony's car in which Nathan had done most of his courting. The boss bought the car for Nathan to use at work and for his son's pleasure the rest of the time. Occasionally Nathan had been able to combine a visit to Hannah with his work, but once she was in hospital his visits had been about once a month and each time with Tony's permission. When Nathan asked him to be his best man Tony joked that, considering that all the courting had taken place in his car, perhaps he should really be the groom not Nathan.

That was all in the past. This morning when Nathan found him in the yard he was instructing the steam-engine driver. The two young men greeted each other warmly then walked back across the yard together.

Tony explained that his father had taken on an urgent contract to fall some dangerous trees leaning over a large house. Tony was planning to use the steam engine winch to guide those trees away from the property as they were felled. Walking on together Tony explained to Nathan how he had deployed the rest of Nathan's staff. Suddenly it occurred to Nathan that his youthful assistant was now twenty-two; at that age Nathan had been in charge of the tree felling work for several years. If the time had come for young Tony to take over that role would there still be a place for Nathan?

***

Returning from her morning walk with Digger, Rachel found two letters waiting for her. She recognised the handwriting on both. The first envelope, small and thin, was from Alexander and the second, a much fuller letter, was in his mother's handwriting. The maid carried her morning coffee tray through to the lounge where Rachel settled down to read both.

Alexander expressed his regret for not coming back for the funeral. Telling Rachel that he understood how much Hannah had meant to her, Alexander paid Hannah a little tribute of his own and wished Rachel well. No declaration of love or even affection, but then on the few occasions that he'd written to her in the past his letters had always been cool and factual.

Lady Wentworth-Jones, known to every one as Lady Louisa, had been a Lady in her own right before she married the Colonel. From the time Rachel first came to live on the estate Lady Louisa always treated her as an equal. During the months Rachel helped to nurse Alexander they also became good friends. Her letter now showed her deep friendship by dwelling for some length on Hannah's sad death. It then went into a different direction: '*Alexander rang me from his club, and it was obvious from the conversation that things are not right between you, or for that matter, the estate. So forgive me if I offend but it's time I told you things that perhaps I should have told you years ago. When Alexander said that he wished to marry you I was delighted. Not only did I know you better than anyone could expect to know their future daughter-in-law but I knew that you were the perfect wife for my son.*

'*Let me try to explain why. The Colonel was a good man but never decisive. Oh, he was all right in the Army; there was either a set manoeuvre for each situation or an order to be obeyed. Later, when those orders conflicted with his conscience, it destroyed him.*' Rachel wondered what was the conflict between conscience and orders that had destroyed the Colonel. Her memory of him was of a kindly old man who wandered around the estate muttering to himself in an absent minded way.

Lady Louisa continued: '*Back on the estate dealing with ordinary people there was no tactical manoeuvre taught in Army Training School for him to follow so rather than deal with a problem he would put it off. I grew up on a country estate and always took an interest in what went on so the steward began to come to me with problems. By the time the Colonel went away to Africa I was managing both the estate and the investments, I knew he was more than happy about it but he never said so. Rachel, you are far better prepared than I was; I'd lived a sheltered life whereas your experience in the Estate Office has prepared you for that role, so now take it!*'

Lady Louisa then reminded Rachel of how she had helped Alexander to recover and learn to walk again. There were a few paragraphs of personal praise that made her blush, then suddenly her breath held tight when she read: '*;You've gone to his weekend house parties, his* *shooting weekends and dressed up for the grand balls just to please him. You've always been so conscious that you were only the Steward's daughter and Alexander was the Lord of the Manor but you are wrong on both counts. Before I appointed your father I had him checked out and I had quite a shock. Your father is the direct descendant of the De Courcy family, who were one of the great landed families in the Midlands. Your line goes right back to the Normandy invasion but why your father has never told you is for him to explain.'*

Rachel re-read the line but couldn't take it in. Her father had always maintained that her grandfather had just been a farmer, and a not very good farmer at that, who'd married late in life. This was all new to her; there must be some mistake.

When she finally turned back to the letter Lady Louisa continued: *'In contrast, on our side the Wentworth-Jones' line only goes back two generations. Alexander's grandfather was in shipping, working from Liverpool; in fact the unsavoury truth is that in his early years he had made his fortune as a slave trader. After it was abolished in the British Empire around 1830 the British Navy tried to impose the ban worldwide by intercepting slave ships on route to America and other destinations. The Colonel believed his father (Alexander's grandfather) somehow evaded the Navy blockade by registering some ships abroad. Anyway, he continued in the trade for some years after abolition. We will never know the full truth about that because it was some twenty years later when he finally married but he married well. That tough old sailor named Jones added his bride's name and became a more respectable Captain Wentworth-Jones but he was still a rough, uncouth old sea-dog. The bride, also well past her first flush of youth, gave him two sons.*

'Both boys went away to have their manners polished at boarding school. When the eldest - who was a bit rough and wild like his father - left school he went in the shipping business with his father, whilst the younger son, the Colonel, was still at school. Even when Captain Wentworth-Jones was a very old man his ships were reputed to still be involved in dubious trading of one sort or other, although the Colonel, being only a boy, never learned just what that trade was. Anyway within two or three years the old man was dead. Sadly, soon after that, whilst still a teenager, the Colonel's elder brother was lost

Again Rachel found it hard to believe, but she knew that Lady Louisa would not have dug out the family skeletons unless they were true.

The letter continued: *'Both boys had been made to sail from an early age but the Colonel hated the sea. Just as one boy loved it, the other always suffered from seasickness and begged to go into the Army instead. When he was old enough his mother bought him a commission and sent him to an officer training college. I met and fell in love with him when he was a dashing, handsome Captain and despite everything I was still in love with him the day he died.'*

Rachel paused, trying to visualise Alexander's father as a young man before reading on: *'Hesston Estate had been in one branch of the Wentworth family for many generations. Although they were only distant cousins of my mother-in-law she had kept in touch. When she heard it was for sale she encouraged Alexander to buy it. It was soon after we'd married so some of the money came out of my dowry, but the bulk of it came from his mother. Yes, the estate was bought with money made originally from slavery! It's our family secret. You should know it but you must keep it, because the locals think the estate came to us down my family line. Even Alexander doesn't know any of this; he just believes that his family owned a small shipping line. Nor does he know about your background. Although I had told him that I would have your family checked out, I didn't tell Alexander what that investigation revealed. I just told him there was nothing there that he couldn't be proud of.'*

It was like a work of fiction to Rachel. She knew that her proud and ambitious husband in some way was a driven man. In the past she had thought it had been just his determination to prove himself fit again. Lately she had begun to realise that it was something more. Lady Louisa was obviously aware of what motivated her son because she wrote: *'Alexander would be destroyed if he knew about his grandfather. He already feels that the Colonel failed in some way because of his breakdown. No matter how I tried to help him understand he just couldn't accept that a serving officer could allow his conscience to interfere with orders. A soldier's duty is to obey, not to question or moralise about those orders. But then the young are always so sure.'*

Rachel smiled when she read: *'I don't think he would easily accept your own family background. He can be so vain at times that it might just make him feel inferior in some way. Anyway I didn't tell him and I don't think you should either!'*

Rachel was feeling numb with the sheer extent of the letter. First the realisation that her family must have something in its near history that for some reason was being kept hidden, and now Alexander's people also had dark secrets.

She walked out into the garden to sit in the gentle September sunshine. Benson, their head gardener, walked over to her to ask a few questions about the flowerbed he'd cleared out. Rachel forced herself to think 'herbaceous' and walked across with him to explain again how she wanted it planted.

Leaving Benson to his work Rachel walked on through the gardens towards the lake. There was a flurry of wings and noise as startled coots and water hens raced across the gardens to splash back into the water. Mallards took to the air with fright to circle overhead before gliding down to land further down the lake. Then a heron, disturbed from fishing among the irises near the bank side, called out angrily as he took to the air with silent, lazy wing-strokes.

Walking further along the lakeside she saw a large pike suddenly strike into a shoal of small fish, causing them to scatter across the surface in a frantic dash to escape. The lake then gradually became quiet again, its inhabitants obviously getting on with their lives, which Rachel realised was what she must do. None of these fish could choose the pool that they were born in; if they hatched out in this pool they had to live out their lives here. She had chosen, perhaps in youthful adoration and love but she had chosen, and now she was here, an energetic twenty-six year old woman. Family skeletons were just dry dead bones; real life was full of today's needs that had to be lived here and now.

Refreshed by the walk Rachel returned to the letter to read even more bad news as Lady Louisa explained, *'I still have a share in the Estate and take an allowance out of it but I take no part in any decisions. Our accountants, Alder and Brockbank, have written to say that our investments are not doing well and have asked to see me. I have no intention of travelling all that way to interfere so I have enclosed a letter giving you full authority to act on my behalf. I know that Alexander has already asked you (if somewhat ungraciously) to sort out the estate, now this letter gives you the right to go much further. Please find out what is going on and sort it out for all our sakes.'*

Chapter Six

Rachel thought that the first thing she ought to do would be to go through Alexander's desk. She'd always respected his wish for privacy but no more. Before that though she must finish reading this letter, which after a few questions about old acquaintances finished on a positive note: *'Ignore Alexander's objections to wires across the park and get the telephone connected, then if you wish to discuss anything with me please do'*.

Alexander's beautiful old roll-top desk revealed a few secrets. Among them was a very sad looking bank statement and a letter dated two months before, from the family solicitors Fenwick and Cuthbert who were apparently responding to Alexander's request for advice in relation to re-organising the estate. It was too vague to make sense to her but it ended by asking him to make an appointment at his earliest convenience.

So he'd been aware of the problems but he'd never discussed them with her; nor seemingly had he got round to doing anything about them. She smiled when she thought about the coming Sunday lunch with her father; the poor man had no idea what awaited him. A feeling of restlessness invaded Rachel's normally relaxed mind so after afternoon tea it took but a few inquiring looks from Digger to persuade her to reach for his lead.

***

On their journey across Cheshire to visit Hannah, Nathan had been a bit scathing about the farmers who were still cutting spring wheat. Even her father had always maintained that spring sown wheat only yielded about two thirds of an autumn sown crop. Usually a farmer grew spring wheat if he failed to get his winter wheat sown before the autumn rain made the ground too wet. When Nathan had said something about late ripening wheat being a sign of slack management she hadn't told him that on the Home Farm they still had two fields of spring wheat to cut. As one field had been cut earlier in the week she walked across the farm to see how the second was progressing.

Putting Digger on his lead so that he wouldn't be tempted to chase a bolting rabbit Rachel was surprised to see that the workers were still enjoying their late afternoon baggin.

Providing the hefty butties was the responsibility of Mary, the wife of Harry Wilson the Dairyman. Not that Mary actually prepared the food herself for she was the cheese maker in charge of all the dairy work. The quality, and with it the price of each cheese, was dependent on her skill and management. In fact Mary took the place of the normal farmer's wife: not only responsible for the cheese-making, she also fed the live-in staff and provide them with baggin both morning and afternoon every day bar Sunday. Then through both the hay and the cereal harvests she provided a late baggin in the fields for all the staff. The fact that much of that food was grown on the farm meant that Mary kept her four dairymaids very busy. Blackberries and crab apples gathered from the field side hedges were preserved along with fruit from the orchard in sealed bottling jars, or made into jam. Longer keeping apples were stored in the cellar for late winter use. Most of that fruit harvest took place through the late summer when the cow's milk production was falling off and the dairymaids had less milk to handle. By Christmas when the bulk of the cows were dried off cheese making would stop altogether, only starting again in April when the cows calved to match their peak milk production with the abundance of May grass.

Thomas allowed Mary a housekeeping budget, so within it the more home-grown produce she made use of the greater the surplus left for her. Vegetables from the garden were salted and stored in deep stoneware bowls. Eggs from the summer glut were carefully placed in waterglass (a preservative) for use in the dark winter days when hens followed nature's pattern and stopped laying.

The skill of any farmer's wife in managing her house budget could make the difference between success and failure of the farm business. Mary's old bones were beginning to feel the constant strain but harvest time baggin would not worry her too much. Two of the girls would prepare it while Mary dealt with the afternoon's milk. Normally early afternoon baggin was taken just before milking commenced. That consisted of a thick cheese sandwich and a big can of tea. At harvest time a second more substantial late baggin was brought to the field by the dairy girls, who stayed on afterwards to help set the sheaves up into kivers.

Rachel had joined in many times. From her schooldays when she first came onto the farm this harvesting tea had always been a happy ritual. The three horses, still harnessed to the binder, would stand munching in their nosebags while the workers sat around on sheaves chatting and joking with each other. This time though the sight of Rachel had the staff jumping guiltily to their feet; even the waggoner hurried sheepishly across to attend to his horses.

Waiting around three sides of the remaining uncut wheat were several village boys. Rabbits, having lived in the growing wheat crop throughout the summer months, now found their home vanishing up the noisy binder. Allowed by Thomas to keep the ones they caught, the boys came after school to give chase to the confused bolting rabbits. From the fourth side, which was nearest the wood, the solid bang of a shotgun told her where Hamish waited.

Walking on round the uncut block of wheat towards Hamish, Rachel was soon in trouble with Digger. He was always excited at the smell of a fox, and now he strained on his leash to attack a dead one lying between the sheaves. Hamish told her, "Arrr I knew he wer' in there so I made them boys stay round th'other end. He crept out my way after th'binder went quiet at baggin time."
Rachel smiled at his dour modesty knowing well that he had probably waited silent and still for two or three hours - just to shoot that one fox.

The harsh realities of country life had been part of her childhood. Most of the tenant farmers, keeping free-range poultry, expected the estate to control the fox numbers. Even she cringed though when two of the schoolboys came chasing past after a three-legged rabbit. The binder's knife-bar took its own deadly toll as the uncut area of wheat became smaller. A sudden burst of boyish shouting from the other side of the standing wheat sent the boys running after another confused rabbit dodging among the scattered sheaves. As she walked back alongside the uncut wheat, another bolted from right in front of Rachel causing Digger to leap on his lead but she just managed to hold him. The rabbit turned towards Hamish who, now freed from the need for quietness, dispatched it with one shot.

Turning her back on the activity of the cornfield Rachel walked towards home feeling the immense pleasure of being part of this living, thriving but always demanding community.

**

The spell of warm September weather broke on the way to church for morning service. The rain took Rachel's thoughts away from the contents of the sermon; instead they were on the amount of corn still to be harvested on the Home Farm. She asked herself why were they were so behind most of the other farmers in the area.

There was no chance to discuss it with her father on the walk home because the westerly driven rain beat against her umbrella and bounced up off the drive to soak her ankles beneath her long coat.

The conversation over lunch was on general topics as Thomas steered Rachel away from any estate subject. The meal over, Rachel poured him a liberal glass of port, passed him one of Alexander's cigars and said, "Now tell me what happened to the Colonel."

"I presume it's the Boer War that you are asking about?" When Rachel nodded he continued, "He had a rough time out there, the Boers refused to fight in a conventional way. I'm no military man so I can only give you my countryman's version of events."

"That's all I want. I need to understand why he came back a broken man."

"The Colonel was sent out to engage the Boers. He marched his men after them for days but they wouldn't stand and fight. Instead they kept on the move in front of the Colonel, tempting him on. When the Boers got into the hills they began to raid his flanks in quick short attacks. The Colonel tried to keep scouts out in front and on the flanks but they were picked off one by one or allowed to see what the Boers wanted them to see. After days of hard marching and constant harassment the scouts reported that the fleeing Boer army was digging in to make a stand near the head of the next valley. The Colonel saw his chance to engage in a set battle, one that he knew how to fight, but it was a trap."

Thomas puffed at his cigar and sipped a little more port until in frustration Rachel asked, "What happened next?"

"It was just a token force in front; when the Colonel engaged them the rest came at the British from both flanks in earnest. There were terrible casualties on our side, but the Colonel, rallying some of his troops, managed to make a stand among some rocks. After several days of pounding and further loss the Boers suddenly withdrew and allowed the few survivors to limp back to base. Although he never talks about it, Hamish was one of those survivors. I understand that towards the end of that action the Colonel saved his life but I've never known just how."

"Is that all or is there more?"

"The Boers could move fast because they were living off the land, replenishing their food stores from the settlers each day. Whereas the British, weighed down with the need to carry every thing with them, were much more restricted. In frustration the British decided that if they swept the countryside clean of settlers then the Boers couldn't keep replenishing themselves. The Colonel, who had been away on leave recovering from that last foray, was then given orders to round up civilians into holding camps. Women and children were held in open country, often with little shelter or food. The Colonel tried his best to do it with kindness but as disease, hunger and the cold took hold he had to watch them die in frightening numbers. He tried hard to get supplies for them but time and time again blundering officials or bureaucracy beat him. In the end he just broke down."

Rachel, having read about that shameful time in British history, could imagine some of the torment that kindly man would have gone through. It was time to top her father's glass up again but he declined a second cigar and sat back relaxed until Rachel asked, "Now tell me about the DeCourcy family."

Thomas rocked forward, his face reddening as he blustered in consternation, but Rachel demanded, "Tell me!"

"Where did you get that name from? It's all in the past! Why bring it all back now?"

"Tell me!"

"My grandfather was both a gambler and a heavy drinker. Alas, in one all-night gambling session he lost all his cash. He was so sure though that he held a winning hand he covered it with his estate. Well, he didn't have a winning hand - and the family lost everything. Well, not quite everything because the winner allowed him to keep one outlying farm to provide a home for his family. Alas, he just carried on drinking and was dead within a few years."

"How big was the estate and where was it?"

"In the south Midlands; I have seen it. It has a lovely Hall, well maintained, with about nine thousand acres of good fertile soil."

"What children were there?"

"Just my father who was in his mid twenties and engaged to a titled Lady. The daughter of Lord Crumstock I think. Anyway, she turned her noble nose up at becoming the wife of a common farmer. Yes, she jilted him."

"Well, then what?"

"Well, being quite bitter my father wouldn't stay in the same house as his drunken father. He took off, travelling around the world. When he eventually returned many years later not only his father but also his mother had died. He seemed to have returned with modest wealth, which he invested in the farm. Amazingly, he not only settled down on the farm but although he was in his late forties he courted and married a widow. That widow, my mother, was also in her early forties, so I think they were both a bit surprised when I came along some two years later. The title had passed on down a different line but it was never explained to me. I just know that my father, your grandfather, claimed not to have inherited a title, nor did he use the DeCourcy name after he returned to England. At his marriage he was just Mr Courtney and would never discuss any of the past with me." Thomas sipped his port thoughtfully. "I knew nothing of this until after he died, which was while I was still at school. My mother then told me what she knew, which wasn't much. Although she did say that father had expected to return from abroad a wealthy man but that he had been beaten up and robbed somewhere on the return journey. It was she who insisted I went to college. Alas, father hadn't been a good farmer or a prudent one for that matter. When Mum died suddenly, while I was still in college, I found the debts were so great that I had no real alternative but to sell the farm and .... Well you know the rest."

Rachel sat in stunned silence thinking so; I'm the great granddaughter of a drunken gambler and married to the grandson of a slave-trader.

Chapter Seven

Bestwick was always at ease with Rachel, but in contrast his somewhat diminutive wife was very shy and quiet. As Bestwick drove them towards Knutsford, Rachel tried hard to get her into conversation but without success. In the end she gave up and just sat back to enjoy the scenery. Rachel knew from Bestwick how they both appreciated the chance of a day in town, so when Bestwick asked, "Are you sure, ma'am, that you will not need the car again this morning?" she replied, "Of course I'm sure. Just drop me off at the solicitors and you can have the car and the day to yourselves." Rachel gave his arm a reassuring squeeze. "I will take afternoon tea in the Fawn and Hound; you can pick me up from there after 4.30."

***

Entering the old Market town of Knutsford, Bestwick turned into the narrow King Street, known to the locals as the Bottom Street, to distinguish it from the parallel but much shorter Top Street or Princess Street, as the more posh inhabitants liked to call it. A hold-up further up the street gave Rachel time to reflect on her studies of Knutsford in her last school year. From them Rachel was perhaps more aware than most of the fantastic variety of architectural styles represented along this one narrow street.

Opposite the Southern end just beyond the railway bridge was one of the oldest buildings. Completed in 1688, the two-storey red bricked Unitarian Chapel was still in use. That it was chosen as the final resting place for the famous Mrs Gaskell when she died in 1865 added to its fame. The other end of the street was equally impressive because the Lodge and imposing gateway to Tatton Park stood on the very edge of the town.

In between, a strange mixture of building styles has made Knutsford the most interesting town in Cheshire. Although most people describe the town as mainly Georgian, in fact the architecture ranges from 17th century cottages near the church to 19th century buildings of a distinct continental flavour. The Manchester businessman, Richard Harding Watt, built these in a bizarre Italianate design. The turrets, towers and red pantile roofs, at first glance seeming out of place, help to make Knutsford unusual if not unique.

Rachel loved the fine traditional 18th and 19th century buildings that grace the Bottom Street. Near the North end a block of silk weavers' cottages contrast with more of the Watt ornate creations, which stand just a hundred yards away from them at the top of Drury Lane. The Ruskin Rooms follow Watt's Italianate style but the next door is a block of cottages that some describe as Art Nouveau.

Although there are these remnants of a bygone small silk industry no other industry encroached on the north side of the town, and Rachel presumed the feudal power of the Egertons of Tatton estate had ensured to that. While still working for her father, a business visit with him to Tatton Park had revealed to Rachel just how ruthless the great landowners had been in the past. Their influence had not just been on the town. In the parkland Rachel walked on the foundations of a forgotten village erased by a past member of the Egerton family, presumably because it interfered with his plan to enlarge the park. Small farms, village craftsmen and cottagers had been moved out and their homes demolished at the landlords whim.

Knutsford's Top Street, which had been developed later than the other, lacked historic buildings. There are though several small lanes or passageways connecting the two streets that Rachel and her school friends had enjoyed exploring. The more important of these lanes were paved with stone sets or cobbled stones while others were just basic cinder tracks. Some led to the back door of businesses or pubs while along another a group of small cottages might nestle round a cobbled courtyard.

When the blockage further along the narrow Bottom Street was cleared Bestwick drove on. It was at the bottom of one of those connecting lanes where he finally parked the Darracq to allow Rachel to alight.

***

Standing back off the street in one of those little cobbled courtyards Fenwick and Cuthbert's Black and white office was more mock than real Tudor. Lifting her longish skirt, which she favoured for formal outings, to climb the four steep steps up to the door, Rachel was aware of how dowdy it looked, peeling paint making the whole place looked scruffy. Inside Mr Cuthbert's office the same aged, dowdy feeling prevailed. Piles of ribbon-tied documents stood on the floor along two walls, whilst in-between them a threadbare carpet marked the path to the desk. Cuthbert emerged from behind more ribbon bound piles (that almost hid his desk) to limply shake her hand and guide her to a chair.

Cuthbert brushed aside Rachel's apology for her late arrival with the explanation. "A backfire from a motor frightened a delivery horse into bolting. Two men managed to catch it but an elderly lady was knocked down and badly injured."

When Cuthbert finally sat behind his desk Rachel was amused to find there was a space through which they could see each other and through it she explained that it was Alexander's wish she take control of the Estate. Mr Cuthbert made suitable supportive noises but when she asked about the letter to Alexander, Cuthbert put on his most unreadable official expression and refused to discuss it.

Rachel tried again. "You've obviously been asked to look into something that has to do with the Estate. If I'm to take control I'll need your help and I expect you to tell me what problems may be facing me."

Shovelling a few papers around he said, "I am sorry but your husband's business must remain confidential."

Passing over the letter of authority from Lady Wentworth-Jones, Rachel said, "That gives me the authority to demand all information relating to the Estate."

Cuthbert read and reread it then gave her a long searching look. "I'd like to ask my son to join us. May I?"

At her nod he left the room and returned with a much younger, taller man who managed both a firm handshake and a fleeting smile, but she noticed that it didn't reach his eyes. After introducing him as his son, Cuthbert senior explained her request. Cuthbert junior put on the same unreadable solicitor look saying, "I have been asked to act for your husband therefore I couldn't poss ..."

Leaping to her feet and lifting her long skirt to stamp hard on the threadbare carpet, she almost shouted, "Look - either I run the Estate with your help or without your help but I am going to run it. Now either you tell me what this is all about or I walk out and take the Estate business with me."

Cuthbert Junior glanced down at her exposed shapely lower leg and then, as he met her angry eyes, his solicitor mask slipped enough for his eyes to twinkle. Turning to his father he said, "I think I can help Mrs Wentworth-Jones; perhaps we should use my office?"

Following him through a couple of doors Rachel had time to

glance around a bright, cheerful office, which had a window overlooking the Bottom Street. Cuthbert Junior picked up the documents he had been working on before being called through to place them neatly alongside some others on a table behind his swivel chair. When he turned back to meet Rachel's amused look he smiled at her unspoken comparison. "Yes, I like my desk clear."

Then pointing to the documents behind his chair he added, "I just let the work pile up out of sight."

Stepping back round the desk, to hold the chair while Rachel sat down, he explained, "I've only been in partnership here for about a year. Before that I worked for a couple of large practices in the City. My Father offered me a partnership when Fenwick retired. By the way, I knew Alexander from our school days, not that we were particularly close friends."

He looked at her for a few moments then added, "When he knew that I'd returned he asked me to take over the estate business. My Father was a bit reluctant - as you noticed he still is - but I did."

Stepping to the door he called to his secretary to bring in the Estate file, then sitting down he asked Rachel again to explain the course of events. Quickly running through the last few days she was aware that he seemed to be thinking more than listening; even when the file was placed before him he only opened it absentmindedly. After a pause he asked, "Are you telling me that the estate is not in profit or is it the farm that's not making a profit?"
"Both."
"Is it - do you think - the general economics of the time or is it the management?"
"Both."
"Alexander said exactly the same! Because I'd been involved with two large estates in my last practice Alexander asked me to advise him on estate management and the possibility of persuading your father to retire." Watching the surprise, if not shock, on Rachel's face he added, "I'm sorry, I know that it's so personal to you but now I've had time to go through both sets of accounts my advice to Alexander would have been that your father should retire."
"I don't know that he's reached retirement age. I'm still trying to come to terms with the fact that Alexander had been aware of so much. In recent years he didn't seem to take much interest in the Estate, and he certainly never discussed any of this with me."

What had her Mother-in-law said in the letter? 'You will have to accept that indecision is part of your man's make up'. Perhaps that was what the row was about - Alexander couldn't bring himself to discuss her father's future with her, nor could he go to the solicitor because then he would then have to make the decision. As Rachel sat thinking it all through Cuthbert cleared his throat to break the silence. "There is more if you would like to hear it?"

"Please carry on."

"I took advice from different sources on how best to run an estate such as yours. The advice back was very clear. The days of an all-round Steward are long gone. Now the practice is to appoint a farm manager who can be answerable to either the owner or the estate agent or both. I say Agent because the thinking is that an estate of this size cannot justify or afford a resident agent and should employ an outside company to manage the estate business."

It was hard to think objectively when the centre of any reorganisation would so affect her father. At the same time her mind was in a whirl over Alexander: did he care enough not to want to hurt her or was he just opting out? She became lost in thought.

Cuthbert had sat patiently thumbing through the Estate file while Rachel tried to think through the implications. Finally, again clearing his throat to get her attention, he asked, "Have you made arrangements for lunch?" Seeing the shake of her head he said, "Perhaps you will join me at the Fawn and Hound?"

As Cuthbert junior guided her to the outside door he seemed to shed his solicitor's deadpan expression but he retained his old world courtesies by holding the door for her. Then, taking her elbow to guide her along the street, the young solicitor again stepped ahead to hold the hotel door. It made Rachel smile with the thought, 'how would he fare striding across the muddy fields and through the woods?'

The black and white timber-framed hotel reflected its age on the inside. Dark oak panelling made the dining room seem distinctly short of light if not dim but the effect seemed to release the formal solicitor further from his professional inhibitions.

Over a rather plain but wholesome meal Rachel learned that Benjamin, or Benjie as he liked his friends to call him, had been a widower for over two years. Perhaps that loss had made him restless enough to leave the City practice and accept his father's offer of a partnership. He chatted on about the town and his growing involvement in many of its affairs, but never once returned to

Rachel's own problems. The meal over he asked, "So what have you decided, what will you do?" Rachel said, "I'm going to walk up the street to the accountants and dig a little further."

"That makes sense, but please, take time to clear your thinking then come to see me before you act."

Alan Brockbank's round, cheerful face welcomed her into a bright, clean accountants' office. The fact that they had met socially on a few occasions helped to dispel any strain. His thick glasses caused him to peer a bit disconcertingly but his ready smile counteracted any embarrassment. He listened to what she had to say, read the letter from Lady Louisa and gave her a long and rather grave look.

Rachel said, "Give me a quick breakdown of the estate's finances."

"I'm afraid both the farm accounts and the estate's are overdue. What we have, and what your solicitor has seen, are some two years out of date and they barely broke even. Judging by the rest of my farm clients I would expect a further decline in the finances of both."

Remembering how her father had been so meticulous and up-to-date over his business records, Rachel found it hard to accept that he had apparently now become so lax.

"I am more immediately concerned about your personal investments. We act as your agents in that we invest your capital on instruction. Before your marriage it was on Lady Louisa's instruction, since then the Captain has instructed us. Of course we give advice and recently we have been advising that your investments are not spread wide enough, and in particular that your two larger investments are not sound. Alas, the Captain has not responded."

"Please explain."

"People keep talking about the possibility of a recession but the American economy is still fairly buoyant as are some businesses here. On the other hand, since the general strike last year many businesses have never recovered and are very undercapitalised. Some of your investments are in those companies and as such are suffering more than some others. You should have sold the shares in the two main ones; now I'm afraid they are worth very little.'

They talked investments for some time, deciding whether to sell or keep each in turn. Alan Brockbank seemed pessimistic about the economy, saying, 'There is a real danger of an American-led depression. If it happens many of our own companies that are already in trouble would soon go to the wall."

Remembering that depressing bank statement, Rachel realised that she would have to cash most of them to release enough funds to provide the estate with working capital. There would have to be another way.

After taking her leave of the accountant she wandered a little further down the street to the town's most distinguished ladies' fashion shop. The owner, who had become a friend through the years, welcomed her enthusiastically. They enjoyed a chat, looked at the latest stock but Rachel wasn't in the mood to try any on and soon headed back to the sedate lounge in the Fawn and Hound.

***

Thomas Courtney, being so proud when his daughter had married Alexander, would never admit to any difficulty in working for his in-laws. Now he saw problems, not just because Rachel was determined to sort out the estate but it was more that somehow he no longer felt his old confident self. Having agreed to install the telephone and to get the accounts finished he then managed to delay his meeting with Rachel for several days.

They finally met in the estate office after Thomas had spent several evenings working through the books. Rachel was shocked to see how physically and mentally drained he looked. The books revealed what their accountant had predicted. Thomas explained, "The wheat market is being undermined by cheap imports; oats are doing a little better but their price is still falling. I'm afraid we're not doing so well with our cheese; it's not just that the price is down, we don't seem to get the highest prices like we used to."

"Well, there must be a reason?"

"I suppose the dairy management has got a bit slack. Perhaps Harry Wilson (the dairyman) is getting past it. He's in his late sixties you know."

Rachel protested, "Is it not more to do with what happens in the dairy?"

"Yes, it's his wife who's the cheese-maker, but I suppose she's also well over sixty. I've talked to them about it." Thomas shook his head as he added, "Without any improvement in the cheese though."

Rachel digested the implications of all that. The Wilsons' son Jack had also worked on the farm since leaving school. He was now married and living in one of the estate's village cottages. Knowing that he was a good worker with a good knowledge of cows, Rachel asked, "Is it not time to make some changes on the dairy side?"

"Do you mean that we should let them retire and let young Jack take over? Because I'm not sure it would be a good idea to bring him into the farm house, with the dairymaids living in and ... well, I think you know what I mean."

Rachel knew well what he meant. The incident had taken place about two years before when Jack's wife had been expecting her first baby. Rachel had heard an old country saying that 'it's a bad time for young husbands – they don't like going without it'. Well, when she'd seen him with one of the dairymaids behind a haystack Jack certainly wasn't going without it. Rachel was a bit ashamed to remember how she'd stood and watched for a few moments. Jack's bare white buttocks rose and fell as the girl clung to his neck, squealing in ecstasy. She felt shocked, not so much at them, for having grown up in the same farmyard as Jack it was not a surprise but at how much fun it seemed to be compared to Alexander's occasional tame, functional lovemaking. Rachel had crept away without disturbing them.

This was not was the first dairymaid that Jack had taken behind the haystack but the others were before his marriage, in his teenage years. He'd even tried it with Rachel but she hadn't been remotely tempted nor had she felt it necessary to tell her father. Young people have to live their lives their own way, to their own standard of morality. But it was different when Jack was married and his wife was expecting a baby. She had to tell her father, as he was responsible for each of the dairy girls' welfare. Having told him only that they had been in a lovers' embrace hadn't altered the fact that he had no option but to send the girl back to her parents. Young Jack had been given a strong warning about his future conduct.

Rachel jolted her mind back to the present and tried not to smile as she answered, "Yes, I can understand what you mean."

Thomas said, "Anyway I'll have think about the dairy side. I can see something has to be done."

"How are you progressing with the retirement cottages in the village?" Rachel asked, knowing from her own observation that the work on them seemed to have stopped.

Again there was some hesitation in his reply: "I've had to set priorities. Which has meant that they'll have to wait awhile."

"They will be needed if we do let one or two older workers retire."

"I know but I have to work within a budget."

Rachel decided to say no more for the time being. The discussion moved on over the rest of the estate staff. The estate's own timber yard hadn't worked for nearly two years. Rachel often called on Old Bill, their head wood-man, so she didn't need to be told that two mild heart attacks would prevent him from ever returning to that very heavy job. His assistant, Clem, was too young and inexperienced to take on the job. "Anyway," Thomas said, "I'm convinced that we can no longer afford to run our own timber yard."

Relieved to get at least one positive statement from him Rachel asked, "Could we rent out the timber yard with an agreement that included doing the estate's timber work?"

Thomas thought a while before saying. "That might work, but it may be hard to find someone suitable."

"I know an experienced timber-man who might be interested."

"Do you mean Nathan?"

Thomas gave her a long thoughtful look before nodding agreement. "Yes, he's a good man. All right, I'll contact him."

Rachel in turn gave her father a long, thoughtful appraisal. Not only did he look tired, his once crisp brain seemed to have lost its clarity. She realised that she had never known her father's age. "How old are you, Father?"

Thomas sat back, seeming to shrink as he slowly answered, "Seventy two."

Chapter Eight

Nathan found that he was on his own again on a Saturday night in a house full of broken hopes. Although this little cottage had enabled his and Hannah's dreams to become plans, those plans had now become part of his nightmare. To get away from them for a time he walked down to the pub for a pint and a chat. Normally a one-pint man he surprised himself that night by drinking three, or was it four?

He couldn't remember but perhaps they helped because sleep came quickly. Then the dreams also came. He was dreaming of the Christmas before their planned wedding. He had stayed with Hannah and her parents for five days, five long delightful days to spend in her company. Lisa Brown always made sure their bedrooms were well apart. Not that it made any difference because, respecting Hannah's Christian beliefs, Nathan promised he wouldn't take her until they were wed. But that night – that night it was a close thing!

It happened after the Browns had gone out to visit friends. Hannah helped him pull the old sofa up close to the log fire. When they snuggled down close together Hannah's lips were soft and warm and her firm, shapely breasts were silky smooth to his caress. As the time went by they slid lower down on the old sofa. When Hannah rolled tight against him Nathan could feel her heart pounding against his chest. Sliding his hand over a shapely thigh down towards her knee he discovered that her skirt had ridden up. As he touched the smooth skin above on that exposed thigh Nathan felt Hannah's heart skip a beat and saw the passion on her parted lips as her hot blue eyes burned into his. He could have taken her, he should have, at least then they would have known what …. Waking from his dream, hot and restless, he thought how strange that all the time Hannah had been in hospital he had somehow shut out his physical desires, but now she had gone his need was unbearable.

Nathan got up to pace the bedroom, trying to convince himself that they were only dreams. But he couldn't live with dreams about the past. Somehow he must find a way to live with reality in today's world.

***

Those dangerous trees that his boss and Tony had undertaken to fall took Nathan away from both the timber yard and his home for the week. Planted a hundred or more years before to enhance the garden surrounding a gentleman's property, they now towered dangerously above the house. By carefully selecting which tree they felled first, backed up by the power of the steam engine winch, Nathan's timber men managed to drop each tree without once hitting the big house. Not that Nathan made the decisions. By deliberately pretending his mind was elsewhere he pushed the responsibility onto Tony, who coped admirably.

Being away in summer when Nathan's cottage stayed reasonable warm wasn't too bad, but now in the autumn five days without heat was too long. Although he had an arrangement with a neighbour who would come in to light a fire on the Friday afternoon when he was away from home, a house needs a fire every day to stay warm and homely.

Nathan thought of this and the damp bed that would again need airing as he cycled homeward from the yard on the Friday afternoon. His first task though was to shop in the village for his weekend groceries.

Feeling a strange reluctance to return to his empty cottage Nathan got into conversation with the butcher who, always ready for a chat, followed him out into the street. They had covered the weather, the government and the growing threat of depression when the butcher, indicating with his thumb his son working in the shop, said, "Did you know that he's getting married in a couple of months?"

"No, who's the lucky girl?"

"It's young Iris Carlisle from th'other end of th'street."

"Where are they going to live?"

"They'll live above shop like I've done. There's only me an't Misses now so we're looking for a cottage."

It took but a few moments for Nathan to consider the situation at the timber yard, the loneliness of his cold cottage and the nightmare memories of Hannah before he said, "I've got a cottage to sell."

The butcher gave Nathan a long look before replying. "Can I walk up after me tea tonight an take a look through?"

There was only time for a quick snack and the skimpiest of a tidy-up before both the butcher and his 'Missis' were at the door. Having heard rumours of how that shop was a little gold-mine Nathan decided to pitch his asking price fairly high. The butcher was in a mood to haggle but when his wife fell for Nathan's oak fittings in the kitchen she completely undermined him.

Nathan not only got his price but he felt an instant relief. Not that he had any alternative plans - it was just that he wished to escape the memories this house triggered.

***

The village where Hannah and Nathan had chosen to live was at the centre of a fairly large parish, which kept the local vicar quite busy. In the past he had travelled around his parish on a sedate bicycle, dignifiedly greeting his parishioners as he pedalled by. They in turn held this mild mannered and always helpful man in complete affection. If his parishioners ever wanted him in an emergency someone or other would know where he was or at least would have seen which way he'd gone.

For relaxation from the cares of his parishioners he liked to take his trout-rod down to the local river. Unfortunately he could only travel the distance of a bike ride. So if old Mrs Thing-a-me-gig needed comfort on her final journey or that young wife from number 17 had been seen fleeing from the house with two black eyes, someone would pedal out and demand his return. He in turn would take down his fly rod, tie it to the cross-bar and, with a wistful look at the river, pedal back more sedately. By that time the old lady had probably gone on into the next world without his comfort and the young wife, back making her husband's tea, would be explaining the black eyes away on the low coal-shed doorway.

Having come from a fairly wealthy family the vicar had been left comfortably off. He could therefore afford to solve his problem by buying a car. For a while the little car provided the tranquillity he had long craved. Oh, he justified the luxury by saying how much quicker he could visit his needy parishioners. In reality though, he would drive out of the village in one direction, then circle round to hit the river well down stream and safely away from his parishioners. Alas, on one such trip he made the mistake of taking his more forceful wife along, she to picnic and read while he fished.

Before then those fishing trips in his little car had been the vicar's only chance of quiet solitude. After that, not only did his dear wife often want to go along, she also got the idea that the children needed to get out into the countryside more. The vicar's protests that seven children and a wife were too much in such a small car were brushed away with "Well get a bigger one then!"

All this was unburdened onto Nathan the following afternoon when he stopped for a chat with the vicar. Having been out with his boss to see some standing timber, on the way back Nathan had asked to be dropped off a few miles outside the village. Mulling over his future now he'd sold his cottage he was enjoying the relaxation of a long walk home in the late September sunshine. The last thing on his mind was to listen to the vicar's troubles until he added, "So I have had to buy a larger car. Do you know any one who wants to buy a small car?"

"Yes, I do, me!"

"Well, it's parked under the trees over there. Go and have a look while I pack my tackle away."

Looking round it Nathan could see the vicar's problem. Although the Morris Cowley had a back seat there was no way one could safely carry seven children in it, as the vicar explained when he walked across. 'I don't put the hood up because with it down I can just about pack the children in standing up. But the hood will come up. Here, let me show you."

Being fairly new the car was priced a bit higher than Nathan really wanted to spend but he knew it was in almost perfect order. The outcome was that not only did they do a trade but also the trusting vicar let Nathan drive him back to the Vicarage before taking the unpaid-for car home with him.

The fire was almost burnt out when Nathan returned to his empty cottage but there was a letter waiting for him. Opening it he was surprised to read of an offer by the Steward of Hesston Estate for Nathan to take over the tenancy of the Estate timber yard. There were various conditions covering the work that the Estate would require from Nathan in addition to the rent. Also, all sawn and unsawn timber in hand had to be taken at valuation, as would the saw-mill fixtures. To compensate for the difficulties of starting a business from scratch Nathan could have the yard rent-free for six months.

Mulling over the Hesston Estate offer while he prepared his tea he resolved to follow it up.

***

After another restless night, when again Nathan dreamt of Hannah's soft lips, Sunday morning seemed empty, therefore he decided to take out his new car for a spin. The timber yard offer from Thomas encouraged him to point it towards Hesston Village.

Neither expecting to meet Thomas nor discuss business, Nathan just drove up to the timber yard and parked. Round the back, six large oak trees lay seasoning while another two were already sawn into planks. They had been restacked with strips of wood between each plank to allow the air to circulate. There was also part of a seasoned ash trunk and two big pieces of elm that also looked well seasoned. Inside, the saw-mill equipment – powered by a substantial diesel engine – would be capable of handling a twenty-foot tree with ease. He was taking a closer look at the engine when Thomas's voice from behind made him jum

After the two men shook hands Nathan said, "I know I shouldn't have come uninvited and on a Sunday but having just bought this car I wanted to try it out."

"It's not a problem," Thomas reassured Nathan, "and I'm happy to talk business".

"I need your assurance that I can buy timber from other sources as well as from the Estate."

"You've got it. Not only that, the mature timber on the estate will be offered at the going rate. But you will be expected to fall, store and saw what timber is needed for the estate's own use."

"All right, but not do it for nothing. I'll expect to be paid a contractor's fee."

"There is something else," Thomas said. "I'd like you to employ young Clem, the assistant woodman. I won't have work for him on the estate if I set the yard out."

They strolled back to Thomas's house together. The tall, distinguished but aging Thomas contrasted with the slightly shorter, lithe vitality of the much younger Nathan. Over a mid afternoon cup of tea the two men came to a provisional agreement subject to Nathan's final decision.

Nathan started up his little car to return to Shropshire.

***

Rachel too had received a letter on the Saturday. Alexander, with his usual terseness, had sent her the list of the gun guests for the coming weekend's partridge shoot. Two local guns would not need accommodation but four married guns would bring their wives to stay over the weekend at the Hall. There was one new name, a Mr Jonson who would be travelling alone and needed accommodation for the weekend. The letter ended with a promise to be home by midweek but no gesture of reconciliation or declaration of love, but then what did she expect?

All the household arrangements were now solely Rachel's responsibility. In the first few years of marriage there had been that live-in husband and wife butler and housekeeper team. Greebs and his wife Millie, had run the house with accomplished ease for nearly thirty years, well before Rachel came onto the scene.

After Rachel lost her mother, that happily married couple had been particularly kind to her. As a result a close friendship had developed, which her marriage to Alexander hadn't changed. Neither they nor she found any strain in the continued working arrangement. Millie, who was the real manager of the house, suddenly became ill and before long was bedfast. Rachel helped Greebs nurse her for many months until eventually the Greebs took up the invitation from their married daughter to go and live with her in Northwich.

While Millie was ill, Rachel and Cook had between them taken over the housekeeper's responsibility. After Millie moved out, neither saw a need to replace her. As for old Greebs, although he had intended to return, after Millie died he admitted that at seventy it was too tiring to work full time. Reluctantly he had stayed on with his daughter but he was full of nostalgic memories of Hesston Hall.

Holding a deep affection for the old butler, who had been a guiding influence through his childhood and a pillar of support through his later convalescence, Alexander readily agreed with Rachel to let the old boy return for special occasions. So a day or two before a weekend house party, or a shooting weekend and even for the occasional dinner party, old Greebs moved back into the Hall. Rachel kept a room just for him then, with his uniform cleaned and pressed, and for those few days Greebs became his old suave self and he loved it.

Even with Greebs in residence there were still plenty of arrangements for Rachel to make; the usual household staff of cook, kitchen maid, bedroom maid and parlour maid had to be augmented for such a weekend. she ran through the plans again on the Sunday afternoon. When she was sure that she had covered every thing she stepped out through the front door for a breath of fresh air.

Remembering that the telephone engineers had erected the poles along the edge of the park, she decided to walk a bit closer to look at their work. She had walked to where the front drive joined the one from both the farm and timber yard when Nathan drove along on his way home. Seeing her he pulled up. Rachel expressed her surprise at the car, at why Nathan was there and even more at the news that he had more or less decided to take on the timber yard.

"Would you like a short run in my new car?"

Rachel couldn't help responding to Nathan's relaxed invitation. "Much as I would like to I think the villagers might misunderstand." Nathan fumbled in front of the passenger seat then, lifting up a pair of goggles and a waterproof hat, said, "If you put these on the villagers will never know."

While Rachel fiddled with her headgear Nathan turned the car away from the village to drive out into the countryside along the traffic-free lanes. When after about twenty minutes they came to a cart track leading through some trees towards a field gate he turned down it and stopped the engine. Removing the hat and goggles to shake her fair hair back into place Rachel said, "Hey, will it start again?"

"Don't worry, this one starts up all right."

Aware of just how hard he had taken the loss of Hannah, Rachel asked, "How are you managing?"

"It's the nights I can't stand so I've sold the cottage. Not that we ever spent a night together there. Its just that there's just too many shattered dreams."

Putting her hand on his arm she tried to say something of comfort. "I'm sure you're right to move. You do have to begin again."

Nathan turned towards her trying to explain and somehow found that they were in each other's arms. Never wanting another woman since receiving that first letter from Hannah years before, he knew it wasn't passion; it was just that Rachel seemed to understand. He was vaguely aware of her slim, attractive figure, of her right breast pressing against his chest, but his thoughts were far away. When he pulled back to look into her upturned eyes it was Hannah's blue eyes looking up into his and it was Hannah's soft lips he gently kissed before jumping out to swing the car's starting handle.

***

Enjoying driving on the journey back to Shropshire, Nathan hated the thought of another night in that house of memories. Lighting the fire didn't dispel the cold, empty feeling inside the cottage. It did allow him though to put the kettle on for a warm drink over supper. Then with his hot water bottle tucked by his feet sleep came quickly.

In the early hours, though, Hannah came back to haunt him. Again he was stretched out on the Browns, old sofa. Again he could feel a firm breast against his chest as he stroked the silky skin on her thigh. Suddenly he sat bolt upright! This time when he was kissing those soft lips it was not Hannah's clear blue eyes looking into his, it was Rachel's hazel brown ones.

Jolted by the compulsive desire awakened by his dream, Nathan paced the bedroom floor disturbed by his thoughts. If he took on the timber yard could he keep clear of Rachel? He knew that he had to! It wasn't just that it could jeopardise his tenancy there; it was that he respected marriage. Not that he had Hannah's deep faith but to him marriage was a sacred union that no one should break lightly and he was well aware that Rachel was going through a lonely and unhappy time. Still, disturbed by his vivid dream, he was even more aware of just how attractive she was. But – and he realised that it was a big 'but' – because he felt not only had he just woken from a dream but also from a long celibate sleep, releasing a physical need that was almost painful. But' no way would he step in between man and wife. Anyway, he reassured himself, Rachel had done no more than offer a comforting shoulder in his hour of grief.

Having deliberately left some tea to drink cold should he need it Nathan went down to nurse the dying fire back to life. Watching the flames flickering up the chimney he mused, over the cold tea, of past opportunities to dally with married women.

Travelling about the district and lodging in many different homes had revealed to him just how many unhappy marriages there really were. For every wife who was so bored with her life that she could make suggestions to a travelling timber man, there had to be an equally unhappy husband who was away doing what?

Perhaps the one time he'd nearly fallen to temptation had been when he was lodging with a young couple where the husband occasionally travelled away on business leaving his very attractive but equally bored young wife. The timber Nathan and his men were felling was over twenty miles from the yard, which was much too far for daily travel. The other single men found lodgings in a boarding house near to the wood, whereas the steam engine driver returned home to his family when he could.

Because it took two men to drive and operate the steam engine Nathan acted as the driver's mate. Travelling out from the yard each Monday morning Nathan stayed in his lodgings on Monday night, then helped to take a load of timber back to the yard on the Tuesday before returning to the wood and his lodgings each Wednesday. More timber was then loaded up on Thursday to be hauled back to the yard on the Friday.

With each large tree weighing several tons that steam engine could barely manage four miles per hour. After a sedate journey of some five or six hours Nathan could arrive looking like a miner just up from the pit. Even the return journey with an empty timber-carriage was little quicker but just as dirty. Lodging separate from his men, Nathan had chosen more expensively than usual, though three nights each week the luxury of running water and a fixed bath was well worth the extra.

The husband of his attractive landlady was away when Nathan got back one Wednesday night, not that he thought anything about it. His bath had been refreshing, his bed was inviting to his tired limbs. Just as he turned back the bedclothes his landlady walked in carrying a hot-water-bottle. Before he could think what to say or do she was close to him stroking and admiring his muscular arms. It had taken all his willpower and a steely grip on each of her wrists to eject her out of his bedroom. The next morning, when he arrived down for breakfast carrying his suitcase, she looked up from the frying pan and calmly said, "Yes, I thought you'd do that."

Nathan recalled that not only was that bored young woman good to look at, she could also cook. Putting a plate of bacon, two eggs and fried bread in front of him she asked, "What are you? Some sort of saint or don't you fancy women?"

"It's just that I've got a girl," Nathan smiled, remembering such a positive reply when at that time he and Hannah had only exchanged a few letters.

***

A gamekeeper's life was a solitary one, although for Hamish, being alone among the woods and fields was pure enjoyment. Few dared be the keeper's confidants. Most of the villagers looked on him as the estate watchdog, spying on both tenants and non-tenants alike. The fact that he usually turned a blind eye to a farmer taking the odd pheasant or villagers snaring a few rabbits to supplement their meagre diet did not count. He was still the man who could end that privilege, even put them in court or, worse, have them turned out off their farm or cottage. Perhaps his wife felt it most of all because by nature she liked to mix and talk but many of the locals were afraid to be too friendly in case they let something slip. Hamish's favourite saying was, "Everybody has a secret, what's yours?"

It followed that when it came to waiting for poachers Hamish was alone. It hadn't always been so. The Colonel in his day had shot much more than the Captain did now. Then not only did Hamish rear more pheasants but he also had the help of an assistant keeper. They could take it in turns to watch, or watch two different places at once and if necessary face the bigger gangs together. When the Captain, after inheriting the estate, reduced the number of shooting days, the young keeper moved on and was not replaced. After that Bill, the old woodman, occasionally helped Hamish but his heart condition now ruled him out.

Hamish desperately needed someone from around the estate whom he could call in when there was a serious poaching threat. In the meantime he'd have to take on these Gypsies on his own. Tonight could just be the night because, with a breeze and a fair amount of cloud to block out the moonlight, it looked ideal for netting partridge. Hamish's skill was his ability to think like a poacher, to imagine where and when a man would choose to take his birds. All he had to do then was to be there and wait.

The keeper set off in the twilight, striding alone towards the stubbles on the home farm.

***

Standing on the drive to watch Nathan's departure, Thomas saw Rachel jump into Nathan's car and began to worry. Working and living in the centre of the estate he couldn't help but notice that things were not well with the marriage of his only daughter. Had he done the wrong thing by offering the timber yard to Nathan? Was it putting temptation before two lonely people?

Since losing his own wife Thomas had come to know what it was like to be lonely, to not be able to share one's thoughts or feelings. Without work to occupy his mind Sunday was always the loneliest day of the week. This Sunday became worse than others, because neither a book nor thoughts of the coming week's responsibilities could take his mind off Nathan and Rachel.

Unable to face the thought of a sleepless bed, Thomas, shrugging on a warm coat, walked out of his cottage and followed the cow lane into the fields.

The evening shadows were changing to complete darkness as he walked between the hedgerows in the cool night air. Suddenly Thomas heard shouting coming from the far side of one of the stubble fields. Hurrying towards the noise he could see what appeared to be three men fighting. It was too dark to make out clearly what was happening but they seemed to be laying about each other with sticks. When one went down Thomas called out a warning and the other two quickly vanished into the darkness of the hedge beyond.

Running forward, Thomas saw a body lying face down in the stubble. Rolling it over he was dismayed to recognise Hamish. As there appeared to be a pulse he took off his coat and folded it under Hamish's head before running towards the farmhouse for help.

When senses began to return to Hamish he sat up with a jerk and wished he hadn't. With his head spinning dizzily he picked up Thomas's coat before staggering towards the field gate. With something to hold onto while his mind became clearer Hamish slowly assembled the memories of that evening. He remembered waiting in the edge of the wood then, as darkness fell, walking across the stubbles. He remembered standing in the shade of a tree watching two men drag a short net towards him. Then his mind seemed blank. Fingering the growing lump on his head, he looked in puzzlement at the coat in his hand as he tried to work the rest out.

He knew who his assailants were and he also realised that by the time he got to the village to rouse out the constable they would be long gone. He could visualise them already muffling their horse's hooves before hitching them into the shafts. Not only would they soon be gone but also they would go silently, "In th'dark no one'll know which way they've gone," Hamish muttered in the night air, "an by daybreak they'll be miles away."

Still puzzled by the coat, Hamish decided it would be better to examine the scene the next day in daylight. As he hung the coat on the gate hinge and turned to make his weary way home to bed Hamish again muttered, 'No, best forget em. I've suffered worse and recovered.'

Chapter Nine

Working closely with someone, even sharing danger together, develops either a strong bond or complete dislike. When the decision as to which way a tree may fall or how a team of horses might react on a steep slope may mean either success or serious injury, a man soon learns whose judgement he can trust. The many years of timberwork had built up Nathan's respect for his boss.

The feeling must have been mutual for the Boss had trusted his oldest son Tony to Nathan's care from an early age. Tony had in turn earned that same respect from Nathan; in fact they had become almost as close as brothers.

These thoughts were swirling around in Nathan's mind when he drove into the timber yard on the Monday morning. A few toots on the horn brought most of the staff out to admire his car. The light-hearted banter from the others as they walked round his new purchase didn't lighten his heavy heart when he knocked on the Boss's door.

"We need to talk about the business."

"In what way Nathan?"

"Young Tony is well able to run the tree felling operation now, in fact if you remember I'd been running it for several years by the time I was his age. You knew that Hannah and me ... well ... we'd planned to start our own business one day. Well ... I think I'd still like to."

"I know what you are saying about Tony but you and me have been together too long not to be able to sort something out. But I suspect you have something more to say."

"Yes - I've been offered the estate timber yard at Hesston. It's nothing like your set-up here but I could handle big trees through it and I wouldn't be so close that I'd be competing with you."

"If that is what you want you have my blessing. When do you want to start?"

"As soon as you feel that you can release me."

He sat back to think for a minute then, leaping to his feet, he came round to shake Nathan's hand. "Go and get started today. I'll pay you six months salary to cover you until you start to make a bit and if ever you need help or advice don't be afraid to ask. Whatever happens, there will always be a job for you here."

Taken back by the generosity of the offer Nathan thanked him profusely then, after a slightly emotional farewell in the yard with Tony, headed towards home. But it wasn't home; Hannah's shadow seemed to be in every room. Relieved that the butcher had also bought all his furniture, he was glad that he could load up what was left of his possessions and never come back. Loading his kitchen utensils in the front seat area then and carefully placed his gardening and tree felling tools in front of the rear seats, then with his bed linen and clothes on top he was away.

Calling in at the Vicarage with a cheque for the car and taking his house keys with a quick explanation to the butcher's shop took but minutes. Aware he was taking some risk by heading towards Hesston without first making a final agreement on the timber yard, but he knew that Thomas was a man of his word, he set out enthusiastically towards a new life.

***

Harry Wilson's round shoulders, caused by a lifetime of pushing into the flank of each cow while he sat on a three-legged stool to hand-milk it, were becoming wearier. The old cowman realised that rolling out of bed before six each morning was getting harder day by day, although he and his wife Mary had done it all their married life. She would light the fire and put the kettle on while he loosed his collie dog and went for the cows. The rest of the dairy staff would be in the yard by 6.15 to guide the incoming cows in their stalls and start on the milking. By the time Harry returned from the field with the last of the cows all the staff would be on their stools milking away. If there were no problems Harry usually sauntered back to his cottage to have breakfast with Mary. It would be a few years since last Thomas had been into the farmyard before breakfast, therefore Harry, who should have been on a stool milking away with the others, could indeed saunter. He knew full well that no one would really challenge the more relaxed approach he'd latterly adapted to his work.

Mary's work as head cheese-maker did not begin until about half way through milking, so each morning she and Harry sat down to a good fry-up. As well as the usual bacon and egg they always had cheese – when it was available their choice was the soft buttery-cheese made from some of the mid-summer milk. That milk, high in butterfat content, did not make into good keeping cheese. The fact that Cheshire cheese needs to mature for a few months before use to

77

develop its flavour meant the high butterfat content in summer milk could cause any cheese made from it to sweat in the hot summer weather. Because of that it was not saleable but it was scrumptious to eat when fried with bacon. Having to provide baggin and feed the living-in staff from a fixed allowance Mary had become canny at using whatever came of the farm at no extra cost. As cheese deemed not fit for sale came free on top of her allowance, the staff had to eat a lot of it. It wasn't difficult for Mary to use her skill to make sure there was always enough reject cheese for her needs.

Trudging up the cow lane towards the night pasture gate as the day broke was just another weary Monday morning for Harry. Suddenly his dog rushed forward to sniff at what looked like a man slumped against the gate bottom. Harry was shocked to find it was Thomas, but as he felt for a pulse he realised that the body was cold and stiff. Jolted out of his lethargy, he rushed back to the yard just as his son cycled in to start work. Harry sent him back to the village to fetch the doctor. Still flustered and unsure as to what he should do next he brought out an old door to act as a stretcher. Then, as the other staff stood chattering and speculating round the body, Harry got their help to carry it into what had been Thomas's house. After leaving them to bring the cows in and start the milking Harry walked towards the Hall to break the news.

***

When she woke Rachel, the maid wouldn't say anything only that Harry wanted to talk to her urgently. Rushing down in her dressing gown Rachel found Harry, cap in hand, standing just inside the back kitchen door.

"I've bad news, Ma'am. I'll tell it to yer' straight Ma'am, it's the Boss, your father, well he's dead Ma'am."

Feeling her knees going weak with the shock Rachel sat down quickly on a kitchen chair. Harry tried to explain how he had found Thomas's body, in as kindly a way as he could, adding, "He weren't there when I looked round at dusk, Ma'am."

By the time she had dressed and walked round to Thomas's house the doctor had already arrived. Inside her old home she was shocked to find the doctor and Harry struggling to straighten out the stiffened limbs on the kitchen table. They drew back with embarrassment when she rushed forward to throw her arms around her father's cold neck. Rachel wept uncontrollably for several minutes over her father's prostrate form before recovering her composure. The doctor would not give a cause of death until after a more complete examination so she reluctantly left them and walked in anguish towards the garden.

Sitting on her favourite seat by the lake Rachel went through some of the joyful memories of her father. That hour gave Rachel time to shed her immediate tears. When Bestwick discreetly coughed she managed to compose herself before he placed a tray on the low table in front of her.

"I've brought you some hot toast, Ma'am."

Then, pouring out a cup of tea he added, "I've been to the post office and rung the Captain. He wasn't there but they're expecting him back soon so I've left a message."

"Thank you, Bestwick."

Discreetly retreating across the garden he frightened a waterhen from among the flowerbeds. Its splash landing out on the lake drew her attention to where a group of resting mallard ducks swam silently together. She knew they would have spent the night out on the stubble fields gorging themselves on the shed harvest grain. Surprisingly, she too felt like eating.

Rachel watched while she ate the warm toast as a great crested grebe, colourful even in autumn, surfaced with a splash just in front of her. It swallowed a small fish before diving down again. When it surfaced further down the lake she knew that she also had to resurface from the depths of her despair. By just watching the wild life on the lake she again felt renewed enough to take on whatever came her way.

***

Having heard the news on the village grapevine and not wanting an expensive funeral going to one of those fancy town firms, the village carpenter/undertaker, Dick Higgins, quickly donned his dark suit before driving out to the hall. Not that Rachel would have used any one else anyway, so she invited him to discuss the arrangements.

***

Nathan's journey to Hesston had been relatively uneventful. The little car only over heated once, which had given him the chance to make up a roadside meal from the remnants of his weekend's groceries.

Arriving in Hesston village by mid afternoon, Nathan drove straight through and on up the Hall drive towards Thomas's office. Although there were no signed documents he trusted the Steward's word on the timber yard. In the countryside a man's word is his bond; many times Nathan bought large blocks of timber on just a handshake. He did think though that Thomas might be more than a little surprised to see him back so soon.

It was Nathan who had the surprise when he pulled up outside the estate office and Dick Higgins walked out to greet him with the news. "Arr, he's gone right enough. No one seems to know how it happened but Mrs Wentworth-Jones has told me that he must lie in his own lounge until the funeral. Anyway I've just got the body ready so how about giving me a lift?"

The two men had co-operated a couple of time when Nathan's company was involved in undertaking, so Joe naturally asked, "Anyway, what are you doing here?"

"I'd come to take over the timber yard but that was just a verbal arrangement with Thomas; now I'm not sure how I'll stand."

"If Thomas gave his word I'm sure that it will stand. I rely on this yard for a lot of my timber, particularly the oak, so we're going to see a lot of each other. You can make a start by helping me get him into this temporary coffin."

With the coffin placed on two chairs beside the table Nathan helped to slide the body into it. They carried the coffin into the lounge where they laid it on two trestles before both standing back in a moment of silent respect.

The undertaker was just explaining how he would make an oak coffin out of wood sold to him some months earlier by Thomas when there was a knock on the door. Hamish stepped in with Thomas's coat. After warmly shaking Nathan's hand he explained as he pointed towards the coffin, "Arr, he must ha' come to me help last night. A couple of poachers laid me out. When I came to I found a coat but it didn't make sense so I just went home. Now I've bin back to look it wer' his coat that wer' folded under me head."

The undertaker asked, "Do you think that they might have attacked him?"

"Arrr no, from th'signs I can see. I'd say more like he put his coat under me and ran for help."

Nathan thought aloud. "That explains what he was doing out there without a top coat on."

By calling on Hamish occasionally through the years he'd lived away from Cheshire Nathan had kept their friendship alive. He wasn't surprised when Hamish asked, "Where are yer' staying then?"

"I'll have to go into the village and ask around."

"Arrr now, we've a bed made up. Yer'll stay with us until yer' finds som'et else, eh?"

***

Rachel had not been allowed to sit and grieve for long. First the Doctor came to report his conclusions. Explaining that because her father had recently been to his surgery complaining of chest pains he was sure his death was from a heart attack. When she questioned him more he told her he had strongly advised Thomas to retire but Thomas had said there were some problems that he wanted to sort out first.

"What problems?"

"He wouldn't say. I warned him that any excitement or over exertion could kill him but he just smiled and told me that he wasn't the excitable kind. Not that I can tell you what he was doing out there in the dark to cause this but I'll sign the death certificate."

After he'd gone Rachel was left to reflect that however lonely she might feel, her father had been even more alone. She'd been his only close relative and yet, because she was also his employer, he couldn't confide in her. She'd been so used to seeing him in full command it was hard to imagine him being ill. On one side she and Alexander had relied on him to resolve their problems, and on the other side the farm staff and the tenants expected him to resolve theirs too. That he'd obviously been ill but couldn't confide in her hurt her deeply.

Some time later Rachel was still trying to think of an explanation as to why her father had been out so late without his topcoat, when the doorbell rang. The maid showed in the undertaker who, without being asked, repeated Hamish's conclusions about the night's events. Dick Higgins also told her that her father was now lying in state and that she could go to him whenever she wished. Going to the door to see him off Rachel was surprised to see Nathan walking towards her.

"I came to say how sorry I am. It must be a terrible shock."

Having mourned alone up to then, Rachel desperately needed the comfort of someone close. She stepped forward without thinking, just wanting to feel the comfort of his arms and sob on his tweedy jacket shoulder. Remembering the vividness of his dream, however,

Nathan stepped warily back and gripped her hand in a formal handshake. As their eyes locked he could see both agony and puzzlement in Rachel's but he didn't try to explain or give her chance to get closer, he just held onto her hand, using it as a barrier to prevent either of them from making any impulsive move.

After a brief moment she asked, "How come you are here?"

"I came to see your father about taking over from today. Will this make any difference?"

"No, but I don't want to talk about it now. Later on you can tell me what you agreed with my father and the estate will stand by it."

"Thank you. Can I do anything to help?"

Rachel had been making a list of phone numbers of the guns invited to the partridge shoot. She was so used to her father sorting out these types of problems she was now uncertain what to do about it. Having put the list down when she came to the door she now reached it from the hallstand, saying, "Yes, will you ring those people to tell them that the shoot's off and tell them the funeral will be at 11 o'clock on Friday?"

Within minutes of Nathan leaving, the telegram boy came to the kitchen door. Having the kitchen maid for a cousin meant that if he went to that door she could exchange his telegram for a large cream cake.

What Rachel read was a brief message from Alexander saying, 'I am so sorry. Coming home. Send Bestwick to Crewe for 7.00pm'. With the feeling of relief that he was coming home there came the realisation that Alexander could have cancelled the shoot, but it was too late to call Nathan back.

***

Nathan was glad of an excuse to go into the post office knowing that it would be a good place to ask about lodgings. First though he thought it best to go round and have a diplomatic word with old Bill, the past estate woodman. Bill soon put him at his ease explaining, "Thomas came round last week to discuss my job with me. I told him firmly that I'd never get back to that sort of heavy work again. He said then he might rent the timber yard it out but I hadn't expected it to happen this quick."

Nathan explained the circumstances and Bill wished him well as he went off to make the phone calls at the post-office.

***

Bestwick was glad to have something to do; all day he'd felt frustrated at not being able to do more to help his mistress. With a quick polish of his beloved car he was off to Crewe station. Arriving early gave him time to walk down the stairs onto the platform. Smoke billowed from the engine as the Captain stepped down from the front carriage and Bestwick, offering his condolences, took his suitcase. Within minutes they were on their way towards Hesston.

Rachel leapt to her feet to greet Alexander when he strode in. He surprised her when he just swept her into his arms whispering, "I am so sorry Rachel, you loved him so much."

It had been a month or more since he'd last held her close. Even then it had been a cool functionary thing for both of them; warmth and response was something she thought had gone forever. After she'd been nestling tight against him for some minutes she felt him beginning to respond to her. For too long she had waited to feel this sort of warm embrace, to feel he needed more from her than just to be a passive housekeeper. Rachel felt the need to hold him close despite her despair, or was it because of her despair? Without trying to understand why, she just let go and curved her body tight to his.

Even during the early days of their marriage his sexual appetite hadn't been high. Although he'd never really seduced her in those first few years, her teenage adoration had meant his very nearness could arouse her. In more recent years his spasmodic lovemaking had become such a functionary thing she'd long since stopped feeling any arousal. Now suddenly she did. Although uncertain whether it was because of Alexander, or guilt at earlier wanting the comfort of another man's arms, she welcomed the dizzy madness. Trying to push her away he said, "We mustn't, not now," but she held on to him, pulling him down with her onto the sofa.

Chapter Ten

Breakfast was a more formal affair when Alexander was at home; the cook in particular enjoyed having to prepare a more substantial meal. There wasn't any blissful closeness across the breakfast table though. The heady passion of last night's reunion had disappeared as Alexander again hid his feelings behind a cold mask. Each time Rachel tried a warm, loving approach she was rebuffed; it was as though he was ashamed of his passion or revealing his need.

They did both linger over their last cup of breakfast tea in a silent sort of companionship, which encouraged Rachel to try to have a serious talk. She began by explaining to Alexander the decisions she'd taken so far relating to the estate but as she started to tell Alexander about the timber yard the maid interrupted. "Sorry to disturb you, Ma'am. Mr Dobson's at the kitchen door asking if it would be convenient to speak to you."

The name sparked an instant reaction from Alexander. "Dobson, Dobson? Do you mean Nathan Dobson?"

"I was just explaining that to you. Father had offered the tenancy of the timber yard to him just before he died. Nathan came to start yesterday."

"Why is he bothering us now?"

"Perhaps we should ask him?"

Having had little personal contact with the Captain since they were boys Nathan felt somewhat self-conscious on entering the dining room. Thinking that she could have saved some of the embarrassment had he come to the front door which, against both the convention of the day and Alexander's approval, she usually answered herself, Rachel tried to put him at ease by asking, "Why the kitchen door? Why didn't you come to the front door?"

"I came to the back door to ask if they thought you were up to seeing me. Until we've valued the timber in hand I can't begin to work in the yard other than go over the machinery. Because of that I've agreed to help the undertaker out this week."

Alexander had seen the understanding look that had passed between the two and almost barked the question. "How can we help you then?"

"Two things, first about the list of guns you asked me to ring. I've contacted them all bar Mr Jonson and no one seems to have heard of him."

Rachel noticed that Alexander put on his most unreadable expression when she asked him, "Who is Mr. Jonson?"

"Never mind that now. What's the second thing?"

"The funeral arrangements. We've been discussing the arrangements for Friday. You had mentioned that you thought your father would have wished his coffin to be carried on a farm wagon. If that's so - then perhaps I could talk to your wagoner to arrange it? Also we wondered if you'd like to walk in procession behind the coffin? If so, do you wish to start from the hall or from your father's home?"

Alexander jumped to his feet in anger. "Why are you interfering in these arrangements?"

"The undertaker's got another funeral this afternoon and he's still working on that coffin. And knowing that I've had seven years of experience of helping to run a funeral service at my last timber yard, we only sold the funeral business when the wholesale timber side expanded substantially, anyway he's asked me to give a hand and it's part of the undertaker's role to help you to …."

When she saw the tension rising in Alexander Rachel butted in. "The Captain and I haven't had chance to discuss the arrangements yet. Please can you give us a little more time to think them through?"

Starting towards the door Nathan paused to say, "Perhaps I should also remind you to think about how you will cater for the mourners after the funeral. What sort of refreshments do you want to provide and where do you want to serve them?"

Aware of the Captain's growing anger Nathan took his leave and drove round to the timber-yard intending to continue working on the machinery but seeing the oily dirt on his overalls when he lifted them off the peg he changed his mind and hung them up again. Hamish had told him where there was a chance of finding lodgings.

From what Hamish had said there was a good chance of lodging with a Mrs Grundy, who was a farm worker's widow in her mid-fifties. Isolated from the village, her cottage was tied to one of the estate's tenanted farms where her husband had worked until his death some six months previously. Normally in those circumstances a widow would be told to vacate her home to allow the farmer to bring in a replacement worker. This time there was a difference because Hetty Grundy worked in the farmhouse and the farmer's third son had recently left school, which provided the frugal farmer with an extra unpaid worker.

With three hefty sons to look after, Hetty's help was highly valued by the farmer's wife, who in turn persuaded her husband to let Hetty stay on as a temporary tenant in the cottage.

Pulling up outside the cottage path Nathan could see that someone had been a keen gardener. Winter vegetables stood in neat rows and the fruit bushes were pruned and tidy. Walking round to the back door he noticed one untidy area in the orchard, where a large old pear tree had crashed down in the recent strong winds.

A tall, slim woman, who looked younger than he'd expected, answered his knock. After he explained briefly who he was and what he wanted, a warm hand shook Nathan's and the door was opened wide. The scullery looked clean as Nathan walked through it into the main kitchen. It too gave the same impression of a good housekeeper. Two homely looking spindle-backed armchairs were placed either side of the recently blacked kitchen fire grate. A scrubbed plain wooden table stood by the window where even the curtains, although patched in many places, looked clean. With his experience of many different lodgings Nathan instantly liked what he saw. To find out more about Hetty he asked, "I was told that you are on your own now; how do you manage to keep both the house and the garden so tidy?"

Smiling at the compliment, Hetty replied, "I lost my husband six months ago but my youngest son's been with me until a month ago, when he got married."

Nathan's expressions of sympathy were brushed away with a shy smile. "It was a shock but he didn't suffer for long and I had the wedding to look forward to. It was my son who tidied up the garden before he left," she smiled again. "He promised to come back to cut up that pear tree but I haven't seen him since his wedding."
"Well, I'm a timber man so maybe I could do that for you."

Up the narrow stairway were two bedrooms. The larger one, which had been the children's, was offered to Nathan whilst Hetty pointed to the other explaining, "When the children were growing up we moved into the small one; I don't want to move out now."

As there were no bathroom or toilet facilities in the house Hetty led Nathan outside to point them out. A large tin bath stood in the outhouse next to a brick fireplace with a built-in cast iron boiler above. Along side it but approached through a separate door was a brick-built earth closet. Indicating a very small pile of logs Hetty smiled hopefully at Nathan, "I'm finding it hard to get enough logs and sticks so perhaps you can help me there?"

They fell into discussion over the different arrangements. Hetty didn't want to prepare a meal for him on the three days that she was at the farm but on Tuesday and Thursday evenings she would cook for him. She would make up a baggin for him to take each day and on Saturday he could decide if he wanted that or he could come back for a midday meal.

The rent was a bit higher than Nathan was expecting but after a moment's hesitation, he accepted and agreed to move in next day.

***

Alexander had become very agitated about Rachel's choice of undertaker saying, "If he needed the help of Dobson he isn't very capable. Well, I suppose it's understandable because he's really just the village odd-job man."

Agreeing with him Rachel said, "He is our village undertaker and if we are part of a village we should support the village craftsmen."

Alexander, with one of his rare smiles, reminded her, "That rule doesn't seem to apply when you go shopping for clothes."

What really got Alexander angry was Nathan's involvement both in the funeral and in cancelling the partridge shoot. Rachel tried hard to explain how lost she had felt without her father and with Alexander being away. Although she dare not say it, she hadn't really known if he would be back at all. Alexander seemed to be mollified until she asked, "Anyway, who is this Mr. Jonson?"

Alexander went very tense."

He's someone I've got to know in the last year." And with that he marched out of the room.

There was no time to sit and think because the parlour maid came in to say that Bestwick wanted to talk to her. "Yes Bestwick?" "Do you still want me to collect the butler today as arranged and, now the shoot was off, do you need my wife to help get the bedrooms ready?"

Confirming both, Rachel went on to ask Bestwick to be ready to drive her into Knutsford later that afternoon. Not that she was in the mood to go shopping but she needed to buy at least one new mourning dress. Then, realizing that she must also explain to the staff what the plans were so far, she called them into the kitchen. "Greebs will be here later this morning and as usual he'll take charge. I don't

87

know how many mourners will need to stay overnight, so Minnie will come in each day to help get the house ready. Certainly the Captain's mother, who will be arriving here tomorrow, will be staying over the weekend."

"Do you want me to prepare food for the mourners after the funeral?"

"I think it would be too much for you, Cook. Although we may not invite the mourners back here the Captain and I have yet to decide how we'll do it. But if we do invite them back to the Hall I'll try to organize outside caterers. Whatever happens you must presume there will be extra at each meal and stock up for additional guests over the weekend."

While she was speaking the front door bell had rung. The parlour maid, having answered it, came back. "The vicar wishes to see you Ma'am, so I've put him in the lounge."

Rachel had never felt close to the vicar. Perhaps because Alexander had had a big say in choosing him the end result was a man reflecting much of her husband's character. The vicar met her coolly with an apology that he had been away on business the day before, which meant that he had only heard the news of her father's death when he return home late. He went on to express his sympathy in a lukewarm manner before discussing the choice of hymns, format of the service and other details. After he had gone she had felt little personal comfort from her priest's visit.

Discovering that Alexander had taken Digger for a walk, Rachel got busy checking through the house in preparation for the coming days. Alexander didn't return until the cook was beginning to mutter about having to keep the lunch warm.

The exercise and fresh air had put him in a better mood, which gave Rachel the chance to persuade him to make various decisions about the funeral or at least put forward her ideas in a way that would make him feel he was making the decisions. Yes, he wanted her father's coffin to be carried into the Hall on the day before the funeral. If Rachel agreed, then Alexander felt that it would be appropriate to all walk behind the coffin and yes, use a farm horse and wagon.

"And after the funeral could we come back to the Hall?" Rachel asked.

"Of course, you would like the mourners to come back to the Hall after the interment."

"Yes and we must bring in some sort of caterer to prepare and serve the food."

The next morning Alexander told her over breakfast that he was going into town. He wanted to talk to his solicitor and he would perhaps call in at the bank. Rachel took the opportunity to ask him if he still wanted her to manage the estate. When he answered "Yes" Rachel explained that the bank had not responded to her letter so she needed his written authority to deal with them. He seemed to hesitate for a while before saying, "Right, leave it to me!"

Digger was as usual ready for his morning walk but instead of heading out across the fields Rachel turned towards her father's house. Deep in thought she walked on past the house and down the short drive to the timber yard.

She spotted Nathan inside standing on the diesel engine plinth completely engrossed in his work on the engine and Rachel was unable to resist watching him. After several minutes he turned to reach for a spanner and saw her. Cleaning his hands on an oily rag he jumped down to greet her. There was a large smudge of black on his nose, which she was sorely tempted to wipe away. That sudden feeling so flustered her that shc had to struggle to marshal her thoughts. Finally, getting control of her inner feeling, Rachel explained the decisions about the funeral and brought up the refreshment problem explaining, "I haven't done any thing about it, perhaps because I don't know whom to ask."

Nathan smiled, "I do know of a company who will come out to the hall and prepare either hot or cold food in your kitchen."

"But will they be free at this short notice?"

"I took the liberty of inquiring and, when they said they were, I asked them to keep Friday free. Subject of course to your final decision."

Rachel suddenly realized just how much she needed someone to think ahead, to anticipate her needs and take some of the load. Trying to hide her thoughts, she asked about the timber yard. Nathan said, "I'm glad you brought that up. It's a pain having to go to the village to use the telephone; can I ask the telephone engineers while they are working on the estate to install a phone in here?" Then indicating a small room on the side of the main building, "I'd like to make it into an office."

"Of course! You said something about valuing the timber in hand - what do you mean?"

"Those trees lying round the back are the only seasoned timber I can work with. I need to pay you their value before I either use them or sell them."

"Can you value them yourself?"

"Yes, but that isn't the way to do it. You should bring in an independent valuer."

"I trust you. You do it!"

"Your father also asked me to fall that blasted (lighning-damaged) ash tree just across that pasture field. I need some ash in urgently because I can work it without too much seasoning."

Rachel agreed to that and also to go with him to look at some other growing timber as soon as she could. Nathan then headed back towards the village to talk to the undertaker about the funeral arrangements. Rachel, in contemplative mood, walked towards her father's cottage.

Sitting in the darkened room with her Father's body triggered many happy memories – the happy times when her mother had been alive and the love and trust her parents had for each other, above all their love for her. Her mother had always made time to listen to her girlish thoughts or fears and after Mother's death her father had done his utmost to take her place. Through the years she'd lived and worked alongside her father their relationship had always been a happy, trusting one. After she and Alexander had become close, especially when Alexander had formally asked her father for permission to propose to her, Father had never complained about the difficult position it placed him in. She knew that throughout the years of her marriage her father must have found it a strain working for his son-in-law.

She lost all track of time as memory after memory flashed through her mind. Loud knocking on the door suddenly brought her back to the present. Her father's secretary, Grace, wanted to know if she should come into the office to work. Knowing that Grace saw her four young children into school before cycling from the village to work in the estate office three days each week Rachel made a quick decision. "Why not take the rest of the week off, then come in next Tuesday as normal?"

Pleased with that arrangement Grace departed, leaving Rachel to have a look through the office.

On the desktop were just his diary and a writing pad. There were two desk drawers, which her father had always kept locked; one contained private papers relating to his employers, who were, of course, herself and Alexander. The other had been used to keep whatever documents her father was working on at the time.

Unlocking one drawer Rachel was surprised to see it held bank statements both for the estate and for the farm accounts. She saw both were in the red and that two debits had been underlined. One was in the Farm account and the other in the Estate's, but both had large sums taken out in the last few months. Had she not recognized her father's handwritten 'what for?' by each debit she wouldn't have known there was anything suspicious about them. So why had Father written his question? What was it that he hadn't understood?

Relocking the drawer Rachel walked back into the gardens to her favoured seat by the lake. She felt amused that when something deep bothered her, this seat seemed to draw her by instinct. That there was something wrong was obvious, but who had drawn out that money and what had they used it for? There seemed to be no immediate answer or course of action other than a resolve not to discuss it with Alexander until she knew more.

The maid interrupted her thoughts. "Mr and Mrs Brown have come to express their condolences, Ma'am. I've put them in the lounge."

Thanking her with a smile Rachel muttered to the distant ducks, "There is one obvious drawback to having a favourite seat - every one knows where to find me."

There was no one she would be more pleased to see. Hannah's parents' handshakes and sympathy were both warm and genuine but they were both ill at ease in the Hall. William Brown in particular sat fidgeting on the edge of his chair, turning his tweed hat round and round in his fingers. Rachel, so used to seeing them full of good-humoured confidence, tried to help them relax. While the maid was serving them tea and biscuits she switched the subject to the estate: "Did you know that Nathan has taken over the timber yard?"

"Yes, he told me when he came out to visit last night. He also said that young Clem's going to work for him."

Rachel said, "Good, I must find out when he's to start. Has Nathan fixed up lodgings?"

"We wanted him to stay with us but he's already got fixed up with Hetty Grundy."

"I think there could be too many memories in your home," Rachel replied with a smile. "Anyway he'll be looked after if he's with Hetty. I'm glad that she's been allowed to stay on in her cottage."

From her school days Rachel had always talked openly to the

Browns and without being aware of it she also spoke less formally when in their company. Trusting them more than anyone other than Hannah, now, without having given it previous thought, she decided to talk openly. "You've perhaps already heard I've taken over the administration of the estate."

As they nodded she continued, "I may bring in an outside agent to manage the estate and then subject to his advice we may employ a farm manager."

Remembering how the Browns had often spoken of their ambition to buy a farm of their own she said, "We may well decide to sell some land. Would you be interested in buying your farm?"
Mr Brown fidgeted about in his chair and his hat twirled so fast that it slipped out of his hand; he took his time picking it up before replying, "Well, maybe."

Knowing it was the most positive reply she was likely to get Rachel got to her feet, smiling her thanks to them. As they made to leave she checked that Mr Brown was going to be one of the bearers before bidding them, "Good day."

Rachel didn't resent the fact that Alexander had failed to join her for lunch. Through the last few years she had become used to eating alone and this time she positively welcomed it. Soon after lunch Greebs, who had taken up residence once again, cut her afternoon's rest short by announcing with his usual dignity, "Bestwick has returned with Lady Louisa; shall I show her in, Ma'am?"
"Of course, yes do."

The two women met like the old friends that they were. Hugs, kisses and deep sympathy from Lady Louisa were so warm and genuine Rachel couldn't help shedding an emotional tear or two. After making sure that her mother-in-law was comfortable in her bedroom, Rachel ran lightly down the stairs to the met by Greebs, who frowned at her lack of decorum before announcing, "There is a Mr Jonson at the door, Ma'am."
"Please show him into the lounge, Greebs."

Going into the smaller day room Rachel ran a comb through her hair and fiddled with her dress to give herself time to think. As she stepped into the lounge she found the mysterious Mr Jonson standing with his back to the door looking closely at one of the oil paintings. He spun round sharply to smile a greeting. She was aware of broad shoulders, lithe movement and a rugged, almost craggy face as he took her outstretched hand.

"Your butler has just explained about your father's death. I am so sorry. I just did not know."

"We've been trying to contact you but …."

"I've been moving around. I am truly sorry to intrude at a time like this. Please extend my condolences to Alexander. Perhaps I may attend the funeral?"

Mr Jonson had reached the door as he asked that question, then at her nod he strode from the room. Rachel found herself almost running to catch up with him and, rather flustered asked, "But have you come expecting to stay?"

"Well yes, but obviously that's out of the question now."

"Any friend of Alexander is welcome in this house. The spare bedrooms are prepared. Please stay?"

"You are really sure?"

"Yes, of course!"

Rachel stepped outside to see him retrieving his suitcases from a racy-looking open-topped car. As he turned to stride back towards her she was aware of the power of the man. It was in his movements, his stride but particularly – as their eyes met – on his face.

Chapter Eleven

When he agreed to help the undertaker Nathan had expected to be involved with some of the practical work, like making the coffin. In reality he had to stand aside or find more menial tasks while the undertaker showed off his considerable woodworking skills.

Realising he was not wanted for his own woodworking skills Nathan had asked how he could help. That was when he found himself organising the funeral. If he was to be responsible for the arrangements Nathan decided it would be better to call on each of the participants in turn.

After explaining to Joe the Waggoner the role he was to take in the funeral Nathan surveyed the Waggoner's mode of dress. The usual old corn sack hanging round his waist like an apron was complemented, because of the rain, with another hooked over his shoulders like a cape. The corners of that sack were tied together under his chin with a bit of binder twine. Then there were the 'yorkies'; half hidden under the sack they were just the best half of a broken leather shoelace tied round each trouser leg below the knee. Not only did they stop Joe's heavy tweed trousers from pulling when he bent down, they also held the bottoms up out of the mud and above the furrow sides as Joe followed the plough.

"Have you got a suit Joe?" Nathan inquired.

"Aye ar'have that, but I anna' got a decent cap," Joe said, doffing an old soiled tweed cap so plastered with years of grease and dirt it was now probably waterproof, "an I canna' afford to buy one."

"The undertaker has got a selection of bowlers, will you wear one of them?"

With that settled Nathan then visited each bearer in turn explaining their need for a dark suit and that it was Rachel's wish to move the coffin to the Hall on the day before the actual funeral. What he didn't say was that he was craftily bringing everyone together to make it a practice for the following day, although he had a bit of trouble when Hamish declared, "Arr I've no need for a practice. I've carried a few bodies in me' time, arrr, an I've no' got a dark suit man, nor owt other than me old tweed keeper's suit."

"Well, what do you wear when you get dressed up then?"

"I wear me kilt and sporran like any proud Scot should."

***

When the day before the funeral finally came the last touches on the coffin took longer than expected. It was mid morning before Dick Higgins and Nathan arrived at the Hall to inform the Wentworth-Joneses of the arrangements for the day.

Later, when they had finished preparing the body and finally placed it in its elegant oak coffin, it got a little frustrating for Nathan. It was time to move the body to the Hall but Dick Higgins was still caressing the final polish to his beloved oak coffin.

Nathan stood back and mentally checked through the arrangements. He had got Rachel's agreement to everything. Joe Candy, the waggoner, was to have his quietest horse hitched to the chosen lorry outside by two and he'd reminded each of the bearers to be here on time. There was no more he could do.

The undertaker was still polishing away when there was a knock on the door. Pulling out his pocket watch Nathan was not surprised to see it was gone two o'clock. Expecting the undertaker to go out to meet the mourners he was even more surprised when he was told to go himself. Strong words passed between them before it became obvious to Nathan that the undertaker just couldn't cope with 'the gentry', as he called them. Nathan wondered how Dick Higgins had managed to pluck up the courage to go to the Hall in the first place, because now it was plain that he just could not face going outside to explain what was happening.

Nathan unlocked the door and greeted each participant in turn, including Hamish resplendent in his kilt. Taking his time to explain again to them to treat today as a rehearsal for the next day's funeral he then went over the details. The Wentworth-Jones family arrived just as he finished and he asked for their approval of those arrangements. Again Nathan was running out of time-filling words when, to his relief, the undertaker stepped through the door and announced that all was ready.

It took a while to get all six bearers to walk in step. The two village tenants and the two farmers had trouble in learning the short instep shuffle needed to carry a heavy coffin. Hamish's military training helped him and Harry Wilson to take the lead place with more confidence. The others were getting the knack of it by the time they lifted the heavy coffin out to the lorry.

Joe Candy looked a different man in his best suit. Without the yorkies round his knees his trousers hung neatly round his ankles while the bowler gave him an added touch of dignity. Joe's choice of horse, the old mare Jewel, also looked resplendent with black ribbons tied to both her mane and tail. She had always been a steady worker but now her weary old legs moved at a very sedate pace. This left Nathan to organise the mourners to walk behind while the undertaker led the cortège at the old mare's dignified pace across to the Hall. The six bearers handled the coffin with much more assurance this time, carrying it from the farm lorry into the hall with a little more dignity. Nathan felt like kicking the Captain when he stood with expressionless military bearing apart from Rachel, who was obviously feeling the strain and showing considerable emotion. *Why can't the pompous ass at least put a supportive arm round her?* he thought. His anger was mollified a little when, after the coffin had been placed in the lounge, the Captain decided to stay with Rachel as she opted to wait there in silent vigil.

Cook had laid on a cup of tea and a scone for the helpers. Lady Louisa enjoyed playing the role of hostess. Introducing herself to Nathan and thanking him for his organising skills, she then drew him across the room to introduce him to Mr Jonson. The two men eyed each other with critical appraisal. Nathan, compact and physically fit, was aware of the swarthy, rugged and perhaps more sophisticated type of man talking to him. He tried to break the ice by explaining, "I am sorry that I couldn't get hold of you to tell you about the partridge shoot. You must have been travelling around a lot?"

"Well yes, I have been moving around. It's not always easy to leave a forwarding address."

Finding his accent hard to place Nathan asked, "Are you over here on holiday or is it business?"

It had seemed an innocent question but Nathan was aware of some caution in the reply: "A bit of both really.

When Nathan asked bluntly, "Where are you from?" there seemed to be even more evasion until Nathan, tiring of the verbal sparring,, went across the room to chat to the bearers and helpers.

Joe Candy looked particularly smart. Even without his bowler hat Nathan could hardly believe the change in the man. Without an old hessian sack tied round his waist Joe looked almost as smart as his horse and lorry. Feeling that compliments were justified Nathan said, "You've touched the paintwork up on the lorry very neatly and the old mare's harness looks as good as new."

"By heck arr, ye canna' beat a bit o' neat's-foot!"

Joe's Cheshire accent was so broad Nathan often had to guess at what he meant, and this time he had to ask, "Do you mean Neat's Foot Oil?"

"Oh arr! I uses it on th'harness, on th'hoss's sprains - and on me own when I have one." Then with a smile Joe stroked his bald head and added, "It'll do owt bar make yer' hair grow."

Nathan realised that without that old tweed cap he was looking at Joe's white shiny forehead for the first time. "I've seen that oil in most stables but I never knew what was in it."

"It's just th'oil from th'foot of a neat, which were an owd name for a cow or ox. It be good stuff."

"Do you use it on everything?"

"Aye ar'do but I'll use linseed oil on th'old mare tomorrow. Aye her coat'ill shine like th'undertaker's boots."

Realising that whatever had put the shine on old Joe's baldhead had also gone on his side-whiskers and moustache Nathan resolved not to get down wind of him for a day or two.

With that practice run, on the day the funeral started out smoothly; certainly the bearers moved with much more confidence. The undertaker gave the coffin a final loving polish in the privacy of the lounge before taking his place at the head of the cortège. Nathan was again left to suggest orders of etiquette to the mourners. He was aware that Rachel was much more relaxed than on the previous day. As he moved among the mourners Nathan received one or two appreciative smiles from her and once, when he turned suddenly, he caught an admiring, lingering look in her eyes.

Perhaps it was his dark suit or his serious funeral voice, but whatever it was he managed to get the many farm workers and other villagers, who had gathered at the Hall to join the cortège, into a semblance of dignified order.

Everything went well, if perhaps a little behind schedule. With the linseed oil glistening in the weak sunshine on her dark, almost black hair Jewel, sensing the importance of the occasion, set a very sedate pace down the Hall drive. The vicar, who expected punctuality, was pacing around impatiently by the time that she led the cortège up to the Lichgate.

Relief that they had reserved enough pews for the family mourners was Nathan's first thought when he saw just how full the church was. His second thought was of how popular Thomas must have been. Even the vicar, in his cold, polished way, expressed similar thoughts, concluding in his eulogy that the number of people revealed just how much the departed Thomas had been liked and respected. The Captain read the lesson with his usual impassive facial expression.

When the bearers finally lowered the coffin into the grave Nathan helped to draw the ropes up and then discreetly retreated. Normally that would be the end of his undertaking role other than making sure that the Sexton was there to fill the grave in but this time he was surprised to see Rachel slip away from the many sympathisers to quietly invite him back to the Hall for refreshments.

Nathan had attended many funerals in the past and therefore was not surprised by the numbers attending a country funeral. Townspeople, other than close relatives and friends, tend to get on with their own business whereas in the country it's just about everyone's business to be there. This was not just because there was the chance to see the local gentry or have a good gossip but because often business was diplomatically conducted between the gravestones. Although telephones were coming into the countryside only a few rich and important people had so far installed them; also, travel was both difficult and time consuming. Here among the throng of locals there was an opportunity to communicate, perhaps to discreetly mention you have a horse to sell or that you may be short of hay for the winter.

The land agents in particular were out in force. By the nature of their business they got to know each other, in fact they had a network of knowledge that they shared carefully within their profession. Nathan had learned to tap that network in his timber dealings, checking whom he could trust or who may have timber to sell. He knew several of the agents present and had done business with some, therefore he wasn't surprised when one of them fell into step with him as they strolled back through the park towards the Hall. Later Nathan took the opportunity to have a word with some of the other agents, all of whom wished him well in his new venture. Before the day was over he had invitations to look over two small blocks of standing trees and was told of some more on a nearby estate.

Being an experienced funeral observer, Nathan found it revealing as to who was chatting to whom. He noticed with some amusement more than one agent making a particular fuss of Rachel.

Although he was sure some of them knew her from the years she had worked with her father, it was more likely that, knowing she was now running the estate, they were angling to become the agent.

It was in his own business interests to move around, to meet old acquaintances and to make new ones but there was one distinguished-looking man who seemed familiar but he couldn't place him. Deciding he must find out his identity Nathan approached him while he was chatting to Mr Jonson. He noted that Mr Jonson sidled away leaving him to be greeted with a warm handshake and a familiar, "Hello Nathan, how are you?"

When Nathan looked puzzled the man laughed, "I'm Mr Ed, lived across the fields from your old farm."

It was Nathan's turn to laugh and apologise. Mr Ed, who was both owner and editor of the local paper, possessed an unpronounceable Polish name, which the locals had got round by calling him Mr Ed. His son Gerald had been a friend of Nathan's before he left the area. Not that they went to the same school, but his home was only a few hundred yards across the fields from Nathan's home.

Pleased to renew his acquaintance, Nathan said, "I spent many happy hours in your home. Although you were often busy Mrs Ed used to give us some great teas."

"Sometimes they were greater than they should have been," said Mr Ed, laughing, "I remember coming home one night to the smell of roast pheasant. A well aimed shot from your catapult as I remember."

"You gave us a real telling off for poaching it! Then you carved up and tucked in with the rest of us."

"It was too good to waste."

"I met Gerald in Shropshire; he was working for the local paper when I was falling some trees there. How's he keeping?"

"He's come back to work on my paper. I wanted him to get some experience with other weekly papers, then if he wanted to, he could come back here."

"And is he back to stay?"

"I think so. Anyway I'm getting ready to take life a bit easier." Nodding towards Mr Jonson, Mr Ed said, "What do you know about him?"

"I've only spoken to him once and I didn't learn very much."

"He seems curious about you; in fact he asks too many questions without giving anything away."

"What about?" Nathan asked.

"About the Wentworth-Joneses, about the estate and the village and where you fit in." When Nathan didn't reply he added, "There is one thing I am sure about."

"What's that?"

"You get to learn accents in my job and his is South American."

A little later Nathan was surprised when the Captain walked across to him and firmly shook his hand. "I must thank you Dobson. I can see that the day would not have gone so well had you not been involved. Well done!"

Before Nathan could do more than smile his appreciation the Captain had moved on to talk to another departing mourner.

The many mourners had begun to disperse. Some to walk home across the fields while others were walking back down the drive towards the church to collect their car or pony and trap. With their departure the real business of a country funeral came to an end.

Nathan knew that, although most had been there to genuinely mourn, some perhaps had just been there to make sure others saw them mourn and for many it had just been a day out with free food and a chance to mix in the complex maze of country affairs.

Chapter Twelve

By Monday morning Rachel's memory of Friday's funeral was a bit blurred. There had been so many handshakes, so much sympathy expressed by so many that individual messages were fused together. One thing that stayed in her mind was a slightly over dramatised thank you and farewell from Mr Jonson. It came back to her at breakfast on Monday when Lady Louisa joined them.

Cook loved to have guests at breakfast. Not that it was ever a formal affair because guests came and partook when they were ready. Had any not eaten by the time Cook wanted to clear the food away she would send a maid up to their bedroom to discreetly inquire if they would like something brought to the bedroom.

Lady Louisa, who usually enjoyed her breakfast in bed, received a bit of light-hearted banter when she appeared at the breakfast table. She took it very well and explained her motive by asking, "Is Bestwick going to be busy today?"

"I have to work on some papers. I can't see that I will be going anywhere," Alexander said before turning to Rachel. "You need to go to the solicitor's soon, don't you?"

"I can't face it today. If you want to go anywhere, Lady Louisa, do use Bestwick."

"I would like to visit some old friends." Lady Louisa looked from one to the other before adding, "In fact, subject to your agreement I would like to stay with Lady Cumfree tonight."

They both reassured her that she was free to have use of Bestwick and the car to do her own thing. With that Alexander left the room to start on his papers.

Pouring a second cup of tea, Rachel sat down again with Lady Louisa. Apparently in a talkative mood the old lady said, "It's time we had a chat. You've been under such a strain that I haven't found time before. Anyway, there's always been that funny Mr Jonson hanging around."

"Why do you say funny?" Rachel asked.

"Because there is something funny about him. Have you noticed that although he is supposed to be friendly with Alexander they don't seem to talk much, do they?"

"No, I hadn't noticed," Rachel said, "but then I haven't talked to him much either. Anyway he's gone now."

"Oh, but he is coming back." When Rachel looked at her in surprise Lady Louisa said, "For the partridge shoot in two weeks time." Seeing Rachel's frown, she quickly added, "But I am sure Alexander will only hold it if you feel up to looking after the guests."

"Well, I suppose after all the hard work put in by the keeper it would be a shame not to hold the shoot. Anyway after breakfast I'm going to take Digger for a walk so I might run into Hamish."

"You seem to have so much to do. Are you sure that you don't needthe car to go to the solicitors?" asked Lady Louisa.

"There're so many other things needing attention. Like appointing an estate agent, looking into the accounts and seeing the bank manager. But I think that they can all wait because today I am just going for a walk."

With that Rachel bid Lady Louisa an enjoyable day and went to put on her tall, lace-up walking boots. But before she could set off Greebs met her with the news that the telephone engineers were there to connect the phone. It took another half hour to sort out which phone and where.

The sound of an axe drew Rachel across the meadow behind the wood-yard. It was one of those warm autumn mornings when the overnight dew lay heavy on the pasture field. Still low in the sky, the sun's rays highlighted the cobwebs that carpeted the autumn grass. Seeing where the two men had walked through the dewy grass, Rachel could easily recognise the difference between Clem's toes-turned-out waddling walk and Nathan's long strides. For a few girlish moments she lengthened her stride to match each of Nathan's but began to feel the strain from those longer strides on her thighs. Drawing closer, she could see two men swinging their axes at the base of a tree. Gleaming muscles rippled in the autumn sunshine as each axe rose and fell in alternate coordinated strokes. Digger bounded up to them causing both to pause and it was Nathan, stripped to his sleeveless vest and glistening with sweat, who turned to greet her.

The sight of those rippling muscles on his lithe, strong body disturbed her; she had never seen Alexander stripped off like that. At the Hall they had separate dressing rooms from which each of them emerged at bedtime, she in a long nightdress and he in an equally long nightshirt. Until that mad fifteen minutes on the sofa a few days previously, what lovemaking they did always took place under the bedclothes where Alexander had never once removed his nightshirt. For that matter he never removed her nightdress either.

While Nathan somewhat self-consciously turned his back to tuck his shirt in, young Clem asked, "Did I do right starting with Nathan today? I'd finished cleaning that ditch out and he needed a hand with this ash tree."

Rachel reassured him, and then as Nathan turned to face her she asked, "Well, what about those other trees you want to see?"

Leaving Clem to finish chopping out the wedge, which would guide the direction the tree fell, they set off together across the fields to a different wood. To Rachel's questioning, Nathan explained his thoughts on how he would run the business, particularly that he wouldn't have sufficient turnover unless he sold a lot of timber direct to Manchester merchants.

They were soon scrambling through bushes and young trees to mark the mature ones they both agreed could be felled. It was a strange hour; Rachel couldn't help remembering the sight of those strong, rippling muscles whilst Nathan's determination to stay clear of her was being undermined by her amenable and yet knowledgeable approach to country life. It was her affinity with the countryside that made him feel so at ease in her company. A few glimpses of a shapely leg as she agilely scrambled among the dead branches and standing trees had a different effect on him. Their eyes made it obvious that each of them was very aware of the other yet both only spoke in business terms.

When they had finished Nathan walked away to help Clem finish falling the ash tree. Turning to watch his long striding countryman's walk take him quickly through the trees, Rachel, disturbed by the strange flutters passing through her breast, sat down somewhat weak-kneed on a log to compose herself. Digger had enjoyed the freedom in the wood and needed a few firm words from Rachel to keep him at heel when she walked back across the fields.

The Home Farm potato harvest was in full swing, no machinery or noise, just eight Irishmen each with a fork and a hamper. Using their forks with a practised, deft short sweep the men made the tubers from each potato plant seem to appear on the surface as if by magic. Hand-picked into hampers, they were then tipped into hogs (clamps) in the field near to where they were dug.

Drawing closer to the workers, Rachel could see old Jimmy

sitting on the hedge-cop by a blazing log fire. Jimmy was the key to the way Rachel's father had worked the Home farm. Without Jimmy her father could never have managed both the farm and the estate. Not that Jimmy was a wage-earning member of their staff; he was a gang master who contracted to do almost all of the farm's manual fieldwork. From planting seed potatoes in the spring, weeding in amongst the growing plants to harvesting them, Jimmy organised his extended family to cope with the peaks and troughs for an agreed lump sum. Hoeing and harvesting the turnips and mangel-wurzels was also done at a separate agreed price. Even the corn harvest depended to some extent on his gang. For it was Jimmy who decided when the sheaves were dry enough to lead home and it was his men who pitched the sheaves up onto the carts. Jimmy or one of his sons always built the corn stacks.

In the past Jimmy's men had contracted to do all the harvest until the Captain finally admitted that his injuries would never let him ride again with comfort. Thomas had taken that opportunity to persuade Alexander to allow him to make a few changes. The first was to agree that, now Alexander had a motorcar, there was no further need for the estate's five carriage horses. With those horses sold off, the head groom retired to a cottage in the village and the under groom moved to a head groom position elsewhere. Thomas then moved the five farm horses into the empty stalls in the Hall stables. There was still room for Rachel's mare, Thomas's trap pony and Alexander's large hunter in the other three stalls.

Thomas, who at the time enjoyed riding round the estate, used Alexander's hunter to keep it in training. The farm waggoner, Joe Candy, from then on cared for those three horses along with his five farm shires. Thomas had then converted the farm stable into a twelve-stall shippen, increased the dairy staff to look after them and from then on involved the dairy workers in the harvest.

Through those early years of her marriage Rachel often rode out with her father on his morning business visits around the estate. In later years, when Thomas rode out less often, the big hunter then became frisky with the lack of regular exercise. Realising that just occasional rides were not an option with such a headstrong horse, Thomas reverted to his pony and trap. At the same time Alexander brought a boisterous pup home; after a few large holes appeared in the garden they named him Digger. Rachel decided that it would be better to get rid of some of his energy out in the fields and started to walk him each morning. From then on the two riding horses lounged fat and lazy in the field.

The end result of all those changes was that Thomas had involved his dairy staff in the corn harvest more and increased the potato acreage to keep Jimmy's family busy. But it was still Jimmy who made the day-to-day decisions. The waggoner was responsible for ploughing and sowing but Jimmy made all other decisions to do with weeding and harvesting of all the crops. It was his expertise that Thomas had relied on through the many years of their unusual working relationship.

Mulling all this over in her mind as she walked towards him Rachel, after a quick calculation, realised that Jimmy must be over seventy. Then, sitting down on the grassy hedge cop next to him, Rachel smiled a greeting, "It's not like you to be resting at midday."
"Me rheumatics is playing me up," Jimmy explained, "Har' to be sure I'm sorry about the Gaffer. He was a fine man; God rest his soul."
"You've worked together a long time. We need to have a chat so that I can catch up on your arrangements."

Rolling a large potato further into the red-hot ashes with a long stick Jimmy indicated towards the working men: "There's nothing that can't wait. I've brought two more grandsons over to get the tatties finished, then we'll get on with the other roots."

He pushed an old battered kettle further onto the red heat at the centre of the fire and added, "That's why we have a fire on a warm day; they brought some real Irish butter over. You can't beat it on the tatties."
"When you've brought me some in the past I've found it tastes strongly of peat. I suppose the peat smoke clings to everything."
"Har' well yes, but ye know, we store it in the peat." When Rachel looked puzzled he added, "When the cows calf in spring we have more milk than we need so we make it into butter, then we bury the spare butter deep in the peat. Har' it'll keep there for years." Nodding his head a few times, Jimmy said, "Don't ye know, it was the butter that got my father through the famine."

From her schooldays Rachel had enjoyed listening to this canny old man. It wasn't often he was in a mood to talk but when he was then she had learned to sit back and listen. This time, with a bit of encouragement, he told how his teenage father had survived the famine.

"His dad was a few years dead, God rest his soul, when the

105

famine struck but his old grandad was still with him. When the blight took the tatties they had very little to eat but, don't ye know, other food could be bought at a price. The old grandad knew where the butter was buried from years back and my father, God rest his soul, would go out in the dark to dig some up."

"But they couldn't live on just butter," Rachel said.

"Har' to be sure no - but he could sell it. There was plenty of food but the English wouldn't let the people have it. That butter money bought some of that food but ......"

"But whose butter was it?" Rachel asked.

"Har' well ye see, some of it was buried by people long dead and some by families who had just died."

"You mean died in the famine?"

"Har' to be sure the famine just made them weak; it was the epidemics that killed them. Whole families were taken, God rest their souls."

"What about your own family?"

"The old grandad went first in 1846, and then father's two younger sisters went in the cholera epidemic a couple of years later. At the end, when there was only father and my old grandma left, my mother, who was the only one alive from her own family, moved in with grandma. She would go out with my father to dig the butter."

"There couldn't have been so much, could there?" asked Rachel.

"Arrr but there was too. Our home was, and it still is, near to Lullymore on the Bog of Allen. There'd been an old monastery nearby and they'd buried the butter too. Don't you know some of it had been buried for a long time? They had some way of marking where it was, which my father worked out. The butter developed a dry skin in the peat, but when that was pealed off it was still sweet inside."

The conversation went on for some time until the kettle began to steam and Jimmy had prodded a couple of potatoes and pronounced them done.

Calling the men over he introduced her to his two teenage grandsons while the other men gathered round. Turning their large square potato hampers upside down the men sat around the fire while Jimmy, spearing each potato with the fork he had used when digging them up, passed a very hot potato to each of them. Butter unwrapped out of greasy paper was also handed round and spread liberally on the cut halves.

Jimmy turned to Rachel and asked, "You'll take one with us, will you now?"

The soft musical accent of the happy family group added to the pleasure of their company. Rachel found that even the strong peat flavour butter seemed to taste all right out in the field, particularly when it was washed down with tea from a battered tin mug.

When she finally got back to the Hall, Cook accepted her explanation for not wanting lunch with an understanding smile, but when she stepped into the study to make the same apology to Alexander (who was pre-occupied with his papers) she got no more than the mumbled reply, "We can have a meal together tonight."

She was still disturbed by the memory of Nathan's company – or was it, Rachel wondered, the sight of his lithe body? Deciding it was better to deflect her mind rather than to try to analyse her feeling she arranged with Cook to prepare a special meal, adding, "And open a bottle of that red wine."

Even when there were only the two of them they always changed for dinner. This time, responding to her restless feelings, Rachel came to the table in the most attractive of her black evening dresses. Perhaps too low cut for someone who was in mourning?

Greebs served the food with his usual awareness of the mood of the table, timing each course to fit in with their conversation. It was wide ranging; she had forgotten just how much she and Alexander had loved to talk in those early days of their relationship, particularly while he was recovering from his injuries. Not that she had ever seen them. At first there had been a nurse to dress the wounds and attend to him in the bedroom and later when they were almost healed his mother had done that. It was only after he had been allowed to get up and his mother had asked Rachel to push him out in the garden that she and Alexander had become really close.

Within a few months they had begun to enjoy each other's company so much that Alexander wanted her with him regardless of weather. On the fine days Rachel would push him out in the gardens or down to the lake; if the weather was bad they sat in the big bay window in the lounge. Her father had always encouraged her interest in world affairs but as an only child and working and mixing with adults, her conversation had always been mature anyway. Even as a seventeen-year-old Rachel was able to respond to Alexander's more worldly knowledge. At the same time she could tell him the news from the estate and village.

Now, as she sat across the table from Alexander, and remembering how intimate those early days had been, Rachel felt that it was a bit underhand trying to recapture them with a low-cut dress and a bottle of wine. But after her strange feelings in the woods that morning she knew that she was in a dangerous mood. Marriage for her was a contract for life but she desperately needed some life in it. That Alexander was responding could be seen in his eyes.

They were soon talking in a way they had not done for years. When she told about Jimmy's family in the famine Alexander tried to explain the other side. "It was the Irish themselves who were exporting food through the famine. They wanted money for it and the starving masses had no money. There was enough food exported from Ireland to have fed the starving poor but the Irish will never admit it. I suppose it's easier to blame the English."

Later Alexander said, "I have to go to France. Something to do with the German problem, although I am only a bag carrier."
"When?"
"I travel up to London on Wednesday but hopefully should be back before the partridge shoot."
"You're cutting it fine; anyway why are you going?"
"It's the top brass really but I'm sort of in support."

The conversation carried on for some time until Alexander responded to Rachel's suggestion that they had an early night. In the bedroom she drew him into her arms, trying to let his passion take control. She could feel his response but he pushed her away and vanished into his dressing room fully dressed. She was undressed and in bed by the time he came out and as usual he was in his long nightshirt.

Through eight years of marriage she had never seen him naked nor had she been allowed to see those scars on his back. Tonight was not to be any different. Alexander's shoulders felt soft and flabby beneath his nightshirt. Remembering those strong, gleaming, naked shoulders in the wood Rachel tried not to imagine just how hard they might feel to her caress. The fact that she had slid under the sheets naked only encouraged Alexander to come to her that much quicker. Before long, Alexander rolled away and was soon asleep while she lay unfulfilled and frustrated with her deepest thoughts. They were not so much about bare shoulders and gleaming muscles but of that glimpse of tender love she had seen on Hannah's deathbed.

Chapter Thirteen

Watching Joe Candy's team drag the sections of the ash tree across from the field into his yard gave Nathan a great feeling of satisfaction. It was not just that he was now his own boss, but more that it was a new start in life. The two young horses moved the big length of tree trunk with such graceful ease that Nathan was hopeful he would be able to haul most of the estate timber the same way. Also, young Clem was proving to be a happy, co-operative worker, although he still had a lot to learn.

Leaving Clem to burn the small waste branches from the tree, Nathan returned to his office to put in a couple of hours on his new telephone. At the end of them he had secured provisional orders for a mixture of different timbers; that way he would increase his turnover by moving most of his timber from the felling site directly to other larger merchants. The estate timber could be used through the yard to supply local people but there was neither the room nor the equipment to handle the larger quantities needed for him to be a financial success.

Although Nathan enjoyed woodwork it would have to be in addition to his main wholesale business. There was a need for farm gates, wheelbarrows and implement repairs but for those he would need to employ a skilled craftsman and he was not sure that he could afford one for the time being.

That problem was solved when old Bill cycled into the yard, stood around chatting for a while and then said, "The doctor tells me I can do a bit of part time work now. I wouldn't expect a full wage; just pay me what you think I am worth. I can't do anything too heavy but the only thing I know is woodwork and I'm going crazy doing nothing."

When Nathan stopped work to give him an inquiring look, Bill added, "I can make almost anything out of wood, from wheelbarrows to gates or maybe do light repairs. My only problem is that I'm not up to heavy work. Now, if young Clem was to do the heavy lifting I could perhaps work a short day? Maybe I could work with him in the yard while you are out in the country looking at timber?"

Nathan liked what he had seen of Bill; perhaps it was simply that he didn't speak with the broad Cheshire accent used by the other locals. It would be some weeks before Bill confided to Nathan that as a boy he had been sent off to a posh school. Before his schooling had been completed the unfortunate death of his father had brought Bill home again to become the breadwinner for his mother and younger siblings.

Although he had taken to Bill, Nathan was still a bit cautious in replying; he needed assurance that Bill was really up to it. He was also concerned if Bill's wood working skills were good enough so when Bill reassured him as to his health Nathan asked him, "What would you need to make a good barrow?"

"I use elm for the body because it doesn't split, ash to give a bit of spring to the shafts and oak for the legs so they don't rot on the ground."

That was the reply Nathan wanted to hear. He had his skilled yard worker. Nathan was relieved he would now be free to get out in the countryside to buy growing timber, organise contractors to fall and haul it.

One of the merchants he had contacted was desperately looking for 'crook timbers' suitable for the ship building industry. Nathan thought the use of steel had killed that trade years before but it seemed not. This man wanted oak crooks for building into the keel of smaller ocean-going ships and what was more he was offering a good price for them. From experience Nathan knew the most likely source would be around these old estates where oak trees had been allowed to grow unmolested for generations. Just a forked oak branch was not suitable. The true ship's crook this buyer wanted came from the bend below the fork rather than above. Usually that shape was found where an old heavy oak branch, having sagged down through the years, had then grown a new strong side shoot upward. Occasionally a woodland tree that perhaps had grown under a taller tree causing it to grow out sideways to reach for the sunlight can also give the right shape. Whichever it was gave an added interest to his timbering.

Although that order would not amount to much in financial returns he was particularly pleased because it fitted in with his winter hobby, which in Shropshire had been to help a couple of local gamekeepers on their main shooting days. Already Hamish had asked him to help out on the estate shoot but he would like to get to know one or two more keepers in this area. Walking across the fields and through the woods on shooting days was the best way to look for those old oaks with suitable ship's crook.

Having tried out the yard's saw bench on one piece of seasoned ash he was pleased how easily the gantry and crane had lifted the heavy timber. The next morning Nathan organised young Clem to lift the seasoned elm trunk up onto the saw bench. Because elm becomes very hard when completely dry the saw would need sharpening a few times before that elm trunk was all sawn into one inch boards.

When Bill cycled sedately into the yard Nathan was relieved for he could then leave Bill to supervise Clem while he drove out to look at some standing trees.

The cast iron wood-burning stove which provided the heat for his office and that end of the workshop also boiled the kettle. When it came to the boil Nathan made up the fire with a few pieces of off-cuts before brewing a pot of tea. Clem and Bill had just sat down on an old saw bench near the stove when Rachel walked in. Young Clem sprang to his feet and offered her a cup. Looking at the three of them relaxing by the stove Nathan remembered a similar scene in the woods years before and resolved not to repeat it here.

He hurriedly poured some tea into a bottle and picked up his baggin bag, explaining, "I have to keep an appointment; I may not be back before you go home."

Seeing his bag Rachel asked, "Is Mrs Grundy looking after you all right?"

Nathan replied with a broad smile as he walked away, "I eat like a king."

The truth was that his landlady Hetty had proved to be a treasure. Breakfast was always on time, his baggin bag filled for the day and on the three nights that she cooked for him the food was delicious. On top of that she was good company, seeming to have the knack of making him feel at home. Perhaps it was her training from years of being in service but Nathan mused that it was more likely she was just an easygoing person and in response he was beginning to feel quite domesticated, taking kindling sticks and logs home most nights. 'Yes,' he nodded to himself, 'it does feel like home – and I must cut up that pear tree next weekend!'

By mid-afternoon he had provisionally agreed terms on one of the stands of timber offered to him at the funeral, subject to going back the following day to mark and estimate each tree. Before that, though, he needed to find a contractor to fall that timber. He had the names of two or three such people who worked in that area. One of them, Luke Jones, had worked with Nathan for several years before marrying and settling down in North Cheshire.

He motored out to the contractor's home where he met Luke's wife and was directed to the wood where her husband was working. Nathan drove across the countryside, found the right block of woodland and then follow the sound of an axe to find the man.

Luke had always been a tough, skilled man with an axe, the sort who enjoys the physical work. Introducing his younger brother to Nathan, Luke said, "Now we work together we only fall on a piecework rate."

"That's all right. I'll go for that but what's your rate?"

"I'd like to look at the trees before we discuss rates. If it's any help I could be free to begin work next week?"

The outcome was that the three of them agreed to meet the following day by the wood where Nathan wanted them to fall timber. They would mark and number each tree as Nathan estimated its value and at the same time try to agree a piecework rate for the job.

Back at the yard, Bill reported that a local farmer had called to see if they could repair a cart shaft and would they also make a new set of shafts for a second cart? Bill assured Nathan they had a suitable piece of ash that would cut into the curved shape of a shaft and on his way home that night Nathan called in to see the farmer and a deal was struck.

From then on the timber yard work began to follow a pattern. Nathan would spend an hour or two at the yard with Clem and Bill although he was still a bit worried about Bill's health. When Nathan questioned him, though, Bill reassured him by saying, "There's no problem! Just the smell of newly worked wood is better than any medicine. Anyway if I feel tired you've told me to take half a day off, if I need anything heavy moving then young Clem does it for me and I have no worries! I just work when I feel like it, and now there's no pressure on me it seems as if it's most of the time."

Nathan now carried his axe and a short crosscut saw in the car with him wherever he went. Sometimes he would need to trim a tree or saw a length of faulty timber off a fallen tree. It became almost instinctive to split up a few logs and drop them into a sack to take back to Hetty's cottage.

***

Those few days Alexander was spending at home were proving

exasperating for Rachel. She had hoped the cosy evening would have brought them closer but, alas, on the morning after making love Alexander was back to his old remote self. When she tried to discuss the estate problems with him he just made a non-committal reply. Trying to encourage him to tell her more about his trip to France got the same cool response. The worst feeling of all was realising that deep down she no longer wanted to bother even to try to get close to him.

The telephone was proving its worth, allowing Rachel to make appointments at the solicitor's, accountants' and bank. Bestwick again brought his wife along to enjoy their day in town whilst Rachel assured him that she would enjoy walking from one office to the other.

Because the solicitor had also handled her father's affairs, that visit took up most of the morning. It was a fraught time digging into the past, which revealed far more than she had expected. For one thing, there was a surprisingly comfortable legacy, although her father had added a footnote advising her strongly against (but not forbidding her from) putting her inheritance into the estate. The surprises in her father's affairs created both complications and implications that would take a lot of sorting out; it would obviously take some time to settle everything up. She could take that time to decide if she should take her father's advice or not. As for the rest, well, dramatic as it was, perhaps she should discuss it with Alexander before saying anything to anyone else.

Rachel's solicitor, who still insisted on being called Benjie, again invited her to join him for lunch. As the lunch progressed he sensed the strains in her marriage and, being a lonely man himself, began to reveal his attraction for her. Not that Benjie was too direct but when the conversation was getting too personal Rachel steered it back to business by asking about estate agents. Benjie switched off the dreamy look in his eyes and told her about the two companies he could recommend. Firmly cutting short the coffee time to send Bengie reluctantly back to his office, Rachel used the hotel telephone to call one of those two companies.

She recognised the name Smith and Brown as a firm that Thomas had done quite a bit of business with. At other times Samuel Brown had earned her father's respect as a worthy opponent on two or three valuation cases. Rachel had met both Samuel Brown and his son Charles on a few occasions during the years she had worked with her father. In fact Charles had developed a bit of a crush on her, which Rachel's father had tried to encourage but any thoughts in that direction ended when Charles went off to the war, but thankfully he came through without harm. Rachel had never responded to him and by the time he returned she was helping to nurse Alexander. Charles had then gone away again, that time to finish his college course. Later she heard he was working in the midlands somewhere.

Rachel was surprised now to be told by his father that Charles was not only a partner in the business but it would be Charles who would handle the estate should she appoint them.

"All right then," Rachel said firmly, "but I particularly want him to meet Alexander before he returns to London tomorrow afternoon, so if you want to act as our agents he must be at the Hall tomorrow morning."

Samuel Brown said, "I'm not sure what his appointments are for the morning, but I suppose between us we can sort them out, so yes, he will be there at the Hall unless you hear different."

That evening, when Rachel tried to discuss her visit to the solicitor with Alexander he just didn't want to know. When she tried again he cut her off in mid-sentence and went back into his study.

The next morning Rachel asked Alexander, "Will you meet the man I think is likely to be our new agent before you catch a train? His name is Charles Brown. My father spoke highly of his company and I knew him slightly before the war."

"I've no time, I've got other things on my mind so you deal with him."

"This is an important decision. I'm not sure I should make it on my own. Surely you want me to choose a man who you can get on with?"

"All right, but just for a mid-morning coffee."

Charles Brown arrived soon after breakfast. The slim, almost skinny youth that Rachel remembered had filled out into a younger version of his father. Although not yet overweight there was the start of his father's jowl and he certainly filled his smart tweed suit. Asking how long the land agent had to spare, Rachel was surprised when Charles said, "I've cancelled all other appointments; I am prepared to spend the whole day on the estate." When Rachel looked surprised he added, "Well, I need to get to know the estate as well as understanding what you want from it."

"Then we will start by meeting my husband before he leaves for London."

Alexander did meet the land agent and made the usual light small chat. He even asked a few sensible questions and then, with his crisp military manner, he left Charles in no doubt that he was in charge but had better things to deal with on that particular day. That left Rachel to deal with the land agent as she saw fit.

When Alexander left them to prepare to catch the train, Charles said, "Before we discuss your plans for the estate I would like to walk it, not necessarily into each farmyard but walk across the fields and get the feel of the lie of the land and how it's been managed. Have you a map I could borrow?"

"Yes, I have a map but I'll come with you."

Looking a little surprised, Charles said, "Are you sure? It will be a long walk."

"I'm sure. I'll tell Cook to prepare a late lunch."

Striding out across the field Rachel said, "It's some time since last we met. How long have you been back in the family firm?"

Charles replied, "I've only been with father about nine months. Before that I worked for a company beyond Birmingham."

"What brought you back?"

"I always wanted to work with Dad but he insisted I should gain experience elsewhere first. He said that I could always come back when I was ready."

"How did you decide when you were ready?" asked Rachel with a mischievous smile.

Charles laughed, "I asked Dad that some years ago. He told me bluntly that I would know because he would tell me and I would not be ready before then."

Charles went on to tell Rachel about his wife, his two young children and his own ambitions before the discussions went back to the estate and the management of the home farm.

It was well into the afternoon by the time they returned to the Hall. By then Charles's highly polished brown boots looked very unpolished and Rachel, having set a good pace, was more tired than she was prepared to admit.

Cook's roast beef dinner held their attention and it was some time before they again discussed business. Charles finally pushed his empty plate away and said, "The first priority is to find a manager for the Home Farm. In fact I might know a man who would be suitable. If we reach an agreement, and of course if you wish to, I can arrange for you to meet him."

By the time the parlour maid brought in afternoon tea they had reached the point of discussing terms for managing the estate. Finally, with terms agreed, her land agent (as she could now call him) went on his way.

***

The following afternoon, when Rachel rang Alexander's office to give him the news, she got a shock. The receptionist answered her request to be put through with, "Do you mean Major Wentworth-Jones?"

Then, while Rachel was still too flustered to speak, the receptionist put her through. Alexander answered, "Major Wentworth-Jones speaking."

"You've got promotion!" Rachel stammered out. "But why haven't you told me before?"

"I only knew when I got back yesterday. I'm sorry there hasn't been any time to ring you."

"But what does it mean?" Rachel pressed him. "Things seem to be happening that I don't understand; tell me, what's going on?"

There was a pause while Alexander cleared his throat before adding, "I have been promoted to Major. Maybe it's because they want me to take a more up-front role this next week. I expect it will sound more impressive when we meet the other people. Anyway, it is long overdue."

Rushing out her congratulations, Rachel then tried again to tell him about her visit to the solicitors. Frustratingly for her he just went on about how much pressure he was under and ended with, "I will be home for the partridge shoot. Bye."

Letting go of the telephone stem, Rachel realised she had been squeezing it so hard her hand hurt. From Alexander there had been no 'How are you coping?' or 'Will you manage to look after the shooting guests?' Not even a 'Do you mind if?' Her anger turned to a mental mockery of the man she had once worshipped. With the promotion Alexander seemed so full of his own importance that even his accent sounded a bit more upper class.

The next morning, feeling that she must talk to someone, Rachel walked with Digger towards the timber yard. Nathan was sorting out a few papers before setting off for the day. He put them down to give her his full attention. Although she wanted to pour out all her problems she hesitated and instead just talked about the estate.

Chapter Fourteen

A day later, having called the staff together to explain that the partridge shoot would go ahead, Rachel told them: "All the usual arrangements will stand, but .... !"

She was amused to see a few raised eyebrows and exchanges of looks when she explained the new arrangements they were to make upstairs. Knowing her staff had over a week to prepare for the shooting guests Rachel escaped from their knowing looks with Digger.

Although many crinkled brown oak leaves still clung stubbornly overhead there were plenty of other leaves to rustle noisily under foot as Rachel, having arranged with her new agent to devote the afternoon to estate business in her father's old office, reluctantly took only a short walk. It was just that she felt she ought to prepare for that meeting by going over the estate books with Grace. Later in the afternoon Charles had also arranged for a prospective farm manager to come and be interviewed by both of them.

Still feeling a need to talk through some of her problems, Rachel wandered into the timber yard on the way to the estate office. The two workmen were busy marking out the shape of a shaft and Nathan was on the phone. With the old battered kettle boiling away it seemed natural for her to put some tea in the pot and brew.

When Nathan put the phone down she took a cup of tea in to him and started to talk about Alexander. Nathan said, "You must be pleased with his promotion. When you next talk to him please congratulate him from me."

"That's the trouble - we don't talk anymore! I've been trying to tell him something all week but he just will not listen."

Nathan held up his hands to stop her, "I'm sorry that things aren't well between you but I can't help you."

When he saw how that hurt her he added, "Look I'll help you with other problems if I can, but you must know I can't get involved in your marriage."

"I'm sorry. I shouldn't have said that. I didn't mean to embarrass you. Please forgive me."

Rachel changed the subject to that of her new agent and his

proposals. Nathan reassured her: "Look, you've chosen an efficient estate agent, you should relax now while he sorts it out." Feeling a bit embarrassed at the strained atmosphere between them he broke off by saying, "I have to go out now."

"And I must take a reluctant dog into the estate office for an hour," Rachel said.

***

When she arrived at the office Rachel was faced with an immediate problem. Grace, who had heard the rumour about an outside estate agent, was concerned about her future. Rachel reassured her as best she could and then settled down to the business of the estate and farm. When they came to an entry for one of those unexplained large withdrawals, Grace just passed over it by saying, "Oh, the Captain made that cheque out."

Rachel decided not to question her further even when Grace said the same about a second large withdrawal.

During the walk back Rachel pondered on what the money had been used for and wandered into the garden. Digger crashed across the newly planted flowerbed in hot pursuit of a startled rabbit only to lose it among some larger shrubs further away. By the time that Rachel had got him back under control and apologised to the gardener the kitchen maid was standing shyly in front of her announcing, "Lunch is now ready, Ma'am."

The afternoon's discussions in the estate office were mainly about property and tenancies. As the time drew near to interview the prospective farm manager, Rachel asked a few questions about him. She was particularly surprised that Robert Towley was only twenty-six. Rachel needed convincing before the interview that he had the right experience. Charles Brown explained, "Robert lost his parents at a young age and was brought up by an uncle and aunt on their Derbyshire hill farm. There were three older sons on the farm leaving no room for Robert on his uncle's farm, but even so he was determined to farm. He had a small legacy and with it he financed himself through agricultural college and then gained further experience working on a mixed farm. Recently he was appointed manager on the Home farm of a small estate in mid Cheshire."

"So why is he looking for a job? And whose was the estate?"

"It belonged to a cotton mill owner. He bought it as a country residence and I suppose as an alternative interest to his main business.

It was all going well until this summer and then the mill owner's daughter returned home from her Swiss finishing school. The girl enjoyed the country life and particularly going for long walks around the farm. It seemed that the number of walks increased when she discovered she could contrive to accidentally meet up with the handsome young farm manager. Anyway the mill owner had great expectations for his only daughter and marrying a humble farm manager was not part of them."

"I can guess the rest."

"No doubt you can. The daughter stubbornly refused to be packed off again to some foreign part so he fired the farm manager. No notice or other consideration just 'Get out'. Robert seemed determined to stay close to his new love and has been helping a neighbouring farmer over harvest. I had a hand in appointing him that time so I'm sure he's the sort of man you want. Perhaps this estate may not be quite as close as he would have liked but it's close enough."

When the interview began Rachel immediately took to Robert. She was impressed with his forward thinking and his perceptive grasp of the Home farm affairs. The fact that he wanted to start the following Monday settled the matter. Rachel decided to move one or two treasured pieces of furniture out of the cottage along with her father's personal things before Robert moved into what would be his furnished cottage.

The following morning it seemed natural to call round at the timber yard to tell Nathan about her new farm manager. In fact she found that most mornings she was unwittingly walking in that direction.

Others had soon realised Nathan could be seen at the yard for the first two hours of the day. On her visits Rachel was surprised to meet several different villagers as well as one or two complete strangers coming or going to see Nathan.

Her agent had told her he planned to visit each tenant in turn through the coming two weeks but declined her offer to accompany him. He did however draft out a letter for her to send to them explaining his appointment and that from the end of the month the estate business would be conducted from his own office in Knutsford. Having signed that letter Rachel realised the Browns would need an explanation as to why she had changed her mind about selling them their farm and resolved to walk over there the next day.

Tying Digger to the yard gatepost Rachel found herself

welcomed into Lisa Brown's home with all the warmth of past years. Lisa sent one of the boys to find her husband before sitting down with Rachel for a heart-to-heart chat. It was obvious Lisa was coping remarkable well with the loss of her only daughter, but then, Rachel mused, many parents lost one child; some mourned two or three. Lisa's solid faith seemed to be helping her to look forward without shutting out her happy memories.

William Brown came in just as the kettle boiled. It was a practised skill he laughingly claimed was achieved by second sight. Unlike Lisa he seemed to be just a bit uncomfortable with her about something. Pretending that she had not noticed, Rachel went on to explain about the agent, her farm manager and Nathan's progress at the yard and then asked, "What do you think – will it all work out?" Reluctant to advise on other's affairs he just said, "Well, maybe."
"About my suggestion that we may sell some land." As she said it Rachel noticed William beginning to fidget. "I've discussed it with the agent and we have decided not to sell."

Before she could add her apologies for changing her mind William Brown, with obvious relief, said, "I'm glad. I haven't got a lot of confidence about farming at the moment. It's not the time to be taking a big risk – and it would be a risk, buying now."

Rachel had always loved this strong, solid farmer. His directness and his honest friendship through the years made her think of him as the substitute for the uncle she never had. They both now laughed together with the relief that they should both have decided the same if for different reasons.

**

On her return walk back to the Hall, Hamish appeared as though he had been waiting for her. He needed to know the number of guns taking part in the coming shoot. He also arrr'd around before saying he was worried about his position under the new agent. Rachel managed to reassure him.

**

Nathan was pleased young Clem shared his interest in shooting. Not that either of them shot much but they agreed it would be fun to borrow some ferrets off Hamish on the odd Saturday afternoon. Ferreting would have to wait, though, because there was no way Hamish would let them shoot anywhere on the estate until after the partridge shoot.

While Clem had been working for the estate, part of his duties had been to help Hamish keep the woodland rides clear. At other busy times he had also helped to build and move pheasant pens and give a hand with other heavy work. It was partly his interest and help that had enabled Hamish to manage the shoot single-handed. But Hamish still considered him too young to take out after poachers.

Asking Nathan to take a Sunday afternoon walk over the shoot with him, Hamish took the opportunity to explain some of the problems he faced running the shoot single-handed as they walked across the fields.

When Hamish pointed to the various shooting stands where the guns would wait on the partridge day Nathan saw they were more or less where they had been when he had helped out as a boy. There were no gun butts like those used on a grouse moor; the guns usually stood out on the open field as on a pheasant drive. The difference was that each stand was carefully chosen so that the guns waited some thirty or forty yards behind a hedge. That way the low-flying partridge should sweep over the fence in range of the guns before being aware of them. Where possible each drive was planned where there was a block of woodland running along one side of the last field leading up to the waiting guns. Nathan didn't need an explanation; because low-flying partridge avoid both woodland and the restriction of low branches, a block of trees helped to direct them over the guns.

Telling Nathan there would be three drives before lunch and either two or three afterwards Hamish went on to say, "Partridge break sideways more than pheasants do. It takes more beaters to cover th'flanks. Young Clem's good at organising that!"

Wondering what he was leading up to, Nathan asked, "What do you want me to do then?"

Hamish cleared his throat with a few arrr's before replying, "I'll be with th'beaters so will yer' load for the Captain?"

"Have you not heard? He's a Major now."

"No I hadna! Major or not ee's still a terrible organiser. The Gaffer used to load for 'im so he could help 'im keep th'guns organised."

Nathan was not sure the Major would be too pleased with this arrangement but in the end reluctantly agreed. He also understood why Hamish had to be with the beaters. Moving the beaters in a straight line and complete silence were the two essential elements for a successful partridge shoot, because partridge fly directly away from danger just one beater out of line could send them off in almost any direction.

Considering the partridge were completely wild Nathan was amazed how many coveys he saw on their walk. Hamish explained it by saying, "Arrr, I just keep down th'vermin and th'partridge look after th'selves."

***

Two days before the shoot, when checking through the preparations for the shooting guests, Rachel was intrigued when Cook asked to have a private word with her. Shutting the lounge door behind her Rachel asked, "Well, Cook?"

"Well, Ma'am, I've known you a long time now so I hope you won't be offended if I say something?"

"You know that you can always speak your mind to me."

Cook shuffled about a bit before saying, "There's talk in the village about you and Nathan. It's none of my business, Ma'am, but I thought I should tell you."

"You're right; it is none of yours or any ones else's business. But I suppose you did right to tell me. Thank you, Cook."

"But Ma'am ..."

"No buts. Nathan's never once acted other than properly with me. I'm not going to change my friends because of village tittle-tattle."

***

Alexander had rung and left a message with the parlour maid to tell Bestwick which train he should meet. He had neither asked for nor tried to talk to Rachel.

Still not having heard directly from him, by the next morning Rachel was in a rebellious mood. Deliberately flouting village gossip, on her way to sort through the last of her father's things she called in to see Nathan but he didn't greet her with his usual warm smile. Instead he somewhat formally invited her into his office then without speaking he gave her the local paper and pointed to the headlines. Rachel's face turned ashen as she read: 'Having accepted the report of the funeral of the late Thomas Courtney (as reported on page 22) the Chronicle decided to investigate his life a little further. The following facts were discovered just as we went to press.

'Although Thomas Courtney was the steward on the Hesston Estate he was not just plain Mr Courtney, his Father had changed his name from De Courcy. The De Courcy family, who own large estates in the south midlands, can trace their line back to the Norman

122

*invasion. There is more: at his death Thomas Courtney or De Courcy
was in fact Lord Gressonham, having succeeded to the title on the
death of his cousin just a couple of months before his own death. His
only daughter is the wife of Major Wentworth-Jones, the owner of the
Hesston estate.*

*'Just promoted, the Major has been out of the country but on his
return the Chronicle intends to investigate why the family kept this
news secret.'*

Aware Nathan was watching her closely Rachel said, "I knew
nothing of this until I saw the solicitor the other day. It appears my
father had only learned about it just a few days before his death. I
haven't even told Alexander yet."

"But you knew before he went off!"

"Yes, but he wouldn't listen," Rachel said in small voice as she read
further: *'It is understood the estates go with the title, which we
understand can only follow the male line. As the Major and Mrs
Wentworth-Jones have no children the search is now on for the
nearest male relative. Whatever happens, the Chronicle believes that
Mrs Wentworth-Jones in now a Lady in her own right.'*

"When you came round to discuss your problems with me you
obviously didn't discuss them all," Nathan said accusingly.

"I'm sorry but I thought it could remain hidden, at least until I'd had
a chance to tell the Major. Anyway, that report isn't very accurate and
my father's right to the title has yet to be proved."

"How do you mean not proved?"

"Well, it seems it was up to my father to prove his right to the
inheritance. The solicitor was working on that proof when father
died."

"The solicitor should have come forward and told you before the
funeral."

Still sounding like a small girl caught out in a misdemeanour, Rachel
tried to explain. "He claims he was still waiting for more information
and felt it wrong to talk to me until he had all the details."

"Has he got them now?"

"Not really. There seem to be some questions that need answering,
which I don't understand."

"How long will all that take?"

"He's very vague, quoting all sorts of legal jargon to me. At the end
I believe it will have to be proved through the House of Lords. Oh
God! What will Alexander say?"

Chapter Fifteen

All estate stewards live between two societies; high society is above them whilst the villagers are happier to keep them at arm's length. A daughter, who also worked in her father's office, had to learn to accept the responsibility demanded in that isolated in-between-land, cut off from many of the intimate secrets of the villagers and yet not part of the higher society. Although that somewhat lonely life had partially prepared Rachel for her married role as the wife of the landowner, the change had still been a tempestuous experience for her. She remembered it now, sitting by the lake in a reflective mood, how in those early days of marriage pleasing Alexander had been her greatest wish.

Slim, smilingly attractive yet with the emotional experience of an isolated country teenager, in those early-married days Rachel was surprised how Alexander was being invited to take her to a whirl of weekend house parties. Had he been invited to so many before the marriage and refused or was it now because of her? Perhaps it was her willingness to listen that appealed to the older men, because she discovered it was they who seemed to be issuing most of the invitations.

For a while Rachel managed to discourage the more amorous approaches. That was until their invitation to the Colonel's.

Alexander had been so determined to make a good impression on his Colonel that Rachel felt obliged to smile sweetly to him. Placed next to the Colonel for dinner and listening to tales of his wartime exploits, she had pretended admiration. Later in the evening the Colonel refilled her wine glass with such enthusiastic promptness that Rachel moved to a chair next to a large potted plant. The plant seemed to be able to take its drink very well.

Earlier the Colonel had persuaded the four male guests to play cards while he innocently pottered back and to with both the wine and the port.

Later, equally innocently, the Colonel suggested that the men would not mind should the ladies wish to retire. Upstairs in the spacious country house Rachel had wished the other three wives a goodnight as each went into their own room and then walked on round a corner of the landing towards her own bedroom. The Colonel unexpectedly stepped into her path from out of a different bedroom doorway. Rachel was bidding him a pleasant goodnight when she was suddenly engulfed in an amorous bear hug. With seemingly practised skill she was whisked sideways through the open bedroom door and in the same move her dress was slipped off her shoulders. That had perhaps been the Colonel's undoing because, balancing on one leg, he tried to kick the door shut behind him while at the same time he couldn't resist looking down at the curves of her firm young breasts. With arms trapped by both dress and bear hug Rachel made the only move possible, she stamped her heel down hard on his other foot.

Without realising it Rachel must have screamed as she fled from the room because one of the other guests, a captain's wife, came rushing round the corner. Back in the safety of her own room that young wife had confessed how the Colonel had tried the same thing with her on her last visit. When Rachel had asked what happened she had shyly confessed that she eventually gave in. To Rachel's gasp of horror she added this advice, "It seems to be part of the sport on these weekends. You either fight them off or succumb (as I did for the sake of my husband's career). The one thing you don't do, you don't get your man involved; that would destroy him."

That young wife, Lucy, and her husband Major Fearnly were now their guests here at Hesston. Although they had become friends, Lucy never revealed whether she had ever gone back to the Colonel's again, though Rachel had long thought the girl's husband seemed to have got his promotion suspiciously early.

Anyway, the next day they had both enjoyed a good laugh when they saw a distinctive limp marring the Colonel's precise military walk. The plant also looked decidedly one sided; seven glasses of wine were obviously over its limit.

The second equally disturbing experience for her happened at the palatial home of a noble Lord.

Rachel wondered why they had been invited. The second afternoon there she found out. On the pretext of taking her to look at some rare specimens of imported shrubs she suddenly found herself cornered in the taller and older shrubs by the portly gentlemen. Rachel's young, agile legs got her out of trouble without any real embarrassment. Then, trying to keep the relationship on a proper footing, she innocently went with him to look through his greenhouses. It had seemed a natural thing to do because she had just taken over running the large Hesston Hall garden and she was genuinely interested, particularly as he was very knowledgeable in what he called new propagation techniques. That was how they had ended up in the potting shed.

His Lordship's propagation technique was soon revealed. He suddenly stepped between Rachel and the door, then, with no more than a wrestled kiss, he tried to give a demonstration. Although trapped with her bottom tight against the potting bench, Rachel found her arms were free. When His Lordship reached down to lift her skirt, Rachel gave him a violent push. Alas, the Noble Lord, more than a little overweight and with trousers down around his ankles, just couldn't correct his balance in time. Stepping nimbly round his prostrate form Rachel spotted a half filled watering can and couldn't resist. She often laughed at the memory of him spluttering as he squirmed his bare bottom about on the cold, wet flagged floor.

Following Lucy's advice Rachel said nothing about the incident to Alexander. Later in the weekend, when passing the potting shed on the way to the tennis court with Lucy, playful giggles were coming from within. She presumed the noble lord was again demonstrating his propagation technique, but seemingly with a more willing student.

Rachel then confessed shyly to Lucy what had happened, including the bit with the watering can. It was about twenty minutes before either of them could concentrate enough to hit a ball.

After those two disturbing experiences Rachel vetted whose invitations they accepted. Alexander, reluctantly agreeing to scale down his social ambitions, now accepted they just invite a group of closer friends to their own weekends. That they were his friends and not hers did not bother her because she knew how moving in different circles would be a major part of their marriage.

From then on their country house weekends, whether for shooting or tennis, developed into a near standard format in whoever's house they were held.

The guests arrived with their wives around mid Friday afternoon. The host and hostess would greet them before the butler showed them up to their rooms, usually followed by a footman carrying matching suitcases.

After a suitable time to freshen up, the guests would come down to the lounge for afternoon tea, when wafer-thin sandwiches would be served, followed by delicious and exquisitely small cakes. Little fingers pointed upwards as the ladies sipped their tea out of the finest of bone china teacups. After a suitable exchange of small talk the ladies would retire upstairs to rest before changing for the evening meal. Meanwhile the men might take a lengthy stroll round the garden before joining the ladies upstairs.

Rachel smiled with amusement because this weekend at Hesston was slightly different. Although the standard butler was here to give some dignity, in fact old Greeb's walk was based more on dignity than movement. The footman carrying the cases was actually the assistant gardener, Reg, squashed into a silly uniform that had barely fitted his teenage figure the year before. The real difference though was that there was no Alexander. Bestwick had driven off to meet the train but had not returned.

The first guests to arrive were Lucy and Major Fearnly, for which Rachel was glad. It gave her and Lucy a chance to have a good gossip while the Major was helping the gardener settle his retriever into the Hall kennels.

The next two couples arrived together but Greebs made one wait while he first announced Mr George and Mrs Eleanor Canterly. George, a shy and rather quiet man who had been at school with Alexander, had recently married an equally quiet girl. They now lived modestly on a small estate in Staffordshire. George also left Eleanor with Lucy and Rachel while he took his own dog round to the kennels.

The other guests, Mr Edward and Mrs ELisabeth Craneby-Brown, were just the opposite. Although Alexander seemed beholden to the husband for some shared wartime experience Rachel found him a bore and his wife a snob. At the end of the war he'd left the army as soon as he possibly could to rejoin his father's merchant bank. The Craneby-Browns appeared to have lots of money, which Elisabeth flaunted far too often. She was certainly too house proud to allow husband Edward to keep a rumbustious and often mud-spattered gundog. Knowing Greebs disliked them, Rachel was sure he deliberately made them wait before announcing them.

Later, the afternoon took its normal course with the usual afternoon tea served in the lounge. Mr Jonson had still not arrived so when the formality of tea was over Rachel joined the other ladies upstairs.

Going to the back of the house to check on Mr Jonson's bedroom she was embarrassed to overhear through the open window the three men talking in the garden below. "Well I never understood how he managed to get back in uniform with his injuries," said one. "If you know the right people," came the reply, "you can get anywhere."

Rachel thought it best if she didn't try to guess who had said what and, changed for dinner, was on her way downstairs when Alexander dashed breathlessly up. "Sorry I'm so late, the train broke down."

"Alexander! We must talk before dinner." But he just brushed past her saying, "No, no! I am going to get changed."

Then, calling back from the landing, "I'll be down in ten minutes." At the foot of the stairs Greebs informed her, "Mr Jonson has gone up to his room, Ma'am."

And so they all went through to dinner together.

Grace duly said by Alexander, Greebs lifted each dish of soup from the maid's tray to place it carefully before each guest in turn then, with the same solemn formality, poured out the white wine. Small talk suddenly stopped when Major Fearnly raised his glass and said, To Alexander, congratulations Major!"

As they all raised their glass and repeated the toast Rachel could see Alexander's chest swelling. She used to think it was courage that had forced him on through the pain but now she wondered if it wasn't just vanity. Mr Jonson interjected "Shouldn't we be including someone else in our congratulations?"

When several guests asked, "Who?" he smiled at Rachel and said, "Like Lady Wentworth-Jones."

Again several asked together, "What do you mean?"

"I stopped in Knutsford to pick up the local paper. It seems there was more to your late estate steward than I'd realised. Lady Wentworth-Jones has inherited her title because her father was Lord Gressonham."

There was an outburst of questions as each tried to ask what it was all about. Rachel saw Alexander's face; it was white, immobile and behind that mask she was sure there was fury.

She felt like crawling down the nearest rabbit hole. However insufferable he may have been, the last thing she wanted was for him to hear this way. Trying to pass it off she said, "I'm sorry you found out. I haven't had a chance even to tell Alexander yet. Anyway it will be some time before we know for certain. Just forget it, this is Alexander's celebration."

But Alexander still sat immobile at the other end of the table.

Glancing round the other happy faces she saw there was a gleam of evil satisfaction on one and wondered again what Mr Jonson was to Alexander.

The guests demanded more of an explanation, and when she gave it they fell into discussion on inheritance of titles. It seemed that there was some variance between the inheritance laws of different Earldoms. George Canterly, claiming some knowledge of the subject, stated, "There are at least two types of Earldoms. The first are called 'Baronies by Writ'. They were awarded in the early Middle Ages to men who had been summoned by Parliament to give advice, but as they are rare it's unlikely to be one of those. I forget what the other sort of Baron is called but they're the usual Earldoms who may have been appointed any time since the Middle Ages. By the way, they can only come down the male line, unlike the Baronies by Writ."

"You mean the first ones can come down the female line?" Major Fearnly asked.

"I believe so, yes," George replied shyly.

"How do you know all this?"

"Its George's hobby." His wife said proudly. "He's always engrossed in some old book or other."

It all left Rachel more confused and determined to discuss it again with Benjie Cuthbert.

The rest of the evening passed without incident until bedtime. Some of the guests were wandering in and out of their bedrooms so Rachel thought it best if she went into Alexander's bedroom with him. But before she could speak he turned on her in a controlled fury. When he finally paused she asked him, "How could I tell you? I tried before you left but you refused to listen. I tried on the telephone but you put it down. I've even tried to contact you these last two days in London but you couldn't be bothered to return my call."

She suddenly felt her own fury rising when he replied, "You haven't tried very hard. You've just done it deliberately to hurt me."

After that Rachel couldn't remember just what she did say. She was sure though that she had told him just how insufferable he was and how through the years she had lived subservient to his every wish. There was a lot more but she could only remember her closing line, "I've been a dutiful wife, running your home and now running the estate. I've come to you when you have wanted me but even that's got less and less and when we do there's no love, it's just a function for you. Well it's a function you can do without from now on because

I'm sleeping in the next room."

With that she stepped into her dressing room, bolted the door on the inside and walked through it into her own bedroom.

***

On the Partridge shoot day Hamish was beginning to worry and it was showing. He'd already explained to Nathan that, because of having to change the shooting day, they had clashed with a neighbouring shoot, which meant they were short of experienced beaters. The fact that the same neighbouring keeper and he usually helped each other out on their big shooting days added to the stress.

The beaters by tradition had met by the side of the Hall where Hamish was explaining the arrangements for the day. Those included instructing Clem to set out straightaway with his party of flankers because they had a long circular walk to get to their places, "An' no talking! Only wave yer' flags if you see partridge coming towards yer'."

While Hamish was talking, not that he said very much, the guests arrived. Those who were staying at the Hall walked round from the front door while the other three guns drove up and began to unload their dogs and guns from their cars.

Seeing the Major had not yet come out, Hamish again went over the arrangements with Nathan. Nathan tried to reassure him: "Yes, he had the whistle. Yes, he would get each gun in place before he signalled to Hamish to start the drive. Yes, he would keep an eye on the new lad who hadn't loaded for them before."

Nathan could understand Hamish's anxiety. In the past Thomas, while loading for the Major, had at the same time discreetly kept an eye the other guns and their loaders. They were lucky all the usual loaders had come and each was greeted in a friendly way by their respective gun. But of course they had an extra loader for Mr Jonson – an apparently bright fifteen-year old who had assured Hamish he had loaded before.

When Rachel joined them with Digger she asked, "Where's the Major?"

Hamish replied, "Arrr he's no' here. We're all waitin'."

Knowing the arrangements Rachel told Hamish, "Then you take the beaters and get in place for the first drive. I am sure the Major will join us in a moment."

With that Rachel walked back into the house. When she came

back a few moments later she walked across to where Nathan was standing away from the others. Speaking quietly she said, "Alexander seems to be acting a bit strangely. I found him sitting in his study just fingering the Colonel's medals."

When Nathan replied, "So what, my Lady?" Rachel just smiled and told him that she was still just Rachel but he said firmly, "In front of others you are 'My Lady' whether you like it or not."

What she did not tell him now was that Alexander only got his father's medals out in times of extreme stress. The two or three times she had seen him looking at the medals had been when he was facing a big interview or some such happening. The strange thing was that each time he had been holding the same medal. It was the Colonel's South African Medal, which also had the Bar of South Africa 1901, awarded by Queen Victoria.

But what was causing her husband so much stress this morning? Surely, it was not just their row? Whatever was troubling him it seemed to have been forgotten when he came out to greet everybody.

***

The layout for the day's shooting was a little like a golf course but there was a difference in that each drive was designed to direct the birds towards the centre of the estate. That arrangement meant that the shooting guests walked only a short distance to their first stand, nor did they move very far between each stand. On the other hand, after each drive the beaters had to go on a fairly wide detour to get into position for the next drive.

By tradition Rachel went with the guns for the first two drives, intending then to return to the house to check on lunch while they held a third short drive. It never crossed her mind to question the morality of shooting; it had been part of her life from a small girl. Although hating to see birds wounded she had learned how to dispatch them with a flick of her wrist. On the other hand death by nature was often far crueller, as proved when she watched a sparrow hawk catch, pluck and eat a squawking starling; it had taken twenty minutes for the starling's cries of pain to finally stop.

Rachel was amused to see Nathan diplomatically organising both the guns and the loaders into their respective places.

By tradition on the Hesston Estate there was a different procedure on the partridge shoot than on the later pheasant shoots. The guns had drawn lots for the first drive. After each drive

Alexander just moved the outside two guns to the middle, which meant that through the day each gun would shoot in every position. Partridge are always unpredictable. Still in their family coveys, they may take off at the start of a drive or run forward before clapping down hidden in the stubble right in front of the guns. When that happened neither the guns nor the beaters would see the birds until the beaters were right on them and then the partridge would burst into flight, skimming the hedge in front of the guns in a frenzy of whirling wings. Ideally the birds shouldn't see the guns until they flew over the hedge and into range. Then hopefully the covey might panic and split, allowing more of the guests to get a few shots.

On the first drive Nathan stood at the outside peg with the Major. One covey, coming early, flew at speed over the middle of the stand. There was a flurry of shots from the two centre guns, Major Fearnly and Mr Jonson, then a flurry of swear words from Mr Jonson. The Major told Nathan to go and sort that out.

It seemed there was a mix-up between Mr Jonson and his loader. When Nathan got to them the lad was still getting a broadside. Intervening, Nathan said, "Come on, its only a misunderstanding," but he soon discovered Mr Jonson was demanding his gun should be handed over in a completely differently way than usual. It took him a while to get the loader into the opposite combination of movements to suit Mr Jonson.

Peace restored, Nathan just got back before two or three coveys burst over the guns. With pheasant shooting the birds usually fly high overhead and then there are always two or three people standing some distance behind the guns waiting to mark and later pick up the dead birds. Because partridge usually fly low they can only be safely shot out in front of the line of guns or behind them, which meant that it was considered safe for the one or two pickers-up to stand beside the guns. The sharp-eyed young loaders usually marked where most birds came down. Then, after each stand, those of the guns who had brought their dogs released them to retrieve.

After that argument with the young loader the drive went without anything amiss, until they moved across a couple of fields for the next drive. Then Nathan noticed one gun in the wrong place. It seemed Mr Jonson didn't like the position of his gun peg because it was on the other side of a hedgerow oak. Nathan found him on George Canterly's peg. When Mr Jonson refused to move Nathan, in desperation, said, "Look I've got the whistle and I won't blow it until you're on your own peg. If that means we stand here all morning, well so be it."

Nathan received a few swear words about getting too big for his boots for a hired hand but Mr Jonson did move. Over his shoulder Nathan noticed Rachel was close enough to hear the exchange but she said nothing either then or later when they were away from the others.

As it turned out, Mr Jonson got more than his share of sport on that second drive when several coveys veered off to his side of the tree. Since he did not have a dog of his own, Rachel took Digger to retrieve Mr Jonson's shot birds. By the time Digger had picked up the last bird the other guns and their loaders were walking towards the next stand. They had to walk down a short, steep, muddy cow path, step through a gap in the hedge and jump a small stream before climbing up the other side.

Leaving Rachel waiting for Digger to carry the last bird, Mr Jonson responded to the Major's call. When he came the Major almost herded him down the muddy cow path to follow the other guns through the hedge. Nathan, standing to one side, glanced back to see Rachel coming with the dead partridge. As he turned back again the Major's feet shot from under him and his hand holding the gun came up. Nathan instinctively knocked the barrel away from Mr Jonson's back as it exploded with a frightening bang. Mr Jonson spun round with a look of frightened horror on his face and in that same instant, glancing down, Nathan was sure the Major's finger had been on the trigger. He looked up to see Rachel's white face frozen in horror. Had she seen what he had? Mr Jonson, although badly shaken, was unhurt. A stray pellet had just clipped the tip of the shoulder of his smart new tweed shooting coat. After apologies from the Major and an explanation of how he had slipped, Mr Jonson walked away in white-faced silence.

The shoot continued without Rachel, who as usual went to oversee lunch preparations. Mr Jonson remained quiet through the rest of the morning. His young loader seemed to now pass the guns back and to just as he required, or at least there were no more curses vented on him. Nor was there any argument as to who went to which stand.

The Major was an easy man to load for, being both a good shot and systematic when exchanging guns. On that last morning drive everyone had fallen into a routine, leaving Nathan time to observe each gun and their response to each other. There was no jollity, just a gentlemanly, cool politeness particularly between the Major and Mr Jonson.

Of course, Nathan wasn't able to see the mood among the guests over lunch for they were inside the Hall, whereas the keeper and his helpers each had their bottle of stout and plate of hotpot round a makeshift table in one end of the stable.

After the beaters had finished their hotpot Nathan watched Hamish set out with his group to push coveys from some outlying fields into the path of the main drive, where they hoped the partridge would settle until the guns finished their lengthy and no doubt more luxurious lunch.

When the guns finally emerged they seemed a little more relaxed. Nathan presumed that they had consumed something a little stronger than a bottle of stout, though there was still a lack of the usual afternoon revelry that he was used to seeing.

Chapter Sixteen

Cook had excelled herself again, preparing a substantial Sunday roast beef lunch. Although Mr Jonson left soon afterwards, the other shooting guests surprisingly seemed reluctant to go. By mid-afternoon, seeing them still sitting around chatting, Alexander suggested that they might wish to take tea before they left. Having told Cook that no one could want to eat again that day Rachel rushed into the kitchen with the expectation that she would have to prepare it herself, but was surprised and delighted to find that Cook had anticipated the need. Both Cook and the parlour maid were putting the finishing touches to a delectable afternoon tea.

Within minutes it was put before the guests in the lounge. When the ladies exclaimed that the small sandwiches were 'exquisite' and the mixture of delicate cakes were 'simply too delicious' Cook was obviously pleased her efforts were appreciated. Rachel was concerned that the guests would be travelling home in the dark but they all seemed to relax and become even chattier as the afternoon tea was consumed.

Eventually, after every one had finally left, Alexander and Rachel settled down to relax, each with a book in front of a roaring fire. In time past they used to break off reading to discuss the merits of each other's books. This was a more silent but still companionable evening with just cheese and biscuits for supper. Alexander, though, drank more than usual; Rachel thought he was perhaps working up to issuing an invitation or even a demand for her to return to his bed, but no; when bedtime came he just bid her "Goodnight" and went quietly to his room.

After an early breakfast Bestwick drove away with Alexander. Rachel then discussed household business with Cook before starting out on her Monday morning walk with Digger and it was in the direction on the timber yard.

Nathan was as usual working in his office. They discussed the success of the shoot for a few minutes. When she suggested to Nathan that perhaps there was some strain when Mr Jonson was around he nodded in agreement. When she tried to discuss the shooting incident he refused to comment, in fact he seemed less talkative than usual.

Presuming he was just trying to sort out his week's work, Rachel made her apologies and left.

***

Nathan stopped work to watch her walk away. Aware of the graceful movement of her slim body and the slight wiggle of her shapely hips as she strode towards the farmyard, he made a new resolve. It was to change his day's work schedule so he might avoid such meetings and the enticing thoughts that seemed to follow.

Calling Clem to him Nathan said, "Sharpen your axe and the long crosscut saw. After our brew we're off to the woods."

Striding across the fields on a dull, murky November day, Nathan explained his plans to Clem, "You and me will fall one big tree or two smaller ones each morning, then I'll leave you to trim them up on your own."

"I can fall these smaller trees on my own."

"No, you can't! You can cut the wedge out if you like but we'll fall them with the crosscut the next day. Each day you'll have one or two to trim up and a wedge or two to chop out and that's it! You then come back to the yard."

"But ... "

"No buts! We work in pairs to fall timber in my set-up!"

From then on the days began to follow a pattern. Once Nathan had attended to any pressing business arrangements, he and Clem strode out towards the woods. Their first task was always to light a small fire then put the kettle on before kneeling down with the long crosscut behind whichever large tree Clem had prepared. Although the sharp saw seemed to glide through the timber it was still hard graft sawing within a foot of the ground. They would soon both be stripped down to their shirts. The kettle was usually boiling by the time they had fallen their one or two trees and so Nathan would stop for a cup and a chat before retuning to the yard. He then had the day free to attend to any business in the yard or drive out to his two contract felling teams.

The one thing Nathan couldn't stop was his thoughts. Conscious that his plan had worked, in as much as he had always left the yard before Rachel started out on her morning walk, but disturbed that he felt a loss, he realised he would need all his resolve to continue to avoid her and avoid her he must.

Nathan's loneliness could have been much worse. Hetty had

proved to be both an excellent housekeeper and an enjoyable companion. Orphaned at twelve, she had been rescued from an austere orphanage by the offer of work from a reclusive widow. There was a cook and two other maids for company and her mistress had not been too demanding. There were also a lot of books in the house, which her mistress encouraged Hetty to read, with just one condition: most mornings Hetty was asked to explain what she had read and give her thoughts on each book when she finished reading it. To an avid reader those sessions were enjoyable because her mistress would explain anything Hetty had not understood.

Taught to cook, to housekeep and to be an interesting companion, Hetty had then disappointed her mistress by falling in love with a mere farm worker. She smiled when she told Nathan this, adding, "But she still gave me her blessing, a full kitchen service and a box of books. She died soon afterwards but I'll never forget her because she taught me so much."

The fact was that Nathan began to enjoy the winter nights sitting in front of a blazing log fire with one of those books. There were still three nights each week when he had to find food elsewhere but on other days there was a hearty meal waiting for him. Hetty never grumbled when he was late or moaned about the sawdust that inevitably fell from his clothes. She just expressed her gratitude for the logs and sticks he brought back and packed up a box of food each morning.

When Anthony drove over from Shropshire at the weekend Hetty kindly cooked them both a meal and agreed he could share Nathan's large double bed. Nathan promised to show his gratitude by cutting up the pear tree on the next weekend. Escorting Tony round his timber yard and later while driving out to one of the timber sites, Nathan swapped memories and outlined ambitions but he was a little cautious, because in the end they were now in competing businesses.

The following week Nathan and Clem felled a large tree each morning. In the afternoons Nathan organised two loads of timber to be hauled away from his other sites and, watching the first load chug off down the road behind a steam engine gave him a real buss of pleasure. He was now really in business.

* * *

The routine of the week had been broken for Rachel by an invitation from Lady Lucinda to a ladies' lunch at her town house. Many of the

Cheshire landed gentry spent much of their year away from home. Much energy was put into partying and entertaining in London while the Riviera or travel in general took up the rest of their time and often their money as well. Some of them only returned to their Cheshire home for the foxhunting season.

To Rachel it was such a waste. Owning a beautiful home with extensive gardens and a vast estate, then to only enjoy it for a few months of each year was to her a sacrilege. The one benefit was that once the hunting season got fully into swing there would be some invitations she could enjoy without Alexander.

Sir Stanley, Lady Lucinda's husband, had inherited his father's industrial empire although Alexander and he had never got on together, perhaps because their interests were so different, with Alexander's army ambitions so far removed from Sir Stanley's industrial schemes. Lady Lucinda, though, always made Rachel feel relaxed in her company, perhaps because neither of them came from the so-called County Set. The only difference was that Sir Stanley's vast wealth cancelled out Lady Lucinda's modest background whereas Alexander's modest estate didn't quite cancel out Rachel's.

Lady Lucinda mixed her guests, both the titled nobility and the more humble locals, with a happy disregard of the pretentious.

When Lucinda's smart butler asked if she wished to be announced by her new title Rachel insisted he ignore any such rumour. Old acquaintances greeted her as usual, most of them expressing sympathy over the loss of her father. But among the so called 'County Set' there was a difference, one or two of them who in the past had hardly bothered to speak to her were now fawning around her. It was some time before she realised what had changed. Could they be so artificial to see only an inherited title and not her? Rachel resolved not to let it spoil her day.

***

Even hardened countrymen seem to be fascinated by the crashing fall of a mighty old tree. Therefore the sound of an axe coupled with the knowledge that there might be a kettle boiling was an attraction to anyone in the area. When working out in the woods Nathan made sure Clem included a couple of extra tin mugs for such occasions.

This Friday morning Nathan and Clem made more noise than usual. A large beech tree, reluctant to fall in the direction Nathan had selected, had rocked back on the saw blade, which meant they had to drive two or three wedges into the saw cut to tilt the massive trunk back in the right direction and at the same time free the saw blade. The sound of sledgehammer striking the metal wedges rang out across the fields like the church bells. Hamish appeared out of the woods to watch the great tree finally fall in the right direction and just after it had crashed to the ground Rachel also came in from the fields.

There was a communal chat around the fire. Hamish however, had a purpose to his visit. "Will yer' no change yer' mind and help me with th'pheasant shoot tomorrow?"

Shaking his head, Nathan said, "I'm sorry. I've got a buyer who wants to see some timber and he insisted on meeting me tomorrow morning."

Rachel looked surprised at the news and asked Hamish, "Will you have enough helpers?"

"Och, aye! We're no' using loaders and I've put th'pegs out for th'guns. Arrr we'll manage Missey."

When Clem went off to refill the kettle from a spring Nathan hooked his jacket over his shoulder, picked up his axe and strode off towards the yard; Rachel fell into step beside him as Digger ran on ahead.

Neither spoke until after they had climbed through the wood side fence before striding out across the pasture field.

Out in the field there was a group of small tree-lined ponds fenced round to keep livestock from getting fast in the dangerous mud. When Rachel pointed to a broken rail in the fence they turned towards it. They both saw the cow at the same time. So deep in the water that only the top line of her back was above the water line, the cow had to hold her head back to keep her nose just out of the water. Pointing to the steep bank in front of the beast, Nathan said, "Clem's got a rope with him. If we drop it over her horns maybe we can pull her round to face this shallow bank where, with a bit of help, she might walk out."

Within minutes he was back with both Clem and the rope. When Nathan's first throw splashed by the cow's head, Digger jumped into the pond thinking he should retrieve it. Nathan ordered Digger back and Rachel held onto the wet dog while he tried again. After a few misses he managed to drop a noose over the cow's wide horns. Taking hold of the rope the three of them tried to get a firm footing among the wet autumn leaves on the sloping shallow bank with Nathan down by the water, Rachel just above him and Clem on the top bank behind

139

her. When they put pressure on the rope not only did it pull the cow's head round it also forced her nose under water. After a few moments of hard pulling the cow, objecting to her nose being held under water, made a violent lunge by lifting her head and splashing out with her front legs, jerking the three of them towards the pond, then when the cow's head swung back towards them, the rope went slack. With that first violent jerk Rachel's feet skidded down the slope then, when the rope went slack, Nathan fell backwards onto her.

Flat on her back and winded by both the fall and Nathan's weight, Rachel struggled onto her elbows as Nathan rolled onto one knee. He was aware that her skirt had ridden up her thighs, of one long shapely leg each side of his knee, of the dirty splashes on her face, even of his hand resting on the ground by her waist but his eyes were locked onto hers. The fact that the look passing between them had passed between man and woman countless time since it got Adam and Eve thrown out of the Garden of Eden didn't lessen the pounding in Nathan's chest.

Clem's repeated shouts of "Swim you beggar, swim!" finally broke Nathan's trance. Leaping to his feet he ran along the bank towards Clem and the cow that had, by violently thrashing out, freed herself from the mud and was now swimming the length of the pond. When the cow reached that end she tried to climb out but again her feet just sank in the mud and, already cold and tired, the effort was too much for her. They took hold of the rope but unless she made some effort there was no way just two men could pull her out.

"At least she's facing the field. We can hook a horse to her now. Clem, go and tell the cowman to bring a carthorse and some help then we'll soon have her out."

As Clem set off at a trot towards the farmyard Nathan turned back to Rachel who was sitting on his jacket at the top of the slope, wiping the splashes from her face. Seeing a dirty smear of mud across her right breast he looked at his arm and realised what he had hit as he fell. He rubbed at the mud on his arm and mumbled, "I'm sorry! Are you hurt?"

Aware of his glance, she brushed at the mud on the front of her jacket before meeting his gaze. "A bit shaken but I've had worse falls from a horse."

Nathan looked down at Rachel's mud-spattered dress and ankles then at his own equally spattered clothes and they both began to laugh. He held out both hands, which she took and came lithely up

140

on to her feet and was coming into his arms, eyes locked into his, when unfortunately as he shifted his balance to hold her one foot skidded down the slope and he was back on his knees. Laughing, Rachel stepped nimbly up to the top of the bank while Nathan, with a wry smile, rocked back onto his feet and followed her. But the moment of temptation had gone.

"The men will soon be back with a horse. I may as well stay and see it through now."

Nathan smiled. "I think not!"

"Why?"

"If the farm men see your wet bottom and my muddy knees, well .."

Rachel blushed, clasped her buttocks and, looking coyly at him, said, "Yes, you're right!"

Then, starting to walk away, she turned to add, "And I'll do a detour away from the farm yard as well."

As she entered the Hall through the kitchen Rachel decided it best to explain her dishevelled state before her staff jumped to the wrong conclusions. They had a good laugh before the maid ran upstairs to run a bath for her.

Sitting dreamily in the warm bath Rachel couldn't help wondering how Nathan bathed. The only other house on the estate with hot water laid on to a bathroom had been her father's. None of the farmhouses had hot water systems so she was sure that no farm cottage would have one, so what did Nathan do? Did he sit in a tin bath in front of the fire? What would it be like to kneel by him pouring hot water over those rippling muscles?

Dressed and ready to meet her guests later in the day Rachel went down to lunch pretending she was used to eating alone. On most days each meal was a lonely affair. Today the mental picture of Nathan kneeling between her thighs disturbed her so much she almost carried her plate through to join the staff round the kitchen table.

She willed herself to try to analyse her feelings: was she falling in love again? Or was it just a physical need Alexander was unable to fulfil? She was in no doubt there was a need and that Nathan could fill it, but was it love? Could you love someone as much as she had loved Alexander and then fall in love with someone else? If one of the staff asked her advice in the same situation she would have told her that it was just a facile feeling that would soon pass. Why did it feel so urgently real for her?

After a quick look round to see that the house was ready for the weekend shooting guests, Rachel relaxed before the lounge fire.

Greebs's discreet knock jolted her mind away from the pond bank and back to reality. "The vicar is at the door, Ma'am."

"Please show him in, Greebs."

"There is something I forgot to tell you, Ma'am. While you were out walking this morning the Major rang to say he was catching an earlier train. Bestwick left to meet it some time ago."

"Thank you Greebs. It will be nice if he is here to meet the guests."

The vicar greeted her in his usual smarmy manner. Although she had insisted the staff still called her Ma'am she had almost given up trying to explain the considerable doubt over her title. Nor was there any point in insisting the vicar addressed her in other than his fawning and superfluous manner. Seating him near the fire she began to ask about village matters. He discussed a few things with her and then, clearing his throat, said, "My Lady, there is something else I should like to talk to you about, but it's a bit delicate."

Expecting some juicy insight into the interesting lives of one of her tenants or maybe one of the staff, Rachel replied, "Come, Vicar, you have always been able to talk to me before. What's so delicate this time?"

He cleared his throat again and shuffled around in his chair, then cleared his throat once more. "There is village gossip about you, Ma'am, I mean My Lady."

"About me! In what way?"

"I am sure there's nothing in it, My Lady, but your name is being linked with Mr Dobson's."

Before today she could have dismissed it with contempt, but now, after this morning? Feeling herself blushing and momentarily flustered she said, "I ... well .... it's just village tittle-tattle. Mr Dobson was engaged to my best friend and now he's working on the estate. I talk to him sometimes, and that's all there is to it."

Showing he had a shrewder mind than Rachel had previously thought, the Vicar asked, "Is every thing all right between you and the Major?"

Had she respected him she may well have confessed all: the coldness of her marriage, her need for fulfilment and the innocent pleasure she got from Nathan's companionship. But after this morning she knew it wasn't innocent, it was dangerous. It was certainly too dangerous to discuss with the vicar. Wondering how many lies she was prepared to tell she replied brightly, "Yes, all is well! Although I do miss Alexander when he's away so much."

"Yes, My Lady, I had noticed he seems to be away more now. He wasn't home last weekend, was he?"

"No, there was a shooting weekend in Shropshire. As you know I didn't go to it, losing my father and all that." Rachel finished lamely while blaming Alexander under her breath for replying to the Canterlys' invitation without consulting her, although she had made up her mind to go and also, to save any embarrassment in someone else's house, to share Alexander's bed. Therefore it had been more than a surprise to receive a letter from Eleanor saying how much she would miss Rachel but she understood, with the loss of her father and all that. The vicar, taking Rachel's silence as an implied dismissal, rose to his feet to make his farewell.

As she watched through the window while he drove away Rachel was surprised to see Bestwick returning with Alexander. When the two cars met on the drive Alexander jumped out to stand chatting with the vicar for few moments.

Still flustered by her own thoughts Rachel wandered aimlessly round the room. She knew that the man about to step through the door was the man she had both loved and wanted to marry above anything else. Now, after being married to him for eight years, how could she have been so excited as she had this morning by another man?

Alexander stepped into the room but before she could greet him he held out a present. Gifts were not normally part of his behaviour, not that he was mean. Rachel was allowed to buy whatever she needed but was not used to gestures of affection. When she stepped close to give him a thank-you kiss on the cheek his arms slid round her waist, pressing her tight against him.

That was the only signal he ever gave to declaring his need of her. She knew then she mustn't think about this morning but must try again to rekindle her feelings for this unresponsive man. Whispering, "I will share your bed tonight." Rachel stepped back to open the small package; a beautiful pearl necklace gleamed before her.

"I thought you should have something fit for a Lady."

"I'm not a Lady yet!"

Chapter Seventeen

As he waited by the pond after Rachel had walked towards the Hall Nathan was surprised to see the new farm manager, Robert Towley, coming down the field towards him. The two young men were only beginning to get to know each other. After the usually greetings Robert explained, "I've got a couple of men bringing the carthorse and a few rails. They can repair the fence while they're here."

Pointing to the fence, Nathan said, "We'll need a bit more room to back the horse in."

Robert turned to kick another two rails down, saying with a smile, "Will that do it?"

The cow came out with little effort. When the horse tightened on the rope the cow, again trying to fight against the pull, lashed out with her front feet, which freed them from the mud and within a second or two she was walking up the bank.

Leaving his men to patch up the fence, Robert started to drive the cow home. When Nathan fell in step beside him he explained, "The walk will warm her up. Anyway, the dairy cows are now inside day and night but there are just these few dry cows still outside, so I'll put this one in the shippen with the others. The heat from them should warm her"

"Will she get a chill?"

"No! They're tough animals. Anyway, if she's inside I can keep an eye on her just in case."

"How are you getting on with your farm plan?"

Robert threw his hands up in a victory salute. "Finished it today! Next week I'll have to persuade Her Ladyship to accept a few changes."

"I think she'll expect you to make more than a few changes."

"I hope you're right. Although there is one change that I'm not looking forward to."

"What's that?"

"Today I have to tell my secretary, Grace, I no longer need her services for more than a day each week, although I think she expects it. It's a shame, though, because she makes a great hotpot."

Robert went on to explain how his secretary, worried about him having to prepare most of his own meals, made a super dish of hotpot each Friday afternoon. There would be one left to simmer in the oven for his tea tonight.

The outcome of their walk with the cow was an invitation to Nathan to join Robert for his hotpot tea. Then as an afterthought when they were parting Nathan asked, "If your secretary ran the estate office for Thomas she must know quite a bit about the timber trade? I'm going to need a part time secretary so if Grace is interested maybe she'd like to call and see me on her way home."

With the mud washed of his hands and face and a change of clothing, which he kept for such emergencies in his office, Nathan put his mind to business. Before the day was out he had agreed terms with his new secretary, enjoyed a large dish of hotpot with Robert and afterwards the two of them spent a couple of enjoyable hours at the local pub.

Friday night was usually bath night but Nathan's apologies for missing it were dismissed by Hetty with a smile – particularly when he pulled a bottle of her favourite stout from his pocket. "And I intend to have a go at the pear tree tomorrow afternoon."

Hetty smiled as she replied, "I know all about a man's tomorrow. Unfortunately I'll not be here to make your dinner. I've got the chance of a lift into town to do some shopping but I should be back by early afternoon. I can make you a hot dish for your tea if you like? If you cut the pear tree up maybe I'll even make you a dish of hotpot?"

Smiling his thanks, Nathan went up to bed without saying anything about that night's hotpot.

Perhaps it was the big dish of hotpot or maybe the two pints of beer stimulating his brain. Whatever, it was a restless night. Several times when he dozed off the thought of kneeling between Rachel's thighs on the pond bank side jolted him awake. Before this he had convinced himself that, because there were too many emotional memories of Hannah clouding his brain, he wasn't ready to fall in love again. Now this was a new dream and it was more than just a kiss. He was kneeling between those long, shapely legs and from the look in her eyes she was not objecting.

In the morning, while driving out to meet his timber buyer, Nathan's mind was still churning over his thoughts and dreams from his restless night. When he ran the timber felling team at his old job the single young timber men working for him often made use of a suitable local lady. Even when his staff moved on to a different felling site in a new area they soon found new satisfaction. Nathan used to smile when he heard them recounting who they had been with and for how much but he had never felt a need for that. Before Hannah there had been other girls but even when he hadn't a girl he had only wanted a relationship or nothing. Now he realised that Hannah's death had somehow released a bottled-up basic urge stronger than he had ever known before. And he wasn't sure his belief in what was right or wrong could be trusted anymore, particularly if Rachel came to him in the woods as she had the day before.

The miles slipped by and he was soon pulling up by the felled timber. Switching off his little car, Nathan said out aloud, "But I don't want a torrid affair with a married woman although I suppose that if she was free maybe I could fall in love again."
He looked at the pile of felled trees and added under his breath, "Heck! She's now a wealthy Lady with a title while I, if I'm lucky, will be no more than a small country timber merchant."

The timber buyer had brought his son with him, "to learn the trade," he said, but as the son was already older than Nathan he wondered what was so special about their particular trade. He soon learned. The father and son ran a furniture making business in Manchester. They were looking for particular oaks with a particular type of grain.

Among the trees already pulled out there was only one that suited them. The two buyers were soon walking through the felled and growing trees with Nathan. There was the strong, pungent odour of a night-foraging fox lingering in the morning dew as the three men looked at each tree in turn. It wasn't long before Nathan realised he was in the company of an expert. Although the old man was really explaining to his son, Nathan heard about different types of burr for different finishes, of how to differentiate between oak trees with one or two dead branches well up the trunk, which could be hollow in the centre and worthless or alternatively might have a sound centre with a brown stain running right down the middle, giving a two-tone effect much valued by this furniture maker.

By the end of the morning Nathan had struck a deal with the furniture maker on about a dozen selected trees but at a price well above what Nathan had first anticipated. And he'd had a free lesson thrown in. The old timber buyer's parting instruction was, "Deliver them before the end of March. That way I know they've been felled before the sap is up."

Nathan asked, "How soon will you use them?"

He replied, "They'll stand for two years before we saw them up. Then we put spacers between each board and let them stand for at least another year."

When Nathan got back to the cottage Hetty had not returned from her shopping trip so he made a cheese sandwich for his dinner. After building the fire up he put the kettle on and walked outside to make a start on the pear tree.

Now that he had his own car he carried both a saw and an axe behind the seats. The saw was an unusual one in that it had an ordinary saw handle on one end and an upright one on the other. which meant it could be used single-handed or by two people as a traditional crosscut.

Hetty returned when he had trimmed off the smaller branches. Within minutes she had changed into working clothes and brought out two beakers of tea. They chatted over their drink for a while and when he started the next cut she took hold of the other end of the saw; with each pulling in rhythm the sharp saw slid effortlessly through the trunk.

Between cuts Hetty explained, "I was brought up on a small farm. Because of ill health my mother was never strong enough to manage any heavy farm work. With my Dad working in a factory each day most of his farming was done in the evenings, so I helped him after school and through the holidays. My Dad always hoped he might get the tenancy of a larger farm, which would allow him to farm full time but it wasn't to be."

"Why, what went wrong?"

"A simple flu epidemic first took my Mum and then my Dad. He nursed her before he was properly better and then went working out in the field. That heart attack ended his dreams of larger farms and put me in an orphanage."

The warm work soon had both Nathan and Hetty shedding jumpers and by then he had realised just how fit Hetty was. Her tall, slim figure disguised the power in her shoulders. When she saw Nathan looking she paused and said, "Yes, we didn't even have a horse. We rolled each haycock on to a stretcher and carried them in one at a time. Yes, I suppose that hard work developed a bit of muscle and since then I've always kept fit."

Later, Hetty went inside to put the promised hotpot in the oven, leaving Nathan to split up some of the bigger logs. It was the sort of relaxing physical work that he found enjoyable. The straight-grained pear logs easily split from the practised sweep of Nathan's axe. It took a little longer to barrow them into the shed.

In the same shed an old cast-iron boiler built over a brick fireplace provided the hot water for both bath night and washday. Before Nathan became her lodger Hetty just warmed two kettles on the kitchen fire and dragged the tin bath into there. Now Nathan carried enough water in from the pump to fill the outside boiler and heat up enough water for both of them. Although bathing in the outhouse meant stepping across the back yard from one door to the other neither of them thought it a hardship. Anyway they had to visit the outside 'bog' before retiring for the night.

Having filled the boiler and lit the fire Nathan came inside for his second hotpot tea in two nights.

They chatted pleasantly over the meal then, as Nathan helped with the washing up, Hetty said, "Do you know there's a rumour in the village about you and a certain lady?"

"She was Hannah's friend, we meet occasionally as we go about our business. We talk and that's all."

"She's a very attractive woman and you are a lonely but virile young man."

"You read too many romantic books, Hetty."

"I might do at that but I've lived long enough to know that a man has needs. A quick wrestle in the bushes could be fun but it could also ruin both your lives."

Nathan said smilingly, "You are beginning to sound like my mother. I think I'll go and check how hot the water is."

When the water was hot Nathan placed the bath in front of the boiler and bailed into it half of the very hot water, then cooled it down with a couple of buckets from the pump. Stepping into the house, Nathan announced mockingly, "Your bath is now ready, Mother."

Sitting in her dressing gown by the fire Hetty, jumping to her feet, cried, "I'll give you Mother!"

Nathan stripped off his own clothes upstairs and came down in just a dressing gown. When Hetty came in he emptied the bath, scraped the coals out to stop the heat cracking the emptied boiler and filled his own bath. After some of the primitive lodgings he'd had stayed in through the years this was luxury just to sit and soak by the warm fireplace. He could have a bath as often as he wanted, Hetty had told him: "That is as long as you provide the logs, fill the boiler and light the fire."

Back in the house Hetty made him a hot bedtime drink, filled the kettle for morning and went upstairs. He sat brooding over his drink for about fifteen minutes before going up himself to slip into bed by the light of the moon.

Again the disturbing memory of Rachel lying beneath him flashed into his mind. He was saying to himself, "Think of someone else," when the door opened.

Hetty, slipping out of her dressing gown, slid naked under the sheets beside him. "I might sound like your mother but I think that I can show you a few things your mother never mentioned."

When Nathan started to protest she leaned over him saying, "I don't expect anything in return or intend to hold it over you. I need a man as much as you need a woman so just enjoy it."

Running her fingers down his body in an experienced manner she whispered, "And it will be better than a furtive wrestle in the bushes with another man's wife."

Nathan did enjoy it. The years of frustration, of unfulfilled desire were unbottled that night. Some time in the early hours he woke to find her gone.

Next morning over a late breakfast Hetty acted as though nothing had happened. When she rose to side away he watched her with interest. Although her slim, almost boyish figure lacked Rachel's curves, her small breast were remarkably firm and he blushed when he remembered just how she had used that slim body.

Sensing his stare Hetty turned and smiled shyly. "About last night; it was good! I hope we can repeat it but I won't tie you down. When you meet someone your own age you'll have my blessing."

That Sunday morning they hadn't bothered to light a fire because Nathan was going to visit his parents and Hetty was going to one of her sons for the day. Although neither of them expected to eat in the cottage Hetty quickly laid the fire, telling Nathan, "If you are back first put a match to it, and then perhaps we can sit and read for a while."

Nathan wasn't back first. He had got a scolding at home for arriving late for dinner and as a result he stayed until dusk. On his journey home he mused how Rachel had dinner in the evening and lunch at midday, whereas farming people had dinner at midday, baggin before milking in the afternoon and then tea when their working day was over at about six-thirty. Lunch wasn't even in their language. No, he would never fit in with the gentry.

About halfway home Nathan's car climbed laboriously up a long incline and started to boil. Thankfully, his mother had put two of her doorstop-sized beef butties and a bottle of cold tea in the car. By the time that he'd eaten, drunk and walked a half mile back to fill the bottle at a roadside horse trough, over an hour had gone by. During that time he didn't see another car. One horseman cantered past without stopping and a family with a pony and trap asked if he was all right. A second pony trap, with just a couple in, stopped just as he was pouring his bottle of water into the radiator. They kindly waited until they were sure the car would go again before bidding him good night.

Despite a heavy driving coat, scarf and gloves Nathan was starved through when he got back to the cottage. Hetty, though, was sitting relaxed and reading in front of a blazing log fire. Smiling his appreciation, he pulled up a chair beside her.

As an active man, sitting quietly reading by the fireside was a new experience and he was surprised how much he was enjoying it. After a while Hetty made them both a drink, then later she went out and poured the rest of the hot water into a bowl in the back kitchen. When she went outside to the bog Hetty filled the kettle on the way in before washing at the sink. Nathan made his own visit outside but had to wash in cold water and when he came back in Hetty had already gone upstairs.

Clouds hid the moonlight as he slipped on a long nightshirt and jumped into bed. Hetty came silently into the room, slid under the sheets and kissed him gently, then whispered, "I think I unleashed something last night that will take more than one night to satisfy."

When his hands hungrily explored her slim body she tugged at his nightshirt saying, "A young bride might be too shy to want you naked but I'm not a young bride."

Chapter Eighteen

After the cow in the pond episode, returning to Alexander's bedroom that Friday night was a daunting experience for Rachel. There had never been any bedtime intimacy, no snuggling up together to share experiences of the day; the whole experience of going to bed together seemed to be slightly embarrassing for him. As a result, for some time Rachel had felt the same, but if she was to save their marriage she had to move back into his bed and to her surprise Alexander excelled himself being both considerate and loving.

***

Accepting that the young pheasant still needed a few weeks to fully develop Alexander decided to delay the full shoot until early December. Instead, he and a few guests would just have a small shooting day round the estate's boundaries and at the same time drive the wandering pheasants back towards the centre of the estate.

That night, after the shoot, Rachel was anticipating that Alexander would revert to his old bedtime ways, neither talking to her nor needing her. Perhaps by Christmas she might expect him to need her again but from his record through the last couple of years even that was in doubt, but as the evening wore on the guests' happy and relaxed mood seemed to affect both her and Alexander. Although the shoot had been only a modest affair it had been enjoyable day, which Cook crowned by serving the most delicious of dinners. Greebs was also in good form, making little quotations while he served each dish and with good wine and good conversation what could be better?

Perhaps Rachel had drunk more than usual because by bedtime she felt not just light-headed but even a little frivolous. Taking her clothes off in her dressing room she suddenly had a mental picture of Nathan's muscles rippling to the swing of his axe and couldn't help but wonder what it would be like to caress them. She pulled on her long nightdress and walked absentmindedly into the bedroom, sliding under the sheets next to Alexander. She was still in a trance, dreamily thinking of rippling muscles, when Alexander rolled over and began to caress her.

Several times over breakfast Rachel caught him looking at her, and each time he quickly looked away. Could it be that her response had triggered a hint of embarrassment on his inscrutable face?

There had been heavy rain in the night but Sunday morning brightened up enough for some of the guests to suggest a walk. When someone mentioned church they all agreed to combine the two and walk through the park to morning service. Although on the evening before the ladies' dresses had followed the latest mid-knee fashion, for church they chose something longer and more formal. The four ladies, the two Majors in dress uniform and the other two smartly dressed young men caused a ripple of interest when they walked up the aisle to the Landlord's personal pew at the front of the church.

Relieved that Mr Jonson had not been with them over the weekend, Rachel was able to relax with the guests and after lunch they spread around the house in smaller, more intimate groups. Walking through from the lounge past Alexander's office Rachel was surprised to hear voices from within. "Well, of course I made inquiries," she heard Alexander say. "But I haven't told Rachel."

"How certain are they?" That sounded like Major Fearnly. "They seem certain Thomas was the rightful heir." It was Alexander speaking now. "When that's finally proved, which should be early next year, then Rachel's claim seems relatively straightforward."

"Where will it leave you?"

"Well, I suppose become a Lord with substantial estates in the midlands." Major Fearnly's voice fell a little, leaving her to guess his next question by Alexander's answer: "There is no doubt that it can come down the female line but Rachel mustn't know any of this yet."

Walking on towards the kitchen Rachel was furious with the deceit of her husband. That he should go behind her back and use his Government connections to probe into her affairs was bad enough but then not to tell her the results, well! Was that what this weekend's gift and loving talk had been about, a title and a large estate? Leaning against the kitchen table, she said aloud, "He's so insufferably ambitious. Just wait until the guests have gone!" Fortunately Cook wasn't there to hear; anyway Rachel could see that afternoon tea was partially prepared.

The guests made their departure immediately after afternoon tea and as she stood outside to wave them off Rachel was surprised Alexander wasn't with her. She was even more surprised when Bestwick drove the Darracq round to pull up near the front door. Alexander came hurrying out with his case saying, "We will just catch it if you motor on Bestwick!" Then, giving Rachel a peck on her cheek, he said, "I can't get back next weekend."

As she watched Alexander climb into the car Rachel wondered if he was running away because he knew that she had overheard him in the study or whether it was the embarrassment of the previous night. "Anyway," she thought, "If it was last night I still didn't get his damn nightshirt off."

On the Monday morning she was still feeling guilty about her thoughts during that mad half hour in bed and, afraid of the embarrassment if she met Nathan, determinedly walked in the opposite direction from the timber yard. When her walk took her towards Claybank Farm she decided to call and have a chat with the Browns. There was the usual invitation in for a cup of tea and, as ever, William Brown appeared as if by magic when the kettle came to the boil. Reminding her that it was the Chapel anniversary on Sunday William Brown asked, "Are you coming this year?"

Despite being a member of the Church of England, Rachel tried to attend the occasional special service in the chapel. Having done that as a girl with Hannah she continued to attend them as the Landlord's wife. "Well yes, I think I am free next Sunday."
"Good, then you'll have a bite of supper with us afterwards?" William asked invitingly.

Rachel went on her way reflecting how the Methodists like to eat. They invited their local preachers round for tea between afternoon and evening services. Then after evening service another bounteous spread would be laid out. Attending their chapel as a schoolgirl she had been amazed at the distances visitors travelled to these special services. Perhaps it was just for the food, but whatever it was she must remember not to have too much tea next Sunday afternoon.

After lunch she rang the estate agent to arrange a meeting with both him and the farm manager to discuss the farm plan.

A telephone call to the solicitor got her no further. Even when Rachel said she had heard a strong rumour to the effect that Thomas's claim was more or less accepted Benjie was still adamant he hadn't received anything official. He had, though, made progress on the rest of her father's estate. There was considerable interest to be added to the figure he had first quoted, he told her, adding, "That money should be in your account before Christmas."

Rachel insisted the farm-planning meeting was held in the Hall.

Not that there wasn't plenty of room in the farm office, there was, but there were also a lot of memories. In the Hall she was in charge and it would do no harm to remind both the agent and the farm manager of that fact.

Robert laid a detailed plan before them listing his analyses of the farm at present, offering his proposed changes both on the farm and to the staff, including a careful detail of relevant costs. It was impressive and Rachel said so before asking, "Why go out of cheese making?"

"Your cheese is only second rate. Mary and Harry Wilson are too old to learn new techniques and young Jack isn't interested in cheese."

"Many farmers are having trouble selling their milk. Can you be sure that you can sell ours?"

"Yes, Ma'am! I have a relative who owns a dairy on this side of Manchester. Not only will he take our milk, he also wants me to try and organise a motor lorry to get more of his milk in direct. He claims the train service isn't reliable enough."

"What about Harry and Mary?"

Robert looked at the agent before replying. "I understood you're doing up some retirement cottages. When they're finished I hoped they could retire there and we could move Jack into the cowman's cottage."

"Wait a minute!" Charles said. "That work was suspended. The estate hasn't got an unlimited budget."

Rachel gave him a firm look before saying, "I thought I had already told you to get on with that work."

And so as the discussion went on Rachel made it clear to both men that she made the final decisions. To her query about old Jimmy, Robert said, "I like old Jimmy but you're paying me to manage the farm, therefore there's no point in paying him to sit on a hedge cop and make my decisions for me."

Robert then went through the various crops, explaining how he proposed to manage them, finishing with, "I will need Jimmy's extended family to do a lot of the harvest work so if you agree I may go over there and pay him a visit."

When he came to the two waggoners Robert was adamant that they both had to go. "Joe Candy is well beyond retirement age and he is a most obstinate worker. His son takes after him. They spend far too much time messing about in the stables when they should be doing other things."

Rachel had to agree and had known that for some time. Mr Brown's men could be working a horse one day and digging a drain the next whereas Joe and his son could always find an excuse to attend to something in the stable.

"Another retirement cottage needed," Rachel said with a smile.

Robert then produced his projected cash flow for the farm. Rachel hadn't expected that. Although Thomas had always worked to a cash flow for the estate he used to say that a cash flow for a farm was a bit like a New Year resolution. It sounded good on the day but would soon be lost in the reality of nature.

Charles Brown, having said very little up to then, started to outline the implications of Robert's proposals on the building requirement. He even listed the effect of Robert's plan on his own cash flow for the rest of the estate, which he and Rachel had already gone through.

It all took up most of the afternoon, through which they consumed a pot of tea and some of Cook's delicious cakes.

After Robert left to walk back to the farm Charles asked, "Well, Ma'am, what do you think of your young farm manager now?"

"He is very impressive," Rachel said, giving him a straight look. "But remember it's also your farm plan.and you both have to make it work."

The estate agent bowed his way out before he got into deeper water, leaving Rachel more than pleased with her afternoon and feeling particularly satisfied that the years in her father's office had given her the experience to grasp the implications of each decision.

***

More work was coming into the yard than Nathan had expected. Making new shafts or doing large repairs on farm carts had never interested the village undertaker. The fact that now more farmers were bringing work to the estate yard was keeping Clem busy, helping Bill. Nathan was aware though that he was he was getting behind his schedule for falling the estate trees. He was still confident that they would fall enough for the estate and his own use but he would like to sell more on to other merchants. His immediate problem was that they were running out of seasoned timber this year.

He mentioned this when Hamish called in at the yard one morning. Hamish, nursing a hot cup of tea between his cold hands, said, "Arrr well, maybe I can help yer' out there if yer'll take a walk with me on Sunday morning."

"Taking a walk with you usually means there's work at the end of it. Is there some this time?"

"Och, aye. A bit of work and a lot of pleasure," Hamish replied as he headed for the door. "An yer'll take a bite with us after if yer' likes?"

**

After a couple of wet days Sunday morning was fine and dry when Nathan parked his car in Hamish's yard. The fierce barking of the dogs was quelled by an equally fierce growl from Hamish, who appeared from behind a building clad ready for the walk.

Letting a spaniel out of its pen, Hamish, with the dog at heel, led Nathan out across an area of the estate that he had yet to explore. When they got to the small lane marking the estate boundary Hamish walked across it, climbed a gate and went into the next farmer's field, explaining as he did so that he was allowed on here to drive his wandering pheasants back towards the estate woods. Then rounding a small copse Hamish pointed to some fallen trees, saying, "Yer'll be glad yer' came now!" Gesticulating round the field he added, "He wants to plough it and they're in his way."

With that Hamish walked off with his dog obviously to hunt more wandering pheasants back towards home while Nathan looked at the trees with interest. There were two windblown massive oaks with uprooted butts standing about eight feet above the ground. Two more oaks had been chopped down and the broken trunk of an elm lay close by. It wasn't hard for Nathan to work out the sequence of events. A powerful wind had swept through breaking the tall elm off above ground and uprooting two of the oaks. The falling trees had taken several larger branches out of the remaining two oaks, which had since been felled. Had they been left standing decay would have set in. A whirl of pheasants' wings made him look up and soon afterwards Hamish came back.

Nathan asked, "They've been lying here for two or three years, so what happened?"

"Arrr well, he'd agreed a sale, then th'buyer wer' taken ill. He'll sell em right to someone who'll move em straight away."

"Will he be in today?"

"No, he'll be at church."

The two men walked on along the estate boundary towards Hetty's cottage, letting the spaniel hunt the rough hedge copse on the way. Several pheasants were frightened back towards the middle of the estate. Seeing Nathan watching his dog work Hamish said, "Have yer' not thought of having a dog yer'self?"

"I have but it's not that easy when you're in lodging."

"Arrr, man, Hetty would'na mind. I know where there's a good spaniel bitch needing a good home. It belongs to a widow and she'll only let it go to a man who'll work it."

When Hamish climbed over a fence into a block of woodland Nathan said, "I'll give it some thought. Anyway, why are we going in here?"

"Arrr, now I did say there wer' some work," Hamish said grinning sheepishly and walking between the trees. He stopped to point at a badger earth: "Hounds are coming on Saturday so can yer' stop th'earths in this wood for me? They're right by your back door."

In his schooldays Nathan had helped him do just that in different woods; it was exciting and an excuse to be out in the woods before daybreak. He wasn't offended at being asked but protested anyway, "So I have to pay twice for those trees do I?"

Hamish just laughed and threw a few dead boughs near each entrance. Nathan did not need to be told that foxes rarely dig an earth themselves, usually relying on a disused wing of a badger sett for their needs. Blocking the entrances in the early hours of the morning after most of the badgers had returned to their beds would help to encourage the fox to spend his day above ground. Then hopefully when the hounds gave chase he would flee towards another wood, giving the hounds both a chase and a chance to make a kill. Meantime the powerful badger would easily push through the one or two dead boughs in the sett's entrance to either leave or enter.

Hamish pointed out two more fox earth/badger setts in the same wood before he led Nathan back to his house where large dish of rabbit pie was a welcomed reward after such a long walk.

Later in the day Nathan returned to a cold, empty cottage to change ready for the Chapel anniversary's evening service and, expecting that Hetty would be returning soon, lit a fire and put the kettle on the hob to warm, thinking as he did so how he felt at home in this little cottage. Perhaps he was becoming too domesticated.

He wasn't looking forward to having supper at Claybank farm. It was not that he didn't like the Browns; it was the other memories that disturbed him. Although he had turned down several previous invitations, this time he thought that perhaps going when there would be other guests present might make the evening passable. First, though, he had to put on his dark suit and attend the service at 6.30.

Sitting on the back row Nathan was surprised to see Rachel walk in followed by her chauffeur, Bestwick, and his wife. When they were seated near the front he remembered Hannah telling him that Rachel came to the occasional special service here.

The service was led by a jovial, ruddy-faced countryman whom Nathan knew to be a provender merchant. The highlight for Nathan was the preacher's illustration of faith: "You farmers know too well that when your cows break through the fence you can do three kinds of repair. If you have no time to spare you just snatch up an old iron bedstead and push it into the gap. The trouble with that is - you usually then forget about it. If you have a bit more time you maybe string a piece of wire or a rail across the gap and forget about that too. Or you make time to do the job properly, stripping out the old fence and replacing it with a new one. When things go wrong in your life do you turn to God for a quick solution and then forget about him? Or do you perhaps make a little more effort to respond to him but inevitably after a few weeks let God drift out of your life again? What you really need to do is to clear out the sin and selfishness of your present life before replacing it with a new lasting relationship with God."

Although Nathan wasn't a regular churchgoer he was sure he had a faith that would last. Then again, all that fence rebuilding would need fencing posts and he should be providing them. Perhaps it wasn't the time to be making business decisions but it jolted him into realising he often refused to buy second-rate oak trees which, although not good enough for the timber trade, could be used for fencing posts.

The service over, Nathan was among the first out through the door and he kept well back away from it. Others joined him for a chat but he stayed back until Bestwick brought up the car and drove Rachel away.

***

The Methodist service was always a refreshing change for Rachel. The singing was enthusiastic, the preachers were usually unconventional characters and the congregation didn't seem as reserved as in the Church of England. Because Bestwick also had friends at the chapel, after the service he chauffeured Rachel to

Claybank intending that he and his wife would visit their friends and then come back for her later in the evening. William Brown was in the farmyard to greet them, saying, "There is no need for that, I'll see that Rachel gets home."

When Rachel protested he waved Bestwick away. "You go off and enjoy yourselves, I'll look after her."

Then as they turned towards the house he added, "Anyway Nathan's on his own, he can give you a lift back."

Rachel realised William Brown must not have heard any rumours about them. Or more likely if someone had tried to tell him William would have refused to listen to tittle-tattle about his friends. She spun round to stop Bestwick but he was driving out of the gate and as he drove away Nathan drove in.

Turning into the farmyard, Nathan was surprised to see Rachel walking towards the farmhouse. He had no idea she would be here for supper and resolved to stay clear of her if he could. He had been watching her in the chapel for the last hour and a half, her poise when she stood up for each hymn, the graceful way she greeted people and the elegance of her every move all revealing her to be in a class above his. Perhaps it was the fact that Hetty had slid under the sheets again last night which, having reduced his mad, urgent needs, now let him think more rationally. Or perhaps the quiet meditative hour in the chapel had helped him to sort out his deeper feelings.

Sitting in the Claybank lounge with memories of Hannah all around him, he realised she had never been in the same league as Rachel. Much as he had loved Hannah, Rachel's vibrant presence made his memory of her seem bland by comparison. But Rachel was out of reach and not just because she was married. He was a man destined to work out his ambitions with an axe in his hand; not for him the grand house or the large country estate.

There were a good number of people in different rooms of the large farmhouse and the food was served to them where they sat. Nathan deliberately moved to another room so he wouldn't be near Rachel through the rest of the evening. There he got into conversation with Bill, and then when Bill went out to look round the cows before going home, Nathan went with him. They forgot the time as they continued their conversation in the warm shippen.

When they did return to the house they discovered that most of the guests had gone. William met them saying, "Nathan I've told Rachel you'll give her a lift home. Is that all right?"

Before he could reply, William was going back into the house for Rachel. Nathan said no more, he just held the car door open for her and put a thick rug across her knees. He said goodnight to the Browns and drove away.

"This was not my idea," Rachel declared and then, turning towards him, asked, "What do we do now?"

Chapter Nineteen

Benjie, her solicitor, rang just as Rachel was about to take Digger for his morning walk. Agreeing to an appointment to visit his office in Knutsford she then walked round to the rear of the Hall to instruct Bestwick as to when his services would be needed. She then left him to finish the Talbot's Monday morning polish and strode out along the back drive with Digger.

When she arrived at the solicitor's office later that morning Rachel was a little annoyed when Benjie's reason for calling her in was to confirm that the inquiries into her father's claim to the title would seem to prove that everything was in order. She had to smile, however, at how long he took to explain it. Obviously, even if she weren't responding to his charms, she would at least provide him an additional fee on a quiet day. And fees can be easily fattened with a little extra talk time. "No, I don't think I have time to have lunch with you today, Benjie." Adding a firm crispness to her voice Rachel left a slightly crestfallen Benjie to buy his own lunch, for she had no doubt the other lunches had been added to her bill.

Later, at her favourite dress shop, Rachel explained, "I'm going to the tea shop for a light lunch but I would like to come back to choose some clothes afterwards. What time do you open again?" That brought a flurry of activity from within and the owner out to greet her. "Yes, my Lady. I can open early after lunch so you don't have to wait, my Lady."

"We've been friends a long time," said Rachel, "and throughout that time I've always been Rachel to you. Even if the title is confirmed I would still like you to call me Rachel."

"Yes, My La ... I'm sorry, I mean Rachel."

Walking into the tearoom caused another flurry of activity as a clean cloth was quickly spread over the choice corner table. "What would you like, my Lady?"

I'd like people to just treat me as they have always done, Rachel thought, but it seems as though I may have to get used to these fawning gestures. When her order for a hot meal had been taken and with a pot of tea quickly placed beside her Rachel had time to think. Not that she wanted to. She had deliberately kept on the move all morning trying not to think of the previous night at Claybank. When she got into Nathan's car she remembered feeling flustered like a schoolgirl on her first date and shyly asking Nathan, "What do we do now?"

When Nathan, strong and resolute, had said, "I'm just driving you home," Rachel remembered saying, "But don't we need to talk?" Nathan had driven on for a few moments in silence before replying, "What do we talk about, that you're a married woman or that your marriage is going through a rough patch? If we stop in a gateway, either a farm worker on the way home from the pub or some other local who knows my car will see us. What would that do for your reputation? No, I'll just drive you home."

Thinking back, Rachel remembered that there was no bitterness in Nathan's words, just an understanding kindness and she trembled at the thought that had he pulled off the road she may not have objected. It was like Nathan to think of her reputation, whereas it would be him who lost out the most. There are no secrets in a country village. Any whiff of scandal would go round like wildfire and would be sure to get back to Alexander. And when it did, well, Nathan would soon be turned out of his timber yard. His dreams of a timber business would go out with him. No, she couldn't let that happen to him.

The waitress broke Rachel's train of thought by serving out her lunch. "Would you like some sauce, my Lady? Do you want more gravy, my Lady?" Rachel hid her irritation with a smile, thinking how Alexander would enjoy this sort of fuss. Yes, he would love being called My Lord. Alexander would really enjoy the pomp and ceremony whereas Nathan? Nathan – stripped to the waist, muscles rippling to the swing of his axe – could Nathan's kind gentleness cope with this artificial pomp? Stop! Stop these thoughts!

Better to think of the dresses she might buy a little later. Tweeds for next weekend at Major Fearnly's. Her present two outdoor suits, hanging to lower calf, were a bit long for today's fashion but they would still do for everyday wear round the estate. Eventually she decided to look for two nice tweedy suits and a new evening dress that gave a suitable look of mourning without being too dull, and mused on about the different dresses she had seen on display before lunch. It seemed that even everyday dress fashion was shorter but she decided it was much more sensible to wear her tweeds around calf length.

But I might be more daring with a dress, she decided, heading back towards the dress shop. The two new tweed suits, one in russet tweed and the other in more traditional green/brown mixture, were soon chosen. With the skirts hanging only to upper calf Rachel worried if they would keep her warm out on the shooting field. The dress shop agreed to stitch a black armband on each jacket while Rachel turned her attention to more sophisticated clothes. It was the roaring twenties, when fashions were changing almost overnight. Two mourning dresses in the latest fashion made a more difficult choice. Mainly subtle mixtures of black and grey with a dash of white in one and hanging just below the knee, both were almost straight with a hint of a low waist. A loose belt hooked around hips made one look really elegant, whereas the other's neckline plunged a little lower than would have been considered etiquette just a year or two earlier. Looking at herself in the mirrors Rachel let the shop owner persuade her that even in mourning she could go with the fashion and show a glimpse of knee as she walked. Her debate between the two dresses was settled by buying both. Well, why not? Rachel thought, I have just inherited a good sum of money and that irritating, fawning Benjie tells me that I could inherit considerably more.

From an extensive selection of fashionable long black stockings Rachel bought silk ones to go with the evening dress and then, on a sudden impulse, some chunkier black ones to wear with her outdoor clothes. Receiving a frown from behind the counter at the thought of them with a russet suit, Rachel smiled, "At least they match the armband."

***

Tuesday afternoon was not an enjoyable event for Rachel. Robert had quite rightly asked her to sit in with him on the staff interviews. When interviewing Harry Wilson she was surprised, perhaps because her father never recorded the age of his workers, to discover that he was older than she had thought. Acknowledging how tired he now got, particularly when he had to attend to a calving cow in the night, the old cowman welcomed the suggested retirement into a smaller cottage in the village.

When they interviewed Harry's son immediately afterwards, Jack was keen to take on the cowman's job, particularly now that the cheese enterprise would stop. Responding to Robert's proposals for more winter milk production, Jack revealed a pleasing depth of knowledge about the different feeding methods needed to produce milk in the winter months. Before he left, Rachel brought him back down to earth by warning him that they would not tolerate any misbehaviour with the dairymaids.

The two waggoners, Joe Candy and his son, were a different proposition. Robert had already explained to Rachel how they were both uncooperative and resentful of him. When the Head Waggoner came in Rachel noticed with a smile that he had left off the habitual sack from his waist. With his hair and moustache slicked down Joe thrust his shiny bald head forward belligerently and said, "My mind is set."

"What do you mean, your mind is set?" Rachel asked.

"I'm no' moving!"

"But if you're retiring we may need your large cottage for a new waggoner. There will be a smaller two bedroomed cottage ready by spring; it will be much nicer for your wife there."

"My lad'll be th'new Head Waggoner an until he gets a wife he'll still live with us so we'll stay put!"

Robert gently said, "We don't know if your son will be the Head Waggoner. We are going to interview him next. We think it best if you and your wife retire to the other cottage. He can still live with you there."

"The job be his by right. He's worked nowhere else, man. How can a young upstart like you come here telling us where we've got to live or work?"

Much as they tried he wouldn't be placated. In the end he did agree to discuss the possibility of moving homes with his Missus.

His son bristled in more or less demanding his rights. And his rights were that they owed him the Head Waggoner's position. Rachel could see he would never be suited and decided it better if she told him rather than Robert but there was no way he would listen to a reasoned argument. Nor was he prepared to work on the farm if not appointed Head Waggoner. In the end he rather rudely told them where to stick their job and walked out of the office and off the farm.

This was the sort of tension that in the past had been sorted out by her father. Knowing it was also the sort of upset that went with a change of personality on any large country estate, Rachel was determined Robert must be allowed to reorganise the farm to make it more efficient.

The rest of the afternoon went without further incident. Two of the dairymaids had planned to leave at the end of the year when all but a few cows would be 'dried off' ready to calve the following spring. There was often an annual change in the young unmarried dairy staff at that time of year. Normally, replacement dairy workers were taken on before the cows started to calve in March; though next year Robert would not be making cheese so he intended to have fewer dairy staff.

The two regular general farm workers were interviewed together at the end. Through the spring and summer months they had an all-embracing role helping whenever needed with both sowing and harvest. In between those seasonal demands, fencing repairs and hedge cutting took up much of their time. The older one, who lived in an estate cottage in the village, could turn his hand to most highly skilled jobs from hedge laying to draining. The younger one, unmarried and living with his parents in their tied cottage on one of the tenanted farms, would also work a horse when a third waggoner was needed. When Robert explained that their role would not change they both smiled in relief.

***

Nathan too had time for reflection on that Monday morning. Hetty, readily agreeing to him having a dog, even suggested it could sleep in the kitchen. He didn't bother about trees when he got to the yard but just set his men to work and drove off to find the owner of the spaniel.

On the journey he dwelt on the happenings of the night before when he had driven Rachel home. Rachel had looked the Lady she was; even without a title she had a presence that would stop any man in his tracks. Although the memory of Hannah was diminishing, it was still strong enough to stand between him and a long-term commitment. Was it enough to prevent him from starting anything with Rachel? No, it wasn't memories but Hetty who had saved him last night. It was she who'd had the wisdom to release his build up of steam, and releasing his frustration had allowed him to think more rationally. Without her Nathan felt certain he would have pulled into a gateway regardless of the consequences. Just as he knew that this morning he would have regretted it. No, a woman of Rachel's quality deserved more than a quick scuffle in the dark, she deserved to be where she was in life, but he did wish she could be happy.

With his mind on other things he did a bit of wandering around the southern outskirts of Knutsford before he snapped out of it. Some strange turreted houses along one road took his attention. Not knowing much about architecture he presumed they were built on the same unusual Italian design he had seen in parts of the town. Realising his wanderings among these upmarket houses had taken him out of Knutsford and into Toft, he turned back to look for a more modest home.

At last he knocked on the right door, which was answered by a charming elderly lady who invited him in and put the kettle on. A quiet, pale, almost sandy coloured Spaniel bitch with darker liver red patches watched him for some time while Mrs Jackson, her mistress, told the story.

"My husband bought her as a pup when he retired and she was his constant companion for over three years. At his side along the river banks through the fishing season, then when autumn came she went with him beating or picking up on one or two local shoots. She even went on his occasional visit to the pub." Mrs Jackson finished by saying, "When my husband died about four months ago, I decided I would only let her go to someone who could give her the same sort of life. My husband used to say she was the most intelligent dog he had ever owned. Bess could even tell what he was thinking."

While she was speaking, Bess walked quietly out to sniff round Nathan's legs. When he reached down to stroke her long fluffy ears she sat down and looked into his eyes, holding his stare. Nathan remembered a saying of his father's: 'You can teach a dog owt if it'll look at you but you can teach a dog nowt if it won't'. Bess's brown eyes held Nathan's for so long he was won over. When he explained his work and his hobbies, her mistress was also won over.

All that remained was to partake of the traditional cup of tea and piece of cake. In fact he had a second piece of cake, sharing most of it with Bess.

When he got up to leave, Bess trotted alongside him and jumped into the car. Although he had been driving with the hood up for a few days, that morning he had decided to enjoy the fresh air more and had put it down again, which meant that he had to tie Bess to make sure she couldn't jump out and also make her sit on the floor by the front seat. It wasn't long before Bess was sitting on the seat by him just as though it was an everyday event.

Driving out to a block of woodland he had been asked to give an opinion on, Nathan parked his car, unfastened Bess and together they went to explore the wood. He couldn't believe how responsive she was to each command. When he told her to seek she scurried, tail wagging, nose to the ground, into the briars. When he said "Sit", she sat with her eyes fixed to his face. "Heel" brought her to his side where she stayed like glue until he released her.

The trees were a disappointment in that they needed at least another twenty years before becoming mature enough to fall. They would be a bigger disappointment to their owner, who was desperately short of cash, but Bess made up for any disappointment by her friendly, responsive nature.

Nathan took time to wander through the trees just to give Bess the chance to have fun, and her fun was to bolt rabbits out of the undergrowth. After about an hour he returned to get his butty bag from the car and then sat on a tree stump to share them with the dog.

Calling on the farmer to discuss the felled trees, he explained his connection with Hamish and was soon walking across the fields from the farmyard. As he strode out alongside the hurrying farmer Nathan tried to learn just how desperate he was to get them moved quickly. When it became obvious that he wanted them moved quickly Nathan pitched his offer quite low. There was the usual half hour haggle before that price was accepted but on condition that they were off the land by Christmas.

After shopping for some clothes in Knutsford on the way back, he called in at a small café for his tea.

When he returned to the cottage at about 6.30 Hetty sat in front of a glowing log fire with the kettle singing on the hob. Bess took to Hetty and she to Bess. Within a few minutes the three of them were sharing the warmth of the fire. Nathan thought, 'If only Hannah could be here to share this; this is what I want, a cosy cottage, my dog on the hearth and a loving woman to share it all with.'

The next morning he hadn't been at the yard long before Hamish walked in. "Arrr, yer' got yer' dog then, did yer?"

"What do you think of her?"

"Well if her's as good as I heard then her'll do."

"She seems remarkably obedient."

"Then yer'll be right for picking up with her a week on Saturday?"

Nathan protested, "Hey, hold on, I've only had her a day."

"Arrr man, yer can't go wrong with a dog like that. Take her for a walk in yer wood tomorrow morning. A couple of farmers are having fox trouble over there so th'Hunt's going to draw it when they hunt nearby. Maybe yer'll block those holes for me, eh?"

"It seems like I get a dog for nothing and then have to pay for her through the rest of my life," Nathan said, but Hamish was already on the move and the only response he got was a throaty chuckle from the keeper's retreating back.

Making up for his relaxing time with Bess on the previous day, Nathan drove out with Clem to work on the fallen timber he had just bought. The rhythmical swing of his seven-pound axe created a feeling of contentment as he trimmed up the large trunks.

The next morning Nathan did as Hamish had asked and went out early to stop the earths. Fortunately it wasn't raining and there was even a hint of moonlight to help and Bess loved it, the darkness, the excitement of different early morning smells and above all the fun of being out in the woods with her new master. Aware of the early-wakening birds stirring in the breaking light, he too felt the thrill of the new morning.

After working on the trees for three days with Clem, Nathan went into the yard on the Friday morning knowing he could now arrange to have them hauled back to his yard.

He decided to take a day away from the yard and drove into Knutsford to ask his bank manager about an overdraft. If he were to expand his business he would need to buy in extra seasoned timber, some of it as ready-sawn boards that were urgently needed for the farm wagon repairs. With an overdraft he could risk buying a larger load for maximum discount. Also, he believed if he bought from one of the yards he supplied with timber then his hauliers could bring them back to Hesston at a reduced rate. Maybe he could persuade them to transport his local trees back to the yard while they were in Hesston.

Nathan was still thinking through those arrangements when Rachel walked into his office. "I think your phone must be out of order," she announced. "I've reported it for you." Passing him a piece of paper, she added, "This man wants you to make and erect an oak gate with two new posts. He's been trying to get through to you all day. When he couldn't he rang me."

He couldn't help noticing how attractive she looked in what seemed a new tweed suit. She in return could see his muscular shoulders set off in the tweed jacket he had bought that Monday. Their silent mutual admiration was only broken when Rachel said, "Bestwick's driving me down to Stafford, where we're meeting Alexander's train before motoring to Major Fearnly's for the weekend." Movement from Bess under the desk caught her attention. When she crouched down to stroke those long ears, Bess in return looked into Rachel's eyes with her big brown ones and won another heart.

Nathan explained how he came to own Bess, agreed to go and see the man about the gates and wished Rachel a nice weekend. As he was saying it, the fact that he could sense the response in Rachel to his unguarded look of admiration sent a tingle down his spine.

Chapter Twenty

Alexander's train was only a half hour late arriving in Stafford, which gave Rachel time to wonder if there was a new relationship between them or whether it was just her husband's ambitious scheming. Watching his tall figure stride towards her across the station car park with Bestwick, she had to admit that he was indeed a handsome man. If only he would show a little more of his feelings, or at least if they could but recapture the closeness of earlier years. But when Alexander slid onto the back seat and gave her a cool, perfunctory peck on the cheek she knew that it was a vain hope.

Surprisingly, they did converse on the journey to Major Fearnly's. Although at times Bestwick touched twenty miles per hour they still had time to watch and discuss the countryside and Alexander even asked about the estate. As she explained the many changes Robert was introducing she was both surprised and pleased at his interest.

He also asked about their shoot to be held the next weekend but when Rachel then asked him about the guests he replied, "Oh, just the usual."

"Does that include Mr Jonson?"

"Yes, I suppose it does. I think he will want to stay over the weekend again."

"I don't think I like him much," Rachel said.

"I'm sorry but he is coming," Alexander said firmly while looking out of the window. From then on his mood changed and their conversation dried up.

On arrival at the large country house, which was really the home of Major Fearnly's parents, the afternoon started in the usual way. Rachel and Alexander made a brief visit up to the bedroom to freshen up before coming back down stairs again for afternoon tea. The senior Fearnlys had again left the house and servants for the use of the Major and Lucy and the staff were, as usual, very helpful to the guests.

The Fearnlys had planned a weekend with more guests than usual, among them a young Captain and his wife whom Rachel couldn't remember having met before. The big surprise, though, was when the Colonel marched into the lounge for tea while she was chatting to Lucy. Noticing that he no longer limped, Rachel said, "Ah, the wrestling Colonel who specialises in ambush." Fortunately, the Colonel didn't hear.

Lucy whispered, "Shush! I hope you don't mind but the Major wanted him to come and I couldn't very well explain why he shouldn't, could I?"

***

Later, when Rachel returned to her bedroom to dress for dinner, she slipped into one of her new dresses. Although the neckline seemed a little lower than she remembered it looked better than when she had bought it and was well aware of the admiring glances it received when she walked downstairs for dinner. The Colonel, who seemed to be waiting for her, held out his arm to escort her into the dining room. Rachel was a bit annoyed with Lucy for seating him on her right but Lucy whispered, "I know you can handle him."

As the meal progressed Rachel realised the Colonel didn't remember her. Anyway, it seemed that once he had caught a glimpse of her cleavage it was all that really interested him. It was so obvious when each time he spoke to her his eyes seldom met hers; mostly they were fixed on the tantalising v in the front of her dress. Not that she was too offended. If I dress to look attractive then I have to expect some response, Rachel told herself.

It wasn't only the Colonel Rachel caught staring; two or three times she noticed Alexander's eyes glued on her from across the table. There seemed to be a hint of excitement about him she found difficult to understand. It was most noticeable when different guests called her My Lady; it was as though there was a newfound importance about her that now somehow stimulated him. Eventually she spoke out loudly for every one to hear. "Please listen. I have not – I repeat, I have not – inherited a title. What may happen in the future, who knows? But it hasn't happened yet and even if it's confirmed I am still Rachel."

Edward Craneby-Brown's upper-class banker's voice cut in, "Yes, all right Rachel! But we know it's a sure thing, don't we?"

"As a banker you should know that a loan is only a sure thing when the last instalment has been repaid. This is nowhere near to that stage, is it?"

The others nodded their agreement.

They had finished the fish course and were well into the main course before the Colonel made a real move. By then he had drunk at least four glasses of wine and the butler was pouring out another. Turning well round, his eyes for once met hers as he raised his glass, "To a pleasant evening together," and at the same time his left hand slid suggestively along her thigh.

Rachel said mischievously, "How is your foot Colonel? The last time we were together you ..."

When recognition hit him he spluttered red wine across the attractive tablecloth.

"He's got a bone. It's got lodged somewhere, hasn't it Colonel?" Rachel explained to the other guests whilst giving the Colonel a hefty slap between his shoulder blades.

The Colonel, red face buried in his napkin, fled the room spluttering loudly. Lucy came round to tidy up as the conversation took off and whispered to Rachel, "There, I told you that you could handle him. Whatever did you do?"

"I just asked him how his foot was."

It was Lucy's turn to flee spluttering form the dining room. Rachel followed on the pretext of looking for a clean napkin and the two girls enjoyed a good giggle in the kitchen.

The Colonel returned in time for the sweet course but studiously ignored her cleavage to talk to the lady on his right.

When the gentlemen joined the ladies in the lounge after their port and brandy, the rather thin young Captain's wife seemed to be paying undue attention to Alexander. From what she could read in Alexander's near inscrutable expression, Rachel discerned nothing more than cynical amusement on his face. Deciding to rescue him, she walked across to sit on the arm of his chair, saying, "We haven't seen much of each other lately."

The girl, giving her a hard look, said as she jumped to her feet, "I need another drink."

The Colonel, bottle in hand, was there in a flash. "Come and sit here my dear." Indicating a low chair he pulled another round to face her.

Again Alexander's gaze fixed on Rachel's cleavage. "Do you like my new dress?" she asked, smiling at the hint of excitement in his eyes.

"You look irresistible, my Lady."

"Oh don't you start," Rachel said, jumping laughingly to her feet, but aware that somehow she aroused Alexander in a way she had not seen before.

***

As the evening wore on she noticed the Colonel keeping the thin girl's glass topped up, and there was no convenient flowerpot close by her. Rachel moved round the different guests, chatting to each in turn. When she eventually rose to retire, the young Captain was deep in conversation with the two Majors but the Colonel and the Captain's wife had vanished.

Passing the billiard room, Rachel heard voices from within and without thinking looked in through the open door. With his back towards the door the Colonel was lifting the thin girl up onto the edge of the billiard table and, from the sound of her tipsy giggles, Rachel didn't think it likely the Colonel would get his foot stamped on. She just shook her head and went up to bed.

Already curled up in bed and half asleep when Alexander came into the room, Rachel was sleepily aware of him moving around the bedroom. Sliding into bed behind her, Alexander suddenly wrapped his arm round her waist to caress her. Never having been a demanding lover, he usually he took 'no' like a tired old dog pretending to want to go for a walk but who was in reality happier to stay curled up by the fire. Waiting drowsily for Alexander to mutter in acquiescence and roll away she was surprised when he came to her with a wildness she had never felt in him before.

She lay awake for a while, wondering if somehow the thought of her inheriting a title was having a rejuvenating effect on him. From at first being sullen and angry about it he had now become almost boyishly excited. Perhaps the thought of becoming a Lord pleases him so much he's now falling in love with my inheritance," Rachel muttered into the pillow. "He's had eight years in which to show his love and now he responds to a stupid title."
That conclusion hurt her deeply.

***

Breakfast was in progress when Rachel walked into the dining room on the following morning. Seeing the Colonel tucking into a hearty dish of porridge, she couldn't resist leaning over his shoulder to ask, "Did you enjoy your billiard game last night, Colonel?"
He spluttered violently but the porridge must have been a little stickier than last night's wine because he managed to get his napkin

to his face without splattering the table.

Hovering nearby, supervising the guests' breakfast, Lucy immediately cottoned on. "Oh, did you have a game of billiards then? How did it go? Did you win, Colonel?"

The Colonel, red faced and still spluttering, reached for the clean napkin from the empty place setting next to his. Rachel avoided meeting Lucy's eyes in case they both burst into a fit of girlish laughter.

**

Nathan's trip into Knutsford was of mixed success. The bank manager, refusing to allow him an overdraft, said, "Look, you've only received a few small cheques yet; the time to think about expanding will be when your business is really turning over some money. You're still in credit so work within it for a while then maybe we can talk again."

Nathan's visit to the timber merchant nearer to Manchester was much more satisfactory. Not only did he get an order for more trees but the timber merchant also agreed to exchange them for the ready-sawn seasoned timber he urgently needed.

Calling in at his hauliers on his return journey he reached another satisfactory agreement. When they hauled in Nathan's next load of timber they would take the seasoned wood back to Hesston and then, while there, haul Nathan's few local trees back to his Hesston yard. It was all amicably concluded sitting round a laden kitchen table before he set off for Hetty's cottage on a dark, murky night.

Cutting across country through Lacksfield village towards Hesston he was motoring down a small narrow lane with the rain dribbling onto his windscreen (the very inadequate wipers were of little use) when, as he rounded a bend between high thorn hedges, he suddenly saw a bicycle without lights coming towards him. Almost onto it before he saw it clearly, Nathan slammed his foot on the brake, bringing his little car to a skidding halt. Alas, the car just bumped into the bike's front wheel, tipping the cyclist off and at the same time throwing Bess from her front seat with a bump.

Nathan jumped out to run round to the front where he found an apparently middle-aged lady struggling to sit up, although with mud on her face, dress and hands it was difficult to be certain of her age. He fussed around as she cried out and held her knee in pain. After a few minutes, with his support she managed to walk round and sit in the passenger seat of the car. Bess wasn't anywhere around and, much as he whistled, she didn't come.

Since the bike looked too damaged to ride, Nathan just leaned it up against the hedge and walked back to his passenger who now seemed more composed and was busy cleaning off some of the mud. "I'm sorry about this. I'm Nathan Dobson. How can I help?"

"I'm Ruth. Can you drive me home please? Anyway it's me who should apologise for having no light showing, my carbide front light flickered out just minutes before but because it was so near home I thought I would manage without a light. Then you came round the bend."

Fortunately, just then little Bess came creeping timidly through the thorn hedge. When Nathan picked her up, Ruth immediately took her onto her lap.

Seeing how his two passengers seemed to be getting on well together, he drove further down the lane to where he could turn his car round before taking Ruth home.

"I didn't see you until I was almost up to you, I'm sorry. But I was going too fast in those conditions," Nathan apologised guiltily. "Is the pain getting any better or should I take you to the doctor's?"

"No, just take me home, please. I'm sorry to be so much trouble."

Nathan was surprised to find that Ruth's home was the Lacksfield schoolhouse situated just out of the village on the junction of two small lanes. After helping her to walk inside he put a match to the table lamp and then lit a second one in the bathroom. There was running water and a bath, something not seen in Hesston village, although he had heard that mains water should reach them in the coming year. When Ruth limped through to the bathroom to clean herself up Nathan made the fire up with a few sticks and when it blazed up he put on what little coal was there and went out through the back door to find more.

With the kettle firmly on the hot coals Nathan set off back to collect the bike. By the light of the car headlights he could see it was just the front wheel that was buckled. It was the work of a few moments to unfasten it and as the rain had momentarily stopped he slid the hood down and loaded both the wheel and the bike into, or was it onto, the car. Now settled after her fright, Bess accepted with relative calm the bike being lifted in above her head.

Back at the schoolhouse Nathan had found a teapot, two cups, some milk, and was pouring on the boiling water when Ruth limped in from the bathroom. With a long, flowery dressing gown hiding the shape of her figure she paused to survey his work and, smiling her appreciation, hobbled to a chair by the fire. Nathan asked as he passed her a cup of tea, "Have you had anything to eat?"

"No, I went to a meeting in the village after school. It went on longer than expected. There are some scones in the cupboard. Would you butter one for me, please, and have one yourself?"

Nathan was soon sitting on the other side of the fire enjoying a delicious scone with his cup of tea and listening to Ruth explain how she came to live there alone. Perhaps it was the shock but as she seemed to want to talk he encouraged her.

It seemed that Ruth's boyfriend Jim had joined the army in the middle of the war when he was just eighteen. "I promised to wait for him and I did but the man who came back was different from the boy who went away. Jim had been through an awful time on the front line."

Ruth went on to tell Nathan how most of Jim's mates had been killed. "Two of his closest friends died in his arms. Jim had been gassed and was in hospital for some time before he finally came back home. With his health shattered and unable to work, he became very bitter." Ruth paused meditatively and went on. "Jim refused to have anything to do with me, telling me to get on with my life without him. I'd just qualified as a teacher so I took a job near his home. At first he refused to even see me, then after a few months when I called round his mother invited me in, and slowly I got him to talk to me again."

Nathan, who had talked to a few war-ravaged ex-soldiers, could easily envisage how the man must have felt.

Ruth sipped her tea before continuing. "After a couple of years he started to do a bit of gardening for a big house nearby. Then I heard there was a vacancy here for a second teacher and when I inquired I found that the schoolhouse was free and they needed a part-time caretaker. It took me a while to persuade Jim but eventually he agreed to marry me and come to live here."

While she had been talking, Nathan realised Ruth wasn't as old as he first thought. There was a hint of sadness about her and perhaps it was that, with the dirt and tears from the accident, that had earlier made her look much older.

Ruth's face seemed to brighten up as she finished her story. "We had a few good years together. Then last year his health failed; then he caught pneumonia ...." Ruth shook her head sadly. "But I've never regretted those years together. I'm sorry. I shouldn't be telling you my troubles."

Nathan said, "Let me wash up these pots."

Brushing aside her protests he carefully washed and dried each pot before asking, "Is there anything more I can do?"

"Well, seeing that you've burned tomorrow morning's fire-lighting sticks, perhaps you can cut me a few more?"

So Nathan went out to the coal shed where he found a few old knotty logs and managed to split enough fire lighting sticks. Promising to bring the bike wheel back in the morning, he left her sitting by the fire.

Thinking about his actions on the journey home he was well aware it was more than just guilt from his part in the accident that was the motivating force. Pulling Bess's ear, Nathan said aloud, "If that had been an old chap of fifty I would have left him to walk home, then perhaps he would learn not to ride without lights. As it was – well, Bess, what did you think about those scones?"

Apologising to Hetty that he had forgotten her usual Friday night bottle of stout, Nathan pulled his chair up to the glowing fire. She looked up from her book with a smile of welcome, dismissed the forgotten stout and asked had he eaten. Nathan told her he had but he wouldn't mind a piece of toast. Hetty cut the bread while he reached for the toasting fork. They sat cosily each side the fire with Bess strategically sitting between them ready to beg from either as Nathan held the long-handled fork to the red glow.

The next morning when he arrived down for breakfast Hetty had already been outside with Bess. "What's the bike wheel in the car?" Feeling a bit embarrassed Nathan explained. "I bumped into it last night so the least I can do is get it repaired for her."

"For who?"

"For the school teacher at Lacksfield."

"You mean the young widowed school teacher? Oooh!" Hetty said, laughing as she raised her eyebrows. "And you've put your new jacket on again."

The trouble with Hetty was that one moment she could sound like his mother and the next become an inquisitive teasing sister. Then in the night she could be something else and although he enjoyed each of her different moods he was often caught out by the rapid change over. Now, seeing his embarrassment, Hetty walked over to him and cupped his face in her hands saying, "Listen, lover boy. If you meet a young lady your own age don't hesitate. In the meantime I'm here." Then, giving him a quick kiss, she added, "And it's bath night tonight."

Nathan drove off to the timber yard to make a couple of phone calls and talk to Clem. He was busy chopping up some timber off-cuts into sticks when Clem challenged him, "Hey, I thought you'd already taken a bag of sticks for Hetty?"

"Yes, but these are for someone else."

"Oh, are they? And there's that bike wheel in your car as well. You're going to be a busy man if you aren't careful," Clem said with humour. Nathan put the sack in his car and drove away, knowing full well that all would soon know his destination.

He had to motor into Knutsford for a new bike wheel, which meant that the morning was well gone by the time he got to Lacksfield school. Ruth greeted him with a smile and an invitation to a cup of tea. She had done her hair differently, he noticed as she bent down to greet Bess before leading them both into her home. The severe schoolteacher bun had been tied in a looser, more attractive manner. There was a more light-hearted look to her attractive face and when he asked after the knee she flirtatiously raised her dress to reveal a very shapely leg with a neat bandage round the injury. "I've put a hotpot in the oven. It will be ready in about thirty minutes, will you stay?"

"Well, thank you. It will take me all of that to fix the wheel and look at your lamp, and yes, I am fond of hotpot."

With a new tyre already fitted the wheel took but a few minutes but the Carbide lamp was a problem. The mechanism was simple: water dripping onto the carbide created a gas, which was released up a thin tube to the flame. When lit it gave off a reasonable light but it took Nathan some time to clean up the simple lamp and get it to work again.

Ruth not only made a good hotpot but she served out a big dish. Watching her busy at the table he couldn't help comparing her to Hannah. Ruth had a very similar figure to Hannah's. She was not quite as tall or slim but she was very much a woman. Although she looked surprisingly like he remembered Hannah, there was a more mature look with a hint of sadness on Ruth's face. At the same time there were flashes of mischief that revealed an impish personality,

178

reminding him of Hetty. Yet Ruth hadn't got Rachel's charisma or poise. Grief! What was he doing comparing anyone to Rachel? He had to get on with life. Anyway, Ruth was her own woman; he shouldn't be comparing her to others when she had seen enough sorrow in her life to mature anyone.

Ruth proved to be an interesting dining companion as Nathan tucked in heartily. She was also such a good listener that by the time he left the schoolhouse he had told her most of his life's story. "Well not quite," he confessed to Bess on the drive home, "I haven't told her about Rachel, or for that matter about Hetty either."

Chapter Twenty One

Apart from knowing he had eaten too much hotpot Nathan was unsure of his feelings on the way home from Lacksfield. This Ruth seemed an interesting woman and the fact that she had known both happiness and sadness gave strength to her character. The loss of a loved one so early in life can take a bit of shaking off, as he well knew. Driving back towards the timber yard he decided that it would be interesting to get to know her better.

Back in the yard it was relaxing to be there alone on a Saturday afternoon. No telephone calls to distract, no staff to instruct, just the smell of newly cut oak and Bess to nose around with him. It was just a matter of checking what seasoned timber was in stock then deciding which repairs Bill could work on and which would have to wait until the bought timber had been delivered.

As there was still some light left in the day when Nathan got back to the cottage he decide to tidy up some of the autumn leaves still lying in the garden. There was something about the dead leaves that excited Bess and she scurried in and out of the pile like a playful young pup. He rolled her over and piled the leaves on to her before she burst out, scattering leaves across the garden. When Hetty called him in for a cup of tea and a piece of cake Nathan, grinning boyishly, said, "Well at least we've moved them."

A smiling Hetty said, "Yes, but where? And would you like hotpot for tea?"

Nathan smiled his thanks but kept quiet about the large dish he had enjoyed earlier, thinking, 'for an honest man there seems to be a lot of things I'm not telling to a lot of people'. While the hotpot was simmering he took a lamp into the coalhouse to light the boiler fire and split up more logs for the next week. He filled the boiler with more water than usual and stoked up the fire before washing, ready for his hotpot. Hetty also dished out a large helping but he faced it with a certain amount of determination.

Conscious of how domesticated he had become, Nathan helped to wash up the dishes, made the kitchen fire up and then went out to see if the bath water was hot enough.

Later in the evening, after both had enjoyed a hot bath, they sat reading in front of blazing fire. Putting her book down, Hetty said, "If you take a shine to this young widow I'm going to miss this. The sticks chopped for me, the blazing logs – and your company."

When he just smiled she said, "I think I should make use of it all while you're still here."

***

On that Monday morning three different farmers came into the timber yard with equipment needing repair. Bill said he could use green ash to repair a set of swingle-trees, which one farmer urgently needed to enable him to hitch his horse team to his plough. The others agreed their repairs could wait until after the load of new timber had been delivered.

At mid-morning brew time Hamish called in and, over a battered tin mug of tea, reminded Nathan about the shoot on Saturday with, "Arrr, man, I'm dying to see how well your little bitch does."

***

It was Wednesday before Nathan drove out to see how his felling contractors were getting on. It was only politeness that afterwards took him to the schoolhouse to see how Ruth was.

Now, hardly limping at all, she looked even more attractive and he couldn't resist her invitation to stay for tea. It wasn't hotpot, but Cheshire cheese followed by apple pie and custard was more than acceptable. Ruth accepted an invitation take a ride out with him on the following Sunday afternoon.

The driving door fastener on Nathan's car began to give him trouble. Worried lest the door came undone when braking he called in at a garage near to Knutsford. The mechanic examined it and said, "It needs a new spring, not to worry. Just make sure you lift the handle each time. We should have it in next week."

***

Apart from having to apologise to the gardener for forgetting to tell Hamish to deal with a rabbit in the garden, Rachel's week was the usual mixture of walks with Digger and preparation for the December weekend guests. On the Thursday before the shoot her usual after dinner rest was interrupted when Greebs, who had moved in to the Hall only an hour before, announced, "Mr Jonson has arrived, Ma'am."

Mr Jonson met Rachel in the lounge with his most dazzling smile. "I hope you don't mind but my car's off the road and I got the

181

chance of a lift here a day earlier than planned. Can you put up with me for a day longer?"

She thought for a moment before replying, "Of course. Your bedroom is prepared but Alexander won't be back until tomorrow."

"Thank you! I'm sure Alexander wouldn't mind my having the pleasure of your company until then."

Thinking no more about it Rachel arranged with Cook for an extra place at dinner and went about her business.

Later, when changing before the meal and conscious that there were just the two of them, she chose one of her more severe high-necked outfits.

Mr Jonson was an interesting dining companion, telling amusing tales of faraway places. After the meal they went through to the lounge to sit near the fire. He went to sit on the sofa then turned and, indicating the other end, said, "Why not join me?"

"Thank you. You were talking about Argentina before. Did you live there for long?"

"For a while, yes. But I'd sooner talk about you."

With that Mr Jonson moved a little closer and lightly rested his arm on the back cushion by Rachel's shoulder. "You make even the plainest of dresses look special. You know, Alexander wouldn't object if we got closer."

Thinking it a strange thing to say Rachel just looked at him, which he took for encouragement and stroked gently down her cheek letting his hand slide down her neck. She jumped to her feet, proclaiming, "I mind though."

She spun round to face him but he just smiled up at her unabashed and said, "Come now, we are both grown up. You are an attractive, hot-blooded woman who doesn't see enough of her man. I'm here and I can give you a much more interesting time than that uncouth woodman you see too much of, so come and sit down again."

It wasn't so much his proposition or his implication but his complete confidence in his charm that got Rachel so mad. "You are my husband's guest and as such you can stay but don't ever try anything like this again."

Rachel had breakfast early while, according to Greebs, Mr Jonson was still in bed. After checking with her staff over the last minute arrangements for the weekend she set out with Digger. This Mr Jonson disturbed her deeply; there was something almost sinister in his relationship with Alexander and, feeling the need to talk it over with someone, walked towards the timber yard. Nathan as usual was in his office and as usual sat back to listen. But all he would say was, "I don't like the man. He's arrogant and a bully."

"Can't you find out anything about him?"

"I'm supposed to be having a drink with Gerald tonight. Maybe he may know something." Seeing Rachel's questioning frown, Nathan added, "Mr Ed's son; he's a reporter on the local paper now. Anyway, I'm picking up with you on the shoot tomorrow so we can keep an eye on him together."

Over a meat pie and a pint Nathan discovered Gerald had more questions than answers. Gerald was also very interested in Mr Jonson, asking, "How did he come to know the Major?"

Asking question after question without response, Gerald finally asked, "Did this man Jonson ever talk about his life in Argentina?"

Nathan replied with his own question, "How do you know the man came from Argentina?"

He just smiled, "We have our ways."

Gerald then went on to ask about the Wentworth-Joneses. Was there any more news about her inheritance? What about their marriage? How often did the Major come home?

"I know nothing about any of that."

"The rumour is that you know more than anyone about her affairs."

Nathan got a bit angry and would have walked out but Gerald apologised and bought him a drink.

***

The weather had turned unusually cold for early December. The ground was frozen hard when the beaters gathered round Hamish on the morning of the shoot. Nathan was apprehensive as to how he and Bess would cope. Although some of the guns had brought their own dogs they could only work those dogs to pick up at the end of each drive but fast-flying pheasants often cross over the guns so high that the shot birds fall well behind, and that was where Nathan would be waiting with Bess.

This pheasant shoot was much more organised than the relaxed partridge shoot. At each stand some fifty yards out from the wood Hamish had put out numbered sticks. The shoot Captain, who in this case was the Major, pulled out a leather wallet containing numbered ivory pegs for each gun to take one in turn. That numbered peg gave each gun his position on the first drive. On the second drive each gun moved to his left two places, which would be repeated again for the next drive and so on through the day. By the end of the day, although each man had shot from a different spot on each stand, they were all still in the same positional order.

Nathan was amused when Mr Jonson drew the next number to Alexander's. Neither man seemed too pleased about it.

Rachel was the only other person picking up with Nathan, although she explained that a local dog trainer would take her place after lunch. Standing some 120 yards back from the guns, they were both out of danger but close enough to see where every pheasant fell. Shooting was strictly prohibited before Alexander blew a whistle for the drive to start. Later, when the beaters came close to the guns, Alexander would blow it again to stop the shooting.

Birds came over the guns at a steady rate, which gave time for them to reload without the use of a loader. Yet because the pheasants seemed to scatter along the line of guns each had some sport. When one pheasant dropped near to Nathan, Rachel held Digger while he sent Bess for it and she made a perfect fetch, bringing the dead bird back and placing it in his hand. Rachel's clap of approval encouraged Nathan to feel a growing pride in his dog while Bess, wagging her stumpy tail furiously, danced around with sheer joy.

By the end of the drive, when Alexander blew his whistle, both dogs had made a few retrieves. The guns had relaxed and were unloading when, with a startling clap of wings, a pheasant burst into the air in front of them. Mr Jonson swung his gun up and dropped the bird. Alexander was furious, shouting, "You don't shoot after the whistle."

Even as Alexander was speaking one of the beaters, climbing through the fence in front of them, frightened another pheasant out of the hedge bottom. When it flew low between the two men Mr Jonson swung onto it, Alexander ducked and turned away in fear but fortunately Mr Jonson didn't shoot. Some of the other guns looked on embarrassed as Alexander strode towards Mr Jonson. Nathan couldn't hear what was said but he thought it would be interesting. On other shoots he'd seen guns ordered to leave the field for a lesser transgression than that.

On the next drive Alexander's two-place move took him to the extreme gun peg on the far end of the line, leaving Mr Jonson on the end peg on this side. In the meantime Rachel, who had also witnessed the interchange, seemed very worried about the relationship between the two men. Nathan tried to pass the whole thing off as just one of those things but Rachel said, "There's more to it than that. He's got some kind of hold over Alexander. I'm getting really worried about it. Try to keep an eye on them both this afternoon, will you?"

How could he refuse? Sharing the excitement together through the morning, each working their own dog and at the same time working close to each other, was triggering little flutters in Nathan's chest.

After lunch, when the guns walked back towards the next stand, Nathan deliberately walked just behind them. Mr Jonson soon fell in step with the Major and before long they were arguing. One attribute of the gentry, which Nathan had often laughed about, was how they could completely ignore their servants. Perhaps having grown up surrounded by members of staff the gentry, when they became adults, continued with a conversation or an argument just as though the servants weren't there. This time Nathan couldn't catch the first exchange so he moved closer to hear Mr Jonson say, "I want it before I leave. It's either that or you know what will happen."
Alexander replied, "I've told you; she has control of both accounts now, so how can I do it without her knowing?"
"That's your problem. But if you don't I'll make sure that not only does she know but every one else will know as well."

When Alexander walked away to check that his other guests found their right pegs, Nathan dropped back to take his place some distance from the guns. Soon afterwards Alexander blew his whistle and the shoot began again.

Nathan was kept busy through the afternoon session. The other dog handler was not as easy to work with as Rachel. On top of that, two runners (winged pheasants) taxed Bess's tracking skill to the limit by hiding among the weeds and briars round the edge of a pond and as a result he only got close to Alexander again on the way back to the gunroom.

After helping to hang the game in the cold room Nathan joined Hamish in the gunroom helping to clean the guests' guns. Pushing the cleaning rod through each barrel, he passed each one to Hamish who checked it and polished on the outside. The Major stepped in to thank Hamish for providing such a good day's sport adding, "You too, Dobson. Your new dog worked well!" Before Nathan could think of a reply the Major asked, "Is that my gun? Good! I'll take a walk with it. Rachel has been complaining about a rabbit in the garden; I might just see it in the dusk."

Soon after he had gone Mr Jonson barged in, asking, "Have you cleaned my gun yet?"
When Hamish nodded, Mr Jonson said, "Right, then tell the chauffeur that I need taking to the station now."

Starting to walk round to the rear of the Hall with that message for Bestwick Nathan was surprised to discover it was snowing and turned back for his topcoat. Not that it was a heavy fall but there was already a thin cover on the path. Hearing a shot from the garden he thought no more about it when he found Bestwick working on the car engine. Bestwick shook his head when Nathan repeated Mr Jonson's request and said, "I've got petrol trouble. It might take me thirty minutes or two hours to get it going."

Nathan explained how the guest seemed very impatient to leave so Bestwick suggested, "Why not take him in your car?"

Nathan was reluctant, for the weather looked bad. After a frosty morning the roads could become icy in damp places and heavier snow clouds were now darkening the last of the evening light. Mr Jonson did seem to be in an angry, urgent mood though so eventually Nathan reluctantly agreed, saying, "Anyway, I'd like to see the back of him."

With Mr Jonson sitting in the front and little Bess sitting on an old sack next to some expensive looking suitcases on the back seat Nathan drove the Morris Cowley out into falling snowflakes. Before many miles the large, wet flakes of early winter snow came down so hard it was almost too much for the simple windscreen wiper. He had difficulty finding the roadside post box for Mr Jonson to post a letter that he seemed to think was important.

Driving in silence for some miles, Nathan took the liberty of challenging Mr Jonson, "What hold have you got over the Major then?"

The way Mr Jonson's head swung aggressively round startled Nathan into taking his eyes off the road for a moment. Then, having to slow down while he tried to re-focus through the blurred windscreen, he added, "I don't like blackmailers."

It was just a shot in the dark but the reactions were completely unexpected. Perhaps Mr Jonson thought Nathan was stopping to have a confrontation because he fumbled in the small holdall between his feet and pulled out a large revolver. "I don't give a damn what you like," he growled, "just get a move on."

Used to the road, Nathan knew they were approaching a humped-back canal bridge. The snow was settling on his windscreen so that he could barely see the road. He was sure the road curved left towards the canal bridge but he could see the roadside hedge going straight on and followed it. The verge widened onto a flat, grassy pathway leading to a gateway, which in turn gave access to the towpath. Increasing his speed, Nathan hit a bump that both rocked the car and rattled his door open. He reached sideways for the door and within a second he was flying through the air.

The Morris Cowley hit the gate with a crash then bounced up across the towpath to dive head first into the canal. But Nathan knew nothing of that.

What was Bess doing on his bed licking his face? Putting his hand up to stroke her long ears Nathan realised she was soaking wet. Then, feeling snowflakes landing on his face, he puzzled as to why they were coming in through the bedroom window. It was only when someone started shaking his shoulder and slapping his face that he realised he was on the ground under the side of a hedge.

Remembering what had happened was a struggle.

Chapter Twenty Two

The next time Nathan came to he realised where he was immediately. The local doctor was sitting on the edge of his bed looking into his eyes, while a concerned Hetty hovered in the background. Sunlight streaming in through the open curtains told him that it must be Sunday morning. He tried to force his foggy brain back to the accident the night before. He could recall being asked if there had been anyone with him and saying yes, then remembered someone saying that they couldn't find his passenger. After that were more vague recollections of a villager driving him and Bess home, but that must have been in the dark last night. Now it was daylight, the snow had stopped and he was bursting for a pee.

The doctor began dabbing something onto the scratches on his face. "You're going to be all right. You have had a bang on the head, which has left you a bit disorientated but it seems to be improving now. I want you to stay in bed for three days and not go near that timber yard of yours at all this week."

While the doctor was talking Hetty had gone down the stairs, but now she was back again, saying, "There are two policemen here wanting to talk to you."

The doctor gave Nathan a long, speculative look and said, "It will be all right as long as they don't stay too long."

"It'll be all right if I can have a pee first." The other two left the room grinning as Nathan reached under the bed for his pot.

Introducing himself as Chief Inspector Shawby, the senior policeman shook hands adding, "I presume you know Constable Wilson?" When Nathan nodded he continued. "About this accident. There are a few matters that we need to clear up."

Nathan held up his hand. "First! Have you found Mr Jonson?"

"Yes. It's bad news, though. I'm afraid he's dead. We think he may have banged his head and drowned because he was still in the passenger seat."

Nathan looked out of the window but the Inspector interrupted his thoughts, "I would like you to tell me just what happened last night. Right from the beginning, so just take your time."

"Well it started to snow ...."

188

"No, go right back to how you came to drive Mr Jonson to the station."

Nathan related how he was in the gunroom when Mr Jonson came in, how Bestwick had an engine problem and so he had volunteered. "Did you hear anything?"

"Just Bestwick telling ...."

"Nothing else? No other noises at all?"

"The Major shot a rabbit in the garden."

"Which Major?"

"Major Wentworth-Jones, of course."

"How do you know he shot a rabbit?"

"Well, that was what he said that he was going to do, so when I heard the shot I just presumed he had."

"Were you in the gunroom when Major Wentworth-Jones came in for his gun?"

"Yes."

"What sort of state was he in? Did he seem upset at all?"

"Not that I noticed but he's always unreadable. Look, what is this? I thought you wanted to ask me about my accident so why are you going on about the Major?"

"Just answer the questions. There was some sort of a disagreement between Major Wentworth-Jones and Mr Jonson, was there not?"

"I think it was just that Mr Jonson swung through on a low bird but he didn't shoot. I presumed the Major had a word with him. It's the sort of thing that happens sometimes."

"Were they not arguing later in the day?"

"I wouldn't know. You'll have to ask the Major about that."

"Where was Mr Jonson when you heard the shot?"

"How would I know? He'd just been in the gun room."

"Yes, but how long after that was it before you heard that shot?"

"Well, I did turn back for my coat so I suppose it could be several minutes."

"Right, let's get back to your car journey."

Explaining Mr Jonson's urgency to catch a train, Nathan described the journey and how, because of the wet snow on the windscreen, he was following the hedge.

"How do you mean, you followed the hedge?"

"Well, I could see out through the side window better than through the windscreen but then I felt a bump, which rattled the door handle. I remember making a grab for it and ... that's it!"

"Why did you grab the door handle?"

"The catch is faulty."

Nathan tried to explain about the garage but the Chief Inspector interrupted, "Were you trying to open the door or close it?"

"What do you mean?"

"Did you fall or did you jump?"

"I'd be a fool to jump into a thorn hedge in the dark."

"Or have a very good reason?"

Nathan answered more questions about the car until he began to feel woozy and protested, "I've had enough of your questions and I still don't understand why you were asking about the Major?"

"The Major was found dead last night."

"When? How?"

"A gunshot wound, in the garden."

Aware of the Inspector's scrutiny, Nathan just lay back on his pillow and said nothing. Taking the hint, the policemen said their farewells.

Hetty brought him a cup of tea and sat where the Inspector had been sitting

"Why didn't you tell me about the Major?" Nathan asked.

"I didn't think you were up to it. It's happened and that's it. Have a rest now and I'll bring you some dinner later."

Relieved there had been no mention of a revolver, Nathan lay back trying to fathom out what could have happened to the Major. Rachel must be so worried. With Jonson out of the way Nathan had thought she and Alexander might put their lives together again but that wouldn't happen now. His mind focused suddenly: 'Poor Rachel, she's all on her own now. I just hope nothing comes out of all of this to spoil her enjoyment when she comes into her inheritance.'

Hetty seemed to be enjoying having Nathan where she could fuss over him. She brought him up a bowl of soup and a beaker of tea then took his chamber pot away to empty it. Later she brought it back and took his dirty pots away.

With nothing else to occupy his mind he lay musing over events, particularly trying to work out if someone with the Major's gun experience could have had an accident or was it the blackmail? What must Rachel be thinking? There was no one left to comfort her now.

Hetty came quietly in. "Oh, you are awake then? Are you up to having a visitor?"

"Who?"

"Your young schoolteacher widow."

"Grief, I'd forgotten. I was going to take her out today."

"Well, you hadn't forgotten last night. You told me about three times so I sent a message to her this morning. Anyway, are you going to let her come up?"

Nathan stroked his fingers through his untidy hair and straightened out the bedclothes. Laughing at his fussing, Hetty went back down stairs.

Ruth rushed in, gripped his hand in concern then chattered on with a mixture of questions and observations. Nathan held onto the hand while he explained about the knock on the head, his scratched face and the Major.

Explaining how she had been told about the accident Ruth brushed aside any danger in riding her bicycle through the thin layer of wet snow to see him – and let Nathan hold onto her hand.

Sometime later Hetty tapped discreetly on the door before walking in with a loaded tray. The two women fussed around, rearranging a small table by the bedside, then as Hetty placed the tray down she said, "I've brought you a cup of tea and some scones."

Nathan smiled in amusement at the best china and at Hetty who smiled again while saying to Ruth, "He seems to like scones, doesn't he?"

"Yes," Ruth replied, "and he seems to like a big dish of hotpot too."

"When have you given him hotpot? Oh, last Saturday! You mean he had a big dish with you at dinnertime?" When Ruth nodded Hetty said, "Did he now! There're some things our Nathan doesn't tell me. Enjoy your tea!"

When she had gone Ruth said, "She's nice, isn't she? You must find it very homely here, she seems to look after all your needs."

Nathan was looking out of the window again.

***

Back at Hesston Hall on the afternoon before Nathan's accident, the guests accepted Alexander's reason for not joining them over afternoon tea. As owners of country houses they knew only too well what a pest a rabbit is in the garden, and once the disagreeable Mr Jonson left the atmosphere was much more relaxed.

Tea over, the Craneby-Browns quickly took their leave and went upstairs to rest before dinner. Eleanor and George Canterly took a more relaxed time over their last cup of tea before also going up to change. Surprised by snow falling so early in the winter, Rachel and Lucy walked out to the porch for a closer look. They were more surprised at how dark it was under the heavy, snow-laden clouds. Rachel asked Lucy to excuse her for a moment and went into the gunroom to look for Alexander. Hamish had just finished cleaning the last of the guns when Rachel asked, "Have you seen the Major?"

"Arrr, Missey, he went after yer rabbit."

"But it's too dark for him to be able to shoot now."

Walking outside to take a look, Hamish replied, "Arrr, I think it is, Missey. Maybe I'll go an' have a look."

Walking back into the main Hall Rachel glanced into Alexander's study, which looked a bit more untidy than usual. Then she saw the Colonel's medals out on the desk. Her knowledge of how they only came out when Alexander was under stress increased her concern.

Major Fearnly, who was waiting for her at the foot of the stairs, asked, "Is there something wrong? Where's Alexander?"

he question was answered when Hamish stepped in through the Hall front door, "Arrr, Missey, prepare yerself; there's bin an accident. The Major's dead."

Taking over with crisp military command, Major Fearnly ordered Rachel to wait inside. Lucy was immediately by her side guiding her into the lounge while Greebs, with an unusual note of urgency, was soon on the phone asking for the doctor and the police. Major Fearnly came back to confirm gently what Hamish had said. When Rachel asked how, he replied, "Alexander obviously slipped on the path, setting his gun off accidentally."

After that the evening was all a bit confusing for Rachel. There seemed to be people coming and going. Then a more senior policeman questioned her at some length. Although she and Alexander had not been very close for some time the shock of his sudden death left her so confused to the extent that she perhaps said more to the policeman than was wise.

The guests all supportively stayed overnight. Rachel was sure Cook must have served them dinner but did not join them. Later, when the doctor visited he must have given her a strong sleeping draught because she remembered no more until Cook brought in a light breakfast.

The morning was well gone by the time Rachel came

downstairs to find Major Fearnly, striding about in full uniform, seemingly completely in charge. There were policemen in the garden poking about in the thin snow, a reporter was asking questions at the door and the telephone was ringing but Lucy steered her into the lounge where Cook brought in a tea tray.

Later, a middle-aged man, introducing himself as Chief Inspector Shawby, asked Rachel, "Are you up to answering some questions, Ma'am?"

"I think so, yes. How can I help?"

"You last saw your husband when?"

"At afternoon tea. The guns don't change for it, we serve it immediately they come in from shooting."

"The Major took tea with everyone then?"

"Yes. Well no, he was there at the start but left part way through."

"Did he tell you where he was going?"

"No. I didn't even notice him leaving. I was chatting to the ladies."

The Chief Inspector studied his notebook for a while then asked, "Did anyone else leave the room at the time?"

"Mr Jonson came in telling me he was leaving before dinner. That was when I noticed Alexander wasn't there."

The questions about who was where and when went on for a while, then the Chief Inspector asked, "Now, what was this row between Mr Jonson and the Major about?"

"A low-flying bird I think, but you must ask Mr Jonson about that."

"You obviously don't know then."

"Know what?"

"There was an accident on the way to the station. I am sorry to tell you that Mr Jonson was killed."

"What about Nathan? Is he hurt?"

"Just a touch of concussion and a few scratches." As he answered, the Chief Inspector was well aware of where Rachel's concern lay. "Mrs Wentworth-Jones, your relationship with Mr Dobson seems to be a very close one, doesn't it?"

Rachel tried to explain about Hannah and the timber yard but it all came out a bit disjointed to the extent that the Chief Inspector asked more questions.

***

Lucy and Major Fearnly stayed on over Sunday night. Major Fearnly secmed to be prepared to make all the necessary funeral arrangements. Rachel wasn't sure if it was what the Army normally did or if it was just because they were friends but it was relieving her of considerable stress.

***

After a restless night, when morning finally came Nathan was ready to get up. When Hetty came in early to check on him he muttered as much but she firmly repeated the doctor's orders. He sank back onto his pillow, well aware of the danger. Some years before one of his workers had suffered a similar bump on the head and, refusing to rest, came in to work the following day. The man collapsed in mid axe stroke. The memory left Nathan well aware of the danger of activity after a head injury.

Hetty brought Nathan's breakfast before dashing off to work and reluctantly agreed he could come downstairs later that morning to make the fire up and prepare a light lunch. But he dozed off again and when he next looked at the clock it was already late morning. Before he could get out of bed he heard the door at the bottom of the stairs opening and a voice calling up to him. The rattle of little Bess's feet on the bare wooden stairs drowned out whoever's voice it was, so Nathan just replied, "Yes, come up."

Bess barged in and jumped affectionately onto his bed but when Rachel walked in Nathan thought he had better push her off again. "The house was empty so I just walked in, I hope you don't mind?" Nathan lay silent for a moment, just looking at her. She was dressed all in black, her unbuttoned coat revealing a high-necked, close fitting dress that was not good for a man who was supposed to be resting. Ignoring his stare Rachel pulled a chair up to his bedside and took hold of his hand before asking, "How are you?"

"Oh, I'm all right, in fact I was just about to get up." But aware of the strain and sadness on her face he said, "I am truly sorry about Alexander. It must have been an awful shock to you."

"Yes, it was. I still find it hard to believe. I keep expecting him to telephone from London." Holding his hand even tighter, Rachel asked, "Nathan, tell me what was going on? Was Alexander being blackmailed about something?"

He had half expected this question but not this soon. "I don't know, but I do know Mr Jonson was not a nice man."

Rachel withdrew her hand and fidgeted about for a moment before asking, "Do you think Alexander's death was really an accident?"

"Oh, I'm sure it was. It's so easily done on an icy path." Nathan tried to sound convincing but he then asked, "Why? What do the police say?"

"They are not saying anything, its just questions from them, but Major Fearnly is adamant it was an accident."

"Well, I'm sure he'll be right."

Rachel, in a surprisingly derogatory way, said, "The Army are always right; it's the way they're trained, they always have to sound positive and convincing."

She chatted on for a while about Nathan, his accident and how was he being looked after and Bess snuggled up to her leg to have her long ears stroked. After a while Nathan rubbed his stubbly chin, saying, "I need to go to the bathroom."

"But you haven't got a bathroom."

"So, then I must take a walk."

Rachel sprang to her feet asking, "What about lunch?"

"We don't have lunch. We have dinner and I'm going to make my own later."

"You get dressed and take your walk while I do you something."

Nathan protested to no avail.

When he walked through the kitchen Rachel was busy cracking eggs. He had been outside and was washing in the back kitchen sink when she called, "I've got a pancake done. If you come for it I'll do you another one."

By the time he had finished the second pancake Rachel had brewed a pot of tea. Pouring it out into two chipped beakers, she sat down opposite, looking serious. "And what about Mr Jonson, was that an accident?"

Nathan had rehearsed his answer to that too but he hadn't anticipated the effect of Rachel's hazel brown eyes watching him while he gave it. "Of course! What makes you think it wasn't?"

He suddenly realised there was a new directness, even boldness, about her. Perhaps she was now free from the restrictions of convention. Whatever it was, she was watching his reactions so carefully he began to feel uncomfortable.

"Have the police been to see you?" When he nodded she continued, "They seem to be very interested in my relationship with you."

"We haven't got a relationship. I just happen to work on your estate and we meet."

Rachel was on her feet carrying the pots to the sink. Coming back, said as she took his hand, "Take care of yourself and thank you for everything you've done for me."

When Nathan protested that he hadn't done anything, Rachel just smiled and bade him farewell.

Still needing a proper wash and a shave Nathan looked at the kettle but it hadn't been refilled. On the way out to the pump he smiled to himself, thinking how Rachel would have to learn a few basic principles if she had to live in one of her own little cottages. The first would be that you refill the kettle every time you use it, and not just refill it but put it back on the hob. Now he wanted hot water and there wasn't any.

While waiting for the kettle to heat up he took Bess for a stroll round the garden where he leaned on the garden gate but he couldn't help thinking of Rachel. Yes, she was both a good friend and a disturbingly attractive woman but she was heading back to a big Hall where her bath would be run for her. Whereas now he needed a bath he had the energy neither to fill up the boiler nor to light the fire under it. Later, after he had shaved and washed up the dirty pots, a dizzy uncoordinated feeling hit him. So he crept back upstairs to bed.

Chapter Twenty Three

The days before the funeral were a strain for Rachel. With the loss of both Hannah and her father she was already mourning two of the three people closest to her, and now she must try to mourn the third. There were no illusions about her marriage, which had become such a bitter disappointment it was close to a complete break up. Perhaps she and Alexander could have pulled it round but she doubted it and now would never know.

There had been so many messages of condolence and many personal callers that the days seemed to fly. The Fearnlys were marvellous, Lucy was a constant source of comfort and the Major had taken over all the funeral arrangements, although Rachel had firmly rejected his plan to carry Alexander's coffin to the church on a gun carriage. Instead Joe Candy would again lead Jewel as he had for her father. The differences were that members of Alexander's Regiment would act as bearers and the Regiment had arranged an undertaker.

There was still the matter of the inquest, which was planned for Wednesday afternoon. Rachel couldn't understand how Major Fearnly could be so sure the coroner would release the body for burial on Friday, though when she challenged him about it he was adamant the funeral would go ahead as planned.

Because her staff were all busy getting the house ready, when the doorbell rang Rachel answered it and was confronted by a loud, brash man who was pacing around and ranting on about his daughter and Young Towley. Rachel protested, "Robert Towley is my farm manager and he seems to be good at his job. His relationship with your daughter is not my business."

"Of course it's your business," the man said aggressively. "You've taken him in and given him a job; if you hadn't he would have been miles away now and this wouldn't have happened."

When Rachel did not reply he continued, "He's still seeing her and he kept her out until three this morning. I want him sacked and cleared out of the area."

Hearing the row, Major Fearnly came out to intervene. His explanation that Rachel was mourning her husband brought a rude retort from the man, which in turn got the Major annoyed. Rachel turned on her heel and went back into the Hall.

She sat near the fire reflecting on how the countryside was changing. The reasons for change went back to the years before the Great War, when there had been over thirty years of agricultural recession. During that time farm rents either didn't rise or in many cases fell, which in turn meant that even the larger agricultural estates were denuded of revenue. Up to the Great War the saving grace for the large estates had been their vast source of cheap labour. Although paid abysmal wages, their vast labour force was held in subservience because most of them were either housed in tied cottages or, if single, they 'lived in' with free board and food.

The Great War had radically altered the rural structure. It did much worse than just take the young male workers away from the country estates; it freed them from the bonded servitude that had been their inherited lot. The few who returned from the mass slaughter in the trenches wanted something better than having to wear fancy uniforms and touch forelocks to the idle rich.

At the same time, throughout the bitter battles in France the officers suffered an even greater percentage of casualties than did the ranks. The German snipers deliberately picked them off. Among the cream of British youth who died on those battlefields were the heirs to many of the great country estates. Rachel could think of several estates in Cheshire which, having been in the same family for hundreds of years, lost their next generation. One leading local family lost thirteen members, a whole generation exterminated on the killing fields in France. As a result some proud families, who had held their lands from the time of the Norman invasion some eight hundred years before, came to the end of their line in those four short years.

It was not just the War though. Through the long agricultural depression leading up to 1914 many country squires continued to live the good life, with a house in London and summers on the Riviera. The entertaining and general lifestyle that went with all of that had drained the financial reserves away so that the loss of sons and heirs was the last straw and they sold up. Rachel remembered reading that throughout the country some twenty-nine thousand estates changed hands during or immediately after the War.

Many of the new estate owners were not country people but hardheaded businessmen who had made their fortunes in the industrial revolution. She knew some of them well. Anyway, she thought ruefully, Alexander's family fitted that description in that the

Colonel had bought this estate, even though it was before the war. Others who had bought estates with no background of country ways could be more arrogant than the old style estate owner and she presumed she had just met one of those today.

Major Fearnly broke into her thoughts by marching back into the lounge. "I've sent him packing," he said briskly, "and I've told that farm manager of yours he will get the same if he brings his troubles here again."

Why do we all call him Major, Rachel wondered as she looked at him. Perhaps it was the fact that when he was first promoted he was so proud that they had all called him by his title and it had stuck. Then she remembered what Lucy might have done to gain his promotion and felt angry at his assertiveness. "Major, you shouldn't have said that to my farm manager. I do really appreciate all you're doing for me but you mustn't interfere with my staff." With that she walked out of the room and, donning walking boots and coat, strode off towards the farmyard.

It seemed strange to pass the timber yard knowing Nathan was not there. How was he going on? Perhaps she should try to visit him again before the funeral.

Rachel found Robert in the shippen, and he immediately apologised about the row. She led him outside away from his dairy staff. "It's not your fault but you will have to decide what you are going to do about it."

"How do you mean, Ma'am?"

"If you're serious about this girl then perhaps you should think about marriage. If that is what you decide then the cottage is here for you."

"You mean it? We can have the cottage if we marry?"

"Of course you can."

Rachel left him looking happier. It felt good to dispense a little cheer at such a sad time.

Those first few days seemed to have run together in Rachel's mind. She found it hard to remember what happened on which day. William and Lisa Brown had been to express their condolences; in fact there were only a few of the tenants who felt they could do that. The rest had written notes of sympathy, of which there were many. she still felt closer to William and Lisa than she did to almost anyone else, although as usual William fidgeted about uncomfortably in the Hall environment while he and Lisa took tea with her.At the end of their visit Rachel did feel comforted by the friendship of these two hardworking friends.

Chief Inspector Shawby had again interviewed her to cross-check different things. "Is it correct that Mr Dobson drove you home from the Browns' farm in the dark one night?" Before Rachel could properly answer he butted in, "You seem to meet him in the woods fairly regularly?"

The Chief Inspector was watching her intently but again before Rachel could answer he went on, "Letting this timber yard to him seems an unusual arrangement, doesn't it?"

Rachel tried to keep control of her growing anger as she replied, "I don't know what you're implying but the yard was a decision my father made just before his death. The estate is like any other business, it must change to survive."

"So you are having money trouble are you?"

And so the questioning went on. Rachel managed to keep control of her temper even though the policeman persisted with questions about Nathan and the estate's finances. His final shot was, "So you can see no reason why your husband should commit suicide then?"

"Good Heavens, no!"

Eventually the policeman thanked her gracefully, reminded her about the inquest and left.

***

Hetty was at home each Tuesday. The farm's big weekly wash was on the Monday now this was her washday. The fire was lit under the boiler for the whites and the colours had been plunged up and down in the dolly tub. But before she could hang them all out on the washing line a flurry of sleet turned to rain.

Nathan had agreed to stay in bed until dinner time but found his morning interrupted when a harassed looking Hetty brought Mr Ed up to see him. The two men exchanged the usual pleasantries before Mr Ed switched to journalism. It was still in a relaxed, chatty manner but Nathan was under no illusions – the editor of the local paper was giving him a going over. The accident, Mr Jonson and the Major's suspicious death were all covered. Nathan, glad of someone to talk to, didn't resent his questions until Mr Ed said, "It's a good job you were knocked out and lying under the hedge by that canal."

"How do you mean?"

"Well, the Chief Inspector's not at all happy with the Major's accident. With your relationship with Mrs Wentworth-Jones you could have had some explaining to do."

"I don't have a relationship with Mrs Wentworth-Jones. I happen to work in the centre of the estate and our paths cross."

"Well, if the Chief Inspector's heard the same rumours I have, then he'll want to know why your paths cross as often as they seem to."

That got Nathan mad enough to tell him to leave but Mr Ed had kept his most explosive question to the end. "What had Mr Jonson got on the Major to be blackmailing him?"

Nathan looked at him long and hard before replying, "Was he blackmailing him?"

"You don't know anything about it then?"

"About what?"

Mr Ed studied Nathan for a moment or two then, pulling a long white envelope from out of his inside pocket, said, "I've had an anonymous letter suggesting some murky deeds in the Wentworth-Jones family history."

Nathan was sure he had seen an envelope looking just like that one somewhere before. Was the one Mr Jonson's posted not long before the crash? But Nathan mentioned none of this. Instead he asked, "What sorts of things?"

Mr Ed got up and paced about the bedroom. Eventually, when Nathan repeated his question, Mr Ed said, "It seems from this letter that the family fortune was made out of slavery. Major Wentworth-Jones's grandfather continued trading in slaves long after slavery had been abolished here. The letter is a bit vague as to where but it could have been to the Southern States of America or even the Middle East. Whichever, it claims the Major's uncle was also involved before he went missing. Yes, it hints he may not have been lost at sea as the family claims."

"If it's true it's all so long ago, what's it got to do with this, now?" Nathan asked.

"The Major was a proud and ambitious man who may not want his family's skeletons rattled, particularly now his wife is about to come into a title and a large estate. It just makes you think, does it not?"

Nathan was looking out of the window as he thought. When he said nothing Mr Ed said, "It could be someone from the past trying to stir up trouble, but who? It's more likely just local tittle-tattle and jealousy but which ever it is – there isn't enough dirt to cause a man to commit suicide, is there?"

Nathan, watching a couple of carrion crows arguing in an oak just outside the garden and without looking away from them, said, "I've seen them peck the eye out of a sleeping lamb. How do you know what goes on in someone else's mind?"

Mr Ed shook his head at that pearl of wisdom. "I don't think there's anything in it. Look, round here we are proud of the Major; he is or was our local hero and I have no intention of destroying that now he's dead. If I went to the police with every nasty letter that came my way – well? Let's just say that I would like to keep this between us for now. Do you agree?"

When Nathan agreed the two men shook hands and Mr Ed went on his way.

Hetty certainly did look harassed when Nathan got down for his dinner. The rain was still coming down steadily, which meant that the week's wash was hanging round the kitchen. The ceiling was too low to suspend a rack from it so she had to make do by other means. Not being used to having a man about the house on washday Hetty had balanced canes between the chairs on which she had hung some of her wet clothes. Nathan had to do a bit of readjusting to free two chairs for the table. He thanked her for both it and for nursing him and promised to make her a clotheshorse for Christmas. Hetty, with her usual efficiency, had put a stew on to simmer away unattended.

Feeling much better after his meal, Nathan put his topcoat on to take Bess out for a short walk. The lane was always quiet, and this time just one local farmer came along; Nathan held the restless pony's head while they had a chat. It felt so good to be outside again, even in the rain, that he walked further than he had intended. When he returned there was the Chief Inspector's car sitting by the garden gate.

The Chief Inspector was soon sitting by the fire watching Hetty do the ironing. The kettle came to the boil just as Nathan took his seat on the other side the hearth. Hetty brewed up and then went on with her work. Her ironing board was just a blanket spread over the end of the kitchen table and there were two irons. Each just a shaped lump of solid iron with a handle and each in turn was placed on the hob to heat up while Hetty worked away with the other.

The policeman seemed to want to get Nathan on his own but when Hetty said, "Don't mind me, I've got work to do," he had no choice but to get on with it.

"We've checked up on the car and it did have a faulty door fasten," he said seriously, "but there are one or two other matters that I want to clear up. About that disagreement you witnessed between Mr Jonson and the Major, what exactly did they say to each other?"

"I was too far away to hear."

"Come now, I can't believe that. You were picking up for the guns so you must have been very close to them."

"We stand a hundred or more yards back, where we hope that we won't get shot."

"This man Jonson seems to be a bit of a mystery man; what do you know about him?"

"I only knew him as some sort of friend of the Major's."

"Did he say anything to you on the journey, like where he was going to or even where he came from?"

Thinking it best if he kept his answers to the minimum, Nathan said, "He was just in a hurry to catch a train."

The Chief Inspector, seeming less than satisfied, demanded that Nathan retold the events leading up to and including his accident. Nathan told it just as he had the first time, still leaving out any mention of blackmail or a revolver but he was jolted when the policeman said, "By the way, we found the gun."

"What gun? Where?"

"His shotgun, it was in the car. A really beautiful gun and in an expensive waterproof case, so it was completely undamaged. Unlike your car."

"Where is my car?"

"We had to examine it somewhere so we took it to the garage. I expect they will need your instructions before repairing it."

Relieved to hear his car would repair, he was beginning to relax, thinking that the policeman had finished, only to be taken by surprise by his next question.

"This relationship you have going with Mrs Wentworth-Jones, you used to meet her in the woods and she often called in at your timber yard. Where else do you meet?"

Nathan got a bit angry at his insinuations. "I've already told you, there is no relationship. You're just jumping to conclusions."

"Oh, come now. A fit, single young man like you who regularly meets up with a young woman? And a very attractive young woman who seldom sees her husband, what other conclusion should I jump to?"

Nathan started to protest when Hetty stepped between them to change irons. Picking up the hot one she spat on it to test if it was hot enough. When it sizzled she said to Nathan, "Tell him about your young widowed schoolteacher."

Before Nathan could answer the policeman asked, "What schoolteacher?"

Nathan was protesting that she had nothing to do with it while Hetty was explaining, "It seems he has a girlfriend. When she heard he had been injured she cycled all the way from Lacksfield schoolhouse in the snow last Sunday morning. I don't think he has any need to meet Mrs Wentworth-Jones in the woods for what you are implying."

That seemed to stop the Chief Inspector going further on that line of inquiry. Muttering his annoyance that the doctor was refusing to let Nathan attend the inquest, the Chief Inspector rose to take his leave.

Chapter Twenty Four

The doctor called in when Nathan was sitting with a book in front of the kitchen fire. First holding up his fingers for Nathan to count, he then moved them sideways, then backwards and forwards before pronouncing, "I think you might live but you still have a touch of concussion. I've already told that policeman you're not fit to attend the Major's inquest this afternoon. Don't go waving a big axe around either, or for that matter don't even go near that timber yard yet."

Having opened the door to leave, the doctor turned back to say, "You would be better not to go to the funeral either. Just stick to walking the dog until Monday."

Not long after the doctor left, William Brown called in to see how Nathan was faring. With his usual timing the kettle came to the boil. Nathan pointed to it saying, "Lisa says you have second sight." William laughed at the thought. "If I had I'd make a lot more money out of farming."

When they were each settled with a cup of tea Nathan again felt the pain of losing Hannah. He would have been proud to have this forthright, solid man as his father-in-law. This week, with time to think, he felt the renewed urge to settle down; it was more than just sex drive. He would happily settle for a cottage like this one with the right woman there to greet him each day. He certainly didn't want a big Hall with dozens of servants or the title that went with it. His thoughts were interrupted when Mr Brown said, "You're not listening Nathan, and I was asking how are you managing without your car?" "I need to sort something out for next week."

Before Mr Brown left he agreed to drive Nathan to the garage on Saturday morning so he could see about his own car or maybe another.

Walking up the lane with Bess the next morning Nathan met Hamish, who was in the mood for a chat. The two men leant over a field gate while Hamish brought him up to date with the estate news. "Arrr I'm having trouble with poachers taking me hares in th'night. Th'beggers hang a net under a field gate and work th'field with a good dog."

Not having seen that method of poaching, Nathan asked, "How

do you mean?"

"Well, when she's chased old Sara'll usually run out through th'gate but err' squeals like heck in a net so there'll be two of em." When Nathan looked puzzled he added, "One to work th'dog an th'other to deal with Sara."

"Anything else happening?"

"Missey cancelled th'Boxing Day hunt meet. Perhaps her'll let em come later?"

"They always turn out at the Hall on Boxing Day, do they?"

"Arrr, make a right mess on th'drive stomping around while they drink their stirrup cup," Hamish said with disgust.

"Are you not going to tell me what happened at the inquest?" Nathan asked.

"Arrr, what would yer' expect with th'top brass involved? Coroner said it wer' an accident."

"How do you mean – top brass involved?"

"Arrr, th'army, Whitehall, they're all same. They want their heroes buried as heroes. Mind you, that policeman didn't like it but when th'coroner asked him if he'd any evidence to say it weren't an accident he hadn't."

When Nathan looked puzzled Hamish added, "Arr,r it were obvious th'coroner had been told to wrap it up that day. He just said how snow must have covered some ice, which the Major slipped on, an th'gun went off!"

"You sound doubtful?"

"Arrr, well he wer' a hero, an' heroes don't shoot themselves, do they?"

Nathan, never having heard what had happened back there in the war to make the Major a hero, asked, "How was he injured?"

"Arrr, he threw himself on a senior officer to protect him and took the blast in his back."

"There was no medal though?"

"Arrr, well, yer' see there wer' some who said he wer' just trying to get away and fell on him. Anyway, it wer' a lucky fall cause that senior officer's now top brass an he's made sure th'Major's to be buried with honour, if yer' see what I mean?"

Nathan saw what he meant and also understood how Alexander had managed to get back into uniform and into Whitehall.

When Nathan explained that he wouldn't be at the funeral Hamish had more derision. "Arrr, our own folks should be putting him away not those regimental bigwigs. I reckon I'll still have t'wear me kilt though."

Nathan laughed and left him to go on his rounds.

A shaft of sunlight breaking through the clouds persuaded Nathan to walk towards the fallen trees he and Clem had trimmed up. As he walked nearer to them he was surprised to hear a steam engine. Rounding the next bend he was even more surprised to see his haulage contractor loading up the oak tree trunks. Both Clem and Bill were helping the two steam engine drivers.

When Nathan walked up they all gathered round him in jovial concern. He assured them that he was feeling much better and the hauliers in turn explained what they were doing. "I brought extra wire ropes, enough to winch the trees out without going off the road, but we've had to drag them along it to this wide spot to load them. You are just in time to watch us load up the last one."

"You must have already taken one load; when was that?"

"We did one yesterday and we spent the night on your office floor. Hope you didn't mind but we needed an early start."

The timber wagon stood on the lane, opposite a firm field gateway. The tree trunk had been dragged up onto the wide grass verge along the opposite side of the wagon. Two strong skids were in place to lead up from the tree trunk to the wagon. The power to load the heavy tree trunk was created by two chains that were already wound separately round and round each end of the tree trunk. Nathan watched as the steam engine manoeuvred into the gateway on the other side. The wire rope was pulled out from its winch on the back of the steam engine and passed up to Clem, who was balancing on top of the two trees already loaded. Clem in turn hung the rope down the far side for the other two men to couple it to the two chains, then the men all stood clear when the steam engine winch tightened on the chains. The action of the two chains unwinding off the trunk rolled it effortlessly up the skids and the heavy tree trunk thumped into place with a wagon-jarring bump.

Nathan walked home a contented man. Not only was his business progressing, he had two good men who could get things done without his constant supervision. He also had to admit that, apart from feeling a bit woozy at times, he had enjoyed these few days' relaxation and these long walks with Bess gave him time to think, time to reassess his life here at Hesston.

Taking the doctor's advice, he stayed away from the funeral.

Hetty though had been allowed to take the Friday off and she gave him a good description of the day. "The church was so packed with mourners that people were even standing round the walls. The six bearers looked funny the way they did a very short stepping march up the church and again after the service when carrying the coffin out to the grave. Young Mrs Wentworth-Jones was dressed in a long black coat and seemed very composed following the coffin, but Lady Louisa was distraught. One of the officers had to hold her arm while Mrs Wentworth-Jones held the other. There were a lot of uniforms about and three or four pale-faced men up from London." Hetty went on through the hymns, the eulogy and ended by describing how moving it had been when the trumpeter played the Last Post.

"Who else was there," Nathan asked.

"Those army men were a toffee-nosed lot and those London men were worse. They said nothing to anyone and soon went off back for their train. There were a good number of the 'gentry' there but I didn't know them. But it was a great day – most of the tenants were there and we all had a good gossip."

She also related more gossip later that evening: "And people kept asking where you were so I just told how the doctor had forbidden you to go. Most of them sent their best wishes."

"That's kind. Anything else I should know?"

"Well, two fatal accidents in one day in a sleepy little village has got people talking. They're a bit cautious as to what they say in front of me but there's a few questions about your part in the two deaths. In fact I overheard one say 'he's been seeing a bit too much of the Major's missus'." Nathan dismissed such talk with a shrug, which prompted Hetty to add, "That policeman was there, creeping about listening. I'm sure he would hear some of the talk."

"He does seem to be a bit suspicious about something so I expect he'll give me another call."

The next morning Nathan was surprised to find that Hetty wasn't up before him. He let Bess out, put a match to the fire and put the kettle on before strolling outside to join the dog. The bacon was sizzling in the pan when Hetty finally came down, complaining of feeling unwell. "Perhaps I'm starting with a cold or something. Make me a cup of my special?"

Hetty had her own mixture as a cure-all for both coughs and colds. When the fruit was ripe in summer she picked a large handful of yarrow leaves and five pounds of ripe elderberry fruit then simmered it with a pound of brown sugar until it was the consistency of honey. Strained and bottled, the mixture would keep for years. Counting aloud as he measured out two dessertspoons of mixture, one of honey and one of whiskey, Nathan chuckled as he poured on the hot water, "If it doesn't cure you at least you'll be ready for embalming."

"And I'll die happy," Hetty said as she took a sip.

William Brown picked Nathan up a little later in the morning as arranged. Nathan quizzed him about the funeral and about the mourners attending. If Mr Brown had heard any rumours he wasn't saying. He just told it straight, about the Regiment's arrangements, about the people he had met there and how well Rachel had coped.

At the garage William went to look at two or three second-hand cars while Nathan discussed the future of his car and was pleased it could be repaired and that it wasn't going to cost too much. The garage even offered to lend him a car while they did the repair.

When Nathan and the garage man walked round the corner, William Brown was looking at a nearly new but slightly battered Morris pick-up. "That would suit you nicely Mr Brown," the garage owner said hopefully.

"Maybe!"

"But Mr Brown, with this open back you can load a sack or two of hen food or an implement part."

"Maybe."

"I'll do a part exchange for your car if you're interested?"

Nathan smiled to himself as Mr Brown shook his head cannily then, without answering the garage owner, asked Nathan, "Do you need a lift back then?"

The garage man was still trying to do a trade "I was going to lend Nathan this pick-up but if you are interested in it I can lend him something else?"

"If Nathan's having it for a week or two then maybe I'll have a run in it sometime."

That seemed to put an end to any hope of a car sale that day so Nathan was allowed to drive away in his borrowed pick-up.

The temptation was to drive round to his timber yard but he knew if he did he would get too involved there. Instead he responded to another temptation and drove out towards Ruth's.

When Ruth met him at the door Nathan was taken aback by how good she looked. It was the first time he had seen her really dressed up. A calf-length tweed skirt with a close fitting knitted jumper revealed her very shapely figure while a brightly coloured silk scarf and a small feathery hat perching at a jaunty angle near the front of her head completed an outfit that combined to make her look years younger than when they first met. His scrutiny was cut short when she shyly slipped her arms round his neck and gave him a kiss. Taken aback he held on to her for a moment enjoying the feel of her in his arms and the firmness of her breasts against his chest. When she leaned back to look up into his face he kissed her again.

"Can I presume from that that you are fully recovered?"

He nodded an answer, "But I might still need nursing for a while yet."

"I think you get enough nursing as it is," Ruth replied perceptively. "And how's your knee?"

"I've still got a bandage on but the pain's gone now. I didn't expect you today. You see, I have some friends calling for me any moment now. We're going into Northwich to do some Christmas shopping." Nathan hid his disappointment by saying; "I'm just pleased to have caught you before you go."

"Why not come for lunch tomorrow?"

When her friend's car pulled up he accepted the invitation and left. He drove away feeling a tingle of excitement at tomorrow's prospects.

Later, after a pork pie and a pint in the pub, he called back at the cottage to check on Hetty. When she declared she felt much better he set off to visit Bill and Katie Brown. Katie said, "Bill's just walked back to the farm for the afternoon milking, but don't go away; stay and have tea with us."

"That's an invite I can't refuse but perhaps I should drive round there and do my stint of milking first."

It was an enjoyable afternoon. Nathan milked a couple of cows, had a chat to the rest of the Browns then motored back with Bill to enjoy the evening with him, Katie and their two young children. It was a relief to discover that the shadow of Hannah no longer seemed to hang over him. Although the memory of her was still very strong when he was with her family, it no longer felt like a knife carving into his chest. At the same time, playing with the two children reminded him just how much he wanted that same fulfilment within his own life.

He reflected on it through the following morning. Hetty was still feeling unwell so he did some housework for her before setting out across the fields with Bess. It had been two weeks since Hetty last slipped into his bed. In those two weeks, not only had two men died, but the death of one of them now freed the woman who again haunted many nights' sleep. Yes, he had woken again to find Rachel so real in his dream. In those dreams he was again kneeling between those long shapely legs on that leaf-strewn bank near the pond. This time, when he pushed Rachel back, he could feel her eyes willing him on. "All right," he told himself as he walked along the field hedge, "I didn't do it. I woke up! But there is neither man's law nor God's to stand between us now."

His thoughts were interrupted when Bess put a startled pheasant up out of some briars. Its cock-cock-cock alarm call reminded him that these were Rachel's pheasants and this was Rachel's land. There were acres and acres of it, plus lots more and a big Hall elsewhere. Did he want to be part of all that or did he want last evening's dream of a small cottage, a loving wife and two or three happy children?

It bothered him all morning, even as he drove out towards the schoolhouse. After his near perfect relationship with Hannah he had begun to worry if he would ever find that same intimacy with someone else. Two questions hovered in his mind: was he falling in love with Ruth or had he already he fallen in love with Rachel? And he wasn't sure of the answer to either question.

Over the meal Ruth told him a little more about herself. She had two brothers, the younger working for a farming uncle and the elder in insurance. Her father had been the village shoemaker who, when work was slack, had helped on local farms. Sadly he died of a heart attack just after Ruth's marriage. But Ruth's mother had been a dressmaker before her own marriage and now managed to support herself.

They talked on about Nathan's business, about the school and even touched onto politics. It was a very easy, relaxed discussion, which revealed to both of them just how much they had in common. After they had washed and dried the dishes Ruth suggested a walk. There was a brief interlude of sunshine to tempt them out but a biting cold wind made them don topcoats.

It was very companionable wandering down the lane together. Ruth, pointing out where different types of wild flowers grew in the season, told how she liked to bring the school children out on nature walks each week through the summer months. Leading Nathan over a stile to follow a path across the fields towards some ponds, again she explained what the children could see on their school outings.

"A blackbird nested in that bush. Two chaffinches scolded us as we walked past this bush but it was a couple of weeks before we saw the nest," Ruth said smiling and pointing through the leafless bush to a now very obvious bedraggled old chaffinch nest.

Sheltered from the worst of the wind in the lee of some bushes they leaned against the gate near to the ponds. "They are lucky children, to be brought out here to experience nature."

Laughing, Ruth said, "I don't have to tell them about the facts of life. It's happening all around them. Last spring I made them all sit on the hedge cop over there, intending to explain about the nesting and breeding season. There was a peewit displaying and calling overhead but what I hadn't realised was that his mate was sitting on the ground just about sixty yards in front of the children. Suddenly the cock bird swooped down and mated her. Well, the kids laughed their little heads off and I never did get to tell them what I'd intended to."

Nathan turned towards her as she also turned. The buttons were undone down the front of Ruth's overcoat so Nathan slipped his arm underneath it and round her waist. They kissed and kissed again until Ruth drew back and expertly undid his coat buttons, saying as she did so, "I can't feel you through this."

Each caressing the back of the other under their heavy topcoats, they held each other close. When Nathan's hands strayed lower he heard a gasp and felt Ruth's body drive against his. Despite his resolve not to rush things he couldn't help his response. For a few moments they pressed hungrily against each other until Ruth pulled back whispering, "It's been so long that I didn't know I could respond like this. Please don't rush me, Nathan, I've only ever had one man. And I want us to be sure before we do anything."

He kissed her gently and took hold of her hand to walk back towards the schoolhouse.

It was only on the return walk he realised from their conversation that Ruth was no longer the assistant teacher. When he asked, she said, "The Headmistress retired earlier this year so they gave me the job."

Chapter Twenty Five

On the day of the funeral everything seemed unreal to Rachel. Solemnly dressed in mourning black she went along with most of Major Fearnly's arrangements although the Army formalities irritated. And yet afterwards it all seemed to relate to someone else.

Although she tried hard to recapture the feeling of her earlier love and admiration for Alexander, it just would not come. All that she could recapture was the cold, inconsiderate side of him. Sitting in church she couldn't help hating herself for having tried to interest and arouse him in recent months, but what really nauseated her was that when Alexander had a last responded it was seemingly because of her inheritance into a title.

Lady Louisa was so heartbroken at the loss of her only son that Rachel found it hard to comfort her. From a tall, upright, dignified lady she had changed almost overnight into a frail and bitter woman. "Why couldn't you have given him a son?" she repeatedly asked Rachel accusingly.

Rachel couldn't very well say, "Well he was never here at the right time and anyway he only came to me about seven or eight times a year". No it was better to let Lady Louisa come to terms with her loss in her own way.

Lady Louisa continued with her bitter accusations: "Why did you not spend more time with him in London?"

Rachel replied, "That was how Alexander wanted it. When I suggested we took a flat there he wouldn't hear of it. Early in our marriage I wondered if he felt I wasn't good enough for his sophisticated London colleagues but he reassured me that it wasn't that and continued to dismiss the idea when I suggested it more recently."

Nevertheless, the funeral had gone well. She had to admit that the Regiment made it into a very dignified and moving occasion. Alexander would have loved all the pomp and ceremony. With the slow march and the haunting sound of the Last Post it had all been a fitting send-off. But she had felt strangely detached from it all.

Through the weekend after the funeral the strain continued. Lady Louisa, still bitter and withdrawn, would hardly speak to her.

Lucy was still very supportive, as she had been throughout the week, but on Sunday afternoon she and the Major left; he to attend to Regimental duties and she to sort out her staff for Christmas. Before they left, though, they had made Rachel promise to spend Christmas with them.

Monday morning had been kept free for the reading of the will. There were just Rachel and Lady Louisa sitting almost silently together in the back of the car while Bestwick drove them towards Knutsford. Lady Louisa's grief kept her quiet but Rachel's silence was from apprehension. She had become convinced there was some dark secret in Alexander's life that might be revealed this day.

At the solicitor's, the unsmiling Cuthbert senior joined his son Benjie in his more cheery office. It had been Cuthbert senior who had originally drawn up the will so he did the reading of it. There was a lot of legal jargon, part of which formalised Lady Louisa's allowance from the estate. There was a very pleasant surprise in that Alexander had a substantial life policy. Rachel had been led to believe that a serving soldier could not get life insurance but Cuthbert senior explained how, after Alexander went to work in Whitehall, he had managed to persuade one insurance company to cover him for a substantial sum. "Under the circumstances I should warn you, though, that there is a suicide clause in it."

Shocked at the implication, Lady Louisa said, "How dare you suggest such a thing? The coroner was quite clear that Alexander's death was a tragic accident. Anyway, he was too brave a soldier to ever do anything like that."

Rachel was aware of Benjie's eyes on her face but she remained silent. After a pause the senior Cuthbert cleared his throat before continuing, "We are not suggesting anything but in a tragic death, even though there has been an inquest; unless the insurance company is completely satisfied they may not pay up."

And that was it. No murky secrets revealed, just a straightforward tidy will. 'Unless it was suicide,' Rachel mused, but she kept her thoughts to herself.

Driving home again afterwards Lady Louisa broke the meditative silence by saying spitefully; "Well, at least you can't cut me off without a penny now!"

"Why would I want to do that? If, as time goes by, you feel that Alexander's stated allowance isn't enough, talk to me about it." Rachel's generous gesture was dismissed with a muttered, "Ohm."

After lunch Lady Louisa stated she would like to return home. When Rachel insisted that she was very welcome to stay longer, the old Lady replied, "There are too many memories here, too many ghosts in every room. I must go away to try to find peace."

***

On the Monday Hetty was still not well enough to go to work so, on his way to the yard, Nathan detoured round by the farm where Hetty worked to explain her absence.

At the timber yard every thing seemed to be in order. Even the staff had drawn their last week's wages. Grace had written it all down in black and white. A farmer had paid a bill in cash; she had paid the men out of it and left the surplus for him. Two large cheques for timber and one smaller one for a repair brought out a smile. At last he had money in hand and now his men were making use of the new timber to repair wagons there would soon be more. Yes, he really was in business now!

***

After a restless night, by Tuesday morning Rachel was determined to find out more about the relationship between Alexander and Mr Jonson. There was only one person with whom she could discuss it. She found Nathan working with his two men at the back of the building. They were using the gantry crane to lift one of his large oaks onto the saw bench. Stopping work to greet her, Nathan apologised for not attending the funeral. Rachel assured him that she understood and she was more concerned whether he should be struggling with heavy timber. When he gave a reassuring smiled she asked if they could have a longer talk.

"When?"

"Can you call round after work tonight?"

"I'm sorry, no. I've to go out to load up some trees from one site and then check on the work at the other. Anyway, Hetty's expecting me back at the cottage for a meal."

"I must talk to you before I go away on Thursday. Could you come tomorrow night perhaps?" Rachel asked hesitantly.

***

It was Wednesday morning before Nathan got into Knutsford to bank his cheques. Afterwards he rushed to do some Christmas shopping before the shops closed at one o'clock. Although Hetty had returned to work that morning Nathan had told her not to bother about his usual baggin bag, so when the shops closed for lunch he decided to relax over a substantial meal in the Fawn and Hound.

Returning to his yard later in the afternoon, he put in a couple of hours' work before it was time to go over to the Hall and see Rachel at six o'clock. First though he had to ring to explain to Ruth why he wasn't calling on her that evening as arranged. He was aware that Ruth seemed a bit quiet when he told her why.

With his collar, tie and new sports jacket on top of clean but slightly battered working clothes, Nathan had easily doffed them to get stuck into some work. Now, to visit Rachel he just brushed the sawdust off his waistcoat and trousers, clipped on his collar and tie, slipped into his jacket and drove his little pick-up right up to the Hall front door.

The parlour maid showed him through to the lounge where Rachel greeted him with a kiss on the cheek. She observed his workday trousers with an understanding smile. This was one of his traits that so appealed to her. He was a country craftsman going about his everyday business, proud of his position in life and finding no need to fawn or put on graces. They settled to chat about everyday affairs until the parlour maid announced, "Dinner is served, Ma'am."

Having dined in some imposing houses through his years in the timber trade, Nathan was well aware of protocol. Indicating a chair to him Rachel took her seat on the opposite side of a beautiful oak dining table. She had chosen a grey and black dress that contrasted with the paleness of her skin above the wide, round neckline. One of the mourning dresses bought after her father's death, she had worn it often enough to have been told many times how elegant and attractive she looked when wearing it. Nathan, although conscious of his gracious dining companion, was not abashed that under his new jacket his old tweed waistcoat and trousers looked rumpled and worn in comparison.

With a dish of soup placed before him he tucked his napkin into the front of his waistcoat and picked up his spoon. After the maid left the room he asked, "So what is it you want to talk about?"

"I am going away to morrow. I'll be staying with Lucy Fearnly for two or three weeks. They seem determined not to let me stay on my own here over Christmas and the New Year. Anyway, I wondered if you would keep an eye on things while I'm away?"

"You've got an agent and a good farm manager, what more can I do?" When he saw the pleading look in her eyes, he added, "Yes, of course

I will."

"I could make it an official position. I need to be able to talk things over with someone I can trust, someone who understands both farming and estate. Would you be interested?"

Nathan wasn't sure and said so.

They discussed the farm for a while, before eventually the maid came in for the dishes. Soon afterwards, Cook strode in with a sizzling hot pheasant followed by the maid carrying the vegetables. Because Nathan had got to know Cook quite well, he greeted her as a friend. Cook in turn chatted away to him and also to Rachel with no hint servility. While Cook was carving up the pheasant Nathan's eyes wandered around the oak-panelled dining room. The beautifully grained oak panels, reaching some six feet up each wall, were the work of a master craftsman. His expert eye told him how each panel had just been sawn out of a great oak tree, but to get that flecking in the grain the panels must have been cut at a slight angle across the grain. Done before powered saws were invented, a boy would have to lie on his back in the sawpit below the bottom end of the long crosscut saw whilst the second, senior, man worked balanced on top of the tree trunk above. He had done a bit of it when he first left school; with the sawdust falling on his upturned face the repetitive pull of the saw had been soul-destroying physical agony.

"That will be all right Cook, thank you. Yes, just leave the cheese on the table and go and have your meal."

"Thank you, Ma'am."

Nathan brought his mind back to the table as Cook left the room. Rachel must have noticed where his thoughts had been because she smiled and said, "It is beautiful, isn't it? Different people have remarked at the quality of these panels. Pour the wine out, will you, Nathan?"

When he put the bottle down she asked teasingly, "Now, tell me about this new girlfriend of yours."

He fidgeted with his knife and fork for a moment before meeting her eyes. "She teaches over at Lacksfield but she's hardly a girlfriend; I've only called on her about three times."

"You should know that among the locals three times is almost an engagement. I've met Ruth so I know how really nice she is."

Feeling uncomfortable with the conversation he remained silent until Rachel asked, "What is it about young widows men seem to find so attractive?"

"Perhaps you're about to find out."

It was Rachel's turn to feel embarrassed. "I keep forgetting. I find the whole experience so unreal. Lucy says I'm in shock but I don't feel that either. Perhaps it's that in recent years Alexander and I .... well, we'd drifted so far apart that I'd learned to live without him and now I can't mourn him. I mourn the memory of what we once had – how can love change to ....? Well, I think I was beginning to despise him."

When he looked a little uncomfortable, Rachel said, "I am sorry Nathan; I didn't invite you here to hear my moans but you are the only person with whom I dare express my thoughts."

The pheasant was delicious, the red wine, to Nathan's inexperienced palate, was equally good, 'but why am I really here?' he wondered to himself.

Rachel must have read his thoughts again. "Nathan, please tell me what you know about Mr Jonson and Alexander? I could see you knew more when I called in to see you. Can't you see I must know what it was all about?"

Nathan, half expecting this demand, had decided to tell her more. "I believe Mr Jonson had been blackmailing the Major but the Major was refusing to pay him any more."

"What was the blackmail about?"

"It seems that there was a murky past in your husband's family, perhaps to do with slavery."

"Oh that, but that was years ago. No one could blackmail Alexander over something his grandfather had done so long ago."

"Suppose it wasn't that long ago? Suppose it had carried on right up to his grandfather's death?"

When Rachel sat back in consternation he added, "In spite of the blockade, slaves were being shipped to the Southern States of America up to the end of the Civil War there, and that was only sixty-odd years ago. Who knows if they weren't traded in some Middle Eastern countries after that? Or if not slavery, what else was he involved in?"

"How do you know so much? Anyway, if what you suggest was true, who could know about it?"

Nathan, ignoring the first question, answered the second. "A relative perhaps?"

"There are no relatives. The Colonel did have an older brother but he was drowned at sea before Lady Louisa married Alexander's grandfather."

"Suppose he didn't drown but lived on? Maybe married and had a family? What was his surname?"

"Just Jones." As Rachel said it realisation hit her. "His son would be Jones's son, Jonson!"

They talked on about the implications, asking each other if someone could be blackmailed over a family's murky past that they had not been part of. In the end it was Rachel who said, "Maybe, if they were as vain as Alexander."

She stood up and leaned over the wide table to remove his plate. Then again, when she reached over with the cheese dish, Nathan couldn't help looking into the wide curve of her dress. Not that it was low, it was just that throughout the evening he had been aware of the creamy white skin below the nape of her neck. Now that he could see a little lower he couldn't help looking. Rachel caught his stare and answered it with an understanding smile. Perhaps the second glass of wine had loosened his tongue or something because he heard himself saying, "You are going to be one dangerously disturbing widow."

As her eyes held his Nathan's only thought was a desire to kiss inside the top of her dress.

Perhaps Rachel read his thoughts again because she began to attend to the cheese on her plate.

Leaving the dirty dishes scattered across the table, the two of them walked through to the lounge. Nathan couldn't resist saying, "There are some good things about living in a big house with lots of servants."

Nather held the lounge door open, stepped into the lounge and turned to close it. Turning back into the room he found that she hadn't moved away and his step back from the door put her right beside him. There had been so many restless nights when his body had yearned for hers; maybe it was the wine or was it that, in releasing his frustrations Hetty had also released his inhibitions? Which ever it was, he didn't hesitate but just slid his arm round her waist and drew her to him, surprised again at her height as her thighs pressed level with his and her lips were just below his. So he kissed them. They both drew back to look into each other's eyes before kissing again.

Rachel drew away and walked across the room to the drinks cabinet. Nathan's mind was still focussed on the sensual sway of her hips when she looked back to ask, "How do you like your scotch?" Then, seeing the lust in his eyes and feeling a sudden urge of wildness, she had to steady her hand to pour out the drinks before carrying them over to the large sofa. His eyes followed her every move. It was Rachel's turn to watch him walk purposefully across to sit next to her. Having seen his gentle side Rachel wondered whether she was ready to feel his masculine power. Was it only a couple of weeks since she seduced Alexander on this very same sofa? She couldn't believe that, with her poor husband in his grave but five days, she was about to take another man.

Nathan reached across to turn her face towards his. His kiss was gentle until suddenly Rachel felt a fire go through him. As his lips slid down her neck to touch the soft, silky skin, his fingers fumbling with the top button of her dress, they both heard the loud Dong! Dong! of the doorbell.

Within a moment the parlour maid was answering it. Picking up his scotch, Nathan jumped to his feet and moved to the big armchair near the fire. Rachel, patting her hair and smoothing out her dress, looked flustered when the maid knocked on the door to announce, "The Chief Inspector is here, Ma'am."

Brushing briskly past the maid the policeman said suggestively, "Ah, I've caught you both together at last."

Before Nathan could say anything Rachel went for the man, "How dare you burst in here with your snide remarks? I have the right to entertain whom I like and tonight Nathan and I have business to discuss."

Nathan sipped his scotch, musing to himself just what business they might have got round to discussing.

The policeman decided to placate her, "I'm sorry, I suppose that I was a bit hasty. I wanted to talk to you again."

"Could it not wait until morning?"

"Not when I heard that you are going away tomorrow."

Rachel, seeming to accept that, offered him a drink, which he refused. The Chief Inspector then asked about Alexander's insurance policy. Nathan listened to the questions and answers until a spark flew out of the fire. Flicking it back in with his fingers, he was aware of the Chief Inspector droning on but his mind began to wander. From the logs blazing in the large dog basket his gaze went up to the impressive mantle piece. That it was of a particular period there was no doubt but he couldn't remember which one. The large oil painting hanging above it was obviously an African landscape. Although the rocks and bush dominated the picture, the two spear-armed natives hunting through the bush on one side whilst a powerful lion sneaked away on the other had a forceful message. Knowing something of the old Colonel's African experience, he could see its meaning and why it took pride of place.

Letting his gaze travel round the other oil paintings he suddenly switched his thoughts back when he heard Rachel say, "We've just spent half the evening discussing the mysterious Mr Jonson."

"And what conclusions have you come to?" asked the Chief Inspector.

"None!" Rachel replied. "I can only presume he was someone from Alexander's past. Maybe they'd met in the War or something?"

Having finished both his scotch and his survey of the room Nathan realised that he had no place here. Not in this room, not in this Hall and certainly not with this woman. Jumping to his feet, he turned to the Chief Inspector. "If you've no questions for me then I'll be on my way."

The policeman said, "Just hold on a minute. I want to know what you've now remembered about this man Jonson."

"Nothing more than I've already told you. He was just a man of mystery to me." And seeing the look of relief at his discretion on Rachel's face, he said to her, "I've thought over your offer to act as some sort of official advisor and the answer is no. I'll happily keep an eye on things though while you're away and I'll always be about if you want to talk to me. I have to be able to work with your staff without them thinking that I'm watching them."

With that he walked towards the door. Looking back to bid them both a goodnight he saw an expression of surprise on the policeman's face but there was disappointment, even sadness on Rachel's.

Chapter Twenty Six

Feeling understandably restless as he drove away from the Hall, Nathan decided to call in at the village pub. It was not just because the Chief Inspector had interrupted his close encounter with Rachel. What also drew him was the fact that the pub landlord, although only licensed to sell drink consumed on the premises, would let him slip a bottle of stout into his pocket for Hetty. The usual mixes of locals were gossiping by the bar, among them Mr Ed and Gerald.

Both newspapermen came over to greet Nathan before Gerald, buying him a pint, pointed to a quiet table in the corner. "I think father expects me to get you tipsy, then worm some great secret out of you," a smiling Gerald explained.

"You keep buying the drinks and I'll think of a great secret for you."

"Seriously Nathan, is there any further development at the Hall?"

"In what way?"

"You know what way. We've two accidental deaths linked together and both are more than a little unusual."

Giving him a hard look Nathan said, "People have been accidentally shooting themselves since guns were first invented and as for motor cars – well, in the years to come when more and more people take to the road you'll probably have a page full of accidents each week."

They sparred around for a while until Gerald gave up and suggested that they both join in the general discussion by the bar.

***

The timber yard was a noisy place when Rachel called in on the way to take Digger out for his morning walk. From the scream of the saw, Nathan was obviously running one of his large oaks through the saw. Nevertheless she decided to try to have a word with him. Nathan pointed to the office and with the door shut she found that the noise was slightly muffled. He shouted an unnecessary explanation, "We're sawing out two gateposts."

The screaming noise stopped, which allowed her to speak above the duller chug-chug of the diesel engine. "I just wanted to thank you again."

"I haven't really done anything."

"Oh, you have! I suspect you've done more than anyone will ever know." When he stayed quiet she went on more shyly, "About last night, I ...."

Nathan butted in bluntly, "I was out of order. We live in different worlds. Much as we get on together I'm no more part of your world than you are of mine."

By then they stood a yard apart with eyes locked on each other. Rachel said, "It is too soon but ... " The sudden scream of the big circular saw drowned out the rest of her words. After a moment of hesitation she threw her arms round his neck and shouted in his ear, "I would have come to you regardless."

Feeling his arms tighten across her waist she, pressing upwards against him, said, "Have a happy Christmas," then, kissing him, she added, "Be kind to Ruth. The New Year will sort life out for all of us."

***

The day did not go well for Nathan. He had to stay longer in the yard than intended and then, when eventually he got out to one of the felling sites, the work to put on a load of timber for the furniture manufacturers was behind schedule. One slightly hollow tree needed a cheese sawing off the butt, and then another to get to solid timber. The brown stain running up the trunk above the hollow place made the tree more valuable but the buyer would only pay Nathan for the cubit feet of solid timber.

After that there was a lot of tugging chains about, hooking them on and off the large trunks and on and off the wire rope to the steam engine. The steam engine belched black smoke, the chains were covered in mud and Nathan had promised to call on Ruth on his way home. By the time the trunks were loaded it was dark so, leaving the others to tie the load down, he split the cut-off cheeses into logs.

Ruth was a bit quiet with him when he first got there but she brightened up with amusement when she saw the colour of his face and clothes.

Refusing her immediate invitation to wash and eat, instead he barrowed the logs into her coalhouse. When he finally sat down at the table, the rabbit pie was more than a little over done. Though she understood she was still quite reserved. He apologised again about not coming the night before and eventually asked, "What is it, Ruth?" Taking a while to answer, she said, "I don't pay a lot of attention to rumours but I am beginning to wonder just what there is between you and Mrs Wentworth-Jones?"

Nathan tried to explain about Hannah's friendship with Rachel, then about Rachel and the timber yard but it all sounded a bit incoherent, especially when Ruth asked, "And last night?"

When he looked a bit flustered she saved his embarrassment by asking, "Anyway, what did you wear to have dinner at the big Hall?"

"I wore just what I'm wearing tonight," Nathan replied with a broad grin, "only they were a bit cleaner last night."

"There can't be anything going on between you then," Ruth observed, surveying his dirty crumpled trousers, "if you went looking like that."

Looking suitably crestfallen, he said, "I've come looking like this tonight hoping there's something going on between us?"

A long look of appraisal passed between them after which her mood changed and the evening passed pleasantly. They even had a cuddle and exchanged a few kisses but it went no further. Although he could sense some excitement she kept it in check, which made him restrain his own desire.

Knowing that Ruth planned to travel home to spend Christmas and the New Year with her mother, Nathan went back to the car for her Christmas present. He had bought her a brightly coloured silk scarf and a bottle of the latest scent from Paris – at least that was what the girl in the shop had told him. "This is for you. Happy Christmas." When in return Ruth gave him a large, beautifully made parcel, he added, "I'm sorry about the wrapping; I was never good at tying parcels. Can I open this now?"

"No, you can't. We'll both open them on Christmas morning and think of each other then."

"I could drive over and see you."

"No, I'd rather you didn't or Mother would be jumping to conclusions."

While driving home afterwards he tried to analyse last night's mad, urgent response to Rachel against his cautious, restrained approach to Ruth. How could he get aroused almost beyond reason then and remain so calm tonight? 'Is it me?' he wondered. 'Is the memory of Hannah still so strong I can never find that kind of love again?' Perhaps the answer was in the two women; one had never known the real fulfilment of a loving partner and was desperate to find it. The other, having known it, so treasured the memory that maybe she now wanted to be sure it would be there again with someone else.

Pulling up outside the cottage he had but one positive thought: 'Well, at least I have over a week away from one and perhaps three weeks away from the other so maybe in that time I can sort out my muddled feelings.'

***

Knowing that the thrashing contractors were working at the Home Farm, Nathan walked along to the stack-yard to take a look. It was a nostalgic curiosity that drew him, because as a schoolboy he had often taken time off school when the thrashing contractor came to his father's farm. Getting up enough steam to drive both the big thrashing box and the straw battener took a lot of fuel. As a boy it had been his job to wheelbarrow loads of both logs and coal to the monster steam engine.

Expecting there to be a few rats bolting as the last of the wheat stack was thrashed; Nathan had left Bess shut in his office. Killing rats encouraged a dog to become hard-bitten whereas a gun dog, so as not to leave a tooth mark on the game it carried, must have a gentle mouth. Better to leave the rat worrying to the cowman's collie dog and his little terrier, which were both on watch when Nathan walked up. When two rats bolted at the same time the dogs split to chase one each. The little terrier killed hers with one crunching bite whereas the collie relied on a vigorous, lengthy shake to kill his.

It was a few years since last Nathan had stood by a working thrashing box. He listened to the rhythmic swish as strong arms drove a pikel into each sheaf and pitched it up onto the machine, followed by the extra hum as that sheaf, with its band cut, flowed evenly into the machine. Grain flowed out into sacks at one end of the machine whilst straw spewed out into a battener at the other. In between, clouds of dust billowed round where the waste chaff flowed into more sacks. Through that dust cloud Nathan recognised old Amos unhooking a full bag of chaff. He was a known local character who followed the thrashing machine for a living. While working at the Home Farm, Amos would rely on Mary for his food, spend each evening in the nearest pub and sleep through the night in the warm fodderbing in front of the cows.

Walking to where the cowman was helping bag up the grain, Nathan had a chat whilst he checked the sample flowing into each sack. Small weed seeds were collected in one sack, in the next came small or split grains whilst the good grain flowed into separate two-hundredweight sacks. None would go to waste; the weed seeds and small grain would be used by Hamish to feed his birds in the woods. Sacks of chaff would be carted and tipped on waste ground around the estate for both pheasants and small birds to pick through. Then when the thrashing machine moved on to the next farm this stack-yard would be full of finches and sparrows cleaning up the residue.

Joining Nathan, Robert explained why he was only thrashing two stacks now. He pointed with his short rat-killing stick to where the battener machine neatly tied the straight straw into long battens, and said, "I had to fill an order for some straight wheat straw for thatching. Then the local watermill desperately needs some oats for horse feed, which is why I've thrashed a stack of oats and another of wheat."

Both men sprang into action when three rats raced away from the stack at the same time. The two dogs chased one each which left one for Nathan and Robert. There was still plenty of boyhood excitement in both men, which is what got them in trouble. Having cut the rat off from going through the fence it dodged back round Nathan, who took a running kick just as Robert brought his stick down. Fortunately it was only a glancing blow but it had him hopping around for a few moments. He decided that, however nostalgic it might be watching the thrashing scene, it would be much safer back in his timber yard, so he left.

***

It was the night before Christmas Eve. Nathan was busy pumping water into a bucket to carry in to heat for their bath while Hetty finished preparing tea. There was nothing in the house to freeze up, no water pipes or tanks, just the old pump outside and they had lagged that. Hetty came out, wrapping a shawl round her shoulders against the night air. Watching him light the boiler fire she said, "I feel as excited as a schoolgirl. It's years since I had three days away from this house. The farm work always kept us here before. Are you sure you are going to be all right until I get back?"

"Yes, of course I am. Anyway, I shall be away for the first two nights myself," Nathan reassured her as they walked back inside together. "You have some fun with your grandchildren. And if I'm home first then I can light the fire and warm the house up for you."

"Hetty turned to look at him. "Home. Is this home to you?"

226

"Well, yes! You've made it a home for me."

"What about these two widows in your life? Which of them are you going to be with over Christmas?"

Laughing at the question, he said, "Just my old Mum and you. Anyway, I can think of three widows and they are all equally dangerous."

It was Hetty's turn to laugh out an answer; "Well seeing as you provide the firewood for all three of us you're sure to strike a spark somewhere."

Hearing Hetty moving about in her bedroom after her bath, Nathan came downstairs and placed her Christmas present, a shawl, on her chair by the fire. He then went out to take his bath. Back in the house afterwards Hetty was waiting to thank him. "It's lovely Nathan, you spoil me," she said, slipping her arms round his neck to give him a kiss. When he held her for a moment he felt her strong, lithe body press into his as she whispered, "You'll get yours upstairs."

***

Disappointed that his car had not been repaired by Christmas, Nathan had to make do in the little pick-up. Piling presents on the floor by the front seat and with Bess sitting regally by him, he set out on Christmas Eve. His first call was on Bill and Katie with a box of sweets for them, a penknife for young William and a small doll for Madge.

Leaving with an invitation from Bill to join him for a day's ferreting at Claybank farm as soon as was possible after Boxing Day, he reflected as to why he seemed closer to Bill's family than he did to his own brother and his family. That there was an age difference between his brother and him didn't account for all of it. Nathan sometimes wondered if his brother was frightened lest he might one day inherit a share in the farm. Or was it his sister-in-law who kept him at arm's length? Whatever the reason they had never been close, but even so he was looking forward to them joining him at his parents for Christmas dinner. Surveying the crudely wrapped presents on the car floor, he hoped fervently he had got one for everyone.

As it turned out Christmas Day was extremely enjoyable. Nathan's mother cooked a delicious goose, the children seemed pleased with his presents and even his sister-in-law was more relaxed and happy in his company. Afternoon milking as usual interrupted the men's day. Willingly joining in, Nathan took a three-legged stool and bucket up to a sleepy-looking cow. As he sat down on the stool someone called out, "Watch that one, Nathan", but they were too late. The sleepy-looking cow, rolling her eye and swinging her leg with practised skill, knocked him tumbling across the shippen floor. Fortunately, all the cow muck had been cleaned out and fresh straw put down just before milking time. Even so, it seemed to give the watching children more fun than any of their Christmas presents.

***

He had intended driving back to Hesston on the Boxing Day afternoon but instead he joined in the traditional day's ferreting with his brother and a neighbour. The rabbits bolted well and Nathan, shooting with a borrowed gun, shot his share.

The day ended at dusk but instead of driving back to Hesston in the dark he again helped with the milking then spent the evening with just his parents. In reply to his mother's persistent questioning about Rachel and the estate, Nathan finally told her about Ruth. That caused a flurry of excitement from his mother and a silent gleam of approval from his father.

An overnight frost made the early morning return journey a bitterly cold one. With a thick rug round his legs and wearing Ruth's Christmas presents of gauntlets and scarf he managed to keep reasonably warm while making good time on the dry roads.

Bill and Clem were waiting with Hamish when Nathan finally arrived at the keeper's cottage. The jill ferrets, muzzled to stop them killing and eating the prey, were ready in their box while the hob was in a separate compartment. As Nathan hadn't got a gun he offered to work the hob ferret, which would be used if the jills trapped a rabbit underground; then he would send the hob down.

The four men worked the ferrets along the many burrows in the big hedge-cops on Hesston Home Farm. Rabbits were not bolting as well as they had in Shropshire the day before. It wasn't long before two of the jill ferrets failed to re-emerge. Nathan presumed they had cornered a rabbit at the end of a large burrow. Tying the long, thin line to the big hob ferret's collar, Nathan released him down the rabbit hole. The theory was that without a muzzle the bigger hob ferret would drive the jills away from the rabbit and stay there himself, then he would then have to dig both rabbit and ferret out.

The theory worked well but it meant he had to dig several holes to follow the line to where the hob ferret held the rabbit. When he finally got there he was pleased to discover three rabbits hiding in the end of the one burrow.

In the meantime the other three men had moved on to the next set of burrows where a few rabbits were shot when they bolted. But again the jills had bottled a rabbit up in the end of a burrow deep below the hedge cop. Nathan put the hob down that burrow and began to dig again. By the end of the day he had done that several times. Although losing count of the number of holes he dug, the friendly rivalry from the other three shooting men plus the fact that he dug out more rabbits than they shot gave him an immensely enjoyable day.

Back at the cottage Hetty had the fire going when he returned. The two of them sat together close to the hot flames recounting their respective Christmases, when Hetty said, "Nathan I've got something to tell you that you might not like."

Nathan, smiling companionably, said, "Well try me."

"It's heavy work at the farm house and I've no security in this cottage so I've given my future a lot of thought. The result is I've taken a job away from here. It's a companion housekeeper position near to Knutsford. The old gentleman lives on his own but he has a cook and two maids living in. Other cleaning staff come in each day so hopefully I shouldn't do too much heavy work."

"It sounds just right for you. I don't blame you for looking for something else; you work too hard now and this cottage is too isolated. Anyway, I can recommend you as a really good companion," Nathan ended with a laugh.

Surprised he was taking it so well, Hetty asked, "But I go at the end of January. What will you do?"

Nathan resolved to give the matter some thought in the coming days. He would have time to think because Ruth wouldn't be back until after the New Year, and Rachel ....? Well there would be no tall, attractive and responsive Rachel tantalising him for another week after that. And what of Hetty? He realised he was going to miss her more than he had at first thought.

Rachel might be right though – the New Year might well resolve their futures.

Chapter Twenty Seven

Not being able to resist any invitation to do a day's beating on a neighbouring estate on New Year's Eve, Nathan found that the invitation extended into the evening. Some of the other beaters pressed him to join in their village New Year's Eve party. It went on a while making it well into New Year's Day when he returned to the cottage.

The next morning Hetty went to spend the day with her youngest son and his wife leaving Nathan with the early part of New Year's Day to himself. The woods and fields beckoned to both man and dog so he responded by taking a long walk across Hesston estate. It wasn't just for relaxation; he particularly went to check round the trees he and Clem were felling. How many were already down, how many more had they yet to fall and were they getting behind schedule?

Glinting on the hoarfrost, the early morning sun highlighted the tips of each tree branch creating a magical scene. To be out in the woods on such a morning was pure enjoyment. Such was his pleasure that, after taking a tally of his trees, he walked on to take a circular tour of the estate. It seemed strange to walk through these woods without meeting Rachel or at least seeing her tall, graceful figure striding through the trees.

Invited to have tea with Bill and his family later in the afternoon, he cooked a simple fry-up for lunch and followed it with a snooze in front of the fire before setting out again. Knowing that Bill would have gone to help with the milking at Claybank Farm before tea, he drove round to the farm to give a hand there first.

Hand milking was time consuming but it was not physically arduous. Spending much of his day on his own he enjoyed the comradeship of working in such a group. And it was good to now be able to go back to Claybank without being overwhelmed with grief over Hannah.

William Brown was more interested in the pick-up than he had let on at the garage. After milking, the Browns all gathered round it discussing its possibilities. Then, at Nathan's suggestion, Bill lifted his bicycle onto the back and jumped into the driving seat.

Taking a circular route round the country lanes gave Bill the chance to try it out. Bill, though, changed the subject: "I told you I thought of applying for the tenancy of a farm on the next estate. Well, I've got it. There's still a couple of details to finalise but, subject to them, I become life tenant of my own farm on Lady Day."

"I'm pleased for you and Katie. Is she keen to go?"

"Oh, yes. We wouldn't be going if she wasn't. We're both ready for the challenge."

"Well, when you move in if I can be of help just say the word."

Over tea the buzz of excitement in the family was infectious; even the children were brimming over with the plans for moving to a new house and farm. Wishing them well, Nathan again promised to give them a helping hand when they took possession in the spring.

The first week in the New Year looked as though it would be much like those in the last year at the timber yard, either working in the yard with his men or driving out to supervise his two tree-felling gangs. The one difference was that he knew which day Ruth would be back in her schoolhouse and organised his day around that.

When that day eventually came it was an emotional reunion but as usual Ruth held herself in restraint. Having known the warm response of Hannah and recently feeling Rachel's urgent need, Nathan began to wonder if Ruth lacked that physical fire. He did, though, enjoy a pleasant evening with her exchanging Christmas stories about their respective families. Eventually, when they snuggled down together on Ruth's small sofa in front of the fire, she kept Nathan firmly under control.

***

The following week Chief Inspector Shawby came into the timber yard a little more hesitantly than when he had barged in on Rachel and Nathan at the Hall before Christmas. Even so, the policeman's observant eyes seemed to miss nothing. Perhaps, though, the Chief Inspector was not so sure of himself among the noisy machinery. Nathan led him into the office before asking, "How can I help you?"

"You'll be pleased to know that we have traced your Mr Jonson. It would appear he was a cousin of Major Wentworth-Jones. Although we've still to get absolute proof of that, we are now satisfied that his surname was Jones and he came from Argentina, where his father had been a successful merchant."

When the policeman paused Nathan said, "You've soon found

all this out. The last time we met you knew nothing about him."

The Chief Inspector gave one of his rare smiles before replying, "Oh, I wouldn't say that; it doesn't do to reveal all we know. We had already found some of his papers in a hotel safe and since then we've discovered more but we're still waiting for more information from Argentina. Anyway, the coroner is happy to resume the inquest; hopefully then the body can be released for burial. We need you to attend that inquest next Friday."

A little excitement came into the week's work on Hesston Home Farm when Robert brought in some steam engine contractors to plough. Owned by two brothers, the two steam engines stood at opposite sides of the field and long wire ropes winched the three-furrow plough back and to between the engines. They moved forward after each pass of the plough. One brother handled his steam engine on his own whilst his assistant sat on the plough to steer it and control the depth. A disgruntled Joe Candy was left to plough the difficult headlands with his horse team after the engines had moved on to the next field.

Nathan saw the long wire ropes stretching across the field and thought of his timber lying deep in the adjacent woodland. After a dinnertime stroll round the fallen timber with the older brother, Nathan had an agreement for them to 'snake out' his timber when the ploughing season was over.

Sharing a Friday hotpot tea with Robert had become a weekly ritual. Over it Robert was explaining how, with one waggoner short, he had no other choice but to bring in contractors to catch up with the ploughing. He then asked, "What do you think about tractors?

"I've never had anything to do with them," Nathan replied.

Robert's face lit up with enthusiasm. "Marshall's stopped building steam engines last year; they're now just making tractors. Maybe I should employ a tractor driver instead of a waggoner."

They discussed the merit of that idea and the changes it could bring to farming until Robert said, "Forget about tractors. I'm getting married in a fortnight!"

To Nathan's congratulations and queries Robert explained, "It will have to be at the Methodist Church because Natasha's father stopped the banns being read in the Parish Church. Now he's refusing even to come to the wedding. Anyway, will you be my best man?"

***

The inquest on Mr Jonson was fairly straightforward. Nathan's evidence was not questioned too deeply; it was accepted that death was accidental and he was soon on his way home again.

On Saturday afternoon he drove Ruth into town to shop. When not actually purchasing they were shop window gazing, discovering each other's tastes and fancies. After afternoon tea in a charming little restaurant they drove back in time to attend a village concert in Lacksfield.

Both had introduced the other to one or two friends throughout the afternoon. By evening Nathan had got used to the occasional raised eyebrows or knowing smile, though from among Ruth's friends there were also one or two searching looks, but Ruth's delightful company made up for any embarrassment.

***

For Rachel Christmas and New Year had been a strain. Not that the Fearnlys' hadn't try to keep her occupied or were not understanding, it was more that she had a dreadful feeling that she should be in deeper mourning than she was. Although at times managing to feel some grief when she remembered the coldness of her marriage her sense of relief was so great that it was difficult not to burst into song, or even dance round the room.

It was strange to be away from Hesston Hall and the estate although she often thought of her staff and of Nathan. Through the last few months she tried to analyse her response to him without success. She sometimes wondered if it was just that, having seen Nathan's tender love for Hannah, she selfishly wanted to experience it herself. Was it now love? Or was it an unfulfilled physical need that made her desperately want to feel and hold a virile, attractive man?

The Fearnlys' home was quite small compared to where they normally entertained on shooting weekends. Even so there was room for the Fearnlys to invite a few friends to visit or to stay while Rachel was with them. In turn she had accompanied them on visits to their friends.

On two or three occasions she had been in the company of one of the Major's fellow officers, a handsome, rather dashing Captain Dewson. As they were the only two unattached among the guests, Rachel and the Captain naturally drifted together. The Captain both attentive and a good listener, and he didn't force onto her.

On the morning of the second day of the New Year, after Captain Dewson stayed overnight at the Fearnlys', he and Rachel took a walk while their hosts were going about their duties. Walking companionably side by side through the fields on a dry but cold morning, they stopped to watch a group of carrion crows arguing among the top branches of a nearby tree. The Captain suggested it looked as though one of the crows had transgressed and the rest were holding a court martial. While standing still they also noticed a group of woodpigeons searching among the fallen leaves under the bare oak trees, no doubt for the remains of last year's acorn crop. It was that kind of morning when she really felt at one with the outdoors.

Rachel strode happily along with the Captain until coming to where a team of horses, just two small fields away, were steaming in the cold air from the effort of pulling a plough. The gallant Captain spread his coat on a convenient hedge bank, inviting Rachel to sit by him.

It soon became plain that watching horses ploughing was not the uppermost thought in his mind. The suppressed feeling of gaiety at her new freedom broke through her inhibitions and recklessly she responded to his kisses and then his caresses.

Afterwards she realised she had wanted to be seduced, to experience something that had never really happened in eight years of marriage, but because her thoughts had been on another time and another man the episode left her feeling empty and sad.

Taking place less than a month after becoming a widow, that brief flirtation left her with a determination not to seek cheap thrills again. Promising herself that from now on risky, wild sexual encounters would be out she decided to return home immediately. The dilemma of how to explain her sudden departure to Lucy was resolved when Rachel rang her solicitor.

Benjie was a little more business-like than usual. Perhaps he now realised that the goose he had thought would lay a golden egg may not lay one after all because he said, "Mrs Wentworth-Jones, I'm afraid I have bad news for you. An heir to your family title has been ˑ he was traced some weeks ago but somehow that ˑ to the people over here."

'o the people here?"

is already on route to England.

ˑe to establish his credentials."

Rachel heard none of it, she

just felt a wonderful sense of relief. Hearing this news made her realise just how much she had been dreading inheriting that title. Only a few days before, the Major and Lucy had persuaded her to go with them to visit the estate and Great Hall she was supposedly inheriting. Under duress she allowed them to drive her right up to the ornate iron gates. Fortunately, the fact that the gates were closed gave her time to think. She smiled remembering how she had got out of the Major's motorcar, gazed up the drive between the two long lines of lime trees for a minute or two before getting back in and demanding to be taken home. Pointing out the beautiful Hall set in acres of sweeping parkland, Lucy pleaded with Rachel, "At least take a look at it."

"It isn't mine yet! It may never be mine."

With that, Major Fearnly reluctantly drove to the nearest hotel where Rachel treated them to a luxury lunch before returning home with no more talk of the possible inheritance.

Something Benjie said on the telephone finally registered, ". ... be at Hesston today."

"Who'll be at Hesston today?"

"Randolph De Courcy, your cousin. I've just explained that he seems worried about how disappointed you must feel and wants to meet you."

Rachel was more disappointed that she wouldn't there to greet him. It would take most of the day for Bestwick to drive over to collect her and take her back to Hesston. Telephoning home with instructions for Bestwick to start out immediately, Rachel also instructed Cook on how to welcome this unknown cousin. Still not satisfied that this new cousin would be persuaded to wait until she returned, she made another telephone call.

***

Nathan was busy going through the paperwork with Grace when the telephone rang. He heard Grace saying, "Good morning, Ma'am .... Yes, he is, Ma'am," before passing the telephone over to him.

Exchanging the usual friendly greetings they inquired how each had enjoyed their Christmas before Rachel mentioned the unexpected visitor coming to the Hall. "I don't know what time I'll get back but it could be late. Would you mind going over to the Hall to look after him?"

Relieved that neither Ruth nor Hetty was expecting him for a meal that night, he replied, "I can keep an eye open for a strange car and wander over there for a chat with him if that helps?"

He could sense the gratitude in Rachel's reply, "Thank you! I'll ring Cook to expect you."

Nathan chatted on for a few moments but as Rachel could tell him almost nothing about her New Zealand relative he became more intrigued to meet the man.

In the timber yard they were tidying up at the end of the day when Cook rang to say the visitor had arrived. Brushing the sawdust off his trousers, Nathan donned his tidy jacket and drove over there. Cook met him at the door, whispering conspiratorially that she had served afternoon tea in the lounge and invited Nathan to follow her through.

A tall, gangly man jumped up to greet Nathan with a powerful handshake and a sincere smile on his weathered face. Introducing Nathan to Randolph De Courcy, Cook left him to explain why he was there instead of Rachel. Nathan's explanation was almost ignored under a barrage of questions about the Courtney family. He tried to get a few questions in of his own but Randolph (as he insisted Nathan call him) just wanted to hear about Rachel. Explaining about Alexander's death and also about Thomas, Nathan told what he knew of Rachel's family background. His cup of tea was almost cold before Randolph apologised and let him pause to enjoy it.

While he tucked into one of Cook's delicious cakes Nathan listened to Randolph De Courcy explain in a strongly accented but cultured voice a little of his own background. His grandfather, who it would appear was also Rachel's grandfather, had lived in South Africa but returned to England leaving his grandmother and their young son out there. Reading about New Zealand, the boy became fascinated with the country, so when his mother died Randolph's father, by then a grown man, travelled to New Zealand at the first opportunity.

Randolph went on to explain how his father became involved with the timber trade there and eventually married and started his own timber exporting business. Following the line of giant Kauri trees as they were felled and the land cleared on New Zealand's North Island, his father moved north across the island until finally settling his (by then) substantial timber business in Northland. Although Randolph worked in the timber business for many years, he chose to start farming when he married. He now farmed much of the land his family had bought and cleared timber off.

Nathan had time to study the New Zealander while he talked and he like what he saw. This tall, slightly stoop-shouldered man, who looked about forty years old, was soon showing photographs of the lovely white-painted veranda running round his home, more faded black and white shots taken in his garden and then of the giant kauri trees that had once grown extensively over the Northland. Even seeing the photographs Nathan just couldn't believe the size of those trees. "They can't be that big, can they?" he asked in amazement. Smiling, he showed Nathan another photo where he stood by the trunk of the largest tree ever to come into his father's yard.

"That tree was eighteen foot in diameter," Randolph said, pointing to his own small figure dwarfed by the massive tree trunk. "I've heard of some even larger."

The parlour maid discreetly knocked on the door to invite them in to dinner. Nathan hadn't realised how quickly the time had passed by, nor had he expected to stay for dinner. But when he protested the maid explained that her mistress had telephoned again to say she would be very late and that they must eat without her.

It was a most enjoyable hour. Cook had prepared an excellent meal and Randolph was the most interesting of dining companions. When the two men finished their meal they moved back to the lounge where Nathan, already having told Randolph about his own modest business, agreed to show him round the timber yard in the morning.

Rachel burst into the lounge full of apologies and bubbling with the excitement of meeting Randolph. Nathan got a peck on the cheek and the briefest 'thank you' before the Courtney and the De Courcy were exchanging their family history. Excusing himself, Nathan headed for the door.

Rachel was so fascinated with Randolph that it took a minute to register Nathan's departure. When she did she ran after him and, catching him by the front door, called, "Nathan, wait!"

Pushing the door to again he turned back to face her but she suddenly felt shy. Although she wanted to explain what a fool she had been a day earlier in Shropshire and how she had been wrong these last few months to flirt with Nathan the words were not there. Instead she awkwardly shook his hand and wished him goodnight and walked back into the lounge where Randolph was up on his feet looking at the African picture. Turning to Rachel with a gesture round the room he said, "So this is the estate grandfather bought with his share of the diamonds?"

When Rachel looked completely bewildered, he said, "Did you not know he had a partnership in a small diamond mine out there? When Grandfather left Africa his partner paid him out in diamonds, then he and my grandmother divided them out between them. My father used what was left of Gran's to set up his timber business in New Zealand. And I'd presumed from what Dad told me that Grandfather returned home to replace the estate his family had lost over here."

Stunned by the implications of his statement, Rachel said, "No! This was my husband's estate; my father was just the steward here. From what little I was told, when Grandfather came back from Africa he just took over the one farm left over from what had been a large estate. He did invest something in the farm but even so, my parents were not at all wealthy. Come to think about it, I do now remember my own father saying something about Grandfather being robbed on the way home."

They talked for a while about the seemingly lost diamonds before Rachel asked, "Why didn't your grandmother come with Grandfather to England?"

"Oh, she was born in South Africa and just wouldn't move. Anyway, from what Father told me his parents were not really happy together. In fact I sometimes wonder if they were legally married because before Grandfather left Africa Gran made him sign before a notary of law as to who he was and that my Dad was his legal heir."

"How do you mean, you wonder if they were married?"

"There's no record of either their marriage or for that matter their divorce but that doesn't mean that both did not happen. Things were a bit primitive in South Africa in those days."

Rachel, realising the implications, laughingly said, "If there was a marriage but no divorce where does that leave me?"

Randolph responded to her humour with, "If there was no marriage in the first place where does that leave me? Anyway, even without a marriage certificate the lawyers here seem to be prepared to accept that, from all the documentations I brought with me, I am the legal heir."

Chapter Twenty Eight

The excitement of meeting her newly discovered cousin kept Rachel up chatting with him into the early hours. As a result she overslept and came down late to discover that Randolph had finished his breakfast and left to visit Nathan's timber yard. Glad to have someone to cook breakfast for, Cook had prepared an inviting range of food for her guest. Rachel decided to enjoy the spoils in a more leisurely but extremely filling breakfast.

She couldn't answer Cook's questions, however, as to how long her guest might stay or even which meals would be taken in the Hall. Leaving her staff to worry about that she donned warm clothes and set out with Digger. At the timber yard Clem told her that the New Zealander had gone with Nathan to fall a tree.

After a longish walk across several fields the sound of an axe drew Rachel towards the felling site. Stepping between the trees, she saw the smoke from the campfire before she saw Randolph and Nathan at work. With coats discarded and shirt sleeves rolled up the two men were completely engrossed in chopping the wedge out of a large oak that would give it the direction of fall. Rachel paused unseen to watch. As each man swung his axe in alternate strokes, she was amused to see the rhythm begin to speed up. It wasn't possible to tell which of them was pushing the tempo but it was obvious they were trying each other out. The taller, gangly New Zealander was surprisingly matching the lithe, graceful movements of Nathan's work-honed physique.

Suddenly the cut was completed and the two men straightened up to smile respectfully at each other. She walked forward. "I see the kettle's boiling so if you two have finished playing boyish games perhaps there's a cup of tea on."

The formalities of brewing up quickly over, both Nathan and Rachel were soon questioning Randolph about timber in his country. With a battered tin mug in his hand he explained how they built a platform round the large kauri trees to enable them to be cut off where the trunk was thinner some ten foot up. Nathan said, "Well, I want all of this tree so it's time we got down on our knees to cut as near to the ground as possible."

Rachel watched muscles ripple again as the two men, each down on one knee, drew the long crosscut saw back and forth through the hard oak. Both jumped back when a ringing crack signalled the end of a great tree. At first the movement in the top of the tree was hardly discernable, then it speeded up and she felt the violent bounce from the shock wave when the heavy tree crashed to the ground.

Grinning boyishly, Randolph said, "Hey, that was fun but I think I'll stick to farming."

Rachel was amazed as to how easily Randolph seemed to fit into her country life. On the walk back towards the Hall the three of them chatted amicable until Nathan left them at his yard. Then Randolph said, "Now let's go see these horses."

With the two horses nuzzling their outstretched hands over the fence, Randolph asked, "Why do you not ride?"

When Rachel explained about Alexander and riding sidesaddle, Randolph said, "Well that's in the past now. If I get them in and groom them can we ride out tomorrow morning?"

"Do you ride a lot?"

"There are just two mornings each week when I have to go into the office; other than those I ride round some part of the farm every morning."

"How big is the farm?"

"Oh, between three and four thousand acres, quite a lot of it still covered with tree stumps."

Rachel asked, "And what kind of business is it that you and your brother run together?"

"It's a bank. My father started it for his loggers when the area was remote from civilisation. Now civilisation has caught up with us we have branches in three different towns. We do alternate days in the office and then meet together each Friday afternoon. The farm and timber businesses are completely separate from the bank and, for that matter, from each other."

***

Nathan watched Rachel walking towards the stables with Randolph the next morning. Although her riding breeches may have been a good fit in her late teens, now, from where he stood, they revealed a little more than they had then.

***

Ruth declined to come to the funeral with him, explaining that she had never met Mr Jonson, or was it Mr Jones? Donning his dark suit Nathan drove over to the cemetery on his own.

With the Chief Inspector looking on from a distance there were just Rachel, Nathan and Randolph to hear the vicar's mumbled committal at the graveside. Nathan smiled sadly, aware that of the three mourners one of them had not known Mr Jonson and the other two had not liked him. Even so, it seemed sad to see the soil pushed on top of a man without one person there to really mourn his passing.

After the funeral Nathan would have gone about his business but Rachel insisted that Cook had already prepared a funeral lunch for the three of them. During it Randolph told them more about his life in New Zealand and how, after tragically loosing his wife, he was bringing his ten-year-old daughter up on his own. Nathan wondered if, with a nursemaid and several servants to help, the 'on his own' bit was strictly true.

Although interested, Rachel seemed quieter than usual until Randolph told them that he had already planned his trip here to look for a suitable school for his daughter. Then she was soon discussing the merits of different schools. As the meal came to an end Randolph, perhaps sensing some undercurrent between the other two, tactfully asked to be excused coffee in the lounge.

In the lounge Rachel turned towards Nathan just as she had done that night before Christmas. He noticed with a jolt that she was even wearing the same grey and black dress. It was those buttons he was fumbling with when the doorbell rang. This time though there wasn't the same electricity between them. She broke the silence: "I'm not going to ask what happened between you and Mr Jonson that night in the snow. Whatever you did I think that perhaps you did it for me. Anyway we've now buried the man and with him I felt I was burying a whole lifetime. Now I feel ready to begin a new life so I just want to thank you again for all your support."

With that she stepped close and, with one hand on each shoulder, kissed him gently on the cheek. Nathan, whose memory of this dress on that heady night had been fuelled by his recent view of those over-tight riding britches, slipped his hands round her waist just a little lower than perhaps he should have. This time, though, there was no thrust of response. Rachel just held his shoulders and gazed into his eyes for a long moment then, giving him another peck on the cheek, said, "Anyway, there's a small gift that I'd like you to have. It's through here."

Following her down the corridor into the gunroom Nathan was surprised when she indicated the gun rack and said, "I've no use for them now, although I may keep one just in case I have a guest who might like to shoot. You told me some time ago you were thinking of buying a gun. Now you don't need to."

Looking at the two twelve bore shotguns standing side by side in the rack and seeing immediately that, although not a matching pair, they were both very expensive guns he said, "No, I can't take one of those! If you don't want them you must sell them."

"It will give me more pleasure to know you have one than selling it to a stranger."

After his further protests were firmly dismissed Nathan came away with his choice of gun and several boxes of cartridge. Rachel called after him; "You can try it out on Saturday because we're having a tenants' shoot."

***

Robert and Nathan had booked a table at the Fawn and Hound to entertain their respective ladies that evening. Nathan decided to stay in his suit and attend to some business in town before picking Ruth up at the schoolhouse.

The two girls had not met before so it was meant to be an opportunity for them to get to know each other before the wedding. Noticing how Ruth was very sociable with both Jasmine and Robert but a bit quiet with him, Nathan wondered about it. Later, when the two ladies retired to the cloakroom, he mentioned Ruth's attitude to Robert who laughed and said, "Perhaps it's that strange perfume I got a whiff of when we shook hands earlier. I know it wasn't Jasmine's and I'm fairly sure it wasn't Ruth's, then you go blabbing on about a gun you've had given to you. Perhaps Ruth thinks you've some explaining to do."

But Nathan knew that he couldn't really explain to Ruth the desperate sexual drive that had almost consumed him after Hannah's death. Nor could he explain the thoughts that had flashed through his mind that very afternoon when for a brief moment his hands had been on another woman's hips. Or that only a few weeks earlier if the Chief Inspector hadn't barged in he might have .... well, anyway, he knew he just couldn't explain all that to Ruth.

At least Ruth had entered into the spirit of the wedding plans with Jasmine. Later, on the way back to the schoolhouse, she told him a little more about the wedding. "Did you know that Jasmine's mother has secretly paid for the wedding dress even though her father won't let her attend the wedding?"

When he steered his car down the country lane without replying, she continued, "It's good of your friend Rachel to hold a reception at the hall for them. It's a shame, though, that there will not be more guests." Relieved to hear Ruth chatting away in a more relaxed manner he said, "Yes, I suppose it is and she's taking trips out to help her cousin choose a school for his daughter."

With a touch of irony Ruth said, "But Rachel isn't really his cousin is she? With different grandmothers they are more like half-cousins!"

Nathan took a few minutes to digest the implications of that.

***

Hamish called in at the yard later in the week to explain about the shoot. "Arrr, there's too many birds left, an Missey does'na want a proper shoot but err'd like that New Zealand feller to have a go, so err's having a tenant's day."

Which was a long sentence for Hamish but it said it all.

Of Rachel Nathan saw but little. She called in at the yard one morning when she and Randolph were on the way to the stables to take the horses out. She told him a little about their planned visits to various schools and explained, "Randolph is staying over the weekend for the tenants' shoot and then, if you don't object, we may go away for a few days to visit schools further down country."

"It's not for me to say if you should go or not, is it?" Nathan replied, but Rachel just looked at him searchingly.

***

A strange mixture of local people gathered on a keen, frosty morning for the tenants' shoot. Some wore ties and smart tweed jackets while others had come straight from the shippens, with the tell-tale cow signs on their clothes to prove it. The mixture of assembled dogs was even more interesting, the pure bred spaniels being outnumbered by a variety of mongrels and one collie. Hearing its farmer owner claim that his dog could find pheasants better then any spaniel, Hamish muttered, "Arrr it can that. I've bin trying to catch the swine at it for months now."

Hamish organised the guns into two parties; he would lead one and Nathan, who had already been asked, would look after the other.

The idea was for half the tenant farmers to stand as waiting guns while the other half, acting as beaters, drove the pheasants towards them. Then each group would change roles for the next drive. No one took it very seriously, which was just as well because most of the dogs were out of control and some of the farmers got completely out of line when they were beating. At different times there were two vicious dog fights among the line of waiting guns, and each time the farmers found the dog fight more fun than shooting pheasants.

Randolph joined in with the company in complete ease. Nathan liked the man more each time they were together. The New Zealander had a bit of trouble understanding the broader Cheshire dialect but then some of the locals found him equally hard to understand.

Back at the Hall for the midday break Cook had heated up a large pan of potato hash, which was brought out to the gunroom where a few chairs had been placed inside and some extra garden seats put just outside. Rachel sat out there among her tenants and laughed more than most about the morning's sport. One joker was suggesting they should forget about the pheasants in the afternoon and take bets on the next dogfight.

Randolph held them enthralled with tales about New Zealand. The farmers wouldn't believe Randolph when he told them he'd never before seen ground so frozen it wasn't safe to ride a horse on. The next few nights of hard frost gave Nathan the chance to get the steam engine across the fields to his furthest felled timber. It was a busy week during which he only visited Ruth once.

Hetty became withdrawn and worried lest she was making a mistake in taking her housekeeping position. Reassuring her as best he could, Nathan understood just how hard it was for her to leave the home where she had spent so many happy years.

The days passed by quickly. Only planning to take a small writing bureau with her, Hetty let her children choose from the rest of the furniture. Nathan, now granted temporary tenancy of the cottage, bought what was left, which were just his bed, the kitchen table and two dining chairs. As he still had the kitchen utensils and a few other things from his own cottage he knew he could manage for a while.

On the Friday night before the wedding he carried in the water and lit the outside boiler as usual. Now through her doubting period Hetty was full of girlish excitement about her move. With all her personal things gone or packed into boxes ready for her son to collect both them and her in the morning, they made use of Nathan's kitchen utensils for supper and breakfast.

To his surprise Hetty also made use of his bed through the night, which was something that hadn't happened since Christmas. One minute she was his lover and the next worrying like a mother at the thought of him being left to manage on his own.

In the morning he said, "Right Hetty, I'm off to work. Take care and if ever you need anything just let me know."

Hetty shed a tear or two before managing to say, "You too. Now go and marry that young widow."

"Which young widow do you mean?"

"The one that you love .... and you should know which one that is."

***

Later that morning when Nathan returned from work the cottage seemed silent and lost without Hetty. Finding the fire nearly out he made do with a cold cheese butty before changing ready for the wedding.

Considering there were only fourteen guests in the chapel Nathan noticed that among them were two very attractive ladies. Rachel, wearing a stylish mourning outfit, looked ravishing but he was more surprised by Ruth, who wore a blue and cream two-piece dress, or was it a suit? He wasn't sure. Anyway, it and the cream hat contrasted against her black hair to such startling effect that he found it hard not to turn round to look while he waited with the groom in front of the altar. Then he had to switch his mind to the business at hand when Jasmine's uncle, in defiance of her father, walked down the aisle with the bride on his arm. The bride looked absolutely beautiful, and not only had this one uncle come to give Jasmine away but his daughter was the bridesmaid.

Back at the Hall the large dining table had been extended and Cook was in her element providing for a real wedding banquet. Even old Greebs had come for the day to act as toastmaster and pour the wine in his dignified but noticeably more unsteady manner. Photographs out on the lawn took some time because each time the photographer got behind the camera someone would crack a joke and their frozen pose would dissolve into laughter. Eventually they all manage to stand still long enough to satisfy protocol. Later Nathan even made a short speech among the informal proceedings.

Much to Robert's pleasure, their oldest son had brought down Robert's uncle and aunt from the hills of Derbyshire. Always grateful to this hardworking couple that had cared for him from an early age, it would have spoiled his day had they not been there. After the uncle, in his broad Derbyshire country accent, proposed the health of the young couple Randolph was heard to say, "I couldn't understand a word of it." Everyone laughed because the Derbyshire people couldn't understand what Randolph said either.

Not knowing many of the guests, Ruth joined in the conversation round the table to great effect. Nathan noticed how she had the knack of getting others to talk. Later he heard her say to Randolph, "Perhaps when you've finished looking at boarding schools you might come to mine to talk to the older children about New Zealand?"

"We have to be back before next week end," Rachel explained, "because the hunt is going to meet at the Hall. Randolph wants to find out what it's like to ride after real British fox hounds."

After the speeches the guests moved through to the lounge. Well, not quite all, because Nathan noticed Rachel and Ruth walking off down the corridor together. Where were they going, what were they talking about? It was the definitive moment for him. What was it Hetty had said? "Marry that young widow, the one you love and you know which one that is." Now, seeing them both together, he still wasn't sure but he did know which one he wanted to share his life. He just hoped the other wouldn't say anything to spoil it.

The pleasant evening over, Ruth stood by seemingly unbothered as Rachel bade Nathan an affectionate goodnight and in turn gave Ruth an equally warm hug. Out in the cold car he wrapped a thick rug round Ruth's legs and got a gentle kiss on the cheek for his thoughtfulness. On the journey back he tried to find out what the two girls had been talking about when he saw them going off together back there in the Hall but Ruth would only say, "It was woman's talk!"

"What the heck is woman's talk?" he muttered.

The schoolhouse fire was almost out; Nathan tried to revive it but in the end decided to go for some fire-lighting sticks. Ruth stopped him and at last he saw the fire he had been yearning to see; it was in her eyes, on her lips as she kissed him and in the way she embraced him. Nathan held her close and whispered, "I love you, Ruth!"

"And I love you too. Forget about lighting the fire, I left two hot water bottles in bed."

Chapter Twenty Nine

Randolph's fascination with old buildings and British history was infectious. When being driven round Cheshire, if he saw an old church he told Bestwick to stop then strode off to look and marvel. The chauffeur tried to avoid driving past one whenever he could.

Rachel took Randolph to Chester for what turned into a long day of Roman history. Bestwick smugly stayed protectively by his beloved car while Rachel (at times trotting to keep abreast) escorted her enthralled New Zealand cousin. Although in places the City Walls were not passable they walked some of the other lengths before looking through the city centre.

***

The Saturday foxhunt proved to be a great success. Red-coated huntsmen intermingling with elegantly dressed ladies in front of the Hall highlighted the pageantry. Less resplendently dressed but sitting confidently on Alexander's hunter, Randolph was fascinated to watch as hounds dodged underfoot while riders exchanged genteel greetings or sipped from the traditional stirrup cup.

At first Randolph, used to rough clothes and hard gallops, thought them a bit sissy looking. But when the first fox broke from the Pool Wood he soon realised he was riding alongside some of the most accomplished and fearless of riders. After months of inactivity his horse became excited at the first sight of the hounds, but when they went on full cry the effect on the horse was electric. Even so, it wasn't long before he was struggling to keep abreast of the leaders. Big spiky British thorn hedges were a new experience but he gamely followed where others jumped.

In the excitement of the chase Randolph's big horse began to pull hard against the reins and the inevitable happened; an imposing hedge loomed in front and his horse, caught on the wrong stride, refused to respond to his desperate pull on the reins. At the last second the horse realised its mistake and stopped, but Randolph didn't!

That there was often a deep ditch behind a British thorn hedge was also a new experience for Randolph. Although it was a fairly soft landing it was an inglorious end to a magical day, but back at the Hall a bath restored his spirit. By Monday he was raring to travel towards Oxford.

Not sure if visiting potential schools or looking into history held priority, Rachel had Bestwick drive them wherever Randolph's whim took him. Randolph explained, "You must think I'm mad but we have no historic building. The only pre-Captain Cook history in New Zealand is a couple of Maori forts. And they're but a mound on which you imagined a stockade."

Fortunately Randolph soon realised that, if they stopped at every interesting building on the way, the journey could take forever. Although declaring that Shakespeare had been boring in his schooldays, Stratford-on-Avon drew him like a magnet. Randolph insisted it was his treat and booked the three of them into the best hotel for two nights, but with his urge to explore he could hardly settle to enjoy his evening dinner.

The next morning they left Bestwick to relax while the two of them set out on foot. The fact that the town had been granted a royal charter in 1198 impressed Randolph's yearning for the past. Their first call was to the 13th century Holy Trinity Church where Shakespeare is buried. For a church to have been built of such a size and splendour was, for Randolph, a clear statement of the wealth and importance of the town even then.

With so much history around he almost galloped from one bit of Shakespearian artefact to the next. Rachel began to realise how his boundless energy and determination to see everything could become wearisome.

***

There was a school to visit on the way to Oxford but it didn't seem to impress Randolph so they were booked in a luxury hotel in Oxford by mid-afternoon.

It wasn't long before they were tramping around some of the Oxford colleges but this time Rachel had her own interest. Although she had not actually applied to a particular college before she lost her mother, this had been the university of her choice. This was a time to indulge in dreaming of what might have been had her mother lived. Sensing her mood, Randolph let her set the pace and because of it admitted he absorbed more of the atmosphere of that beautiful city.

Although they stayed in the city for most of that week, Rachel managed only the briefest of telephone conversations with Hesston

Hall. Not having travelled much, this trip meant as much to her as her cousin. When later he became more fascinated with the small villages along the Thames Valley she was equally enthusiastic.

Randolph wanted to go further down the Thames but Rachel reminded him that they had to visit a high school at Bath. And when they did he loved it at first sight, although Rachel wasn't sure if it wasn't just the fact that some of its buildings dated back to the mid-nineteenth century. Or perhaps it was their sports tradition that made Randolph decide he had finally found the school for his daughter.

Afterwards, tramping around the beautiful city of Bath, she realised just how well read her New Zealand cousin was. According to him, both Jane Austen and Dickens used Bath as a setting in some of their books. Later he walked on Roman-laid stone flags with a deference that impressed her. He would have stayed on to study all the historic buildings from Roman Baths to Georgian crescents,but Rachel decided that three weeks away from home was enough.

***

Making a brief telephone conversation to Hesston Hall to instruct her staff to expect her home the following day, she had Bestwick deliver Randolph to the railway station, saw him safely onto the London train and turned the car in the direction of Cheshire.

Refreshed after a most interesting tour ,Rachel, although keen to get back to Hesston, broke the journey to stay the night in Kidderminster. The next morning, when they had been on the road for over two hours, she suggested to Bestwick that they would take break for a relaxing lunch. He said, "I presumed, Ma'am, that you would want to get back for the wedding?"

Rachel leaned forward demanding, "What wedding?"

"Nathan's! It's this afternoon at two o'clock," and sensing her astonishment said, "I am sorry, Ma'am, I thought you knew."

Realising Bestwick must have kept in touch with home more than she had, Rachel told him to drive on while she thought.

Thoughts of a relaxing lunch were cancelled when she told Bestwick to pull in at a small café. Over a dry sandwich he tried to reassure her that he could get to the Chapel on time.

Changing from the back seat to sit in the front she managed to inject a greater sense of urgency into him. Even so the journey seemed endless. Rachel's thoughts were equally without conclusion.

That Nathan was marrying Ruth jolted her out of the happy,

detached mood of the past weeks. She brooded inwardly, why had she told Ruth that Nathan was just a good friend? Why? Why? Is it because, she wondered, that I've only just woken up to what my heart has been telling me for months? "But why couldn't he have waited?" Rachel unthinkingly said, to Bestwick's embarrassment.

From the outside the Chapel seemed quiet; the service was obviously in progress. Rachel pushed through the door into the nearly empty chapel just as the minister said. "If any man has any reason why ...." The words were lost to her pounding heart. Knowing she must object now or forever remain silent she just froze, unable to make the protest rise from the tightness in her chest. The rest of the exchange of vows was lost in unreality until the minister said, "You may now kiss the bride."

Feeling her knees weaken, Rachel sank down onto the end of the nearest pew, oblivious of the signing ritual. The change of music and the sight of Ruth and Nathan walking arm in arm towards her finally jolted her back to reality. They faced each other in the aisle, uncertainty showing on all three faces. Ruth's mature beauty was not lost on Rachel as she suddenly reached for Ruth to give her a kiss and hug before gripping those strong muscular arms to give Nathan a peck on his cheek. As soon as the bride and groom stepped away from the church door Rachel slipped past them and ran.

Although there had seemed to be very few guests at the wedding, the next day everyone seemed to know the details. After the Sunday morning church service people seemed to be taking an almost vindictive delight in discussing details of the wedding with Rachel. That the honeymoon couple were spending just one night at the Fawn and Hound before returning to their home in the schoolhouse was among many of the gossipy details she heard.

When Monday morning finally came Rachel couldn't help walking Digger towards the timber yard. Not that she wanted to – in fact walking in through the door she wanted to be anywhere but there. Nathan just turned on his stool to look at her without speaking. Feeling her throat tighten as the colour drained from her face, she finally blurted out, "Is that what you wanted?"
He stood to walk towards her, "I needed someone to share my life, my dreams – a home – maybe children."
"What about love?"
"You think that I don't love Ruth?"
Rachel turned and fled.

Chapter Thirty

After her trip away from Hesston Rachel found that there were a few things needing her attention on the estate. Various decisions asked for by her land agent about the estate's business would be relatively easy to deal with. First, though, she needed to respond to Benjie Cuthbert's invitation to visit his office in Knutsford.

Now there wasn't going be a title, or the inheritance that went with it, settling the final parts of her father's estate was relatively straightforward. Benjie produced various documents needing her signature before handing over two pleasantly large cheques. The first completed Thomas's affairs and the second was the settlement of Alexander's life policy.

When again Benjie invited Rachel to take lunch with him she thought, 'Why not? I'm now a woman without a man. Although I wept over my husband more when he was living than after his death I mustn't now weep over Nathan!' Agreeing to meet him later for lunch, she walked across the street with the confidence of a comfortably off young widow and deposited the two cheques at the bank before walking on to the accountants.

Where to invest the inheritance seemed to be a difficult question. Alan Brockbank, peering at her through his thick glasses, warned of uneasiness in the stock markets. Although interest rates were very low he was afraid of serious recession. Rachel left his office with the decision as to where to invest undecided.

Lunch in the Fawn and Hound followed by a serious visit to the dress shop was equally cheering. Perhaps the most pleasing thing of all was that the toadying 'My Lady' title had been forgotten; she was back to being just Rachel or Mrs Wentworth-Jones. Her refusal to wear the traditional severe black mourning clothes, long favoured by many older widows, still raised a few eyebrows although she looked for suitably sober yet attractive everyday dresses. The short, straight silhouettes then in fashion suited her tall figure and to her surprise there was a good selection in her size. Perhaps the dress shop, knowing of her reluctance to have her clothes tailored, deliberately stocked a range in her size. Nonetheless, it still took the fashionable black stockings to add that extra widow's demeanour.

With all her personal shopping completed Rachel instructed Bestwick to take her back to the accountants. Although neither could anticipate how serious a stock market crash would be or if there would even be one, even so Rachel accepted his advice to keep most of her funds in a cash deposit for the time being.

While catching up with her business decisions through that week she managed to avoid meeting Nathan again. On the other hand, Randolph gave a pressing invitation for her to join him in London, which he repeated again in the week. On Sunday, having taken Digger for an early walk and attended church, Rachel had just finished a lonely lunch when Randolph rang again. Although she was not sure if it was wise to let him get so close, there was no way she wanted to spend another week avoiding Nathan.

***

Travelling to London by train Rachel was a little surprised when Randolph met her and outlined his proposed itinerary. It included a visit to Cambridge before travelling along the east coast, and he had bought a car so he could drive himself.

***

Marriage suited Nathan. Although the schoolhouse was not his ideal home it was warm and cosy. One of the highest compliments that could be paid to a Cheshire housewife was to say, "She keeps a good fire" and Ruth – thanks to Nathan's endless supply of logs – 'kept a good fire'. Through those cold winter nights the low settee was put to good use in front of that good fire. Obviously already an experienced lover, Nathan surprised Ruth both with his ardour and apparent competence. Compared to her first husband's frailty, the sight of Nathan's strong, hard, muscular body stripped off in front of the fire fascinated her.

Of Rachel Nathan saw nothing. From a chance meeting with Bestwick he learned that she had been travelling down the Eastern side of the country with Randolph for a couple of weeks and had now returned to Hesston. Although Randolph came across for a chat, Rachel either deliberately avoided him or their paths did not cross.

Within days Randolph's title was confirmed and they were away again. From the estate staff Nathan understood Rachel had gone to advise on altering and decorating the Hall for the new Lord Gressonham. Nothing was said but he did begin to wonder about the relationship between them.

As for the timber business, it progressed solidly. That refusal of an overdraft earlier on had not restricted him too much. Orders came in steadily, customers paid promptly and his bank manager began to smile when he called.

There was another timber yard right nearby called the Elmwood. Nathan knew little about it other than that it seemed not to compete much with his business. When he was offered two or three blocks of growing timber by land agents who in the past had sold to the Elmwood timber yard he begane to wonder about it but was surprised to receive a fairly urgent request to call there.

The owner, Ben Jackson, a short, stocky man in his early sixties, welcomed Nathan warmly. He explained how it had been his policy to use mostly locally grown trees but now, because he had been nursing his wife through a long and painful illness, he had failed to buy ahead and was running out of timber. The outcome was that Nathan received a substantial order, mainly for oak but some ash and sycamore were included. He came away both pleased and envious. The envy was for that well equipped yard which, although not substantially larger than his at Hesston, contained much more modern machinery. The main saw could be set to cut up a whole tree with little physical effor.t With the business situated on the edge of town, there was a large service counter with plenty of trade customers.

That order prompted Nathan to bring one of the plough team's steam engines a back. The long wire ropes could reach in among the growing trees to snake out Nathan's heavy timber much more efficiently than the farm's horse team. Clem worked with the two steam engine teams to supervise and sort the different trunks, easing the eventual task of loading.

It also brought about a meeting with Rachel. He had walked across the fields to check how the steam engine team were progressing and had just finished instructing the men when she came through the trees towards him. They shook hands, exchanged pleasantries, then moved to a nearby log to sit and chat. Whatever strain there had been between them on their last meeting had long gone. Now their relationship was back to being both relaxed and congenial. In answer to her questions he brought her up to date on various events around the village, in particular how his business was progressing. Rachel then told him about some of the interesting places that she and Randolph had visited. When he said, "You seem to get on well with Randolph," there seemed to be some hesitancy in

Rachel's voice. "Yes, we have a lot in common, and he just happened to be here when I needed a change. Anyway, how about Ruth and you? Is there any sign of a family yet?"

"We're trying!" Nathan replied with a bashful grin.

They parted on a cheery nod to walk off in different directions. The fact was there had been no thought of family planning between him and Ruth. They both wanted children sooner rather than later and Ruth agreed that when it happened she would need to give up her job and with it the schoolhouse. Nathan was keen to look for a house immediately but Ruth, more reluctant, cautioned him, "It's not always that easy; let's wait a while."

***

After a couple of weeks of solid hard work and a really enjoyable home life things changed dramatically for Nathan when he called in on Ben Jackson. The relationship between the two of them had developed beyond just business. Ben, relying on a manager to run his day-to-day business, had spent more and more time with his wife. Now that was over (Nathan had attended the funeral the week before), Ben was devoting more time to his business and that was when he discovered that his manager had been, to use his words, "Dipping into the pot!"

Ben Jackson went on to explain, "I was planning to retire before I knew my wife was ill. I'd intended to make my manager a partner, with full control and all the profits, but to pay me a small rent."

"Did he know this?"

"Yes! We'd discussed it, agreed terms and I'd bought a small cottage so he could move into my house here."

"So what happened?" Nathan asked.

"I suppose he couldn't wait to get his hands on the money. Perhaps because of my wife I've let setting up the partnership drag on too long. Anyway, he's dipped into the pot in a fairly big way."

"What are you going to do now?"

"Offer you the tenancy of both the yard and house!"

It was the last thing Nathan could have expected. When he didn't reply Ben added, "And I want to settle it fairly quickly. I have a brother out in New Zealand who I haven't seen for thirty years."

Everyone's going to New Zealand, Nathan thought. Rachel, who had called in at his yard for a chat, told him that she was thinking of going with Randolph when he went back to fetch his daughter.

Nathan's thoughts flitted back to the offer. He wanted the security of owning his own house and, if possible, his business premises as well. He now said as much to Ben.

The outcome was that Ben offered to sell him both the house and business if he could afford them. Nathan replied, "I'll have to negotiate with the bank first."

Ben did a circle round his office before saying, "I'll be your banker! You can pay me over a period of eight years."

Nathan accepted subject to Ruth's agreement. He respected Ruth's judgement, treating her as an equal partner in the decisions within their lives.

When he did tell Ruth he got the most surprising answer. "I've got something to tell you. I've waited until I was sure before telling you – I have been carrying a child since our honeymoon!"

From then on things moved at a fast pace. The school governors, seemingly confident of finding a replacement, accepted Ruth's resignation from the end of that term. Within a few weeks Nathan had taken over the business and he and Ruth moved into the timber yard house. Now there were three extra full time workmen but with them came a cash turnover that left a comfortable margin at the end of each week.

The Hesston yard also became busier. By injecting capital into the estate Rachel had galvanised her new land agent into activity. The retirement cottages were reaching completion, several separate farm tenants' building repairs were in progress and part of the Hall garden fence was to be replaced with new oak rails. Most of the timber for this estate work came through Nathan's yard.

The plan was for Ruth to take charge of the Knutsford timber yard office leaving Nathan, who appointed a foreman from among his Knutsford staff, to spend some time in the Hesston yard.

Some of his timber buyers did not want timber felled while the sap was up in summer months, which meant that Nathan had to lay his felling teams off for a while. Luke Jones and his brother, keen to earn some money in other ways, took on the task of splitting and erecting the rails for the Hesston Hall garden fence.

Overseeing all this work, it was inevitable that Nathan would meet up with Rachel. Intrigued to know more about her planned trip he asked about New Zealand. When she replied enthusiastically he asked, "And what about you and Randolph? You seem to be getting close. Are you going to become Lady Gressonham after all?"

Looking a little flustered, Rachel called Digger to heel and set off across the fields.

***

With two separate businesses on the go the telephone, if at times unreliable, was invaluable. After leaving the timber yard unattended for a few hours, when Nathan and Clem came back from the woods the phone was ringing. Clem took the call then rushed back to Nathan, shouting above the noise, "You must go home now – Ruth's been taken ill! They've been trying to get us for hours!"

When Nathan arrived back at home he found a neighbour looking after the house. She explained that the doctor had just left and that Ruth had had a miscarriage earlier that morning. He rushed upstairs to find her sobbing despairingly into her pillow. Trying to comfort her, he told her there would be other times and other babies but she seemed inconsolable.

Insisting Ruth stay in bed, the doctor organised a local woman to come in each day for the length of her convalescence while Nathan, although prepared to look after her, was persuaded to go to fetch Ruth's mother.

With two women in the house Ruth convinced Nathan that he should get on with running the business. Because of that he missed the doctor's daily visit until the fourth day, when he returned to the house just as the doctor came down stairs. He had several questions to ask but one was uppermost, "Why's Ruth so distressed? Surely we can try for a baby again?"

The doctor seemed to hesitate for a while before clearing his throat, "I am worried about your wife. She's running a temperature today, which is not good. Anyway, after three miscarriages it may not be wise to have another pregnancy."

He demanded the doctor explain further. Realising that Nathan did not know about any previous miscarriages, the doctor explained briefly and left.

Nathan was stunned. That they would not be able to have children was a blow. That Ruth had not trusted him enough to tell him she had miscarried twice in her previous marriage was a bombshell. In turmoil he left the house, jumped in his car and drove away.

Overhearing the conversation without realising its implications, Ruth's mother went back upstairs and, trying to reassure Ruth, said, "The doctor's explained everything to Nathan. He'll understand now why you are so upset."

Realising that he would also know of her deceit, Ruth sprang out of bed and ran downstairs calling out to him. When she heard the car start up she dashed out into the yard only to watch it speed away down the road.

***

Bess, now practised at not being left behind, had jumped in the car as Nathan opened the door. Nathan parked the car down a small lane and the two of them walked into the Hesston woods, one in tail-wagging enjoyment, the other in black despair. Believing their marriage had been based on love and trust, the sickening truth that it seemed to be based on neither hit hard. Without trust there was nothing left.

Knowing Rachel had left to join Randolph to prepare for the New Zealand trip Nathan tramped through the woods, not expecting or wanting to meet anyone.

It took a couple of hours of solitude to shake him from his despondency and clear his thinking. There was no doubt in his mind as to what he had to do, which was to put aside his doubts about his love or Ruth's trust and try to make the best of his marriage. After all, he and Ruth could still be happy without children if they were determined.

The doctor's car was in the yard again when he returned home. His mother-in-law met him, explaining that Ruth had collapsed outside and was now very ill. Explanations as to why she was outside kept Nathan occupied while they waited for the doctor to come downstairs.

When the doctor eventually came down it was not good news. Ruth's temperature, which had earlier risen to a dangerous height, was now falling alarmingly. After promising to be back in a half hour the doctor left to make another call. Nathan went up to comfort Ruth. Not prepared for how ill she looked, he sank onto the bed beside her. Grasping his hand, Ruth whispered, "The doctor said he thought I lost the other two because Jim had been gassed. Knowing how much you wanted children I should have told you about them."

"I forgive you and we've still got each other. Just get better."

"I didn't tell you about our baby until I'd gone well past the time I lost the others. I thought I was all right this time then ...."

Reassuring her how he needed her regardless, Nathan stayed with her until the doctor came back. By then Ruth was barely conscious. The doctor checked her temperature and pulse then ushered him outside. "There's nothing more that I can do. When complications set in like this the end comes quickly."

"How do you mean – complications?"

"After a miscarriage sometimes all the placenta fails to come away. When that happens it can trigger infection, which can then spread very quickly. I've done all I can."

Ruth woke sometime later, smiled weakly up at Nathan and whispered, "Thank you."

He watched, heartbroken, while the life breath gradually left his lovely wife.

***

As the new Lord Gressonham, Randolph was an impressive man. Unconventionally likeable in his approach to his peers, he also had the ability to enthuse those who now worked for him. Particularly he wanted to entertain, to have the great Hall ringing with music and laughter before he returned to New Zealand. He insisted that Rachel returned to act as the hostess for the occasion, not just on the evening of the ball but he expected her to oversee the preparations as well. It was beginning to irk how he now seemed to presume he had first call on her time.

That Rachel and Randolph were obviously close was noted by all and the fact that they were not first cousins added to the gossip. Rachel ignored such rumours because throughout the time they had travelled together he never once made an advance to her. Now, as his guest preparing for the ball, she realised he was becoming attracted to her. Although admitting that he was an engaging and likeable character she was having second thoughts about travelling with him to New Zealand.

Still dressing attractively but demurely in a widow's darker colours, Rachel was surprised when her height of fashion straight-silhouetted dress seemed a bit tight around the waist, rather more so than could be blamed on the rich food Randolph insisted she shared.

On the night of the ball more than one attractive lady flirted with Randolph. Perhaps they had awakened him, or perhaps it was the closeness of Rachel when the two of them danced the last dance together that aroused him. Whatever the trigger, the result was that, after the last guest left, she found herself in his arms. Deciding to allow him a kiss before telling him that she had changed her mind about going to New Zealand, Rachel was suddenly swept off her feet and carried up stairs. Ignoring her struggles he took the stairs two at a time and dropped her on the bed and then straightened. With a questioning smile he said, "You can't say that the idea hasn't crossed your mind?"

"We can't, I'm with child!"

"You're having a baby?"

"Yes!"

"How? When?"

"I am recently widowed."

Propped on her elbows, Rachel said, "I'm sorry Randolph but I was going to tell you tonight anyway and also that I've decided I'm not going away with you."

He turned and walked out of the room.

The following morning, when Rachel was sitting up in bed nibbling half heartily at her breakfast, there was a knock on the door. A subdued Randolph came in at her invitation, "Why couldn't you have told me before?"

"I just didn't know before. I've never been sick or felt any signs other than I've been putting on weight."

"But surely your monthly ...." Randolph, stopping in embarrassment, then said, "Well, I have been married."

"I first missed a couple of turns over Christmas, so when I got back home I went to see my doctor. It was about six weeks after losing Alexander and he was sure I wasn't with child. He told me not to worry and that they would start again in a month or two. He said the shock of losing a father and a husband would throw any woman out of cycle."

"But now you're sure."

"Yes."

Randolph took her hand and kissed it. "It makes no difference. I've become very fond of you, Rachel."

Realising what he was going to say, Rachel tried to stop him but he gently placed his hand on her lips and said, "Will you do me the honour of becoming my wife?"

He took Rachel's refusal very well and understood her need to return to Hesston immediately. They parted with some sadness, both aware of what might have been. She though, knew that the dazzle of marrying into high society would never make up for a lack of true love. But then was true love beyond her now?

There was something she had not told Randolph, perhaps because it had only become apparent to her in this morning's early sleepless hours. On that New Year's visit to the village doctor, after he had looked at her for a moment or two, his exact words were, "You've been a widow for six weeks and by this time, knowing you're in good health, I could tell by just looking at your face. And I can assure you Rachel – you are not six weeks into a pregnancy." Perhaps because he had been a close friend of her father's she felt too embarrassed to tell him about that scuffle with Captain Dewson some four weeks later.

***

Rachel arrived back at Hesston tired. Still unsure as to how to explain her predicament, she ate a small supper before going up to bed. It wasn't until the next day when she had finished breakfast that Cook came in looking serious. Cook fumbled over the right words to break the news about Ruth's death, which had been just two days before.

Despairing for Nathan but unsure how she should express her sorrow, Rachel walked outside with Digger. Surprisingly, there was Nathan's car going towards the timber yard. Without hesitation she strode after it.

Clem and Bill were engrossed in their work so Rachel walked past them towards the office. Nathan turned from his desk to look at her for a moment, then suddenly he was up on his feet and they were holding each other. Trying to mutter words of comfort she felt his strong arms squeeze her words back into thoughts. Was it was less than a year, it seemed like a lifetime, since Hannah's death when they first held each other like this? Feeling the security and strength of his arms she knew without doubt that this was her man and shed a tear. Pulling out a slightly grubby handkerchief, he tried to comfort her but Rachel was not just sobbing for his loss. Feeling her bump pressing against him she realised that when Nathan eventually emerged from his grief he would be free but she had now placed a barrier between them that was insurmountable.

Chapter Thirty One

After that visit to the timber yard Rachel walked across the fields with her mind in a whirl, unsure if she wanted to let people presume she was carrying Alexander's child yet unsure if she could live with the truth. The village doctor agreed to see her that afternoon. When he did he took one serious look and said, "Well you are now! I can't understand how I missed it before."

"You didn't miss anything, it was me. I didn't tell you the whole truth."

The doctor sat quietly while an embarrassed Rachel confessed. After he had checked on the dates and briefly examined her he said, "Yes it does seem that the father is Captain Dewson. Do I take it that you don't really want to marry him?"

"No, but I'll have to think about everything because I'm not sure I want to tell everyone the truth."

"It may not be necessary!"

"But doctor, the truth will come out when the baby is born."

"Not necessarily."

When she looked mystified the doctor said, "Look, there's only three and half weeks' difference and who knows just when a baby will come? At least wait a while before you tell anyone."

"But I'm being dishonest."

"So? You'd be surprised how many times I have this sort of a conversation. You have to decide what's best for your baby."

Getting to his feet to shake her hand, he said, "Promise me you'll wait a week or two and come and see me again before telling anyone."

***

Steeling herself to attend Ruth's funeral, Rachel slipped into a rear pew in Lacksfield Church. Thinking of Ruth, of her sweet yet strong personality, Rachel wept for her and for Nathan who had lost so much. She watched Nathan's sad figure walk up the aisle after the coffin but avoided looking at him after the short service when he followed the coffin out towards the door. Her intention had been to let the mourners follow the coffin out and then slip away hopefully unnoticed. Out in the graveyard Rachel found her path blocked as the bareheaded mourners stood silently watching the coffin lowered into the grave. The birdsong coming from the graveyard trees seemed a poignant send off. Then it was over yet no one moved. Eventually Nathan began to walk through the mourners, thanking each in turn for coming and still Rachel was hemmed in. When eventually there was a gap to slip through there was Nathan facing her and without thought they were in each other's arms, "Oh, Nathan, you've lost so much." Smiling into her red-rimmed eyes, he touched her bump and said, "And you've gained so much. Alexander would have been thrilled." His smile vanished again as a tear trickled from her sad eyes.

***

And so Rachel walked out with Digger each day. It was May; the countryside resonated with wonderful spring songs of birds celebrating the breeding season. On the garden lake newly hatched broods of ducklings scurried across the lake's surface after insects. Crazy coots lived up to their name, attacking any bird that came near to their beautifully striped chicks.

When Lucy rang to ask after her health Rachel told her about the baby. Lucy, immediately presuming it was Alexander's, congratulated her enthusiastically.

On another morning Hamish appeared out of the trees with a rare smile. "Arrr, Missey, the Major would have bin pleased. This estate'll go on now."

Keeping her promise to the doctor was not as hard as expected. She was determined that the first person to be told would be Nathan, because there was no way Rachel was going let him hear through village gossip, and yet how could she tell him? How could she tell someone who had just lost what he treasured most, his wife and unborn child, that her baby came from a casual, furtive scuffle?

Her dilemma still unresolved Rachel's walks got longer, partially perhaps because in the Hall Cook seemed to give her the occasional long, reflective look. Out in the fields there was no need to hide her guilt. One morning, while holding onto Digger, she watched two hares, now without the madness of a March courtship, chasing each other round in circles until the chase ended in gratifying passion. That their passion lasted longer than hers had with Captain Dewson reminded her as to just how silly she had been. Had it been one of the dairymaids on the farm she would have lectured her on irresponsibility.

Then a letter arrived from Lady Louisa. It was so full of

grandmotherly congratulations that Rachel had to smile. Although Lady Louisa did scold her a little for not telling her the wonderful news sooner, the rift between them was healed.

The wonderful feeling of approaching motherhood compensated for the misery of her deception. It was beyond anything she had expected. Through the barren years of marriage she had tried to be indifferent towards having children but now she realised that those thoughts had been some sort of protection against the disappointment of not conceiving. Perhaps that yearning for more excitement in her marriage had been nothing more than the need for this fulfilment.

When a letter arrived from the dashing Captain Dewson, Rachel realised she could tell no one the truth until she had replied to him. Obviously Lucy had told him the news and he had jumped to a guilty conclusion but there was no real affection in the letter. There was, though, the offer to meet her for a discussion and he had even signed it David. It was funny, Rachel thought, I'm having a child by a man whose Christian name I've never spoken, not even on that eventful frosty morning.

The greater dilemma was not how to tell others but how to reply to the handsome Captain. She knew only too well he was indeed a dashing, all-action type of man but was there any depth to him? A second week of long walks and troubled thoughts passed by without any resolution. Then Lucy rang. "You remember Captain Dewson? Yes, well, he's had an accident."

"What sort of accident?"

"Apparently he was training a young Army horse over jumps; no one knows quite what happened, they just found him lying by a fence. A broken neck I think."

The earpiece slipped out of Rachel's hand as she slumped down off the telephone chair.

The chambermaid, who was probably listening to the conversation from behind the door, rushed in to help. Before Rachel recovered, Cook was by her side and between them they almost carried her to the sofa.

***

Bestwick drove Rachel across to Leicester on the day before the funeral. She to stay overnight in a hotel ready for the morning service while Bestwick drove off to look up a distant cousin.

The Regiment put on the usual pageantry for the funeral of a serving officer killed on duty. Watching David's heartbroken parents following their only son's coffin, Rachel saw that in their grief they were also proud. In the eulogy the vicar, mentioning Captain Dewson's humble background, placed great emphasis on his many achievements, particularly his outdoor activities of shooting, riding and mountaineering. He ended with, "No challenge was too great for this adventurous young man."

And that's what I was, Rachel thought, just a challenge. Again she watched David's parents by the graveside, his mother sobbing while his father tried proudly to match the uniforms around him and square his shoulders too. Walking from the grave she knew that the truth would make a now dead hero into a bounder in his parents' eyes. It would not ease their pain, it would just destroy the old couple's proud memories.

***

Back in the Hesston doctor's surgery, after the usual health questions, he asked, "Well, who have you told?"

"No one."

"I didn't think you would."

"But ...."

"No buts. We'll face it out together in a few months' time."

***

For the second time Nathan was living in a house full of memories, of hopes lost. This time, though, the house being part of his dream timber merchant yard, it perhaps saved him from despair. Whatever was the reason, within a couple of weeks he lost the intensity of pain he had felt after losing Hannah. Instead there was an inner deadness, which he could not explain, and it made him feel guilty.

Throwing all his energy into the business brought some relief from his strange guilt.

Nathan's visits to his Hesston yard were curtailed by the illness of his Elmwood foreman. A tough ex-soldier who had fought in the trenches through the latter few months of the War, suddenly started to shake when he had to meet with a customer. Liking the man, Nathan agreed he should go on paid leave but at the same time he knew that his business could ill afford such unusual generosity.

Nathan managed to find two local women, who took turns to 'do for him' as they liked to put it. So his house was clean, his washing done and even the occasional hotpot was left simmering in the oven. But he tried not to stay in too often on his own. The only food most pubs served was a meat pie or occasionally a lump of cheese. It took a while to find one where there were neither maggots on the cheese nor green mould on the pie. Not that he tried to drown his sorrows; it was just that he needed companionship without close commitment or questions.

He was reminded again of Hetty when, having received a congratulatory letter from her on his marriage only a few weeks previously, now a sympathy letter came in the post. He wasn't sure that he wanted someone else in Ruth's house but as the days went by he realised that it was no life on his own and Hetty was the ideal housekeeper companion. Eventually he plucked up courage and drove round to visit. A maid showed him into the parlour, then an extremely smartly dressed Hetty breezed in, gave him a hug and a kiss, then rang a bell to order tea before sitting opposite him for a serious chat.

Although sympathetic, Hetty's bright and lively personality soon had the laughter lines showing again around Nathan eyes. Feeling his spirit lifting, he became more determined than ever to invite her to move, and then he noticed the ring. Seeing his glance she said, "Yes, look at it, isn't it great?"

He held her hand to examine a beautiful diamond.

"Yes, we're getting married next month. Aren't I lucky? Jim's a wonderful man."

"I'm delighted for you, Hetty. Where is Jim?"

"He's out playing golf this morning. Oh, Nathan, Jim's so kind ..."

When Hetty babbled on about her future husband's many qualities Nathan, though pleased for her, knew he had lost.

***

Short, stocky Ben Jackson bustled into the Elmwood yard full of renewed energy. "Listen, Nathan, I've put off going to New Zealand until later in the year. My brother tells me I'll enjoy it more through their spring and summer. I'm bored now. I need something to do."

With Ben back running what had been his own yard Nathan was free again to motor towards Hesston more often. Checking on his men who were still working on the split oak railing fence round the Hall gardens it was inevitable that he should meet Rachel.

As they talked pleasantly together she could see the

unhappiness in his drawn features. Nathan, though, found it hard to fathom Rachel. She was obviously glowing with good health but he detected a sort of distance between them, almost as though she was shutting him out. The fact was that as the months sped by Rachel became more detached, from the affairs of the estate and particularly from former friends. It was the oft-repeated suggestion that at least she would have a living memory of, if not an heir to, Alexander that drove her to seek the solitude of fields and garden.

Under Robert's management the home farm was improving and this year's crops looked extremely promising. Harry Wilson had retired and his son Jack was now in the cowman's cottage. The farm milk, now picked up each morning by a motor wagon, went into the outskirts of Manchester. Robert had bought a tractor and hired a driver instead of a waggoner. It was all change with lots of other improvements taking place across the estate. Yet as her time came closer Rachel became more fearful.

***

When the garden fence was finished Nathan was walking back from doing a final inspection when he noticed Rachel sitting by the lakeside. He had done his calculations from that fateful day of the car crash and knew Rachel must now be overdue.
"May I join you?"
At Rachel's nod he sat on the other end of the garden seat.
"I was just dreamily watching waves lapping gently by my feet."
"It must be hard, going over your time."
"It's harder than you think."

Hearing the sadness in her voice he reached out and touched her shoulder. In response Rachel turned her tear-stained eyes to meet his. They held that pose for some time, one wanting to help but not knowing how, the other wanting to confess but afraid that it would send him away for ever.

***

Too tired to do anything but too worried to relax Rachel sat restlessly in the lounge working out the time from the day before Alexander's death. She was now ten days over and beginning to despair, not so much for herself – a healthy baby would fulfil her need – but the truth of her conception would hurt so many other people. Then the parlour maid broke into her thoughts by showing the doctor into the lounge. "Let's have a look at you then?" He said cheerily.

266

Afterwards, still smiling, he said, "You've not altered much."

"What will I do now? I can't hide the truth any longer, can I?"

Taking a small bottle out of his bag, the doctor said, "This is something I use on very rare occasions."

"What is it?"

"Just drink it and then I'll tell you."

When Rachel pulled a face at the taste, he smiled. "It's a herbal mixture I learned about many years ago. One of the local gentry went on a long trip abroad and while he was away his wife managed to conceive by the neighbouring farmer." The doctor's smile became a throaty chuckle. "She visited me in the same despair that you're in now and I couldn't help her. Amazingly, two days later she gave birth to a healthy boy so I challenged her, and she told me she'd visited an old herbalist in the next village. I decided I'd visit the same old lady. It took a bit of persuasion but eventually she told me the ingredients."

"Does it work?"

"I very rarely use it, but yes. The only trouble was, that neighbouring farmer had black, curly hair and stuttered and the boy, who's now in his early teens, also has black, curly hair and stutters."

Trying to laugh, Rachel had to hold her bulge when it hurt.

"Your man hasn't got black, curly hair and a stutter?"

"Hadn't – he's dead!"

"Oh, I'm sorry. That explains something, though I would never have asked."

***

To continue the pretence of dates Rachel had engaged a nursemaid some three weeks earlier. Coming from a genteel family who had suffered financial misfortune, this delightful nineteen-year-old with little to do but wait occupied some of her time by distracting Clem in the timber yard. Bill was heard declaring, "The sooner this baby comes the better and then perhaps we might get some work done."

And come it did, quite dramatically some two days after the doctor's visit. Realising that a small baby some two weeks late might start the tongues wagging, the village doctor called in at the post office on his way back from the Hall and casually said, "Well, there's now a daughter up at the Hall, only six pounds five ounces but then with all the walking her mother's done it's a wonder she's even that heavy."

Whether it was due to the gossipy postmistress or not, people did seem to accept that the baby was normal if just a bit late. As for

Rachel, with little Miranda cuddling in her arms, it was like a miracle.

Although frustrated, through her confinement Rachel took seriously the doctor's warning that one of the side effects of his herbal mixture meant that she must take even more care. Because of that it was about three weeks before she walked out into the garden gently pushing the pram. With several letters to read she let Miranda gurgle happily away while she sat by the lakeside and opened them. The first one from Lucy revealed how frustrated she was with her own unfulfilled motherhood, her letter babbling on about visiting Rachel to see who the baby looked like. There were other letters of congratulations but the one that Rachel left to the last was from Lady Louisa. It read, '...I'll arrive on Thursday. I'm so looking forward to seeing and holding my only grandchild that I can hardly ...' Rachel's eyes filled with tears.

***

It had been a bad few weeks for Nathan. Within a month Ruth would have been giving birth to his baby and he began to feel real grief again. He recalled a conversation they had had just a few nights before Ruth lost the baby. She had said, "I suppose you want a boy, don't you?"
He replied, "I want a healthy baby and you to come through it all right."

He remembered Ruth's challenge, "Well, if you really want a girl you can prove it, if it is one, by buying her first dress."

When Nathan heard that there was a baby girl at the Hall not only did he want to congratulate Rachel with a gift but he also needed to lay his own memories to rest. After nearly three weeks he finally summoned the courage to actually go into a baby clothes shop and buy that little dress.

That afternoon when his strong boots crunched across the Hall gravel he was not expecting to see Rachel but just to hand his present in at the door. Surprised at being directed towards the garden by the parlour maid, Nathan, dressed for work with rolled up sleeves on a clean collarless shirt, clutched a roughly tied parcel containing that little pink dress. Pausing to make manly clucking noises into the pram, he said, "What a beautiful little girl. Alexander would have been pleased ... Why the tears?"
"Because it isn't his."

As she blurted out the story, Rachel became more distressed.

Nathan was soon on the seat holding her hand. It ended by her sobbing on his shoulder, "How can I tell Lady Louisa Miranda's not Alexander's or tell David's parents ...? I can't even tell Lucy; she's too close to the Dewsons. There's only you I dare tell."

"You shouldn't have carried that burden alone. I was here, you could have told me sooner."

"I wanted to but it's so sordid."

He kissed her gently. "Nothing about you can ever be sordid. As regards who you tell - tell no one. It would only cause pain; just let it stay between us."

***

Three months later the local paper ran a little feature:

We have reported at different times the sad loss of both the father and husband of Mrs Wentworth-Jones. Interwoven around those stories at the time of the death of Major Wentworth-Jones was the saga of whether Mrs Wentworth-Jones had inherited a title or not. That the title was later proved to belong to a distant cousin from New Zealand must have added to her loss.

Now we are pleased to report not just one happy ending but two. First, the christening of Miranda, the daughter of Mrs Wentworth-Jones and the late Major Wentworth-Jones and secondly, the announcement of the engagement between Mrs Rachel Wentworth-Jones and Mr Nathan Dobson, proprietor of the Elmwood timber yard.

***